Fatal
Legacy

Rebecca Deel

ISBN: 1979790795
ISBN-13: 978-1979790796

DEDICATION

To my sons.

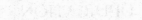

ACKNOWLEDGMENTS

Cover design by Melody Simmons.

CHAPTER ONE

Del Peterson grabbed empty book boxes from the back of her SUV and thrust them into the hands of her cousin, Ivy Monroe, and moved the remaining boxes to the ground before closing the hatchback. The sultry July afternoon generated heat and humidity typical in Otter Creek, Tennessee and had baked the area in unrelenting waves for three weeks with no rain predicted in the near future. Out of her vehicle for two minutes, and she needed another shower, this time a cold one.

"This is a massive house, Del. I'll bet the library has more than a couple bookcases. You sure we have enough boxes?" Ivy's voice registered her skepticism.

Del eyed the gray stone structure as they crossed a flagstone path and climbed stairs to the shadowed porch. "Judge Reece says I won't be interested in his mother's entire book collection. She was an eccentric collector."

"Is that a nice way of saying she never threw any books away, whether they were good or not?"

She shifted her load of boxes to one hip and rang the doorbell. Big Ben chimes sounded from the interior of the home. Behind her, Ivy laughed. Del's own lips curved. Mrs. Reece had been one of her best customers at Otter

Creek Books. Widowed three times, each husband left her a tidy fortune which she invested even as she reclaimed her first husband's last name. The octogenarian had stopped in every couple weeks to buy more books. She had loved murder mysteries.

Similar to a very handsome cop who stopped in every few days as well. Josh Cahill hadn't shared Mrs. Reece's tastes for cozy mysteries, though. He preferred edgier, hard-boiled mysteries and thrillers.

Del dragged her attention back to her cousin's question. "Mrs. Reece kept the books she enjoyed. The rest she traded for newer books or donated to the library. Judge Reece wants me to evaluate his mother's hardback collection for him. He doesn't read genre fiction and wouldn't know if a mystery is valuable or not. I'm to give him an estimate of the value and tell him which volumes to keep."

"Book snob, huh?"

"He prefers biographies and history."

A shadow darkened the frosted glass. Judge John Reece opened the door and motioned them into the foyer. "Thanks for coming out so quickly."

"Your mother was one of my favorite people. We had some long conversations discussing books we read."

"Her death was quite a shock." Reece shook his head, eyes shadowed with sorrow. "Mother lived in this house for fifty years and had never fallen down either of the staircases, even when she was pregnant."

"Do the police know what happened?" Ivy asked.

"They think she stumbled in the dark, perhaps tripped on her robe's hem." He sighed. "Well, come to the library. Mother had a lot of books. I'm afraid you have much work ahead of you."

"I visited your mother several times, Judge Reece. And you're correct. This is going to take several hours." Del and

Ivy trailed the judge down the marble floor hallway. He opened another door and ushered them inside.

Two stories of books, paperbacks, hardbacks, every imaginable color and size, greeted Del's gaze. Nothing in the church-sized room was out of place. Serious book envy hit Del again. "Incredible."

Ivy dropped the load of boxes she'd carted in. "Judge Reece, I didn't realize your mother had so many books."

He laughed. "Most people collect normal things like coins or stamps. Mother collected books."

Del placed her own boxes on the floor and moved further into the room. She knew several customers who would love to boast about a library like this. "When do you need the assessment completed?"

"I'm here until the end of the week. After that, I'm due in court."

"We'll do our best." Three days. She was glad to have Ivy to help with the mammoth task. While her cousin was a rabid romance fan, she had read her share of mysteries over the years as well. All Del needed was an extra pair of hands to help her sort paperback books and pack them for transport to her store.

"I know I asked you to assess the value of Mother's hardback collection, but as you're sorting, would you mind boxing them? I thought I would have enough time to do it myself, but I have business to complete before I return to Washington, D.C."

Del and Ivy exchanged a look. No way she and her cousin could manage this by themselves. "We can do that, but we'll need more boxes and more help to finish in time."

"Bring whatever help you need." Judge Reece dug into his jacket pocket and handed Del a key. "I'll be in and out until my flight home. This will make it convenient for you to sort and pack around your own schedule instead of mine. I realize you still have a business to run. I have book boxes stacked in the formal dining room. At the hallway, turn left and go straight back. Dining room is on the left." He glanced at his watch and grimaced. "I'm meeting with Mother's lawyer in a few minutes. I'll grab my briefcase and go. Lock up when you leave."

Del stared at the judge's retreating back.

"We'll need an army to box these books by Friday."

"I'll ask Madison and Nick if they will help after the store closes." Madison Santana, Del's business partner, and her husband, Nick, had become good friends over the past year.

"Maybe they'll bring Madison's brother. With all those muscles, he's perfect to haul heavy books around." Ivy grinned. "Perhaps he'll grab a certain smitten bookseller, throw her over his shoulder and ride off with her."

Del frowned at her cousin. "Grab a box."

She studied the room's layout. The hardbacks occupied the top three shelves of each bookcase. The other shelves held paperbacks of all colors and sizes. Hardbacks first, she decided. The paperbacks were unlikely to be valuable, just well loved by the appearance of some of them. She spotted a step ladder with rollers near the far wall.

"Where do we start?" Ivy bent and lifted a stack of empty boxes.

"Left side behind the door. Hardbacks first." Del walked to the ladder and pushed it across the room. "Let's grab my laptop and our water from the car. After, why don't you find more boxes? The ones we brought are good for paperbacks, but not the heavy books."

"Aye, aye, Captain, ma'am."

Del rolled her eyes and retraced her steps down the hall with Ivy close behind. At the front door, hand on the knob, she heard a peculiar coughing noise. "What was that?" She turned, searched the darkened hallway.

"I don't know." Ivy started down the hall, stopped. "Should we check on the judge?"

Still no more coughing. Hmm. "Must not be serious."
She shrugged. "We'll check if we hear anything else." Del
walked out the front door and stepped into nature's sauna.
She unlocked her SUV and, after handing a bottle of water
to her cousin, took a minute to drink half a bottle of water
and retrieved her laptop from the backseat. As she closed
the door and relocked her vehicle, an engine revved nearby.
A black truck drove by on the street in front of Mae
Reece's house. At first, Del thought it was Judge Reece
going to his meeting, but the driver had dark hair where the
judge had snow white hair. The driver, face partially
shadowed by the bill of his ball cap, scowled in their
direction and accelerated.

"Who was that?" Ivy asked, gaze tracking the truck
until it turned right at the street corner. "Not your biggest
fan, is he?"

"I've never seen him before." She led the way to the
library. "Once I set up my computer, we'll start." Good
thing she'd charged her laptop before leaving home this
morning. Del unzipped her case, pulled the laptop from
inside, and flipped open the lid. Computer ready, she turned
toward the hallway.

Ivy climbed down the ladder with an armload of
books. Del hustled to the foot of the ladder. She reached up.
"Let me have those. You should have waited for me."

Ivy laughed. "Yeah, like we've got so much time to
waste. Can you believe the judge wants us to box this
whole library? There's got to be over 30,000 books in
here."

Del scanned the shelves again. Ivy's estimate might be
conservative. "We'll draft help. I'll climb the ladder and
hand books to you. Record the books. I'll look up their
values later." That part of her job might have to wait until
the judge returned to the nation's capital. "You type faster
than I do."

"Some excuse. You want your hands on those books instead of the keyboard."

Del grinned. "Caught me."

They worked for a solid hour before they were interrupted by the phone ringing. Del had just climbed off the ladder to give her legs and back a break and was nearest the phone. It kept ringing.

"Should we answer it?" Ivy asked. "Maybe it's Judge Reece."

"You might be right." She reached for the handset. "Reece residence."

"Good afternoon. I'm looking for Judge Reece."

Del searched the desk for paper and pen. "He's in a meeting. I'm not sure when he'll return. I can take a message."

Silence greeted her for a moment. "I see. My name is Seth Brady. Judge Reece was supposed to meet with me an hour ago about his mother's estate. Will you have him call my office to reschedule?"

"Sure. I'll leave him a note." Puzzled, Del clicked off the handset and wrote the message on a piece of paper she found in a desk drawer. She turned to her cousin. "That was the lawyer's office. Judge Reece didn't show for his appointment."

"Wonder what happened?"

She headed for the door. "I'll leave the note on the desk in the office. That's the most likely place for him to see it." Del headed down the hall, checking doorways as she passed various rooms. She located the dining room with the huge pile of book boxes. They would need all those and more to box the books.

She located the office across the hall from the dining room. Del cleared the threshold and stopped, nose wrinkling. What was that smell? Reminded her of a sewer. She crossed the room and laid her note on the desk. She turned to leave and saw a pair of men's shoes on the floor.

Del hesitated. Cold chills crawled up her back. She forced herself closer to the shoes. Rounding the desk, she froze. Hands clamped to her mouth, she backed away from the sight of Judge Reece sprawled on the floor, a red hole in his forehead, a pool of blood under his head.

Joshua Cahill crawled closer to his quarry. As long as the culprit didn't go any further, this call was almost a wrap. If he didn't know better, he'd swear he heard his six foot four brother-in-law laughing from across town in his council meeting. Ethan Blackhawk, police chief of Otter Creek and husband to the youngest of Josh's triplet sisters, Serena, had tangled with this problem many times over the past two years.

You would think Mrs. Wilson would be more careful. He huffed out an exasperated breath when the object of this call stared at him in disdain. "Come here, Fluffy. Your human mom is about to have a heart attack worrying you'll fall from the tree." In Josh's opinion, if the cat climbed up into the tree, he could climb down when he wanted. Fluffy was a dumb name for a male cat. Maybe Fluffy hid in the maple tree so often because his name embarrassed him.

Josh adjusted his legs for a more secure hold on the tree limb and reached into his shirt pocket for his stash of cat treats. Nothing else worked in getting Fluffy from the tree unless the fire department came with the ladder truck. Unfortunately for him, the guys were out on a call. A brush fire out on Highway 36. With this long dry spell, the firemen had been busy.

He extended his arm, cat treat in his hand. "Come here, buddy." Fluffy gave a dainty meow and crept closer to Josh's hand. "That's it, fur ball." As soon as Fluffy crawled within reach, Josh lifted the feline into his arms and fed him the treat. He took a minute to scratch the sweet spot on the cat's head and was rewarded with a rumbling purr.

With a soft chuckle, he shifted the cat to one arm and scooted toward the tree trunk and ladder. A minute later, Josh placed the tabby into Vera Wilson's arms.

"Oh, thank you, Officer Cahill. Fluffy was so scared."

Josh restrained himself from rolling his eyes. "Not a problem, ma'am. How did he escape this time?"

"I was unloading groceries and he darted from the kitchen, to the garage, and into the yard."

He studied Mrs. Wilson's vehicle. "You have a small car. Why don't you close the garage door before you unload groceries? Maybe we'll keep Houdini in the house that way."

"Why, I didn't think of that, young man. Yes, I think I will try that."

"Excellent. I'd better get back on patrol, Mrs. Wilson. See you later."

"Thanks, again."

One more scratch, this time under Fluffy's chin, and he slid behind the steering wheel of his vehicle. Josh grabbed a bottle of water and polished it off before notifying dispatch he was back on patrol. As he drove down the street, he grinned. If his Delta team could have seen him rescuing a cat that probably didn't want to be rescued, they'd have been rolling on the ground, howling with laughter. Yeah, tough former Delta warrior Josh Cahill, now a tree climber, cat rescuer, and ticket writer. This job was not in the same league with his Delta years.

It was good to be home, though. Much as he'd loved the adrenaline ride of Delta, Josh had missed his parents and his sisters. Eight years in the Rangers and five in Delta was enough. He'd lost many good friends in the Sand Box. After his leg injury, he'd known it was time to step out and let younger men take the lead. The Army had agreed and released him. Had to admit, though, he missed the action. Pulling over DUIs and chasing down speeders just didn't have the same adrenaline rush as facing insurgents with an RPG aimed at you.

He drove down Main and headed toward the town square. Braked at a stop sign, dispatch broke into the radio chatter.

"Unit 6."

Josh grabbed his radio handset. "Unit 6. Go ahead."

"10-59 at 3365 Morningstar Lane."

"10-4."

Josh flipped on his lights and sirens, turned right and stomped the accelerator. He swerved around vehicles that were too slow to merge right, frowning. A dead body at the Reece place? Who could it be? Mae Reece had passed away a week ago. The whole town had turned out for her funeral. He half listened to the radio chatter, but heard no further information.

Two minutes later, he pulled into the long driveway of the Reece estate and stopped behind a familiar SUV. His gut tightened. Couldn't be, he told himself. And then he saw Ivy Monroe barrel out the door and vault down the steps toward him.

He shoved open his driver's door and met Del's cousin at the foot of the stone stairs. "Ivy, you okay?"

She nodded, eyes wide. "It's Del."

Josh's heart squeezed. No, not Del. "Where is she?" He couldn't lose anyone else.

"Follow me. I'm too rattled to give you directions. You'd end up in the Bermuda Triangle if I tried." She darted ahead, through the double doors and turned left into another room.

Library, Josh noted as he scanned the room, hand on his weapon. He spotted Del, arms curled around her stomach, shoulders hunched tight, seated in an armchair near the window. Thank God. He knelt in front of her. With a soft voice, he said, "Hey."

Del stirred, lifted her gaze to his. Her face was colorless, eyes vacant.

Definitely in shock. He could help with that, but he needed information first. "Del, are you okay?"

She blinked.

Josh took her hands in his. Ice cold. He squeezed. "Are you hurt?"

Another blink, then she shook her head. A deep breath. "Josh?"

"I'm here, sweetheart." Now where did that come from? He'd never called Del Peterson anything like that. If it made her more comfortable with him right now, he'd call her every sweet name he could think of. "Talk to me. What happened?"

She shuddered. "Judge Reece." Swallowed hard.

Josh's eyebrows rose. "What about him?"

"He's dead."

He stood. "Can you show me where he is?"

Del nodded, her hair rippling with life in the waning light from the window, and rose to stand in front of him.

"Ivy, wait for the ambulance. It should be here soon." Slipping an arm around Del's waist to steady her, Josh walked his favorite bookseller down the hall. Within a few feet of an open door on the left side, tremors started to ripple through Del's body. "Easy, Del. You don't have to go inside the room. Just show me which one. This place is big enough to get lost in."

He didn't think she paid attention to anything he said beyond not returning to the room with the judge's body. She leaned harder into his side. "Where do I go from here, beautiful?"

Her eyes darted toward the room nearest them.

Josh noticed a desk with a computer sitting on top of it. Looked like an office of some kind. "In there?" After getting a nod, he steered her back to a nearby chair and eased her to the cushion. "Stay here."

He scanned the office as he stepped through the door, noted the shoes sticking out, rounded the desk. Josh blew out a breath and reached for his portable radio. "Dispatch, this is Unit 6."

"Unit 6, go ahead."

"ETA on ambulance?"

"Three minutes."

"Copy. I need a detective and the crime scene team to 3365 Morningstar Lane. Also notify Chief Blackhawk."

"10-4."

Josh took a minute to study the scene and body visually before heading back to the woman with her face buried in her hands. He needed to secure the crime scene and that meant getting Del and Ivy out of the house. "Del, come with me."

She raised her head to stare at him. "Don't we need to wait for the ambulance?"

"We'll wait in my vehicle." He held out his hand to her. "You're my priority right now." No one could help Judge Reece.

Del stared at his hand a moment. She drew a deep breath and reached for him. Josh helped her stand and walked her through the front door and down the steps to his SUV. He seated Del in his front passenger seat and motioned Ivy over. "Stay with her."

Knowing Del needed a blanket despite the July heat, Josh opened his hatchback and pulled out a blanket which he wrapped around Del, and cranked his engine to get the air conditioning going for Ivy.

The approaching sirens grew louder until they were silenced at the entrance to the Reece driveway. The ambulance pulled in followed by another police SUV. The driver's door popped open and a lanky red-haired detective crossed the pavement to meet Josh at the back of his SUV.

Josh nodded to his other brother-in-law, Rod Kelter, and motioned the ambulance attendant toward Del and Ivy.

"What's the situation?" Rod pulled off his mirrored sunglasses and slid them into his pants pocket.

He glanced at the open door of his SUV and moved out of hearing range of the women. "Del found Judge Reece's body in the office." Josh rubbed the back of his neck and turned his gaze toward Del. "Rod, it looks like he was assassinated."

CHAPTER TWO

Rod blew out a quick breath. "Great. I planned to take Megan out of town this weekend. A surprise trip to Florida."

"Good luck with that. If it's not your job, it's hers." Josh's sister, Megan, was editor of Otter Creek's local newspaper, though she'd sold off the quirky printing presses a few months back and gone to online subscriptions and for those die hard paper-and-ink readers, a neighboring town's paper did the print run. "You could foist this off on Nick."

The detective grinned. "I'll tell him you volunteered his services. I'm sure Madison will be glad to cook for you in appreciation for your thoughtfulness."

Josh grimaced. "You have a mean streak." Madison was well known county-wide for her culinary skills. More often than not, her cooking efforts ended up in a visit from the fire department. His long-suffering brother-in-law Nick had pretty much banished the woman he adored from the kitchen except to operate the microwave.

More sirens cut off as cruisers swung into the drive and parked at odd angles. Rod waved over another patrol officer. "Don't let the women out of your sight. Don't let them talk about what they've seen, not to each other or anyone else. Ethan should be here soon. Send him in as soon as he arrives. Josh, let's go."

Another glance assured him the EMT was still working with Del and Ivy. The thought of leaving them with another officer left him uneasy. He followed Rod inside the stone mansion.

"Which way?" Rod asked.

Josh inclined his head toward the hall. "Straight down the hall. Third door on the left."

"Did Del say anything about what happened?"

"I didn't ask. I had her show me where the judge's body was located and hustled her and Ivy out of the house."

"I don't think I've met Ivy. Who is she?"

"Del's cousin. She's working at the bookstore until she starts teaching at the community college in the fall."

Rod paused in the doorway of the Reece office as Josh had done when he first crossed the threshold.

"Do you know who's been in here?"

"Del and me for sure. The killer. I don't know about Ivy. Probably not, though, considering she's hyper." Not like Del. He'd never seen her almost incoherent. He didn't like it. His jaw tightened. He'd like to have an up close and personal discussion with the person who'd caused her so much fear. That was unlikely, though.

Rod stepped further into the room, rounded the desk, stared down at the body of Judge Reece. "No weapon?"

"No."

"Killer probably took it. I'll ask Del if she saw one or maybe picked it up."

"Be careful with her. She's pretty fragile."

Rod shot him a glance, eyebrows raised. "Have you ever known me to be abusive with a witness?"

Josh's face heated in the air conditioned room. "Sorry. Del's a friend."

"I like her too, but I don't think in the same way you do."

"It's not like that," Josh said. Not that he wasn't interested. Timing hadn't worked out to pursue it yet.

"If you say so." Rod's tone indicated a clear disbelief in his statement. Great. No doubt his reaction to Del would end up fodder on the family grapevine in the near future. He'd have Serena and Madison on his doorstep in the next few days if they resisted the temptation to harass him over the phone. His mother wouldn't be far behind them.

Footsteps echoed on the hardwood floor behind him. He turned and eyed Police Chief Ethan Blackhawk as his long strides ate the distance between them. His brother-in-law didn't look happy. "Do I earn brownie points for calling you away from the mayor?"

"Oh, yeah." Ethan scowled. "His Honor was on a roll today. His nephew is earning a steady supply of speeding tickets lately and racking up more than his share of DUIs on the weekends."

"Must be police harassment," Rod said, his done dry. "Did he want you to wipe the record clean?"

"Why else would he pull me aside after a town council meeting? I'm not his favorite person."

"What did you tell him?" Josh asked.

"His nephew could get in line behind Megan to pay the speeding tickets and if he got pulled over for another DUI, I would personally throw him behind bars."

Rod whistled. "Better watch your back, Ethan. His Honor is likely to start up another campaign to replace you as police chief."

"So he threatened. What do we have?"

Rod stepped aside and motioned Ethan further into the room. "John Reece. Federal judge. One shot to the forehead. No other signs of trauma. Del Peterson found the body."

"Josh, what do you see?" Ethan asked, his dark gaze probing.

He snorted. "Light switch shot. Close range."

"Light switch?" Rod's gaze shifted between Ethan and Josh. "What is that?"

"One shot between the eyebrows turned off his lights. Permanently." Josh said. "Sure kill shot."

"Did you talk to Del?" Ethan asked.

"Enough to find out where the body was and to get her and Ivy out of the house."

Ethan sighed. "This is going to get messy, fast. A federal judge's assassination means we'll have the feds breathing down our necks. U.S. marshals will be all over this case since it's their jurisdiction. The FBI will be right behind them. They won't be able to resist sticking their nose into everything."

"And messing it up," Rod muttered. "Craig Jordan will be in our faces in the next 48 hours."

"Sooner, I'd say."

Josh grimaced. He'd heard stories about Jordan. None of them were good. The fed made no bones about using anyone and anything necessary to achieve his objectives and close his cases. Two of those cases had involved Serena and Megan. The special agent was not a favorite of the Otter Creek Police Department.

"Let's get the coroner out here so our crime scene unit can get started. Anything you learn, I want to know about yesterday. Clock's ticking, Rod." Ethan turned to Josh. "Let's go. I want to check on Del, then return to the office and clear up paperwork before the feds camp out in my office."

Josh trailed the police chief out to the driveway and his SUV. The EMT was putting away his medical gear in the ambulance. Ethan walked up to Del and knelt, putting him at eye level with her.

"How are you feeling now, Del?" He clasped her hand in one of his. "Better?"

She nodded. "Oh, Ethan. It was terrible. Poor Judge Reece."

"I know. I'm sorry you saw that. Look, Del, trauma affects people in different ways. If you need to talk to someone, I've got the names of several counselors we recommend."

"I'll be okay." She gave him a ghost of a smile.

Ethan reached into his pocket and pulled out a business card. "Call me if you need me." He stood and strode back to Josh, glanced at his watch. "You off shift?"

"Yes, sir."

"It will be a while before Rod can talk to Del and Ivy. Someone needs to stay with them. Do you want me to assign the responsibility to one of the other patrolmen?"

Josh's gaze returned to the bookseller. Something inside him rebelled at someone else being responsible for Del's safety. If he stayed, he could listen to Rod's questions and Del's answers. "I'll stay."

He nodded. "Good enough. When do you go back on duty?"

"Not until Sunday night. I'm on third shift next week."

Ethan clapped him on the shoulder, spoke a word to another officer, and left.

Josh returned to his SUV and knelt beside Del, gaze scanning her face. "It will be a while before Rod can shake free. Would you and Ivy like a cold drink?" He figured sugar and distance from the crime scene would help her recover. Waning daylight hadn't done much to negate the brutal heat, but he suspected the gentle bookseller would prefer to be outside than near the office where she could see and hear the crime scene people.

"We would appreciate that as long as it won't be too much trouble."

"It's no problem. I could use something myself." His black uniform drew heat and he was sweaty all over, especially under his bullet-proof vest. Josh stood and, stepping away from his vehicle, called one of the uniforms nearby and put in a request.

Ten minutes later, a patrol car rolled to a stop. "Order's up, Cahill." Swanson grinned and handed over the sweating six pack of Coke.

"Thanks, man." He bumped fists with his friend and the prowl car eased around the drive and back to the street before taking off in a cloud of dust and swirling lights.

Josh retraced his steps to Del and Ivy as the coroner's van pulled to a stop behind the ambulance. "You may not drink the real stuff, but trust me, you need the sugar to combat shock."

"It's fine," Ivy said. "As long as it's cold."

"Thank you, Josh." Del's gaze connected with his for a heart stopping moment.

He gave a nod and moved a short distance away, enough to give them privacy yet still be within his hearing so he could monitor their conversation. He quartered the area. Nothing. Somewhere nearby, though, a killer walked among them.

Del sipped the last of her Coke, glad the shaking had stopped. Though he hadn't said much to them since arranging for the cold drinks, Josh hovered nearby, watching everything. His stance and constant visual scanning told her he was still on alert. His vigilance made her feel protected, cared for.

Just doing his job, she reminded herself. Don't read anything into it. Wishing she wasn't just a job to him wouldn't make it so.

Activity near the front door drew his attention for a second. He turned and approached them. Kneeling so close she could see multiple colors in his hazel eyes, Josh studied her face for an instant. "You look better."

"A cold Coke cures everything. Didn't you know that?"

Humor sparked in his gaze. "Can't say I've heard that one. My mother and sisters swear chocolate cures all ailments. I'll make a note of your preference."

More activity drew her attention from his gaze until his hand cupped her cheek and turned her face back to him. His action shocked her. He'd never touched her beyond accidental brushes that happened when people were in the same vicinity, occupied the same retail space and a few lunches shared with his family. "Josh?" she whispered.

"Look at me, sweetheart," he murmured. "Ivy, eyes on me. Tell me how my favorite bookseller is as a house mate."

Ivy laughed. "Before or after her morning cup of green tea?"

"Oh, man." Josh grinned, his gaze fixed on Del. "Another tea drinker. No wonder Serena loves you. What do you have against a good cup of coffee?"

"Too bitter for my taste."

"Maybe I can change your mind about that. What else, Ivy? Any secrets I can use for blackmail?"

"She has a weakness for apple pie and ice cream of any flavor." Ivy smiled. "She likes chocolate, but her favorite food is Mexican. She's not really into flowers."

Josh's eyes widened. "No flowers? That's a surprise."

Del's cheeks burned. "The scent gives me a headache."

"Guess that's why you don't wear perfume."

She didn't think he'd noticed her at all, yet he paid enough attention to notice that? "You don't wear cologne, either." A noise behind him made her jump.

Josh brushed his thumb over her bottom lip. "Right here," he said. "I dropped the cologne habit in the Army. Didn't want to announce my presence to the enemy. Ivy,

what does she collect? My sisters and mother all collect
something different. What's Del's thing?"

Her cousin laughed again.

"No," Del said. She couldn't shift her gaze or face
toward her cousin to warn her about keeping her mouth
shut. Josh had both hands on her face now.

"Another minute, okay?" His gaze drifted from her
eyes to her mouth. Del fought against the instinct to wet her
lips, but oh, man, she wanted to something fierce.

Desperate to get attention off her and her preferences,
she said, "Tell me something about you."

He grinned. "I like to read."

"Something I don't already know."

"My drink of choice is coffee. Plain. No fancy stuff
like Maddie tries to shove on me. I'm a night owl."

"Favorite food?"

"Mexican, but the Army taught me to eat anything that
doesn't eat me first."

Ivy grinned. "Perfect. Maybe you two should go to
dinner together."

Del's cheeks burned hotter. "Ivy!"

A couple vehicle doors slammed nearby. Josh glanced
over his shoulder and, with a brush of his thumbs over her
cheeks, stood and moved back. Out of the corner of her
eye, Del noticed the coroner's van moving, the ambulance
close behind. Her gaze darted to Josh. He winked at her and
turned to survey the surroundings once again. So what was
that about? While she wanted to believe the handsome cop
saw her as something more than a friend, she knew better
than that.

Rod Kelter approached the SUV at a fast clip. "How
are you now, Del? Able to answer a few questions for me?"

She nodded, shrugged off the blanket Josh had draped
around her shoulders.

"Good. Let's go inside, ladies. You could fry an egg on
the sidewalk today."

Del stood, surprised to find her legs shaky. She grabbed the car door to steady herself.

"You okay?" Josh shifted closer.

She straightened, forced herself to release the metal frame. "I'm fine." One step after another, Del made her way to the mansion's entrance. The closer she drew, the more dread curled in her gut. She didn't want to be in the same house with Judge Reece's body. Stupid. Not like a dead body could hurt her. But the visual she couldn't get out of her head made her want to throw up.

One step inside the doorway and tremors wracked her body.

"Del."

Josh waited until her attention centered on him rather than on the beehive of activity down the hallway in the study. "The coroner took the body with him."

She closed her eyes a moment, relief flooding her system, calming the tremors. "You distracted me."

"You didn't need another memory to deal with."

"Nice work," Ivy said.

Del blinked away the forming tears. "Thanks." He was right. Seeing the body wheeled down the stairs would have added more sleepless nights to what she feared already would be a string of them.

"Let's go to the living room," Rod said. "Might as well be comfortable while we talk." He led the way into the gorgeous room and dropped into a brown leather recliner near a couch of similar material. The detective pulled out a small notebook and pen. "Why don't you start at the beginning, Del? When did you arrive?"

Del huddled into the corner of the couch, wished she could run away from the questions and bloody memories. "Around two o'clock. Ivy and I were supposed to be here at noon, but a shipment of books arrived later than normal. One of my customers was anxious for this particular shipment and we were swamped at lunch today." She drew in a deep breath. Man, she needed to slow down and answer Rod's questions without rattling on about stuff that didn't have anything to do with Judge Reece. "Sorry," she murmured.

He smiled. "So you arrived around two. What were you and Ivy doing here?"

"Oh, Judge Reece asked me to evaluate Mae's book collection."

"And pack up the library," Ivy added.

Rod's eyebrows shot up. "Big job."

"I planned to draft help," Del said. "He wanted the books packed by this weekend."

"Huh. Okay, we'll come back to that. Walk me through what happened from the time you arrived to when you called us. You arrived at two. Who let you in the house?"

"Judge Reece."

Josh straightened from the wall he'd been leaning against.

"You talked to him?" Rod asked.

"For a few minutes."

"What about?"

"His mother. He mentioned how shocked he was that his mother had fallen down the stairs." She glanced at Ivy, seated to her right. At her nod of agreement, Del continued. "He showed us into the library and left."

"Did he say where he was headed?"

"He had an appointment with his mother's lawyer," Ivy said. "He said he needed to grab some papers in the office before he left."

"Any special reason he wanted you to pack up the books?"

"Multitasking," Ivy said. "Del rocks at that."

"Mae loved books." Del smiled. "She was an equal opportunity collector, but she especially loved paperbacks.

She also had some very valuable hardbacks, first editions that were worth quite a bit of money."

"And what exactly were you supposed to do for Judge Reece?"

"We were recording all the hardback books for him. I was going to look up their values after we'd packed them in boxes."

"Judge Reece had scads of book boxes for us to use," Ivy put in. "There's a mountain of them in the dining room across from the office."

Rod made some notes and pinned Del with sharp gaze. "What about the other books? The paperbacks?"

"Mae left them to me. We were book buddies, always swapping book recommendations."

"Why not give them to her children?"

"None of them were readers, except for Judge Reece and he didn't read fiction."

"I see. So the judge showed you to the library and went to retrieve his papers. What time was this?"

Del scrunched her forehead. "Maybe 2:15." She glanced at her cousin. "Does that sound right?"

Ivy nodded.

"What did you do after Reece left you?"

"Packed books," Ivy muttered. "In case you wanted to know, hardbacks weigh a ton when you're hauling them down the ladder."

Rod chuckled. "I'm familiar with that. My wife, Megan, has quite a collection of her own. If we ever move to another house, I'm hiring movers to come pack her books and haul her stash to the new place."

"No, wait," Del interrupted. "Don't you remember, Ivy? We had to return to the car to get my laptop? We drank some water, came back inside, then got to work."

"Okay. So that was around 2:15. Your call to dispatch came in at four. What made you go into the office?"

Del swallowed the bile pooling in her mouth at the memory of Judge Reece's body.

"Del?" Rod leaned over and laid his hand on her knee. "You all right?"

"Sorry," she whispered.

Rod sent a pointed look to Josh. Seconds later she heard the front door open. He was leaving? Odd, but she felt abandoned. Del grabbed Ivy's hand. She hoped her cousin's grip would keep her grounded in the present instead of mired in the past.

"Stay with me," Rod said. "Don't think about that yet. I only want to know what sent you to the office."

"Phone call from the lawyer's office. He didn't make it to the appointment and the lawyer was calling to check." She gave the lawyer's name. "I thought he would see the note if it was on the desk."

Josh came back in, two more Cokes in his hand. He opened one of the drinks and handed her the bottle, passed the other to her cousin. "Sip it slow, Del."

She nodded, took a couple sips, waited for the nausea to subside. A deep breath, then, "I don't know what's wrong with me. I'm not usually so sensitive."

"Shock in your case." Josh snorted. "Just about any strong scent does Serena in. If I don't watch it, she'll turn me into a vegetarian soon."

Rod grinned. "Amazes me that she's made a success of her personal chef service when she has trouble cooking beef."

"That's when her tea drinking habit is the heaviest." Josh grimaced. "Nasty stuff."

"I'll second that." Rod studied Del a moment. "Ready now?"

She nodded.

"So the lawyer called, said the judge had missed his appointment. What did you do next?"

"Took a message and went to the office." Her heart thumped harder. She didn't want to do this, but she knew Rod needed all the information he could get from her and Ivy to find the judge's killer. "I walked into the office and saw his shoes." Del stopped. Her hand clenched around the bottle.

A rustle of movement behind her, and Josh's cold hand cupped the nape of her neck. Somehow either his presence or the touch of his cold hand grounded her, chased away the shakes and unsettled stomach.

"Did you touch anything?" Rod asked.

"No."

"What about you, Ivy? Did you go into the office?"

She shook her head. "Del wouldn't let me once she saw Judge Reece. We called you guys from the library."

"Think carefully before you answer the next question. Did either of you hear a gunshot?" After a negative response from both, he asked, "Did you hear anything unusual or out of place?"

"We didn't hear anything," Ivy said.

Del frowned. "Nothing except that weird cough."

Josh's hand tightened on her neck.

"When did you hear the cough?" Rod asked.

"Maybe 2:20. We were at the front door to get my laptop."

"Did you hear anything else after the cough?" After a negative head shake from her and Ivy, the detective leaned toward her. "What about before when you were in the hall? Did you hear the judge talking or maybe movement?"

"Nothing."

"You didn't go check out the noise?"

"No," Ivy said. "We didn't hear it again. Why? What was that noise?"

"You didn't hear a gunshot at any time?" Rod pressed.

"Rod, you're scaring me." Del's voice shook. "What did we hear?"

A quick glance at Josh, then, "The coughing noise was probably a suppressed gunshot."

CHAPTER THREE

So close. Josh wiped the sweat from his brow as he followed Del's SUV. If Del and Ivy had checked on the judge or lingered at the front door, they might have seen the killer. He or she would have killed them as easily as he'd dispatched Judge Reece. From his observations at the crime scene, the killer surprised the judge. No argument, according to Del. No sign of a struggle.

Though he remained close to the SUV, he scrutinized the traffic. No one revealed interest in their two-vehicle caravan. They arrived without incident at Del's two-bedroom bungalow located on Evergreen Road.

Josh turned off the engine and climbed from his vehicle. Del and Ivy lingered on the walkway. He extended his hand to Del. "Keys. I want to check the house before you enter."

"Why? We didn't see the killer, so he couldn't have seen us."

Not necessarily. That thought made his stomach churn. "Better to be safe."

"I hate this."

Josh stilled. "You don't want me in your house?"

"I hate that searching my home is necessary. What if someone is waiting and hurts you?"

"I'd prefer he come after me instead of you or Ivy. I can take care of myself." Except when he'd zigged instead of zagged in the Sand Box and taken a career-ending bullet in the leg. Josh was agile enough for law enforcement, but not for Delta. He wiggled his fingers. "Keys, beautiful. I don't want you and Ivy in this heat long. It's brutal out here."

She dropped her keys on his palm.

"Any pets?"

She shook her head.

He opened the door, slipped inside, listened to the silence. Nothing appeared disturbed. Knowing a killer had been near the women hours before, he searched the house, weapon in hand.

No one lurked in Del's home and her backyard was empty of anything except a flower garden and bird bath. He smiled. For a woman who didn't want to be given flowers, she didn't skimp on the yard.

He slid his weapon in his holster and motioned the women inside. "All clear."

Relief washed over Del's face. "Thank you for checking."

"Not a problem."

Ivy took Del's laptop. "I'll put this in your room before I change clothes. I can't wait to get out of these sweaty things." She paused at the hallway entrance. "Thanks for everything, Josh."

He studied Del's face. Still too pale. "Will you be okay?"

"Sure."

He tilted his head. "Why don't I believe you?"

"Maybe because I don't almost witness a murder every day."

She shouldn't have seen anything like that. Sure, death arrived for everyone. Violent death was altogether different. "Time will dull the memory. In the meantime, you'll have vivid dreams, nightmares. They're normal."

She wrinkled her nose. "I was afraid of that."

"Where's your cell phone?"

Del pulled her phone from her pocket and handed it to him. Josh keyed in his name and cell number on her speed dial and returned her phone. "Call my phone."

He saved her contact information. "Call me if you can't sleep or become uneasy. I live a few blocks away and I can be here in under three minutes. I'm also off duty until Sunday night."

"Thanks." Her voice sounded choked.

He reached for the doorknob, stopped, turned back. Leaving her in tears didn't feel right. He leaned down and whispered in her ear. "You have an amazing teddy bear collection. If you sweet talk me, I'll show you my cars if you promise not to rat me out to my sisters. They believe I gave my cars away before I left for boot camp."

Del grinned. "Deal."

Much better. "Working tomorrow?"

"I wouldn't miss it. The Christie Club's meeting at ten o'clock."

"Christie Club?"

"Some mystery readers wanted to form a book club but couldn't bring themselves to call it the Murder Club. They were afraid Ethan might object to the name."

"Ruth must be part of that group." Ethan's aunt was a bestselling cozy mystery writer.

"They're armchair detectives and Ruth has turned them into a sounding board for her books. Those women have plotted all kinds of murders." She shook her head. "I would hate to make them mad. They could plot the perfect crime."

"Do they read only classic murders?"

Del laughed. "These ladies love Robert B. Parker, John Sandford and a whole range of cozy mysteries, too. They love the challenge of solving mysteries before the killer is revealed by the author. They read more books than you per week."

"I might drop by tomorrow." He paused. "These murder experts will want details about today. It's best not to talk about it with anyone outside the investigation."

"Okay." She bit her lower lip. "Josh?"

"Yeah?"

"Would it have made a difference if I had checked on the judge?"

Other than her being as dead as Judge Reece? "No."

"But if I had called an ambulance?"

"He died instantly, Del." Josh cupped her cheek with his hand. "Call me if you need anything." He pressed a kiss to her forehead and left.

After showering off the day's sweat, treating a scratch from Fluffy, and heating a meal left in his freezer by Serena, Josh grabbed his cell and called Ethan. "Update?"

"Too early. How are Del and Ivy?"

"Ivy's okay. Too soon to know about Del. She was pretty shaken."

"Shouldn't have been exposed to any of that," Ethan said.

Josh heard the anger in his brother-in-law's voice. No doubt, Ethan took the assassination personally. He especially wouldn't like the fed interference sure to descend on them. "The feds will want to interview Del and Ivy?"

"Count on it."

"Any chance I can sit in on that?"

"Something you need to tell me, Josh?"

His free hand fisted. "No."

"I wouldn't let the feds talk to the ladies without me or Rod there," he said, voice soft. "What's your stake in this?"

Josh sighed. Should have known Ethan wouldn't let this drop. He couldn't explain his protective tendencies with Del, even to himself. "Del's a friend. I was first on scene. Makes it personal."

"If something changes, I need to know. Cops make mistakes when the stakes are personal."

He tightened his grip around his cell. "Right. You can tell me about that from personal experience, can't you?"

Ethan chuckled. "I asked for that, didn't I?"

"We're just friends."

"I want to know if that changes. Got me?"

Stubborn man. "Yeah, I got it." Josh ended the call and decided to call it a night. He'd be lucky to get in four hours of sleep before the dreams chased him out of bed.

He woke two hours later at his cell phone's first ring.

Del turned over and punched her pillow into a new position. Didn't help. Every time she closed her eyes, she saw John Reece's face, the hole in his forehead, the pool of blood under his head. She swallowed hard. If she didn't find a way to calm her mind and keep it focused on something else, she'd end up barfing. Again.

Del threw back the covers and swung her feet to the floor. She glanced at the clock. She had to get up in four hours to be at the store on time and she wouldn't have help aside from Ivy and Madison. Maybe a cup of tea would help her sleep. If nothing else, she'd grab a book, prop her feet up and indulge in a little relaxation. A cozy mystery sounded perfect.

Unable to think of anything better, she eased her door open and listened. No movement from the guest room. Good. She padded into the kitchen and, working from memory instead of her kitchen light, grabbed a mug, filled it with water, dropped in a tea bag, and slid it into the microwave.

She considered a light snack, immediately rejected the idea. The thought of food made the nausea swirl in her stomach. The way she'd felt the last several hours, she might be ready to eat in a day or two. The microwave beeped. Del yanked open the door, hoping she caught it before the sound woke her cousin.

She tossed the tea bag in the trash and carried her mug to the living room. With the lamp on the lowest setting, Del settled deeper into the cushioned chair, propped her feet up and grabbed the latest Laura Bradford mystery. She'd stopped reading at a good place and wanted to finish the book. Sleep seemed elusive tonight anyway.

Two chapters later, a noise outside yanked Del from the Amish mystery. She listened a minute, heard nothing else, and wondered if her imagination was playing tricks on her. Josh had told her skittishness was normal. Maybe a neighbor's dog was in the front yard. Blue, the blue heeler that lived next door, was a regular visitor. His owner never remembered to latch the gate.

Satisfied with that explanation, she returned her gaze to the page. Another noise drew her attention, this time from her backyard. Heart pounding, Del dropped the book on the end table and turned toward the French doors that led to her patio. Her eyes widened. The security light was out. She'd just replaced that bulb last week. It was possible the bulb was a bad one, but could she take that chance? The light had been on when she made her tea.

Feeling stupid, she dropped to her knees and crawled from the living room to the hall. The doorknob on the French door rattled. A burglar? Really? After the crappy day she'd had? Del hurried to Ivy's door and opened it. "Ivy," she whispered. "Wake up."

Her cousin sat bolt upright. "What is it?"

"I think somebody's breaking in. Come with me."

Ivy threw off the covers and jammed her feet into slippers. "Did you call the cops?"

"Not yet. Come to my room. I left my cell phone on the charger. We'll call from there." Del shut the door behind her cousin, locked it and raced across to her nightstand. She snatched up her cell and, with her eyes on her bedroom door, hit her speed dial.

On the second ring, Josh answered the phone, sounding fully alert. "What's wrong, sweetheart?"

Sweetheart. She loved sweet names like that. If only he meant them specifically for her. But Josh Cahill called all the women in his life by sweet or funny names. "Someone's trying to break in my back door."

"Where are you?"

"Bedroom. Ivy's with me."

"Can you climb out a window without being seen?"

"The window is on the back wall."

"Do you have a gun?"

"No." Glass shattered in the other room. She gasped.

"Talk to me."

"He broke the glass."

"Can you open the window without alerting the intruder?"

"I think so."

"Get Ivy to help. Make it look like you escaped. Then both of you hide in your closet. Don't come out until you hear from me or one of the other Otter Creek officers that you know. Do you understand?"

"Yes. Ivy, we need to open the window." She raced across the room to help. Hot, muggy air filtered into the room as she grabbed Ivy's hand and dragged her into the large walk-in closet. Del shut the door and pushed her cousin toward the back wall, thankful she'd taken time to straighten it up earlier in the week so they didn't stumble over stacks of shoes. She sank to the floor. "We're in the closet," she whispered into her cell phone.

"Stay put, Del. I'll be there in less than a minute."

"Okay. Josh?"

33

"Yeah, sweetheart?"

"Hurry."

"Almost there. Just hang on."

Over their open cell connection, the police siren sounded loud and clear. She also heard Josh talking to someone, asking for backup at 2416 Evergreen Road. Must be talking to the dispatcher.

Wood splintered nearby. Her bedroom door? Del reached over and gripped Ivy's hand. If they made noise, the intruder would know they were still in the house.

A soft curse sounded as a police siren cut off. Footsteps pounded across the floor toward the back wall. Then nothing.

Over the phone, she heard Josh yell, "Police! Freeze!" and then the phone connection dropped.

"What's happening?" Ivy whispered in Del's ear.

She gripped her cell phone harder though she pulled it away from her ear. "I heard Josh yell for somebody to freeze and then the call dropped." Del shuddered, gripping Ivy's hand tighter. Together, they sat in the dark and waited.

After what seemed like hours, they heard movement in Del's bedroom. Hardly daring to breath, she watched the closet door. Was it Josh or the person who'd broken into her home? If this was the burglar or Judge Reece's killer, she and Ivy had no way to escape. Had something happened to Josh? She drew in a sharp breath. She couldn't think like that or she'd drive herself crazy. He was a cop, a good one from listening to Ethan, Rod, and Nick talk about him. He knew how to take care of himself.

Footsteps moved closer to the closet. Del pressed against the back wall. The doorknob turned.

CHAPTER FOUR

Flashlight in hand, Josh approached the closet. Fellow officers were searching the neighborhood for the escaped perp. He caught a glimpse of the guy, not that it helped since he wore black, face covered by a ski mask. Though tempted to chase the perp further, he worried about Del and Ivy. He didn't intend to lose anyone else on his watch. If this guy killed Reece, Josh would have another crack at him. It was only a matter of time. If the killer tried for Del tonight, he wouldn't give up easily. But why come after the women at all? Del and Ivy didn't see him. Was he covering his bases? Or was this a string of bad luck?

He snorted. The chances this was a coincidence ranged somewhere between zero and nil, and nil was out of town. In his military and law enforcement experience, nobody's luck was that bad.

Gripping the heavy duty flashlight, he stepped to the side of the door, aimed his light toward the back of the closet, flung open the door and turned on the light. Two women raised their hands against the blinding light. He didn't see any obvious injuries. Safe. Thank God. "You're safe now."

Del surged to her feet and raced toward him. He had just enough time to plant his feet before she threw herself into his open arms. Shudders wracked her body.

Josh wrapped his arms around her. "You okay?" After receiving a nod despite tightening her grip around his waist, he turned his gaze toward Del's cousin, making her way out of the closet. "What about you?" He eased Del to his side and, after stuffing the flashlight into his pocket, extended his arm to Ivy. She slipped one arm around Josh, the other around her cousin. "Ivy?"

"I'm fine. Scary few minutes."

His arms tightened around them both. Josh was so afraid he'd be too late to save them. The whole time he'd jerked on clothes and careened down the deserted streets toward Del's place, he imagined various scenarios, all bad. Then he saw the perp race across the yard. Incredibly fast. The way he moved reminded Josh of his special forces days.

That reminder was the reason he'd dropped the chase when the perp disappeared in the woods. If this guy was a professional, he could hurt or kill the women in seconds. The haunting thought had driven him to check on them, praying he'd arrived in time.

The timing had been close enough he had to concentrate to drag his heart rate down from the stratosphere. Not normal for a sharpshooter.

Out in the hall, someone called his name.

"Bedroom on the right," he responded. Ivy eased away from him. Del, though, burrowed closer, burying her nose in his neck, still shaking. "Everything will be okay, baby," he murmured against her ear. "I won't let him near you or Ivy."

"I know," she whispered. "Thank you for coming so fast."

Josh cupped the back of her head, threading his fingers through her rumpled hair. Footsteps sounded behind him. He turned his head, nodded to Rod Kelter.

"They okay?" Rod assessed what he could see of Del and turned his attention to Ivy.

"We're okay," Ivy said. "Scared."

"Understandable." Rod eyed Josh. "You arrived fast. On stakeout?"

"I live a few blocks away. Del called me." Josh rubbed her back. "I was first on scene, couldn't wait for backup."

The detective didn't make further comments. His gaze rested on Del. "I need to ask you and Ivy some questions, Del. Why don't we take this somewhere more comfortable than your closet?"

"Where?" She lifted her head from Josh's shoulder.

"Living room. Intruder came in the back door."

"Can we change clothes? I'm not comfortable answering questions in my pajamas."

"Don't touch anything in your bedroom. Same for you, Ivy."

"I left the closet and dresser drawers open when I went to bed." She grinned. "I'm not the best housekeeper."

"Ten minutes long enough?" Rod asked.

Del nodded.

With a pointed look at Josh, Rod left the room.

Ivy eased past them. Her soft footsteps faded as she crossed the hall.

Josh eased Del back, nudged her face upward with his fingertips under her chin. "Better now, sweetheart?" She didn't look as though she was going to fall apart anymore.

"Sorry. I lost my composure for a minute."

"You're entitled."

"Josh, thank you. I don't know what would have happened if you hadn't been so close." She leaned up and kissed his cheek.

He stilled. Heat flooded his body that had nothing to do with the hot, sultry weather on this muggy night. When she started to move away, he captured her face between his palms and leaned down to press a soft kiss on her lips. Her startled gasp made him smile. He'd been wanting to do that for months. Though he hated the circumstances, he didn't mind introducing the idea of seeing him as more than a friend. "I'm glad I was close." He tapped her nose gently. "Get dressed, beautiful. Rod's not a patient man." Knowing he needed to leave the closet before he pushed things too far too fast, he turned and strode away.

Rod waited at the end of the hall. Yeah, he figured the detective wouldn't let this pass though maybe he was more interested in Josh's perspective on what happened rather than dogging him about this thing with Del. His brother-in-law may push, but it wouldn't make any difference. Josh didn't understand what was happening yet. He'd been blindsided by his favorite bookseller the first time he saw her and reluctant to explore it too closely since Del's business partner was his sister, Madison. He'd hate to cause dissension between them if he and Del tried a relationship and it didn't work. Too late to back out now, he supposed.

"Sit," Rod said. "This is my first week in a while for night duty."

Josh dropped onto the couch and stretched his legs in front of him. A long night for both of them. He didn't need much sleep, but two hours was a little less than he was used to. Guess he'd gotten soft since leaving the military. "I start third shift again next week."

Rod snorted. "You like night duty and don't have a wife waiting at home."

Josh cringed. "I don't want to hear about your wife keeping your side of the bed warm, buddy. That's my sister and I definitely don't want that visual in my head."

"Sounds like you introduced that picture into your brain all by yourself." He dug into his pocket for a notebook and pen while yawning. "Start at the beginning. When did Del call?"

"Couple minutes after two. Told me someone was breaking into her house."

"You the one who told her to open the window and hide in the closet?"

Josh nodded. "By the time Del called me, they couldn't leave the house without the perp seeing them. He broke one of the glass panes while she talked to me. House is too small for them to leave Del's room unseen at that point."

"Smart advice. If this was Reece's killer, they wouldn't have stood a chance against him. When did you arrive?"

"At 2:06. I spotted him running across the backyard. Black pants, black shirt, black ski mask. Six three or four, about Ethan's size. Not an ounce of fat on him. I followed, but this guy was fast, light on his feet. Almost no discernible sounds as he ran." Josh frowned. "He reminded me of some of the guys I used to work with in special forces."

Rod's eyes narrowed. "You think he's ex-military?"

"Wouldn't surprise me. This guy melted into the shadows, Rod. He moved like a well-trained spec ops soldier."

"If you're right, Reece's killer is as dangerous as they come."

Ivy hurried into Del's room and skidded to a stop. "You're not dressed. What's wrong?"

"What isn't? We almost witness a murder and less than twelve hours later somebody breaks into my house. I used to feel safe in this town. I'm friends with cops, including the chief of police. I've never been anywhere near a crime yet within the space of a few hours I'm exposed to two major crimes?"

"Must be a coincidence, Del."

"I don't buy that." Del stood, grabbed clothes and her tennis shoes, headed for the guest bathroom. "Tell Rod I'll be a couple minutes."

Though she wanted to slam the door, Del refrained. At first, she'd been too frightened to feel anything but sheer terror. Now, she was furious. Almost witnessing Reece's murder was bad timing. This latest incident made her blood boil. Why would someone break in to steal? Jobs were available in Dunlap county, many suitable for either skilled or unskilled labor.

What did she own that anyone would want? Her television wasn't new. She wasn't obsessive about music so she only played the radio when she needed musical entertainment. The only thing she invested money in, besides her store, was books and the teddy bear collection. Her cheeks flamed. She was still a child at heart. When she collected enough unique bears, Del donated them to the hospital or the police for traumatized children.

These incidents might frighten her cousin into going home to Nashville. Ivy needed a new start, away from her abusive ex-boyfriend. She deserved better than that jerk. If Ivy went back home, he'd pressure her into taking him back, no doubt promising to change.

Del scowled. He'd promised before, but he wouldn't control his mouth. No, Lee Hall never hurt Ivy physically, but he tried to change her cousin to suit him. She wanted her cousin to stay. She'd missed spending time with her while the jerk had been in Ivy's world. He'd slowly but surely cut Ivy's friends and family from her life until she discovered his actions. Del loved having her cousin back. She didn't want anything to send her home.

Del yanked on her clothes and shoes, ran her fingers through her hair and called it good. No use worrying about her appearance. She would look like the walking dead at the store in a few hours, but that was too bad.

She opened the door and traipsed to the living room where Ivy, Rod and Josh waited. Del's gaze collided with Josh's warm hazel eyes. He stood and gestured to the couch.

"Come sit with Ivy." He scanned her face. "Ready for your second police interview in twelve hours?"

"I'm afraid we won't be helpful. We didn't see anything."

"So Ivy said." Rod's pen hovered over his notebook. "Start from the beginning."

Del told the detective about her sleeplessness and decision to read. "I heard something outside."

"What?"

She thought a moment, analyzing what drew her attention from the book. "Shifting rocks in my driveway. I thought it was the neighbor's dog until I heard a noise at the back door."

"What did you do?" Rod asked.

"Crawled to the hallway and ran to Ivy. Felt stupid, too."

"Sounds smart to me."

"You weren't here when I thought I imagined everything."

"Your instincts were right. It was a good move, Del."

Josh, who stood behind the couch, laid his hand on her shoulder and gave a gentle squeeze. "Always pay attention to your instincts. Better to be embarrassed than to brush off warnings from your subconscious and end up hurt or worse."

Del shivered. If she'd ignored her subconscious, would she and Ivy be dead now? Not if this incident was a burglary. Would a burglar break down her door? Didn't they just steal and run?

Rod flipped to a new notebook page. "What happened after you reached Ivy's room?"

"I woke her up. We ran into my bedroom and locked the door. I called Josh."

"What did he tell you?"

"Leave by the window."

"Could you?"

She shook her head. "My window is on the back wall, the same side of the house as the French doors. The burglar was back there. While I was on the phone, the glass broke. Guess the burglar failed at picking the lock."

"Your French doors have a standard lock. Any self-respecting burglar would be inside in a minute or less."

Del closed her eyes. "Thanks for trashing my security even more."

"The dead bolt slowed him down. The best dead bolt locks with a key. You should change the lock for your own safety."

Another shoulder squeeze from Josh. "I'll take care of it, Rod. I'm upgrading her security."

"Hey, I'm not made of money."

"Don't worry. We can do many simple and inexpensive things. However, you need a security system, sweetheart. I know some guys who will set you up at cost. They owe me a few favors."

"You don't have to do that," Del protested.

Ivy patted her knee. "Say thank you and shut up."

The lack of sleep and stress made her grumpy. Del sighed. She needed to accept the new security measures with grace instead of grouchiness. "Thank you, Josh."

"I'll make calls in a few hours and start the process."

Rod cleared his throat. "Back to your story, Del. You called Josh and, while you were on the phone, you heard glass breaking. What did you do?"

"Opened the window as soon as he was inside. We hid in the closet."

"What did you hear?"

"Footsteps in the bedroom, cursing, then nothing. Right, Ivy?"

"He kicked the bedroom door in," Ivy added.

"He?" Rod glanced up from his notes. "Definitely a man?"

Del replayed the events in her head. "The floor creaked in the hall and in front of my closet. I hear the creaks when my brothers step on those boards, but never with me or Ivy."

"Did you hear enough cursing to determine if the voice was male or female?"

Ivy grinned. "Male. Deep voice. Salty language. He wasn't happy about us being gone or the police arriving."

"Did you leave the closet before an officer told you it was safe?"

Del shook her head. "Josh said to stay hidden until he or an officer I knew arrived."

Rod grinned. "Doesn't mean you listened to him."

Josh snorted. "Del is not Megan, bro. She doesn't look for trouble like my sister."

The detective turned his attention and question to Ivy. "What about you?"

Another head shake from her cousin.

"When you left the closet, did you notice smells that were out of place?"

Del paused. Her face heated remembering her source of comfort and safety. Josh's arms. She remembered the scent of his soap. Not what Rod meant with his question. "Nothing."

"Ivy?"

A frown marred her beautiful face. "There was a sharp scent, not one I recognized."

Rod jotted a note, looked up again. "Anything else stand out?" When he received a negative response, he asked, "Did you hear anything before Del came to wake you?"

Ivy shook her head. "I wouldn't hear a bomb go off."

Rod closed his notebook. "Pack a few necessities."

"Pack? Why?" Del asked.

"Two reasons. One, this is a crime scene. The CSI team needs to process your place. Second, your home is not secure, especially since your French doors are compromised."

"We'll find a motel with a vacancy." Del dreaded the hassle though it was for their safety. She wouldn't risk herself or Ivy.

"Not a motel," Josh said. "You're coming with me."

Del straightened and turned around to stare at him. "What?"

He tapped her nose again. "Trust me. You and Ivy pack what you need for a few days."

"What are you planning, Josh?" Rod's eyes narrowed. "You know how small towns talk, man. You can't take Del and Ivy in like stray puppies. The news will be around town before sunset."

Josh dragged his attention from the hall. "With both of them staying and a home invasion here, I don't think the town biddies would faint. However, I won't place Del in an uncomfortable situation." Especially now that he'd made the first move to change their relationship. At least, he hoped Del interpreted that peck on the mouth as a game changer. He sure had. And he couldn't wait to kiss her again. Patience, he reminded himself. He'd had months to think about dating Del Peterson. She'd had less than an hour. "Mom and Dad have room and I'll be able to stay when I'm off shift. They also have a top quality security system. If this guy gets through that system, he'll still have to go through me."

Rod frowned. "Think this was a stupid burglar?"

"I noticed a broken lock pick in the door knob. That plus the dead bolt slowed him down enough for me to arrive in time before he reached them. It's good Del couldn't sleep. Otherwise she and Ivy would be dead."

CHAPTER FIVE

"Are you sure your parents won't mind?" Del asked. "I hate to inconvenience them."

Josh turned into the driveway of his childhood home. "I called and cleared it. Mom loves company. She says the house is too quiet now that we're gone. We drop in all the time and when I'm tired of my own company, I stay a few nights, especially when Dad's out of town. Mom doesn't sleep well when he's gone."

Maybe she could do something to repay their kindness. "Do your parents read much?"

The SUV cruised to a stop. "Mom loves to read mushy stuff."

"Woman after my own heart," Ivy said from the backseat.

Josh grinned. "She carries her Kindle everywhere, but she also loves paperbacks. No hardbacks, says they're too heavy. Dad reads a lot of history. Why?"

"I'd like to repay them for opening their home on short notice. I have books in mind they might like."

"They'll appreciate it, but don't feel obligated. Really, sweetheart, they don't mind." He nodded toward the open back door, light spilling onto the deck. "Mom's waiting for us."

"It's 4 o'clock! She should be sleeping."

"Go on inside." Josh threw open the driver's door. "I'll grab our gear and be right behind you."

As Del and Ivy climbed the deck steps, Liz Cahill opened the screen door and waved them inside.

"Come in." She smiled. "I'm so glad Josh brought you to us." Liz's gaze searched Del's face. "Are you all right, honey? Josh told me what you've been through. I am so sorry."

Tears burned her eyes. "Thanks," she choked out. A tear slipped down her face which she brushed away. She couldn't break down now. Josh would come in the door any second. She didn't want him to think she was a wimp.

A second later, soft arms enfolded her. "It's going to be okay, Del. Josh and my sons-in-law will catch this man."

Del heard the screen door open behind her. Footsteps drew near.

"Everything okay, Mom?"

"We're fine, love. Del's in Serena's room. Madison's room is ready for Ivy."

"Dad up?"

"He just finished his shower. He said for you to go up as soon as you arrived."

Del drew back as Josh's footsteps faded into the interior of the house. At least she didn't have to explain tears to the tough cop. Nothing seemed to faze him. Then again, she didn't know him well, something she would love to remedy. Maybe that kiss signaled a change in their relationship. Probably wishful thinking, though.

Liz turned to Ivy. "Your turn, Ivy." She hugged Del's cousin close for a minute. "Now," she said as she eased back, "what would you girls like to do? Sleep or watch the sun rise? We can sit on the deck and listen to the birds as the world awakens."

"You don't have to entertain us," Ivy said. "Go back to bed."

Liz grinned. "I can't. My sweet husband is leaving for Nashville in an hour. I was already awake when Josh called."

"Are you fixing breakfast for him?" Del asked. She and Ivy could help with that. She wasn't a chef like Serena but she could find her way around the kitchen.

"Would you girls like to help make a batch of waffles."

"Absolutely," Ivy said. "As long as coffee will be ready soon, I'm game."

"Me, too," Del added. "Would your husband like an omelet, too?"

"He might." A smile crossed her lips. "Josh would appreciate your efforts. My son can put away food. Actually, all the men in our blossoming clan are hearty eaters."

"Must be nice," Ivy groused. "If I ate like that all the time, I'd wear every pound on my hips."

Del's gaze snapped to her cousin's face. She hated that haunted look in Ivy's eyes, her self-esteem in the basement. What would turn that around for her? "Open your eyes, Ivy. You need to gain a few pounds. Men like something to hold onto, don't they, Mrs. Cahill?"

"Please, call me Liz. Men like hugging a woman bigger than a twig. Let's start on breakfast, ladies. Ivy, the coffee's in that ceramic container. Del, search the refrigerator for omelet ingredients. I'll work on the waffles. We might have twenty minutes before Aaron and Josh are ready to eat."

"Dad?"

"In here, son." Aaron Cahill poked his head out of the bathroom, shaving cream covering half of his face. He glanced at the bedside clock. "You made good time."

"Sparse traffic this time of morning."

"That's why I leave this early when I attend banker meetings in Nashville. Traffic is gridlocked from seven o'clock on."

Several of his friends worked for Fortress Security, based in Nashville. Those guys did some serious black ops work, something Josh missed. Though Fortress had offered him and his Delta unit jobs, he hesitated to start that part of his life again. He still had some hard things to work through. He also didn't want to leave his family. He'd spent long years away from them. Life had moved by so fast. When he was released from the Army, he realized his parents were aging. After so many years away, he wanted to spend time with them, offer help when they needed it. The truth was he missed them while he'd been deployed all over the globe.

"How are Del and Ivy?"

"I thought they were holding up okay, but when I came into the kitchen Mom was holding Del. She was crying." It ripped at his heart out to see her tears. He wanted to be the one Del turned to when she needed comfort. Stunning and scary thought.

His dad froze. "Your mother was crying?" He grabbed a hand towel, ready to wipe shaving cream from his face. His father hated when his mother cried. No doubt he planned to charge downstairs and fix whatever was wrong, no matter what it took.

"Del was crying."

His father's tension eased away. "Ah. All the stress?"

"She seemed okay earlier."

"Hits them like that sometimes. Liz has a knack for drilling down to the emotions pretty fast. Also, Del doesn't have her mother close by. Your mom's a good substitute mother." Aaron eyed him. "What do I need to know, Josh?"

His father didn't miss a trick. Josh checked that the door was latched shut and moved two steps closer to his father. "The man after Del and Ivy is a professional, Dad. He's dangerous. Maybe former military."

Aaron straightened and swiped off the remaining streaks of shaving cream. "You saw him?"

"From a distance. Dude's fast, moves like special ops."

"I don't want your mother alone at night."

Just what Josh was thinking too. "How long will you be gone?"

"Three days. Do I need someone to cover this trip? I'm sure Dave would go. He's ambitious, pushing hard for his own bank pretty soon. It'd be good for him."

"You need to go this time, Dad. You said this meeting concerns coming changes in banking regulations. I'm off duty for the next three days. If I can't be here at night for some reason, I'll have Ethan, Nick or Rod stay. If we catch him, there won't be any danger to Mom or the women."

"If anything happens or something changes, I want to know immediately. Nothing is more important to me than Liz's safety."

"I'll watch over her. You have my word."

Minutes later, he and his father joined the women downstairs in the dining room. "Breakfast smells amazing, Mom. Waffles and omelets? I'll have to add another mile to my run."

Liz smiled. "Another pound or two on your frame won't hurt. You haven't regained the weight you lost after your leg injury."

Josh snorted. "Between you and Serena, I'm not going hungry. She keeps a closer eye on my calorie intake than I do. I'm exactly where I need to be."

"If you say so, love. Try one of the omelets. Del made them."

"Is that right?" Josh selected one, slid it onto his plate and passed the serving platter to his father. "Omelets are a weakness of mine."

A knock sounded at the back door followed by footsteps in the kitchen. Ethan strode into the dining room. "Morning, folks." He bent and kissed Liz on the cheek and shared a handshake with his father-in-law. "Heard you had some excitement over night, Del."

"I've reached my quota of bizarre happenings this week."

"Did you rest after Rod turned you loose?"

"We didn't try," Ivy said. "Since we were too keyed up, we helped Liz fix breakfast."

"Have you eaten, Ethan?" Liz asked. "We have plenty."

"I planned to pick up something. Serena had to be at the grocery store as soon as the doors opened."

Knowing his brother-in-law had an ulterior motive for dropping in, Josh steadily plowed through his meal. If he had information Josh could act on, he might miss a few of those meals his mother was so worried about.

"You're already here. Might as well eat before your day spins out of control." Aaron waved Ethan to a chair beside him and went to the kitchen for another plate and utensils. "How about some coffee, son? It's the Home Runs blend."

"No better coffee than that." Plate filled, Ethan set to work on his food. "Del, Rod gave me a run down of what happened last night. You up to telling me what happened in detail?"

"I don't have much to share."

"Go through it anyway. Sometimes witnesses remember things when a little distance separates them from the actual event. Shock dulls memories and you and Ivy have had more than your share of upsetting events since yesterday afternoon."

As Del rehashed the events, Josh watched her face and body movements while finishing the last of the omelet. He'd never eaten a pizza omelet before, but it was amazing. The closer she approached the point in her story where she called him, Del's coloring paled and her breathing grew more shallow. She was more upset about the break-in than she was letting on.

Josh hated the necessity for her to retell the story over and over, but Ethan was right. Details came back to crime victims with a little distance from the event. Too far from the event, details would fade.

He noted her full plate. She hadn't managed more than a bite or two of the waffle and that many of the omelet. Frowning, he nudged her plate closer. "Your body needs fuel though stress masks hunger. You need to eat, Del." Josh glanced at Ivy's plate. "You, too, Ivy. You don't eat enough to feed a bird."

"I'm just not hungry," Del whispered.

"Try, baby," he murmured. With a pointed look at Ethan to knockoff the questions for now, he went into the kitchen and dug around in the cabinets for his mother's tea stash. He dumped a mint chamomile tea bag in a mug of water, slid it into the microwave, and nuked it. When the appliance finished, he grabbed a spoon, a packet of natural sweetener and carried them back to the table. He placed the mug in front of Del. "Serena swears by this stuff. Says it's the only thing that settles her stomach."

"She ought to know." Ethan grinned.

"How's my baby girl this morning?" Aaron asked.

Ethan's face lit. "She's great. Busy with Home Runs. Serena added a new family to her cooking rotation last week so she's scrambling to fit all the cooking in for the week."

At the look on his face, an invisible band tightened around Josh's heart. Quite simply, Ethan adored Josh's sister. He'd felt the same way once about a woman while he was still in the Army. Josh had thought Emily was the love of his life. Turned out he was wrong. His gaze drifted to Del.

Ethan turned his questions to Ivy. "You and Del didn't see the man who broke in. Did you notice anything about the footsteps?"

"Like?"

"Was the rhythm of his steps even?"

Josh's attention shifted to Ethan. "Did you pick up his tracks?"

"Left shoe impression is deeper than the right."

"An injured right leg?"

"That's my guess. Not sure if he sustained an injury during his escape this morning or if the injury is older."

Josh scowled. "He didn't limp when he rabbited this morning. I couldn't catch him. I'd hate to see how fast he is without the injury."

"He slowed about three hundred yards after you turned back. That's when the injury showed in his tracks."

"Hope he hurt himself when he dived out the window at Del's."

After Ethan finished the last of his waffle, he inclined his head at Josh. "Got a minute?"

"Sure." He followed his brother-in-law outside to the deck. "What's up?"

"Got word the feds will descend on us late this afternoon. Our least favorite fed is leading the charge."

Josh groaned. "Craig Jordan?"

"Afraid so." Ethan's sharp gaze studied Josh's face. "U.S. Marshals are making noise about taking Del and Ivy into custody as material witnesses."

He rubbed the nape of his neck. "Del isn't going to like that."

"Won't stop the feds. Any op Jordan has his hand in never turns out quite like he plans. Del and Ivy might need an escape hatch."

"I'll take care of it."

"Thought you might."

"You want in the loop?"

"Not until the plans are in place. Right now, I need deniability." He grinned. "Later, all bets are off."

"Roger that." He'd begun planning for such a contingency after answering Del's original call at the Reece place. Josh was well acquainted with the snafus that occurred any time Washington political cronies involved themselves in military or law enforcement affairs. "I might need some time off if Jordan or his marshal buddies screw this up."

"More like when, not if. I'll make sure your shift is covered. If I can't get someone else to run patrol, I'll do it myself."

Josh's eyebrows shot up. "Serena okay with that?"

Ethan shrugged. "Part of the job description. If she can't sleep, she'll go on patrol and sleep in the SUV. She's done it before. Listen, Josh, if this goes bad, you'll need help. Most of Otter Creek's officers aren't trained to deal with this kind of threat. I can help and I'd trust Rod and Nick at my back any time, any place."

"Somebody has to run the department." He glanced over his mother's flowers and shrubs. "I have some people in mind."

"When your plan's in place, I want verbal reports. Nothing on paper that the feds might trace. For Del and Ivy's sake, I hope we don't need the extra precaution. But their lives may depend on those contingency plans. Keep your head in the game. Distractions could kill you or the lady."

If Josh's assessment of the killer was accurate, all of them would be lucky to escape from this conflict unscathed.

CHAPTER SIX

"Remember the rules, Del?"

Del scowled at Josh as he turned off the SUV's engine. "Don't leave the store unless I tell you or one of your brothers-in-law so I have a bodyguard. You will bring lunch. And above all, do not answer Megan's questions for the newspaper. You went over those rules a dozen times in the last hour. And by the way, Joshua Cahill, I don't want fifteen minutes of fame based on Judge Reece's death or an inept burglar."

Ivy leaned over the backseat. "I'm going in. Looks like Madison opened the store." With that, she threw open her door, grabbed her purse, and scurried inside Otter Creek Books.

Tension ratcheted up a couple notches in the silence as Del fumed. Normally, she wasn't bad tempered. Lack of sleep plus one crisis after another added up to a major case of grumpiness.

"Look at me, sweetheart."

Josh's quiet voice sent regret zinging through her. "Sorry," she murmured. "I know it's not your fault."

He cupped her chin and turned her face toward him. "Yeah, it is. I'm handling this situation like I would an op with my men. We planned missions, practiced, then ran them in our heads repeatedly until when the time came to execute, it was automatic. Things still went wrong, but we anticipated most contingencies. I want to keep you safe. This is the only way I know to accomplish that task."

"I want out of this padded cage and I want my life back."

"We'll get there. Humor me. I have errands to run, but I'll return by noon with lunch. Any requests?"

"Nothing heavy."

"I know what to bring for you both, then." He smiled. "Better go inside. Ivy's watching me pretty close through the window."

Del crossed the sidewalk into her store. A couple steps inside the doorway, and the knot in her stomach began unraveling. The scent of books always did that for her. Reminded her of summer vacations when she lost herself in a great mystery. Like Ruth Rollins, she loved tracking murderers through the pages of a story. Hunting killers in real life was another thing altogether. Fictional criminals couldn't kill you. The one who cut short John Reece's life was all too real, though not a glimpse of him anywhere. Almost like a ghost.

"Iron out your differences?" Ivy asked.

"My fault." Del skirted the counter and headed for the office, her cousin on her heels. She threw her purse into a drawer. "I don't remember ever feeling so out of control. My emotions swing from contentment to anger with a glance. Josh will think I'm nuts."

Ivy dropped into the chair in front of Del's desk. "From what you said about his family, they've been through the wringer with all the sisters and their husbands."

"The path of love for the sisters was rocky. Ask Madison to tell you her story." She smiled. "It's your kind of book."

"I might do that."

Del glanced at her watch. "Won't be long before the Christie women show up." Knowing them, they wouldn't wait until the official starting time before they arrived and began the questions. She had a feeling Ruth Rollins would be the first one through the door, hot on the trail of a plot for a new book.

Customers drifted in and out, some purchasing books, some browsing and doing their best to learn what happened with Judge Reece. So far, the grapevine had missed the early morning excitement. Wouldn't last. She figured noon at the latest before the news broke around town.

Fifteen minutes before the Christie ladies were due, Serena Blackhawk arrived, two trays in hand, one loaded with assorted cookies, the other bearing blueberry muffins. She laid them on the coffee bar counter which separated Del's bookstore from Madison's yarn shop, the Bare Ewe.

"Morning, Del." Serena smiled at her, sympathy in her blue eyes. "Heard you and Ivy had more excitement over night."

"Your brother came to our rescue."

"He's good at that." She removed plastic wrap from the trays and rounded the coffee counter to brew a pot of coffee for the store's customers. "Ruth asked for cookies and muffins for this morning's book plot discussion." Serena wrinkled her nose. "For some reason, the scent of cookies and muffins is bothering me today. Want any tea?"

"Sounds perfect. Josh made mint tea that tasted wonderful."

"Excellent suggestion." Serena smoothed her blond hair behind her ear and pulled two mint tea bags from the dispenser on the counter. "I'm looking for a good book for Ethan's birthday. Any suggestions?"

"A new Clive Cussler book came in yesterday. He'll like the latest John Sandford, too."

"I'll take both. Maybe we can introduce him to a new author soon." She laughed. "Not that he has much time to read these days. He's always at someone's beck and call."

"Does he like his job?"

"Most of the time. He hates the politics, though. Ethan's a cop at heart, not a politician. He'd love to pass that responsibility to someone else. Too bad it's part of his job description."

Del considered her recent interactions with him. "He's good with people. This isn't just a job to him. Ethan seems to care about those he encounters."

Serena's face glowed. "Thanks for saying that. I think so, too."

"You're totally in love with him."

"He's amazing. I'm so blessed to have him in my life." Serena checked the two mugs of tea. "The magic elixir is finished brewing. You want sweetener?"

"Serena, I didn't expect to see you this morning." Madison Santana mooched a cookie from the tray. "You brought my favorite cookies. I adore these chocolate chunk delights."

"Special request from Ruth."

Del's gaze shifted between the sisters. The Cahill triplets were identical except for personality and Madison's facial scar and a limp, leftovers from a devastating car accident a few years earlier.

Madison eyed the tea in Serena's hand. "Feeling okay?"

Serena shrugged. "A little upset stomach."

"What about you, Del?" Madison leaned closer to Del's mug, sniffed, and locked her blue gaze on her face.

"Short on sleep, but otherwise fine."

"Nick's on duty. He'll check on you during the day."

Del smiled. "Aw, come on. Fess up. He might say he's checking on me, but we all know Detective Santana is looking for any excuse to steal a kiss from his wife. That man is smitten."

Serena laughed. "She's got him nailed, Maddie."

A subtle glow lit Madison's face. "Like Ethan is any different."

Ivy drifted up to the counter. "Okay, enough already. You're making the single women in the room envious. Cookies."

"If you want chocolate chunk, grab one now. Madison is crazy about them."

"Don't blame her. It's chocolate."

Serena finished her tea. "On that note, I'm off. I have Josh's meals to cook this morning. Can't let my brother starve." With a wave at one of Madison's customers who called out to her, she left the store and drove away in her yellow Volkswagen Beetle.

Two minutes after Serena's car left the town square, Ruth Rollins strolled through the door. Del drew in a deep breath. "The grilling begins," she murmured to her cousin.

After watching Del go into her store, Josh backed into the town square and drove to Highway 18. He needed to make purchases without leaving a trail. Feds were nosy.

On the highway, he accelerated. He checked frequently for tails, was relieved not to spot one. He doubted the murderer would follow him. A small smile crossed his mouth. Not yet, anyway. At some point, they would meet face to face. Josh welcomed the opportunity as long as Del and Ivy weren't in the line of fire.

He pulled out his cell phone and punched in a number.

"Major, been a while."

Josh grinned. "Too long, Alex. How you been?"

"Bored. Got something interesting for me?"

"Maybe."

"When and where?"

"No questions?"

"What will I need?"

Just like that, his battle buddy committed to an unknown op, like he'd never left Delta. Man, Josh missed his unit. The men he served with always watched each other's backs. His unit followed his orders without question. Though he loved being a town cop, he wasn't used to a small playing field. In Delta, their field was global.

"Personal security detail. Have to work around Uncle Sam's assets."

Alex groaned. "Which ones?"

"Marshals, FBI."

His friend muttered a few choice words about the competence of the alphabet agencies. "Still in Otter Creek?"

"Yep. This may turn out to be nothing, but my gut says otherwise."

"Your gut saved our hides more than once. I've got some time. Why don't I come down. The guys have been kicking around an idea, one you might want in on."

"I'm not interested in full-time black ops work right now, Alex."

"I'll fill you in later." The sound of a keyboard clicking drifted through their cell connection. "I need to wrap up a couple things. Look for me around six."

"I'm staying with Mom for a few days. Dad left this morning for a three-night trip."

"Oh, man. Time with the amazing Liz Cahill."

Josh snorted. "You want her to feed you."

"Guilty. Hey, you told me to keep my hands off Serena and now she's married to that big bruiser, Blackhawk. Surely your mother will take pity on me and feed me. I can't remember my last home-cooked meal."

Alex Morgan didn't have family, at least none who acknowledged his existence. They disowned him when he joined the military. Senator James Morgan wanted his son to be more than a front-line Army grunt. Fifteen years of silence from his parents and older brother. No one crossed James Morgan's wishes. Their loss, Josh thought. Alex Morgan was one of the finest men he knew.

"Mom already thinks you're one of her own. She'll expect you to stay with us at the house." Alex could help him keep watch tonight.

"I'll bring my Go bag. Want me to alert the rest of our unit?"

"Roger that. Fully loaded Go bag, Alex. The perp is trained. See you at six."

Josh ended the call, gut churning. He prayed all this precaution was unnecessary. However, he wasn't willing to risk Del's life by being unprepared.

Thirty miles later, Josh exited Highway 18, drove into Westchester and parked in the lot of a big box store. He bought two pre-paid cell phones, then drove to the gun shop across town. He needed supplies not on the Otter Creek police department's normal supply list.

He pushed through the front door and hailed a few retired military guys who liked to hang out in the shop with Harry Willis, the owner. "Where's Harry?" he asked.

"In the back getting your gear ready."

Josh wound his way through the store, stopped twice to look at a Desert Eagle and a Sig. Later, he reminded himself. He didn't want to be gone from Otter Creek too long. He knocked on a door that was always locked. "It's Josh."

A series of locks clicked and the door opened to reveal the gray-haired former Marine. "Bag's ready." He closed and locked the door behind Josh. Harry's sharp gaze settled on Josh's face. "Flashbangs, grenades, C-4, detonators, ammo. Need weapons? Got a new Ruger."

"Add it and more ammo. Rope, two Mylar blankets."

Harry added the supplies and said, "Ruger's out front."

Josh slung the bag over his shoulder and followed him from the storeroom. With no customers other than the former military personnel hanging around, Harry relaxed his vigilance. Those guys would watch for customers or nosy law enforcement personnel. Josh's lips twitched at the irony since he was now law enforcement. Harry didn't seem to mind since he knew a little about Josh's military background.

The store owner unlocked the gun case and pulled out the weapon for Josh to examine. The Ruger fit his hand like it was made for him. "Very sweet, Harry."

"If you want to swap it for something else, bring it in after your op."

"Who said anything about an op?"

Harry gave a bark of laughter. "This stuff ain't standard cop equipment, son. You got a good team backing you?"

"The best. We've been through many firefights together."

"Watch your six. If you need something else, get in touch. We'll settle the tab later."

With a nod, Josh left the store and piled the gear into the hatchback of his SUV. A glance at his watch and he slid into the driver's seat. He'd been gone long enough he was feeling twitchy. He should head back to Otter Creek. One more stop to pick up lunch, then he'd check on Del and Ivy. Didn't matter that one of his brothers-in-law would have been in touch at the first sign of trouble. He had to see for himself they were okay. He knew in his gut trouble was coming and he didn't want to be separated from Del when it struck.

CHAPTER SEVEN

As the last of the Christie Club members exited the store, Del dropped onto a stool at the coffee bar. "I thought they would never leave."

Ivy grinned. "Ruth Rollins is very persistent."

"I was afraid to turn my back. She followed me all over the store and peppered me with questions. Now I know where Ethan learned his dogged persistence. I've never seen her so frustrated."

"I wouldn't want Ethan, Rod, or Josh mad at us for spilling information about the Reece murder."

"I'm surprised Megan hasn't tried to weasel answers from me."

"Just a matter of time."

The bell over the front door rang. Del turned, expecting to see Josh. Instead, Detective Nick Santana walked through the door, sunglasses pushed to the top of his head, a bag from Burger Heaven in one hand, two drinks in the other. The scent of grilled hamburgers with a side of fries reached her nose before Nick did. Oh, man, that smelled great. Her stomach, however, knotted, confirming the wisdom of asking Josh for a light lunch.

"Lunch with your wife, Nick?" Ivy asked.

"Best part of my day." He eased onto a stool next to Del. "Ethan told me what's happened since yesterday afternoon. You okay?"

"Sleep deprived and grumpy."

He turned to Ivy. "What about you?"

"Ditto, except I'm not grumpy."

"Staying with the Cahills should help you sleep better. Nobody will slip past Josh." He studied Del's face. "If you want to talk, Madison and I want to listen. We've been through similar circumstances, got the scars to prove it."

Tears burned her eyes. "Thanks."

"We'll find this man and nail his hide to the wall." His expression hardened. "He'll make a mistake and we'll nab him."

Madison finished ringing out a customer with a huge yarn order and walked into her husband's open arms. "Hi, sweetheart."

A brief kiss, a longer one, followed by Nick's husky voice. "Ready for lunch?"

"Starved. Ruth's band of murder plotters descended like vultures on Serena's cookies and muffins. I only scored two cookies before they were gone."

Nick chuckled. "Bet the intrepid ladies were buzzing about Reece's murder."

"They ganged up on me," Del complained.

"Not surprised. Too bad Ruth is over seventy. She would have been a great cop."

"Enjoy your lunch. I'll watch the yarn store until Annie arrives."

"Are you sure?" Madison asked. "The bookstore's been busy all day."

"We'll handle it," Ivy said. "Your helper should be here soon."

Nick slid from the stool. "Come on, beautiful." He handed Madison the bag of food, grabbed the drink holder in one hand and slid his free arm around her waist. "Yell if you need us."

She waved them on. Ivy sighed watching them, wrapped up in each other. Made Del's heart squeeze to see their happiness. "Sweet."

"Think there are other men like him left in this world?"

"I do." She wanted to see the same happiness on her cousin's face one day. "The right man is out there, Ivy. Don't settle for less than the best."

Her cousin propped her chin on her hands. "Don't worry. I'm never settling again. I learned my lesson with Lee."

The front door opened. This time, Josh strode through with his own bag and drink carrier. He scanned both sides of the busy store. "Can you break for lunch?" he asked.

"We're watching the yarn store for Madison. She and Nick are in the back."

"If we eat at the coffee bar, we can watch both stores."

"What's for lunch?" Del peeked at the bag. "Nick brought Madison food from Burger Heaven."

Josh froze, one hand in the bag. He glanced her direction. "You want lunch from there? We can save this for later."

"You seemed to know what my stomach might tolerate when you left this morning."

He shrugged. "Serena loves this deli. Says they have the best grilled chicken salad wrap. She's hoping to sweet talk the owner into sharing her recipe." He slid one wrap to Del, one to Ivy, and pulled out a third for himself. "I brought iced blueberry tea."

"Oh, man." Ivy moaned as she unwrapped her lunch. "This smells fabulous. Who needs Burger Heaven?"

Del sipped the tea. Oh, boy. She closed her eyes. This was so good.

"Like it?" Josh asked.

"Incredible." She opened her eyes and smiled. "Thank you."

Karen Kendall, one of Madison's favorite yarn customers, strolled through the doors. "Hi, ladies, Josh. Where's Maddie?"

"Lunch date with Nick," Ivy said. "Need something?"

"My yarn order came in. Can you find it or should I stop by later?"

Ivy waved Del off. "I've got it. Eat." She glanced at Josh. "Make her."

Josh saluted. "Yes, ma'am." He turned his head in Del's direction. "You heard the lady."

She rolled her eyes and peeled the paper covering from her wrap. "Ruth came with her cronies today."

"How did it go?"

"I probably have grill marks all over my body. Those women were merciless. I didn't cave to pressure, much to Ruth's disgust."

Josh laughed. "Good for you. Anything else happen?"

"Like what?"

"Anything make you uneasy?"

She scowled. "The day is still young. The way my life is going right now, the next crisis is due to hit soon."

Del and Ivy took turns answering questions, deflecting curious inquiries, and checking out customers. Throughout their meal, Del noticed Josh scanning the store and the street. What or who was he looking for? The man who broke in last night wore a mask.

Annie Jenkins breezed through the door. "Sorry I'm late." She blew her silver corkscrew curls away from her mouth, brown eyes twinkling. "My dog escaped from the backyard again. I swear that mutt is part mole. Every time I turn around, he's running around the neighborhood."

"Why don't you get a GPS tracking chip for his collar?" Josh suggested. "You'll be able to find him when he escapes."

The grandmother of four tossed her shoulder bag in the cabinet under the cash register. "Great idea. Don't know why I didn't think about that before." She grinned. "I don't want to add to your pet rescues."

Josh groaned. "Fluffy and I spend too much time together. I have a scar collection from rescuing that stubborn feline."

"You, Josh Cahill, are a softie."

"Don't spread that around town. I'll never hear the end of it."

"You kids finish lunch. I'll cover the register."

"I'm finished." Ivy crumpled her trash and threw it in the waste can. "I'll unpack boxes from yesterday's shipment, Del. Finish eating." She left Del and Josh alone.

He polished off the rest of his wrap and policed his trash. "She seems better this afternoon. So do you."

"Cops have dropped by all morning. I think the only person who hasn't is your sister, Megan."

He snorted. "She just put the weekend edition of the paper to bed so your reprieve is almost over."

"I don't want another inquisition. The Christie Club was brutal."

"Tell her to harass her husband or Ethan for information." He studied her face. "Will you answer two questions?"

"I'll try."

"Good. One easy. One hard. Which one's first?"

"Hard."

"Think back to yesterday at the Reece place. You and Ivy said you didn't see the shooter. Did you see anyone before you went in the house?"

Del thought through their arrival. Broiling heat came to mind, but no people. "No one."

"You returned to your vehicle and retrieved your laptop. Did you see anyone then?"

She started to say no, stopped, frowned. "A man in a truck drove by."

"Recognize him?"

She shook her head.

"Description?"

"A baseball cap left most of his face in shadow. He did have dark hair, a square jaw."

"Caucasian?"

"Yes and he was muscular. Not as much as Ethan or you. He looked tall. The top of his head nearly reached the cab's ceiling." She sighed. "This can't help Rod."

"Never know. What about the truck?"

"Black. Late model Dodge. Crew cab."

His eyebrows shot up, amusement glittering in the depths of his eyes.

"What?" Her face burned. "My brother has the same truck."

"Rod will have more questions for you."

"What's your easy question?"

"Is Del your given name?"

Del laughed. "Oh, no. I'm not going there."

"Come on. Your name can't be that bad."

"Your name is normal." She smiled. "Figure out my name."

He stared a moment. "I'm a cop."

"No cheating by looking it up."

He nodded. "I love a challenge. What's my reward for getting it right?"

"What do you want?"

"A date with you."

Del's heart hammered in her chest. "Deal. What's your penalty for each wrong guess?"

Josh stilled. "Do I have choices?"

"I'm debating between requesting a real kiss or asking a question."

Heat flared in his beautiful hazel eyes. "Don't waste your reward. I'm more than happy to exchange real kisses with you anytime, penalty or not. I'll answer a personal question for each miss." He paused. "At least, I'll try. I may not be able to answer some questions."

Ivy's laughter had them both turning their heads toward her as she carried a stack of books to the register. "This will be fun to watch. Josh, the deck is stacked against you."

"Kisses from a beautiful woman, guaranteed conversation, and a promise of a date. How can I lose?"

Del thought she'd just been played, but couldn't figure out the catch.

Josh noted Serena's yellow bug in the parking lot at his apartment complex. Maybe she knew Del's real name. Wasn't cheating by looking her up in the system. If he found out early, he could still tease her with outrageous guesses and add levity to stressful days. Military and law enforcement personnel had a macabre sense of humor. Like he told Ivy, he couldn't lose.

He switched off the engine and opened the hatchback for his Go bag. He needed more supplies and clothes. If the Feds made trouble as he and Ethan anticipated, Josh could buy more clothes anywhere. Some supplies secreted in his apartment would be harder to locate on short notice without attracting the wrong type of attention.

He closed the hatch, locked his SUV. He climbed the steps two at a time and slid his key in the lock. The smell of burned food hit him as soon as he opened the door. He frowned.

"Hey, squirt, if that's a new dish you're trying out, I'll pass on a taste test."

Silence greeted his sarcastic comment. His brow furrowed. "Serena?"

Not good. Josh dropped the bag by the door and pulled his Sig. Tension knotted his gut. Could the killer have targeted him, but surprised his sister? Serena had no chance against someone ruthless. She had courage in spades. Courage, however, wasn't bulletproof.

Quickly, Josh cleared his living room and small dining room. Made his way down the hall to the two bedrooms and bathrooms. Kitchen. Only place left besides the laundry room. With silent steps, Josh covered the few feet to the kitchen. He waited a few seconds. Heard nothing and peered around the corner into the room.

The room was empty. Two pots were simmering on the stove. A third must have boiled dry because black smoke rose from the pan. He frowned. Where was his sister? He moved around the island to turn off the burner.

His sister lay still as death, crumpled in a heap in front of the stove. "Serena!"

Shoving his Sig into his holster, Josh dashed forward, turned off the burners and dropped to his knees. Hand trembling, he pressed his fingers to the side of her neck, blinked away the sting of tears when he felt a steady heartbeat. He didn't see visible injuries.

Josh grabbed his cell phone and punched in Ethan's number.

CHAPTER EIGHT

Ethan's desk phone rang. "Yeah, Trudie?"

"Sorry, Chief, I know you asked not to be disturbed, but Special Agent Craig Jordan is demanding to see you."

A flash of irritation rolled over Ethan as he glanced at the clock. He'd figured on at least another three or four hours before the Washington boys made an appearance. "Five minutes, then you can send him in."

He dragged one hand over his face. Turf wars with Craig Jordan. Not something he wanted to deal with again. Ethan grabbed his cell phone and punched in Rod's number.

"Kelter."

"The fed invasion has begun."

"Who?"

"Jordan."

"Not my favorite fed in the world," Rod almost growled. "He knows more ways to screw up a case than to solve one."

"I have three minutes. Anything new to report?"

"Just left the bookstore. Josh learned Del and Ivy saw a man driving by the Reece place yesterday."

Ethan straightened in his chair. "Enough to give us a description?"

"Wore a Yankees baseball hat which left his face in shadow. Drove a black Dodge. Couple of uniforms are canvassing the neighbors to see if they can give a better description. Ethan, if he's the shooter, he knows the women saw him. He'll keep coming after them until we stop him."

"Gives the feds more leverage to take them into custody as material witnesses."

"Can we stop Jordan from taking them?"

"Delay, maybe. This man might be a neighbor driving past. If a neighbor can identify the driver, we'll keep Jordan from taking them. If Jordan connects the break-in to Reece's murder, we have no chance at keeping their safety in house."

"What if we tell Jordan the women are already in protective custody?"

"Doubt it will fly. Get here as soon as you can."

"Two minutes."

Ethan clipped his phone back onto his belt and opened his office door. "Have a seat, Agent Jordan." He didn't bother offering his hand to greet the man. Didn't feel like offering the perspiring man a cold drink either. Feds were tough. No need to coddle them. "What can I do for you?"

"I'm taking over the Reece murder."

Ethan dropped into his desk chair and eased back. "Will your team analyze the crime scene and body?"

"They'll arrive in a few hours. I was wrapping up a case not too far from here."

"Lucky us," he murmured. "I assume you want a copy of everything we have so far."

Jordan's smile came across as smug. "We'll double check your findings, of course."

"Tax dollars put to their finest use."

"Any witnesses?"

"Two women were in the house, but saw nothing. Wrong place, wrong time."

"I want their names and contact information if they aren't already in your report. I want to interview them myself."

"Of course." Ethan didn't mention the new information Rod had passed on minutes before. What Jordan didn't know he couldn't pursue yet. In the meantime, he and his team could double check Otter Creek's findings. Never hurt to have another set of eyes on the evidence. The longer Ethan delayed Jordan from taking Del and Ivy into protective custody, the more time it gave him and Rod to arrest the shooter. This might be a fed matter, but it was still happening in Ethan's jurisdiction.

Rod knocked on the office door and slipped inside. He dropped into one of the two chairs in front of Ethan's desk. He nodded at Jordan. "Made good time. Running this show by yourself, Jordan, or are you bringing the whole circus?"

Craig Jordan scowled. "The Reece case is mine, Kelter. Federal judge, federal case, federal jurisdiction."

"Overstepping your bounds, Jordan. The U.S. marshals have responsibility for judge safety," Ethan said. "Can't resist sticking your nose into this one, can you?"

"Look, I know you might have a few hard feelings, Blackhawk."

"A few hard feelings?" Ethan's eyes narrowed. "You almost got my wife killed in that fiasco with Hans Muehller. I'm not likely to forget that. Despite your cowboy tactics, I'll give you what help I can. Keep me informed of your findings as you learn them. Any interviews you conduct will include one of my people."

"Wait a minute."

"My town, my people. You want to talk to my citizens, one of us will be with them. End of discussion." At that moment, Ethan's cell phone rang. He unclipped his phone and glanced at the display. He frowned. Josh. Ethan stood. "I need to take this. Excuse me a minute."

He walked into the bullpen and closed himself into the empty office next to his own. "Blackhawk."

"I need you at my place. Now."

On the move, Ethan yanked open the office door. "Why?"

"I found Serena unconscious on my kitchen floor."

Breath froze in his lungs for an instant. "On my way." He raced past the bullpen, his desk sergeant, and out into the heat. Cranking his SUV, he peeled out of the parking lot, hit his lights and sirens and sped down Main Street. She hadn't been sick when he left the house this morning. His heart thudded against his chest wall. She was everything to him, his greatest gift. The possibility that something or someone might take her from him made him feel sick.

Eight minutes later, Ethan swerved into the parking lot and ran up the stairs to Josh's home. His brother-in-law opened the door before he had time to beat on the door.

"Living room," was all he said.

Pushing past him, Ethan strode into the living room and spotted his pale wife laying on the couch, pillow beneath her head, scowl marring her beautiful face. He dropped to his knees, raised a shaking hand to push aside her bangs. "What happened, baby?"

"I must have a stomach bug. I've been guzzling mint tea by the gallon today." She sent an apologetic glance at her brother. "I might be a little dehydrated. I kept throwing up. I think I cleaned up everything. Sorry, Josh."

He grinned. "No problem, squirt. What's a little puke between siblings?"

She laughed, then moaned. "Don't make me laugh. My stomach muscles are sore."

Ethan studied her pale face. "We need a doctor to check you."

"I'm fine, Ethan."

He framed her face with his hands. "I need a doctor to tell me you're okay. You scared me."

"Ditto," Josh said, his voice soft. "Put the man out of his misery, squirt. I bet Ethan can pull some strings and get you checked out in under an hour."

"But what about your meals? I'm right in the middle of cooking."

"I may not be here much in the next week or so. Depends on what happens with Del. Come back later in the week if you feel better. I'll clean up the kitchen and put everything away for now. What we shouldn't keep, you can pitch. Deal?"

Serena sighed. "Okay."

Some of the tension left Ethan's muscles. He'd been prepared to fight her to get her cooperation. He slid one arm under Serena's knees, the other under her back and lifted her. "Don't," he said, short-circuiting her protest. "I need to hold you." Maybe then the invisible band around his chest would loosen enough for him to breathe again.

He carried her down the stairs and placed her in the passenger seat of his SUV. After strapping the seatbelt around her, Ethan turned his head and brushed her lips with a gentle kiss. "I love you," he whispered. If anything happened to her, he didn't know what he would do, didn't know if he could survive without her now.

"I didn't mean to scare you, love."

He made himself move back though he wanted to do nothing more than gather her as close to him as possible. "Let's make sure you're all right."

On the way to the doctor's office, he called Dr. Anderson's receptionist and was told the physician would see Serena as soon as he could get her there. He pulled into the parking lot. "Don't move," he ordered. "I don't want you hitting the pavement if you should pass out again."

"How magnanimous of you." Sarcasm practically dripped from her words. He grinned at her snippy attitude.

They walked into the building that housed John Anderson's medical office. His receptionist waved them through to an open examination room. Anderson's nurse, Stacey, breezed in the room, stopped short when she noticed Ethan standing beside the exam table. "Chief Blackhawk." She looked between him and Serena. "Which of you is Dr. Anderson to see?"

"Serena."

"Tell me the details. He should be in shortly to check her."

Minutes later, John Anderson knocked on the door of the exam room. "What's this about you passing out, my dear?" He listened to her explanation, then said, "Let me examine you and we'll talk, all right? Chief, wait in my office across the hall."

Though Ethan was reluctant to leave his wife, he knew Anderson would take good care of Serena. He trudged across the hallway and settled into a chair and waited what seemed like hours. His muscles twitched with the need to move so he gave up the fight and started pacing. He rubbed the knotted muscles at the back of his neck. What was taking so long?

Finally, the exam room door opened and footsteps approached the office. The physician poked his head in the office and motioned for Ethan to follow him. Tension twisted Ethan's gut. He stepped through the doorway and drew up short at the sight of his wife, sitting on the table, her face buried in her hands.

Alarm roared through him. He hurried forward, cupped his hands around her shoulders. "Serena, what is it? What's wrong?" All he could think in that second was she'd been diagnosed with cancer. Whatever it was, they'd deal with it together.

She lifted her face. Tears poured down her cheeks, but there was a huge smile on her face. "Nothing is wrong. In fact, everything is absolutely perfect."

Puzzled, he turned toward the grinning doctor. "Doc? Care to enlighten me?"

"Congratulations, Chief Blackhawk. In seven months, you're going to be a father."

CHAPTER NINE

Josh scraped the last of the mysterious burned mass from the pot and dumped the mess into the trash. He suspected the pan might be toast, but he'd try cleaning the charred metal before he pitched it in the trash. While he scrubbed, he wondered what the doctor would say about his sister. He hadn't been that afraid for her since she'd been taken by Muehller.

More scrubbing led him to the conclusion that the pan was a lost cause. He dumped murky water down the drain and slid the pan into the trash bag near his feet. He'd need to stop by the kitchen place off Main Street in the next few days and buy a replacement.

He glanced at the clock. Almost time for the bookstore to close. Why didn't Ethan call? Maybe Dr. Anderson was busy. Serena wouldn't be happy if she wasted her afternoon in the waiting room. He grabbed the trash bag and hauled it to the dumpster.

Josh grabbed the rest of his gear, stuffed it in his Go bag along with clothes, and locked up. After storing his gear in his SUV, he cranked the engine and reached for his phone. He punched in Ethan's number.

"Yeah?"

Josh frowned. What was up? Ethan sounded strange. Squealing and laughing in the background? "Where are you?"

"Bookstore."

"You took Serena from the doctor's office to the store? She must not be that sick."

"You driving?"

"I'm headed to the bookstore myself."

"I'll talk to you when you get here."

Josh was about to ask for details when the call ended. Okay, that was odd. More than a little worried, he put the SUV in gear and pushed the speed limit to the store. He found a parking space close by and jogged up the street half a block. He shoved his way through the front door and stopped. His mother and all three sisters were huddled close together, Serena held tight in his mother's embrace. Tears flowed freely from all but Megan. No surprise. Meg didn't cry easily. She did, however, sport a huge grin on her face. Huh. So whatever news came from the doctor's visit, it must not have been bad.

He located Ethan sitting in an armchair nearby and made his way to his side. His brother-in-law sat with a cold Coke in his hand, his expression somewhat blank. "Hey, man, what's going on? Is Serena okay?"

Ethan's gaze dragged up to Josh's face. "She's fine."

He frowned. She'd been out cold on his floor not two hours ago. "What did the doc say?"

"Serena's pregnant."

Stunned, Josh turned to the knot of women that now included Del and Ivy. His heart squeezed. His baby sister was having a baby of her own. "Does Dad know?"

"We left a message for him to call when he gets a chance."

Josh clapped his brother-in-law on the shoulder. "Congratulations, Ethan."

"Thanks. Can't take it in."

He chuckled. "Drink your Coke. Got a feeling this is just the beginning. Wait until the baby gets here."

Ethan groaned. "Please, I haven't processed the fact we're having a baby yet, much less what happens in seven months."

"You do remember the squirt is one of triplets, right? Wonder if multiples run in the family?"

His brother-in-law paled. "Don't go there."

Josh laughed and turned toward the group of women. Serena noticed him approaching and broke away from the pack. She grinned and hurled herself into his open arms. He wrapped her close. "Congratulations, sweetheart. You're going to be an amazing mother. Just spare my old heart and don't pass out again. Don't think I can take it."

"I'll try."

His gaze rested on Madison, noticed tears on her face. "Is Maddie okay?" he murmured. He knew this day would come, but this must be so hard for his tender-hearted sister. Madison's car accident a couple years earlier resulted in injuries which prevented her from having children, something he knew still grieved her.

"I called Nick from the doctor's office. He promised to be here soon. Ethan and I told Maddie before anyone else." Serena tightened her grip around his waist. "She's happy for us but the memories hurt."

"She'll be okay. We'll all help. The most important person in her corner is Nick. He adores her, squirt. He'll help her get through this."

Serena nodded and pulled away. "It's so unfair for Maddie. She deserves everything."

"She's very blessed and it won't take her long to remember. Let her be part of the plans and preparations." He nudged her toward Ethan. "I think your husband needs a little care right now. He looks shell shocked."

"Don't worry. I have plans for that man."

"Please. I don't want to know."

Serena grasped Ethan's hands and urged him to his feet. "Come on, handsome. Time to celebrate. Can you knock off early?"

Ethan sighed. "The feds arrived just before Josh called."

"You're the chief of police. The Washington boys can wait until tomorrow. Besides, isn't Rod with them?"

His gaze drifted over Serena's face, softened at her glowing expression. "He can handle them. You're more important to me than the job. The feds will keep." He grinned. "This provides a great excuse to ignore them until tomorrow."

After another round of hugs from the women, Serena and Ethan left, holding hands.

"That's a welcome surprise," Liz said, her arm around Madison. "Enough bad things have happened in this family to last a lifetime."

Megan grinned. "Wish I'd had a camera in the room when Doc Anderson told Ethan he was going to be a father. He still looks like he's in shock."

Madison brushed away a tear. "I hope Serena's baby is a girl. She'll wrap her dad around her finger."

A mischievous grin from Meg. "I hope she has twin girls. When they turn sixteen, Ethan will greet every date with his Glock."

"Wicked, sis." Josh shook his head.

She sniffed. "He deserves it for giving me grief about my driving."

"You're lucky I haven't caught you speeding, snoopy. I won't be as nice as he is."

She rolled her eyes. Meg turned to Del and Ivy. "Sure you won't reconsider an interview?"

Del shook her head. "Sorry, Meg. Orders from higher up the food chain. No interviews."

"Who?"

"We're not confirming or denying any names," Ivy said. "We aim to protect the innocent and the guilty."

"Pseudonyms for Ethan and Rod?" Meg countered.

Another round of laughter and Meg left with their mother, talking about the new nursery that Ethan and Serena would now have to put together. Josh waited until Del and Ivy were both occupied helping customers to approach his remaining sister. He didn't have to say anything, simply opened his arms.

"You okay, sunshine?" he murmured against her ear.

"I'm happy for Serena and Ethan." She burrowed tighter against his chest. "But it hurts."

"You don't lack courage, Madison Santana. You look soft, but have a steel spine and a golden heart. You'll come through this even stronger, beautiful."

She gave a watery laugh. "How do you always know the right thing to say?"

"I know you."

The bell over the door rang and Nick strode through. He took in the scene. "Madison." The detective covered the distance between him and his wife in a few long strides. She loosened her hold on Josh and dived into her husband's arms.

He folded her close. "Is Annie still here?"

"In the back."

"Ask her to close for you tonight." He leaned down and brushed his lips over hers. "I have plans for you, Mrs. Santana."

She grinned. "Sounds interesting. I'll see if she can help." She looked over at Josh. "Thanks," she murmured and hurried down the aisle toward the back.

"I don't know what you said to her, but thanks," Nick said. "I expected this to be harder for her."

Josh shrugged. "Just reminded her of some things I admired about her. Got special plans?"

"I knew this day would come and I've been making plans for a while. All that matters to me is that I have her. This is my time to remind her of that. I'm taking her out of town for the night."

He got the unspoken message. No calls for this one night. If anything happened, he'd call Rod.

Madison moved down the aisle, shoulder bag in hand, and pressed against her husband's side. "Ready. Annie will come out front in a minute."

Nick looped his arm around her shoulders. "Get ready to be spoiled, baby. Later, Josh."

Josh turned to see Del watching the couple as they exited the store.

"Is she okay?"

"Nick will make sure she is." He studied her face, noted her fatigue and pallor.

"I can't imagine what you thought when you found Serena on your floor."

Fear the shooter had targeted him and attacked Serena instead. "You ready to close?"

Del turned, looked around the bookstore. "It's empty for the first time today."

Josh's cell phone chimed. A glance informed him Alex had crossed the Dunlap county line and would be in Otter Creek soon. Josh punched in his friend's number. "I'm still at the bookstore."

"Be there in ten."

He slid his phone back into its carrier. "Let me help you close, sweetheart." He wanted to leave when Alex arrived. Del and Ivy shouldn't be near the store when Rod turned the fed loose. He'd promised to let Josh know when he finished briefing Jordan. That was probably the only heads up he'd get. With careful maneuvering, he'd keep Del and Ivy from the circus until tomorrow.

He helped Del lock the doors and count out the register. "What about the bank deposit?" he asked.

"I'll put it in the night drop," Annie said. "I have to drop off the Bare Ewe's receipts."

Del smiled. "Thanks, Annie."

A knock sounded on the outside door. Ivy looked up from washing the coffee pot, stared. Josh grinned. His backup had arrived.

Del studied the man who pounded on Josh's back in a male greeting that would have knocked her breath from her lungs. He was Nick Santana's height, around five feet eight and had a dark complexion like he spent time in the sun. Combined with his dark hair, she wondered if Cajun was in his background.

She suspected he had served with Josh. There was something about him. The same movements and awareness of his surroundings as Josh and Ethan. Former special forces? A dangerous, but honorable man. Otherwise, Josh wouldn't treat him as a long lost brother.

"Who is that?" Ivy whispered, eyes wide.

"He's something, isn't he?" She grinned. "Maybe he finds art historians fascinating."

"Nobody finds art historians fascinating, especially not a man like that."

Interesting response from her man-shy cousin. Many honorable men populated the world. Ivy had landed a dishonorable one. Del was grateful her cousin had wised up and seen the true Lee.

Josh approached the coffee counter with his friend. "Del, Ivy, meet Alex Morgan. He's going to give me a hand with your security. This is Del Peterson, bookstore owner, her cousin, Ivy Monroe."

"Del, we appreciated the books you sent our unit. Made long hours pass quicker." Alex turned his attention to her cousin. "Ivy." When he smiled, Ivy nearly dropped the coffee carafe. Del could see why. The guy had a killer smile. He turned to Josh. "Sit rep, Major. Here or at your mother's?"

"Too many windows here. Makes me twitchy. Ready to leave, Del?"

She handed the deposit bag to Annie, who listened to the conversation with frank interest.

Ivy replaced the carafe on the burner and turned toward the office. "I'll get our bags." Del noticed she avoided eye contact with Alex, who watched her retreating back. A minute later, her cousin returned with her handbag and Del's. "Ready."

"Stay close, Alex," Josh said.

"I've got your six."

Josh hustled Del and Ivy to his SUV. Despite the lingering heat of the day, Del shivered. No matter how much she told herself she was imagining things, she felt as if the killer hid in the shadows, watching, waiting for an opening. She glanced at her cousin. Maybe she should send Ivy home for a week or so. That would place Ivy in Lee Hall's path, though.

"No," Ivy said, frowning. "You're not sending me home for my own safety."

"Wouldn't you feel safer out of the killer's reach?"

"I'm not taking trouble to Nashville. I don't want to add another layer to an already bad situation at home."

"What do you think, Josh? Shouldn't we send her home for a while?"

"You want the truth?"

A chill swept over her body. "Always."

"If the shooter is after you both, there's nowhere to hide. We have protection in place and know the score. No one will be watching out for her in Nashville. Ivy would be an easy target."

"I'm safer here than at home," Ivy said. "Besides, I broke the lease on my apartment, Del, and I won't stay with

Mom. She'll push her own agenda and I just left that pressure cooker."

Del sighed. She didn't blame Ivy. Marigold Monroe loved Lee Hall, couldn't understand why Ivy broke off her relationship with him, and made it her mission in life to reunite them. Del thought Aunt Mari was more interested in Lee's fortune than his personality. Her aunt loved to spend money and no doubt had planned to use Ivy's unlimited expense accounts if she'd married Lee. She'd done the same with Ivy's own accounts until her cousin received a call from the bank, questioning a number of purchases which maxed out her credit card. Ivy had cut up the card and moved her accounts to the bank in Otter Creek.

"I'm only concerned for your safety."

"If things get too hot here," Josh said, "I'll take you someplace safe, Ivy."

They pulled into the Cahills' drive a few minutes later. "Mom's already here. Go on in."

Del hesitated, hand on the passenger door. "Trying to get rid of us, Josh?"

"Yes, ma'am."

At least he was honest. She didn't want to hear Josh's suspicions. Later, she'd dig up enough courage to confront the issue. Not tonight, though. Del was too tired to deal with it. After she got some sleep, Josh better have answers, good or bad. She wanted in the loop. After tonight. "What's a sit rep?"

He chuckled. "Military shorthand for situation report."

"Tomorrow, I want a sit rep. Will you tell me?"

"What I can," he said and climbed out of the SUV.

"That answer had enough holes in it to drive a semi through," Ivy complained.

"Tomorrow, we'll learn the information we need."

"Secrets bite when you least expect."

Ivy ought to know. "Let's go inside, see if Liz needs help."

They climbed the deck stairs and opened the door. Scents of garlic bread, tomato sauce, and Italian seasonings greeted them. Del breathed deep, her stomach rumbling.

Liz turned, smiled. "Hungry?"

"Everything smells fantastic," Ivy said.

"Lasagna and garlic bread. Where are Josh and Alex?"

"Outside. They'll be in soon. Need help finishing dinner?" Del asked.

"Salad fixings in the refrigerator if you want to put one together."

They dropped their handbags in their rooms, washed their hands, cut tomatoes, mushrooms, and cucumbers, tore lettuce, and shredded cheese. As they finished the salad, Josh and Alex walked into the kitchen, duffel bags over their shoulders.

"Alex." Liz hurried to Josh's friend. Alex dropped his bags and wrapped heavily muscled arms around her, lifted her from the ground in a bear hug. "It's great to see you. You've been away too long."

Del frowned. Tears in his eyes? She must have imagined it. A glance at Ivy, though, showed she'd noticed the same thing. There was a story here, an interesting one. Maybe one of the questions she asked Josh should cover his friend's relationship with the Cahills.

"Didn't want to wear out my welcome."

"We always want you here, son, for as long as you can stay. Did you bring your appetite?"

"Yes, ma'am."

"Dinner's ready. You boys stow your gear and we'll eat."

"Same room as last time," Josh said. He led the way up the stairs.

Del and Ivy carried food to the table and poured iced tea by the time Josh and Alex entered the dining room. Alex claimed the seat beside Liz. The food was passed quickly and after the first bite, Alex moaned. "Liz, marry me."

She laughed. "Silly boy. You're out of luck."

"Kick Aaron to the curb and run off with me. I'll treat you like a princess if you cook for me all the time."

Josh thumped the back of his head. "Stop hitting on my mom."

"How can I resist her, Major? She's beautiful and cooks."

"Idiot," he growled, though his eyes twinkled.

Conversation during dinner stayed light. Liz shared Serena's news with Alex and a lively discussion of baby names ensued. Del's sides ached at the outrageous suggestions from Josh and Alex.

The house phone rang and Liz rose to answer. Her soft murmur made it apparent she was talking to her husband. "Wonder what your father will think about the baby?" Del asked Josh.

He grinned. "Dad hasn't said anything, but he wants to be a grandfather." His smile faded. "He was heartbroken over the loss of Madison and Luke's baby."

"Knowing your dad, he'll be concerned about Maddie now," Alex said.

"It's nice that your parents care so much," Ivy said with a sigh.

A haunted look came and went in Alex's eyes. Del wondered what caused him so much pain. Definitely one of the first questions she would ask Josh.

A cell phone chimed. Ivy jumped. She dug into her pocket and checked the screen. She frowned at Del. "It's your mother."

Oh, man. She hoped her mother hadn't heard about the murder and break-in. But why contact Ivy instead of complaining to Del about keeping secrets?

Ivy rose. "Excuse me." She walked toward the living room.

"Think she's heard?" Josh asked softly.

"I hope not. If she has, she'll load the car and come to protect her baby. Or worse, send my brothers with shotguns."

From the living room, Ivy's end of the conversation rose in volume. "Aunt Dee, stop screaming. I can't understand what you're saying."

Fear gripped Del's heart with icy fingers. She jumped to her feet and dashed to the living room, Josh and Alex crowding in behind her.

Ivy's face was white. "The police were just there?" A look of horror dawned on her face. "No! It's not true. I didn't call you because it's not true. No, ma'am, I'm not lying to you. Aunt Dee, take a breath. Listen to me." She stopped a moment, closed her eyes. "Del is not in Oakwood. She didn't leave Otter Creek. I'm looking at her now." She shook her head, pulled the cell away from her ear. "She doesn't believe me, keeps sobbing, demanding to know why I didn't call her."

"About what?"

"A fire at your place. The firefighters found a body in the house."

CHAPTER TEN

Josh's fists clenched. A body? Alex shook his head. Didn't take a genius to know the fire and body might be connected to Del's situation in Otter Creek. Could be bad luck, too. He sighed. Not likely, much as he wished that were the case.

Del grabbed the phone. Before she spoke, Josh reached over and pushed the speaker button. Broken sobs sounded throughout the room. He nodded at Del.

"Mom?"

A strangled gasp, then, "Del! Baby, is that really you?"

"There was a fire at the house?"

More sobs, quieter now. "The police are here. One of the detectives wants to talk to you."

A few thumps, then, "Ms. Peterson, Del Peterson?"

"Yes, I'm Del Peterson."

"This is Detective Milo Tyler, Oakwood Police Department. Ms. Peterson, there was a fire at your residence here in town. I'm sorry, ma'am, but the house is a total loss. The fire crew discovered a body in a bedroom. The neighbors thought they saw you in the home during the past two days. That's why we contacted your mother."

"Well, obviously, I'm not there, Detective Tyler."

"Ma'am, do you have any idea who this might be? The body is female."

Ivy grabbed Del's arm, eyes wide. "Do you think it might be Lily?" she whispered.

A low, distressed cry had Josh reaching for Del, drawing her into his side so he could support her physically if she needed it. "Detective, my cousin Lily Delray stayed in the house from time to time. She had a restraining order against her husband, Charles. I gave her a key a year ago when she needed a place to recuperate after a fight with her husband landed her in the hospital."

"We'll send a unit over to check on her whereabouts. Give me a number where I can reach you, Ms. Peterson."

She glanced at Josh, got his nod, and rattled off her cell phone number. "I want to speak to my mother again, please."

"Del, are you really okay, honey?"

"I'm fine. I promise."

"I need to see you. Come home, at least for a day."

Josh understood the need to see her daughter, but he wasn't sure he could take Del out of town, not with the feds here. Del's gaze sought his, a question in her beautiful eyes. He leaned close, his mouth brushing her ear. "Don't know if we can."

Del shivered. He pressed a soft kiss to her temple. Yeah, he felt the same way. Whatever was between them was growing fast.

"I'll try, Mom. I don't know if I can get away right now. I'm behind on ordering and stocking and I'm processing a thirty thousand book donation to the store. If I don't take care of that, I'll be living in my garage while books take over my bungalow."

More quiet sobs. "I need to hold you in my arms, Del."

"I know. I'll try."

"If you loved me, you'd come home."

Cold. Manipulative. Josh tugged Del closer, wrapped his other arm around her. Emotional blackmail at its worst. He rubbed her back, waited to see how she dealt with this latest move. Though his family smothered him at times, he was grateful they never used emotional blackmail.

"I'll call you later, okay?"

"I want to see your face. Otherwise, don't bother to call."

"I can't believe she said that." Ivy shoved the phone in her pocket. "She been taking lessons from my mother?"

Del gave a watery laugh, buried her face in Josh's neck. "They are sisters."

"Everything okay, son?" Liz asked as she walked into the living room, cordless phone in her hand.

"Not sure." Nothing was wrong on his end except for a need to wring Dee Peterson's neck for hurting her daughter.

"Your father wants to speak to you." She handed him the phone.

Del started to move away. Josh pressed his hand against her back, a wordless command to stay. Not like he'd share anything private with his father while his mother listened. Del sighed and rested against him. He liked that. She fit as if made for him. Dangerous thought. He couldn't afford distractions and Del was definitely a distraction. He pulled his focus back on target. "Yeah, Dad?"

"Anything new happening?"

"Unconfirmed."

A pause, then, "Something new is happening but you're not sure if it concerns Del and Ivy?"

"Yes, sir."

"Do I need to come home?" Alarm rang in his father's voice.

"Not yet." An unspoken warning to stay packed and prepared. "There's been some trouble at Del's house in Oakwood. Not sure if it's related."

"I want to know the minute you figure it out."

"Roger that."

"Give the phone to your mother. Watch your back, son. I love you."

"Love you, too." He handed the handset to his mother. He grinned. "I think he wants to whisper sweet nothings in your ear." Josh laughed at the blush staining his mother's cheeks though she grinned, her face lighting up. No question in his mind that his father and mother believed the other to be the love of their life.

"I'll clean up," Ivy said, moving toward the dining room. "Looks like everybody's finished with dinner. That conversation with Aunt Dee stole my appetite."

Alex followed on her heels without a word. Neither Del nor Ivy would be left alone until Reece's shooter was behind bars or in the morgue.

Left alone with Del, Josh lifted one hand and cupped the nape of her neck. "Talk to me, baby," he murmured.

"I'm okay."

"If something hurts you, I want to know about it. And I know your mother's theatrics hurt. Is this normal with her?"

"Since my father died."

"Is it the same with your brothers?"

"Unfortunately. They're all married, though, so they have families of their own to take care of. Gives them an excuse to ignore the demands."

"You have a life."

"Not according to Dee Peterson. Since I'm the only daughter, it's my job to cater to her every wish."

"Was she like this before you lost your father?"

"Oh, yeah. The only difference was Dad caved to Mom's every whim. We were all devastated to lose him to cancer, but Mom's been lost without her soul mate."

"You can't fill the gap. No one can replace the love of your life."

Del eased away to lock gazes with him. "Personal experience?"

He'd told her not to hold back the truth. Had to follow his own rule. "I thought I had. Now I wonder if it was the real thing." He bent and placed a soft kiss on her lips. "A discussion for another time, okay?" he whispered. "Do you want to see your mother?"

"She has high blood pressure. I don't want to cause her a stroke or heart attack." Her troubled gaze locked with his. "Is there any way I can see her, even for a couple hours? Oakwood's not far."

"The distance isn't the problem. The feds are. The FBI's in town already. U.S. marshals may be here by now. They want to interview you and Ivy." And most likely take them into protective custody, though he didn't plan to share that with her now. Ethan might hold them off another few days as long as the feds didn't discover the fire in Oakwood and the break-in here. An accidental fire killing her cousin would be a tragedy, but explainable bad luck. If the fire proved deliberate and connected to the case, the Washington elite would whisk Del and Ivy into protective custody.

He didn't want Del out of his sight until the shooter was caught or taken out. "I'll talk to Ethan, see if he thinks we can avoid the feds another day. If he clears it, I'll take you to Oakwood tomorrow."

"Remember the deal we made regarding my name?"

His eyebrows rose. "Want to back out?" Had she changed her mind about getting to know him?

"Modify it."

"Can't change the rules midstream, sweetheart."

"Conversation's the point, right?" She leaned closer to whisper, "Would you mind if I asked a question or two about your friend?"

Josh stilled. Del wanted to ask questions about Alex? He fought against the unexpected surge of protectiveness for Alex and unwelcome flood of jealousy over her interest in his friend. He wasn't sure he was man enough to step back while Del decided if she wanted to pursue his best friend. "Why?"

"He has a story and Ivy's fascinated with him. I don't want her hurt."

One by one, his muscles unclenched. "He's a great guy. She could do a lot worse than Alex Morgan."

"She already did and has the scars to prove it."

Josh's face burned. Some idiot had hurt Ivy? "I'd class Alex with my brothers-in-law any day. Ask your questions. I'll answer if I can without breaking a confidence. Okay?"

Sure the shock of the call was past, Josh nudged her toward the kitchen. "Help Alex and Ivy while I contact Ethan." He wasn't sure his brother-in-law would be available, not if his sister's expression was anything to go by when they left. If not, he'd call Rod.

He punched in Ethan's number. Three rings in, his brother-in-law answered, voice gruff. "New development. You want an update or should I call Rod?"

"Talk to me."

He explained about the call from Del's mother and conversation with the Oakwood detective. "Del wants to spend a couple hours with her mother. Can you keep the feds off our backs a few more hours?"

"Jordan will be interfering with his own crime scene people tomorrow morning at least. What's your take on the situation in Oakwood?"

"Hope it's a coincidence, but my gut says otherwise. Probably a ploy to flush out Del and Ivy."

"Be ready for an ambush, most likely on the way back."

"Agreed. Do we go or stay?"

"Go. Have Del and Ivy turn off their phones. If the feds learn they're in the wind, at least they can't track them. Be back before nightfall. I can't keep Jordan on a leash any longer than that."

Del hunted for a comfortable spot. Despite the fabulous bed, plush quilt, and cool temperature in the room, sleep was elusive. Again. With a sigh, she threw back the covers and sat up. She was exhausted, but couldn't slow her mind enough to sleep.

A cup of tea? Liz told her to make herself at home. She knew where the tea was kept. If that didn't work, maybe Aaron had a hammer she could use to knock herself out. If she went home with raccoon eyes, her mother would worry more. She didn't want to add fuel to her mother's arguments for her to move home. Wasn't going to happen. Del loved the bookstore and, to be honest, she loved being away from the Dee Peterson pressure drama. Yes, it was meant letting her brothers deal with Mom. They could handle it. She did it for years after her father passed away. It was their turn.

Del slid her feet into slippers, snatched up her robe, cinched it, and opened the bedroom door. A quick glance told her Ivy was sound asleep. Good. Her cousin was a bear when sleep deprived. A smile curved her lips. She wasn't sweet after a short night, either. She moved down the stairs.

A soft light glowed in the living room. She peered around the corner and spotted Josh sitting on the couch, doing something with his gun. She frowned. It was in pieces. She stepped onto the main floor.

Josh glanced over. His eyes widened. "Hey, beautiful. Everything okay?"

"Can't sleep. I came down to make a cup of tea." She moved closer. "What are you doing?"

"Cleaning my weapon."

Unease whispered through her. "What if you need to use the gun while you're cleaning it?"

Amusement glittered in his eyes. "I have a backup weapon in a holster at my ankle. You worried I won't be able to defend you properly?"

Heat swept over her face. "You don't need a gun to defend me if it was necessary."

He grinned. "Correct."

"Can I see what you're doing?"

"Sure." He motioned her over. "Army taught us to clean our weapons frequently. I spent a lot of time in the Sand Box and needed to clean out the grit so my weapon wouldn't misfire." He shrugged. "Could have been the difference between life or death for me or one of my men."

She drew in a deep breath to reply to his statement and froze.

Josh stood, alert. "What is it?"

"The metallic scent. That's what I smelled in my bedroom the night the burglar broke in."

He reached for a bottle from the coffee table and uncapped the top. "This?"

Del sniffed and reared back. "That's the smell. What is it?"

"Gun oil." He looked at her, his expression growing grim. "Your burglar had a gun. Most burglars don't carry them. If they're caught, they'll get less jail time if they don't have a weapon."

Her stomach clenched. Confirmation that her home invasion wasn't a burglary gone wrong. She needed that tea. "I'll make my tea." If she was lucky, she might sleep tonight. After that bit of information, she had her doubts.

"Want company?"

"I'd like that." Who didn't want a handsome man to distract you from scary thoughts? "Do you want tea as well?"

He chuckled. "Sorry, I'm a cold, sweet tea man. I'll grab a Coke and join you after reassembling my weapon."

In the kitchen, Del located Liz's tea stash and settled for one with Valerian in it. Smelled horrid, but might help her sleep. Her mother used the same tea. Thinking of her mother made her heart squeeze. She tried to call before she went to bed. The call went to voice mail. She didn't leave a message because if Dee Peterson knew something, she gossiped. Josh didn't want her sharing too much information. Silence was their best advantage.

The microwave signaled the heating cycle's end for her bedtime brew. She settled at the island as Josh padded on sneakered feet to the refrigerator and grabbed a soft drink. He took a deep drink before sitting on a barstool beside her.

"Why can't you sleep?"

"Worried about Mom."

"It's what she wants, you know."

"Mom's a master manipulator. She and Aunt Mari both should have their picture next to the dictionary definition."

Josh glanced at the clock. "Is this a good time for my first name guess?"

"Sure. I'm ready with my first question."

"Delaney."

She snorted. "I wish."

"Ask your question, beautiful."

He needed his eyes checked. At this time of morning, she wasn't beautiful. "When Alex hugged your mother, his facial expression revealed a deep emotional connection to your mother. Why?"

"You don't ask easy questions, do you?" He sighed, turbulent emotion on his own face. "Alex's family disowned him when he joined the military. He's had no contact with them in fifteen years."

Tears pooled in her eyes. No wonder Alex looked so touched. Liz Cahill treated him like she did Josh. "So heartbreaking for him. Never receiving mail or packages while deployed must have hurt."

Josh grinned. "I told Mom and Dad about Alex after the first mail call during boot camp. They started sending him letters and boxes, too. They sort of adopted him. Mom collects strays. That's how she sees Ethan, Nick, and Rod, too. Alex still isn't sure how to deal with it, but Mom and Dad think of him as theirs. He enjoys the Cahill clan whenever he comes in."

Though her mother's theatrics drove her crazy, Del was thankful to have her, especially with her father gone. She and her brothers indulged Mom too much. At least they had each other, unlike Alex. "I'm glad he has the Cahills. No one should be alone in the world."

His lip curled. "If you knew his family, you wouldn't say that."

"Why?"

"A question for another night, sweetheart. It's an ugly story that should come from him." He inclined his head toward her mug. "Finished?"

"I'll put this in the dishwasher and get out of your way."

"For the next two hours, I'll be reading a book between perimeter checks. You're no bother. Want to talk more?"

She wanted to stay with Josh, knew it wasn't wise this time of night. "Rain check?"

"Sure." He walked her to the stairs. "If you can't sleep, come back down." He grinned. "I'll read you the Army field manual. Guaranteed insomnia cure."

"If people knew the sleep secret, drug companies would lose millions of dollars each year. I planned to look for a hammer if the tea didn't work."

"And do what?"

"Knock myself in the head."

"Ouch. Trust me, the Army field manual will do the trick." He framed her face with his hands. "Get some rest, sweetheart. Tough day tomorrow." Josh leaned down and dropped a butterfly kiss on her lips.

A small smile curved her mouth. "You promised a real kiss. When will you deliver?"

"Want a real kiss, huh? Not tonight." He wiggled his eyebrows. "Something to look forward to tomorrow."

Anticipation splashed through her veins. "Tomorrow?"

He nudged her up the first step. "See you at breakfast."

Five hours later, Del stumbled from her room clad in jeans, tennis shoes, and tank top paired with a button-up shirt. In deference to the killer heat and humidity, she'd pulled her hair into a ponytail.

She knocked on Ivy's door and poked her head in. Her cousin was tying her own tennis shoes. Ivy had paired jean capris with a turquoise t-shirt. She looked cool and comfortable. And well rested. Del wished she looked that perky.

Sympathy crossed Ivy's face. "Didn't sleep?"

Del scowled. "I slept."

"How long? Five minutes?"

"Four hours."

Ivy cringed. "Hope there's more Coke in the refrigerator. You need caffeine."

"You saying I'm grumpy?"

Her cousin darted out the door and down the hall. Halfway to the first floor, she called back, "You need a nap."

A soft chuckle behind Del had her face flaming. She whirled to see a damp-haired Josh striding toward her in black jeans and a black t-shirt. "Why don't you look tired? You slept fewer hours than I did."

"I'm used to four hours a night." A hint of shadow appeared in his gaze before he blinked and it was gone as if never there.

Something to ask later. "What time do we leave?"

He checked his watch. "Thirty minutes."

She frowned. "Won't Alex need sleep first?"

"Unlike you, he fell asleep as soon as his head hit the pillow and didn't wake until time to relieve me. In the military, you train yourself to sleep whenever you have the chance. He'll be fine. Come on. I smell Mom's country breakfast. Ham, biscuits and gravy, bacon, hash browns, and eggs. Nobody does breakfast better than Liz Cahill." He paused. "Except Serena, when she's not feeling pukey."

Del preceded him downstairs, brewed more tea, filled a plate and sat in the dining room with the rest. She wondered if someone else would drop by this morning.

Sure enough, with her plate half empty, a knock sounded at the back door and footsteps crossed the kitchen into the dining room. Rod Kelter kissed Liz on the cheek and greeted the others at the table.

Liz patted the place next to her. "Have a seat, son. Would you like a plate?"

"I hadn't planned on stopping here, or I would have skipped the cop shop food."

"Serena baked this morning?"

"No, ma'am. She's feeling pretty bad this morning. Ethan's staying with her until the worst is past. One of the third shift guys stopped by the Donut Den."

Josh leaned back in his chair. "You have news?"

"Fed crime scene analysts will start at the Reece place this morning. Jordan's making noise about interviewing Del and Ivy." He smiled, a hard light in his eyes. "I had no information about Del's whereabouts today. Same goes for Ivy." His direct gaze included them both. "Make sure your phones are off until further notice. If you're around town, avoid the station and town square. Don't take either of your vehicles. I don't want to know whose wheels you take. The U.S. marshals roll into Otter Creek this morning. They'll want face time as well."

He returned his attention to Josh. "Plans in place?"

"Want info?"

"Tell Ethan. The still shell-shocked police chief received a call early this morning. Oakwood's arson investigator found traces of accelerant at Del's house."

Del straightened. "Someone set the fire?"

"Did the shooter try his skills at arson," Josh asked, "or was it the victim's ex-husband?"

CHAPTER ELEVEN

Josh held out his hand to Del. "Ready?"

When she nodded, he threaded his fingers with hers and tugged her outside to Alex's idling SUV. He kept Del between his body and the vehicle. He hurried her to the backseat, boosted her up and slid in beside her.

She looked puzzled. "Safety," he murmured. "Go," he said to Alex.

Smooth as silk, the SUV rolled down the drive and into the street. Josh scanned their surroundings. He figured at some point today they might have an encounter with the shooter. Probably not until they left Oakwood. He couldn't be sure they would take the arson bait. Everything in Josh rebelled at taking Del and Ivy into further danger though he appreciated that they wanted to reassure Mrs. Peterson. He wouldn't let down his guard until they returned to Otter Creek.

Beside him, Del shivered.

"Cold?"

"I feel like someone's watching my every move."

Rebecca Deel

Josh felt the same. He and Alex didn't know yet who they were up against. Made protection more challenging when each person was a possible threat. "Alex's ride has bullet-proof windows and armor plating." Didn't mean a tango couldn't take them out, but it would be harder to do damage. If the shooter had an RPG, Alex's reinforced ride wouldn't be enough protection. While he knew the SUV's limitations, Del didn't. She relaxed against the seat. At least he'd given her some measure of security.

The drive passed with a few comments between the women. Josh and Alex continually scanned their surroundings. No messages from either Rod or Ethan. All in all, Josh considered the first half of the trip a success when they drove down the main drag of Oakwood. Del provided directions to her mother's place.

Minutes later, they parked in the driveway of a two-story brick home with a wraparound porch. Flowers in planters decorated the porch every few feet. Bushes provided landscaping for the yard. Del grew up in beautiful surroundings. The neighborhood appeared to be a good one in which to raise children.

Ivy reached for the door handle.

"Wait." Alex's voice rang sharp in the SUV's interior. He stepped out, closed the door behind him.

Ivy scowled.

Josh reached over and flipped her hair. "He's your bodyguard, Ivy. To stay safe, do what he says without question. If you don't, it might cost not only your life, but his as well."

"I hate this." Her hands fisted on her thighs. "We were in the wrong place at the wrong time. I don't want you or Alex hurt or killed because of that."

"Trust us to do our jobs and we'll all have a better chance at getting through this unscathed." Josh prayed his statement was true. If his suspicions about the shooter being former spec ops turned out to be accurate, doing their

104

job would become harder. "When Alex gives us the all clear, we'll go inside."

Two minutes later, Alex opened Ivy's door and held out his hand. "Stay right with me." He helped her to the ground and kept her body between his and the vehicle. They circled the back and stopped at Josh's door.

Josh got out and motioned to Del. She slid over the backseat and placed her hand in his. "Whatever happens inside, I've got your back, sweetheart. If the situation becomes too much to handle, we'll leave. No more than an hour, okay? Detective Tyler wants an interview. I didn't set a definite time, but the sooner we leave Oakwood, the better." His skin crawled. Not a good sign.

"Thank you."

"Don't thank me yet. Day's still young." Too many things could go wrong. He helped her to the driveway. "Inside." He and Alex kept the women between them and hurried to the front door. Del shoved her key in the lock and threw open the door as Josh had instructed her on the drive over. Once the door closed behind them, Josh drew a deeper breath. He held Del in place until his partner gave the all clear to move. Alex pulled the drapes to prevent the shooter from getting eyes on them and took up position to the side of the window.

Alex signaled they were clear to move. Josh removed his hand from Del's arm. "Stay away from the windows," he murmured.

"Mom?" Del called. "Where are you?"

"Del! Oh, honey." Footsteps echoed down the hall and stairs. A petite, blond fashion plate hurried into the living room and came to an abrupt halt at the sight of Josh and Alex. Her astonished look morphed into one of welcome. "Del, you didn't tell me you were bringing Ivy and some new friends."

She smiled. "I didn't tell you I was coming either. Don't I get a hug or anything?"

Josh darted a glance at Alex. His friend rolled his eyes and resumed surveillance. Del couldn't have told her mother they were coming. Mrs. Peterson wouldn't answer the phone when her daughter called the night before or this morning. Made no sense to him. His parents kept their cell phones handy and charged the entire time he'd been deployed. No matter what time he called, his parents answered their phone within two rings.

Dee Peterson's face pinked. She wrapped her arms around Del for a moment. "I'm glad you came home." She turned and enveloped Ivy in a hug before turning to face Josh. "Introduce me to your friends, Del."

"This is Josh Cahill, Madison Santana's brother, and Alex Morgan, his friend."

Josh shook her hand. "Nice to meet you, Mrs. Peterson. Hope you don't mind us tagging along."

"I'm always happy to meet Del's friends. Would you like iced tea?"

"Sounds great, ma'am. Thank you."

"I'll help you, Mom." Del trailed her out of the room.

Josh shifted position to keep her in sight, pleased to notice her step toward the cabinets near the kitchen window, then abruptly change direction toward the refrigerator.

She nudged the door closed with her hip, a full pitcher of tea in her hands.

"Here." Josh hurried forward. "Let me take that." He carried the pitcher to the counter where Mrs. Peterson lined up five glasses. "Would you like me to pour, Mrs. Peterson?"

"No, thank you. We'll be along shortly."

"Yes, ma'am." Josh turned, winked at Del, and left the kitchen. He returned to the same place as before, one defensible and close enough to reach Del in seconds if they came under attack.

The living room was so silent, Ivy startled when he appeared. Her gasp earned him a glare from her and his friend. Josh's eyebrow rose. Alex was feeling protective after having known Del's cousin less than a day? He grinned. Couldn't happen to a better man. Ivy hadn't been in Otter Creek long, but he suspected she was a keeper.

Josh studied Ivy. "You okay?" he asked, voice soft enough not to carry into the kitchen.

"Sorry," she whispered. "I keep waiting for the other shoe to drop, you know?"

"Let us do the worrying. Your job is to act normal."

The rest of their visit with Mrs. Peterson passed without incident until Josh signaled Del it was time to leave.

"We need to go, Mom," Del said, standing. The rest of them followed suit.

"Oh, but I thought we could spend the day together, Del." Mrs. Peterson's eyes filled with tears. "You just arrived. Surely you and Ivy can stay for a while. There are plenty of things for your friends to do in town if they don't want to stay here. I'm sure listening to women gab isn't something they'll enjoy."

"I can't stay this time, Mom. I have to return to Otter Creek. Remember all those books that are taking over my house and store?"

"They can wait, Del. I can't. Who knows what tomorrow holds? I might have a heart attack overnight."

Josh's jaw tightened. He wouldn't let Del be blamed for their fast departure. Her relationship with her remaining parent was important to her. "It's my fault we can't stay, Mrs. Peterson. I need to return to Otter Creek." He held out his hand to Del's mother. "Thank you for being so gracious to unexpected guests. Please, come to Otter Creek soon. My family adores Del and would love to become acquainted with you."

Dee Peterson's smile reminded him why he loved Del's. It lit up the room. A few more tears and recriminations, and Josh and Alex escorted the women back to the SUV.

Safely inside the vehicle, Del drew in a deep breath, tilted her head back against the seat.

If safety hadn't been an issue, Josh would have enjoyed his time in Mrs. Peterson's company. She was a gracious hostess and an interesting conversationalist. After the shooter was behind bars, he'd suggest bringing Mrs. Peterson to Otter Creek for a weekend. She might like spending time with his sprawling family. Loneliness must be an issue as all her children were out of the house. Bound to leave her too much time to worry.

"When it's safe, we'll bring your mom to visit."

Del nodded, not opening her eyes. Alex cranked the engine and set the vehicle in motion. About the size of Otter Creek, it didn't take long to reach Oakwood's police station. He found a parking spot near the front entrance.

Inside the lobby, Josh showed the desk sergeant his badge. "Detective Tyler is expecting us."

The officer examined his credentials, nodded toward the double doors on his right. "Bullpen. Last desk on the left, near Lt. Wood's office. Go on back."

Through the doors, the noise level picked up from various phone and face-to-face conversations. Two men sat handcuffed beside desks. Josh steered Del and Ivy away from the men and a woman who cursed an officer typing his report. A bald man occupying the last desk glanced up, noticed them approaching, and stood.

"Detective Tyler?"

"Help you?"

"Josh Cahill. This is Del Peterson, Ivy Monroe, and Alex Morgan."

Shouting erupted as one of the cuffed men bolted from his seat and raced for the doors. Alex shifted position automatically, making himself a barrier between the women and the rest of the room.

Milo Tyler muttered a curse. "Zoo in here today. Let's go in the interview room where we won't have to shout to be heard." He led them around desks and down a hall. After opening a heavy wooden door, he ushered the group inside. "Have a seat. Be back in a minute."

Josh knelt beside Del, studied her closed expression. Stress. More days of unrelenting pressure waited. He tucked her hair behind her ear, and dropped his voice to a whisper. "Tyler will record the interview. Don't volunteer information, but answer his questions."

The detective returned, carrying two folding chairs in one hand and a file folder in the other. Josh sat on one chair beside Del while Alex settled on the other side of Ivy.

Tyler closed the door and dropped into a chair on the opposite side of the table. "I'm recording this interview. Helps me keep the notes straight." He placed the folder on the table, gaze fixed on Del's face. "Ms. Peterson, who wants you dead?"

Del drew in a sharp breath. "I thought this was an arson case with an accidental death."

The detective narrowed his eyes. "You haven't been in town for months. Someone trashed your house before it was torched. The M.E. dug a 9 millimeter slug from the vic's brain. Overkill for someone who likes to watch stuff burn."

"She's not a hostile witness, Detective," Josh said. "Del's offering her help. As you mentioned, she's been in Otter Creek for months. Who would have a grudge against her after all that time in another town?" His voice, though soft, conveyed a clear warning.

Del would hate to be on his bad side. Did the detective realize who Josh was, what he had been? Though not sure of the specifics, she recognized an extraordinary awareness not present in most of the law enforcement personnel she knew. The result of his specialized military training, she suspected.

"You're positive the arsonist didn't panic when he discovered a woman in a supposedly empty house?" she asked. The idea that Reece's killer murdered someone in her home made Del physically ill. Whether the victim was Lily or someone else, she didn't want circumstances in her life to spill onto an innocent.

"Evidence indicates the killer shot the woman, then ripped your house apart. Trashed every room. Not the work of a panicked arsonist. It was cold, calculated. Lucky you weren't at home or you'd be the one on that stainless steel slab at the morgue."

Del swallowed hard against the surge of choking bile. Under the table, Josh clasped her hand in a tight grip. Drawing strength from his wordless support, she raised her gaze to Tyler's. "Have you identified her?" She waited for Tyler's reply, stomach knotted. Del didn't want the victim to be Lily. Logic told her, though, her cousin's luck had run out.

"I just informed the immediate family. Vic's name is Lily Delray."

Ivy covered her face with her hands, shoulders jerking with silent sobs. Alex slipped an arm around her shoulders. To Del's surprise, her cousin turned toward her bodyguard and let him fold her into an embrace. Del was too angry to cry. Soon, though, she'd be still enough to grieve the loss of her cousin.

"M.E.'s sure this wasn't a domestic?" Josh asked.

"No signs of injury except the gunshot."

"So the shooter surprised her or she knew him. Is it possible Lily's husband scored a gun, shot his wife, and burned the place to cover his tracks?" Alex asked.

A look of frustration crossed Tyler's face. "I wish. Like nothing better than locking up abusers. Delray's alibi is iron-clad. He was in Atlanta with a group from his work. They took the company van, didn't return to town until after the fire was out. I'll ask you again, Ms. Peterson, who wants you dead?"

"I don't know."

"Or won't say."

Heat burned her cheeks. "He killed my cousin, a woman who cried when she saw an animal in pain. Lily had no defenses against her own husband much less a total stranger. She didn't deserve to die like that."

Josh's hand tightened around hers. She'd made a mistake, one Detective Tyler was sure to catch. He narrowed his eyes. How could she deflect his attention without lying?

"He? How do you know the killer is a man, Ms. Peterson?"

"A generic term, Detective. I don't know who the killer is."

"You're experiencing trouble in Otter Creek."

A statement, not a question. Rod had mentioned Tyler to Ethan. Did he know about Reece's murder or the burglar? Local law enforcement people must share information. They didn't seem to respect the federal officials, though.

Josh had warned her not to volunteer information. She suspected Ethan hadn't shared much, either. Would the FBI or U.S. marshals know about her house fire? Oakwood was a small town and an arson fire that destroyed a resident's house was big news. Would the feds check?

If Tyler knew about Reece's murder, he would ask more questions Josh didn't want her to answer. So she'd dangle the burglary in front of him. No proof the burglary was related to the murder. Didn't take a genius to connect the two events since her life to this point had been entirely forgettable. The detective couldn't know what had transpired in the last three days. He was fishing. She hoped. If he discovered she held back information, he might throw her in jail. Not a phone call she wanted to make to her mother or brothers, a situation sure to send her mother's blood pressure through the roof and provide her brothers with blackmail material for life.

The whole experience might give her mystery group a charge. They'd be the first to attempt springing her. Her luck, they'd bake a cake with lock picks in it and extend her time as a guest of the Oakwood P.D.

"That's true." Josh's hand clamped like a vise around hers. Del fought to keep her expression placid. "My home was broken into a couple nights ago." Tyler studied her face as sweat pooled at her lower back.

"Anything taken?"

"Police arrived before the burglar did more than break the glass and slip inside."

"You home?"

Josh's grip on her hand eased. Good. She'd guessed right about the burglary. Careful answers might help her avoid jail.

"I woke Ivy. We called for help from my bedroom."

"Coincidental to have an officer on patrol that close to your house." His expression made it clear he believed that situation unlikely.

"I was the first officer on scene," Josh said. "I was off duty and live a few blocks from Del."

"Catch him?"

"Rabbited as soon as I arrived."

"Know what he wanted?" Tyler directed his question to Del.

"He didn't have a chance to take anything. Scared us, though." Del wouldn't share about the burglar's gun as it would cause more questions than she wanted to dance around. She prayed the question-and-answer session was almost over.

"I bet." The detective leaned back in his chair, arms folded. "Had a run of bad luck this week. Any chance these incidents are related?"

Del shrugged. Better to do that than give herself away. She wasn't a good liar. Pastor Lang would be pleased.

Without repeating the question, Tyler turned his inquiry to Josh.

"No proof either way."

"Holding back on me, Cahill?"

"What makes you ask that?"

"Don't believe you boys are along for the ride today." His gaze assessed Alex. "More like bodyguards."

Josh grinned. "Both, Detective."

Tyler snorted.

"That hurts." Amusement colored Alex's voice as he stroked Ivy's hair. "Only stupid men would let Ivy and Del slip through their fingers. The Army drummed stupid from us in boot camp and the Sand Box."

"How long were you in?"

"Twelve years," Josh said. "We finished?"

"What's your hurry?"

"Sun's going down. I'm afraid of the dark."

Tyler rolled his eyes. "Yeah, we're done. You think of something else, Ms. Peterson, call me. Same goes for you, Ms. Monroe."

Ivy turned toward Tyler, face pale and wet. "If we remember anything, we'll call. Lily's killer deserves death row." She wiped traces of tears from her face with Alex's handkerchief.

"On that we agree." The detective grabbed the file at his fingertips and stood. "I'll walk you out."

Josh waved him off. "You have more important things to do. Chief Blackhawk will be in touch, Detective. He'll expect progress reports."

A wry smile crossed his face. "Your chief was quite clear about that. Seems like a good man."

"The best."

Two minutes later, Josh crawled into the back of the SUV beside Del. "Good job, sweetheart. Honest without sharing too much. You're a natural."

"I don't ever want to do that again."

"I thought he'd haul us off to prison," Ivy muttered.

"Both of you conducted that interview without a hitch." Alex's gaze seemed to focus on Ivy a minute before he returned his attention to the road leading from Oakwood. "Detours, Major?"

"Del, ready to head back to Otter Creek?"

"I thought you had an appointment." Del frowned. "We could have stayed longer with Mom?"

"Technically, I don't have an appointment. You do."

"With who?"

"The feds. They'll be livid that no one knows where you are." He shrugged. "Doesn't bother me to keep them dangling a while longer, but Ethan and Rod are pushing it to give you this much time."

"Let's go home, Del." Ivy sighed. "What's the worst that can happen? We'll give them the same unsatisfactory answers we've given everybody else and they'll go away."

Del hoped that was the case. The way things had been going lately, she was afraid to believe it. She noticed the telling glance Alex shot Josh. "What's wrong?"

"The feds might take you into custody as a material witness, baby. Especially if they connect your midnight visitor to Reece's murder."

"We don't know that's true," she protested. "It could be a coincidence." She knew the chances were slim, but Del didn't want to leave her store and her readers. She loved her job. She also needed the income to pay bills. Padlocking the doors and moving home was not an option. She also had Ivy to think about.

"Don't set your heart on staying free," Alex said. "We'll do what we can, but we're limited beyond going on the run with a target on all our backs."

"It won't come to that."

Josh didn't answer.

Del sighed and turned to watch the darkening sky. A gloomy silence fell in the SUV, unbroken except for faint road noise. Alex drove well. He navigated traffic like a driver with serious training. Twenty miles from Otter Creek, a cracking sound drew her attention. Before her eyes, the front windshield spiderwebbed from right to left.

CHAPTER TWELVE

"Down!" Josh shoved Del and Ivy flat on the seat. He considered making them unbuckle and crouch in the floorboard, discarded the idea. If Alex lost control of the SUV, they might wind up in a rollover. He wanted them belted in for safety. "Don't raise up until I tell you it's safe."

"What's happening?" Ivy asked, voice tight.

The SUV leapt forward. "Bullet hit the windshield," Alex said, voice grim.

"Are you okay?"

"I'm fine. Stay down so I'm not worried about you or Del."

Josh's grip tightened on his weapon. The bullet had been aimed at his side of the vehicle. If not for reinforced glass, he'd be dead. Was their perp arrogant or that good a shot? Either way, he could have hit Del. His jaw flexed. Shooting through glass messed with bullet trajectory. One miscue and Del would have left the SUV in a body bag.

"Change of plans?" Alex asked.

"Negative." Josh reached into the luggage area and grabbed his Go bag. He jammed his hand into the side pocket, seized night vision goggles and slipped them on for a minute. He scanned the area for heat signatures. Nothing. Didn't mean the shooter wouldn't try again before they made it to Otter Creek. Nearly impossible, though. Probably wanted to scare Del and Ivy, maybe get lucky and take him out. They would be vulnerable with him down.

Even if he succeeded, the shooter was an idiot to discount Alex. His partner didn't run from a fight. Ever. Alex Morgan tracked terrorists and captured or killed them. In Josh's mind, the shooter fell into terrorist category.

"What now?" Del asked.

He stroked her cheek while scanning their surroundings. Alex had his hands full driving at top speed over unfamiliar roads. He'd dispatched warlords and terrorists while driving in war-torn countries during his military stint. If that became necessary now, the women were in dire straits.

"We burn rubber for the next eighteen miles. Once we cross the town limits, we'll be harder to pin down." He unclipped his cell phone from the holder and hit his speed dial. Ethan answered on the second ring.

"Blackhawk."

Must have one or more feds within hearing range. Didn't matter if the Washington boys knew they were en route. His priority was Del and Ivy's safety. "Coming in hot. We took a hit to the windshield on Highway 18 twenty miles out."

"Injuries?"

"Negative. Ride's reinforced."

"ETA?"

"Ten."

"Roger that." The noise level rose dramatically. Ethan must have moved out into the bullpen. "Back door. We'll be ready for you."

"Feds?"

"Ready to tear a strip off our hides. If you planned on federal law enforcement, better try another career path."

Josh chuckled at Ethan's cheerful response. "I'll make a note. How's Serena?"

"Pukey, amazing."

Guess the shock was wearing off. Ethan was perfect for his baby sister. He treated her like a princess, loved her as his most precious gift. Serena looked upon him the same way. "Told Dad about the baby yet?"

"He's creating a list with names for more than one baby." Ethan's tone was tinged with amusement. "I hope the effort's wasted."

"Five minutes."

"We'll cover you," he said, and ended the call.

Josh leaned forward. "Drive to the back of the police station." He gave terse directions. Alex weaved through slower moving town traffic, muttering under his breath while swerving into the opposite lane to by-pass an ancient pickup doing ten miles under the speed limit. Tires squalling, Alex rounded the corner and guided the SUV into the back lot of the Otter Creek PD. At the gate, Josh leaned forward, waved his card in front of the scanner, and the iron gate swung open. Alex's vehicle halted far enough away from the building to allow Ethan to open the door. Four other officers, weapons drawn, provided promised coverage. Two feet to safety. A lot could happen in two feet.

"Can we sit up?" Ivy asked.

"Give me fifteen seconds to take position," Alex said. He turned off the engine, freed his weapon, shoved open his door, slid to the asphalt. After scanning the surroundings, he rapped on the glass.

Josh opened his door. "Slide to me. Rod's waiting inside."

Del sat up, her gaze locked on his. "What about you?"

"Behind Ivy, sweetheart." He climbed out, helped her to the blacktop. An officer hustled her inside to safety. He turned to Ivy. "Your turn, kitten. Same routine."

She scrambled across the seat and grasped Josh's extended hands. Alex drew her under his arm and hurried her inside the station.

"You, too," Ethan said. "You're not going hunting while you carry a badge."

A flame burned in Josh's gut. He wanted to do just that. If he did go hunting, though, someone else would be tasked with Del's safety. He scowled. Not going to happen. Unless the feds placed them in protective custody. Inside, his brother-in-law led the way through the station to his office.

"Where are Jordan and his flunkies?"

"Dinner. We don't have long. Tell me."

For the next few minutes, Josh gave his report in rapid-fire fashion, much like his reports to his commanding officers in the Army. Ethan sighed, ran his hand down his face. "You know what's going to happen."

"Can we avoid it?"

"Doubt it. Jordan's being hardnosed about this."

"What about hassling his crime scene team?"

"They finished despite his interference."

"Where are Del and Ivy?"

"Interrogation." He held up a hand before Josh spewed any blistering words. "It's the safest place. No windows and controlled access."

"They've been through so much already. Can the fed session wait until tomorrow?"

Ethan sent him a pointed look. Yeah, he knew better. Didn't mean he liked it. "Would the marshals allow them another night before taking them into custody?"

"No, they wouldn't." A deep bass voice sounded from Ethan's doorway. A six foot, barrel-chested male with brown hair and eyes stood in the doorway wearing a dark suit, white shirt, dark tie, and black shoes. Typical fed uniform.

Behind him, a blond male assessed him with an icy blue gaze wearing identical attire. The growing sneer on his mouth conveyed the marshal's attitude about Josh's request. Jordan wasn't the sole hardnosed fed in town. Young, too. Probably a rookie with the accompanying attitude.

"Josh, meet Marshals Ken Burns and Stone Vance. Gentlemen, Officer Josh Cahill."

Josh figured the blond was Stone. Couldn't see the middle-aged guy sporting a yuppie name like Stone.

Blondie said, "You've already hindered our investigation. We're racing the clock to track down Reece's killer."

"Join the line of excellent people working on that."

Anger flushed his cheeks. "Trail's already cold thanks to your department's inept investigation."

The other marshal held up his hand, stopping his partner's tirade in its tracks. "Enough, Stone. Not their fault Jordan got the jump on us. My apologies, Officer Cahill. No disrespect intended. You've got to understand where we're coming from. Judge Reece was a friend."

"He was a good man," Ethan said. "This is personal for us. We want this shooter behind bars. If we can help, we will."

Burns shifted his attention from Ethan to Josh and back. "Where are the witnesses?"

"Interrogation room. Down the hall, first door on your left." Ethan smiled, more a baring of his teeth. "The ladies need a meal. You will let them eat before questioning them."

"Wait a minute," Stone blustered. "We have jurisdiction over Reece's murder. You can't prevent us from questioning the witnesses."

"Not negotiable, Vance. Their well-being is my responsibility. They eat first."

"We can wait a few more minutes, Chief," Burns said. "Is there an office we can use to check in with our supervisor?"

Ethan inclined his head to the right. "Office is empty right now."

"Thanks." With a nod, he preceded his partner next door. The wooden door shut with a soft click. An angry voice sounded muffled through the walls into Ethan's office.

"I'll take care of dinner," Josh said. "You or Rod need anything?"

"We grabbed dinner while the marshals ate theirs."

"Where's Jordan?"

"Chatting up a waitress at the diner."

Josh grinned. "You have a spy?"

"Whole town's in on it. I spread the word he might cause trouble for Del. Reports started the minute he left his hotel room."

"Chief Blackhawk, you're getting the hang of small-town living."

He snorted. "Get going. The marshals might give us a few minutes. Doubt Jordan will be so accommodating."

"If the feds grow impatient, don't let Del and Ivy talk to them alone."

Ethan stilled. His gaze raked over Josh's face. "Your friend is sweet on Ivy. You interested in Del?"

"Don't know if it will go anywhere, but I want the chance to find out."

"Your objectivity's shot."

"Your objectivity took a hit a couple years ago. You didn't step aside either." Josh moved in closer. "Don't ask me to do that, Ethan. Not as my boss or my friend. I'd prefer to hide her and track the shooter. I'm giving us and the feds a chance to find this guy before I bring in my team. I'm not losing Del."

He watched Josh a minute, then said, "Your plan better be set when you return." He headed toward the interrogation room.

Josh left the station and stopped at Burger Heaven. Back at the station, he found his Go bag in Ethan's office. He closed the door and blinds, and located two tracking devices. He slipped them into the pre-paid phones he bought for Del and Ivy.

He stashed both phones in his pocket and retrieved the food from Ethan's desk. A stop by the vending machine netted four Cokes. In Interrogation, Alex and Ivy sat on one side of the scarred wooden table. Del waited alone on the other side. Rod rested one hip on the table's edge while Ethan lounged against the wall near the door.

"Text came in a couple minutes ago," Ethan said. "Jordan was at the cash register."

"Stall. Del and Ivy haven't eaten since breakfast."

"Don't know how long Jordan will cooperate."

Rod stood. "I'll help." He grinned. "Love to tangle with that lame fed. Might call Meg. She'd appreciate getting in a punch or two at him."

"My money's on my snoopy sister."

Rod chuckled and left the room. Ethan leaned in close to Josh's ear. "Jordan won't let you stay for the interview. Don't make an issue of it," he murmured. "Pick your battle. This one isn't the place to dig in. The feds will take them into custody as soon as the questioning is finished. I'll get you a few minutes with Del before they're under wraps. Make those minutes count."

"Thanks."

Ethan closed the door behind him.

"What's going on?" Del asked. "Does he know something he hasn't shared?"

Josh handed Alex a couple Cokes and unpacked the food bags. "I brought cheeseburgers with everything on them."

Alex dug into his burger. He chewed, swallowed, grabbed a couple of fries. "Oh, man, I've missed these burgers."

Josh unwrapped a cheeseburger and took a bite of his own. Nobody else grilled hamburgers this good in town. He dreamed about the taste of these while deployed. The chow hall never came close to Burger Heaven. He took the seat beside Del and nudged her with his elbow. "Eat, sweetheart. We'll have company before long."

"Is that what Ethan said?"

"Feds aren't patient."

She frowned, but picked up her hamburger. She and Ivy finished the last of their fries when a sharp knock sounded on the door. Ethan came into the room followed by Burns, Vance, and Jordan. From his brother-in-law's expression, his last few minutes hadn't been peaceful.

Josh stood. "Jordan."

Craig Jordan scowled. "Cahill. What are you doing here?"

"Dinner."

"Take a hike."

Heat burned Josh's cheeks. He wished for a couple minutes with the cantankerous fed. End up in jail, though. Jordan wasn't one to let an insult or a punch to the gut pass without reprisals. "Does this mean we're not friends anymore?"

"I'm not friends with cowboys who play by their own rules."

He grinned and gathered the trash. "Don't know what you're missing."

"Reams of paperwork explaining why I didn't follow protocols."

"No imagination." Josh turned to Ethan. "Okay if I bring in more Cokes?"

"They just finished dinner," Vance protested. "An obvious ploy to delay us. Again."

"Josh," Del said, voice soft. "It's okay."

"No, baby, it's not." He crouched at her side. "Jordan and company will need you to go over the day you found Reece, several times. Carbonation will settle your stomach." Had she understood his unspoken message to talk about Reece and not the break-in or shooting incident?

She swallowed hard. "Good idea."

One look at Alex had his friend standing. He laid a hand on Ivy's shoulder, squeezed. "Back in a minute."

Jordan frowned. "Don't you have anything better to do, Cahill? Surely some cat needs saving."

Josh narrowed his eyes. So, Jordan had been checking up on him. "I'm off duty. If Fluffy or his friends need hauling out of a tree today, I'll be sure to pass them your number."

Alex returned with two more cans. He gave one to Ivy, the other to Del.

"Blackhawk, take your two flunkies and get out."

"Not happening, Jordan." He smiled. "One of us stays with them or I'll remind Del and Ivy about their right to legal counsel." Ethan motioned for Josh and Alex to leave the room.

Josh brushed his lips over Del's. "I'll be waiting," he whispered and stood. At the door, he glanced at Del. Uneasiness filled her gaze. He winked at her and closed the door.

Jordan's words, though muffled, seeped from the room. "If I didn't know better, I'd think you were avoiding us. I'm sure Blackhawk informed you that such behavior would land you behind bars for obstructing justice. Now, let's begin."

His hand gripped the doorknob, knuckles white. As a friend, he longed to whisk them away and hide them. As a cop, he understood questioning was necessary. Posturing or not, the more people working Reece's case, the faster law enforcement could chase down leads. Del and Ivy's safety depended on them capturing or taking out the killer. Turning, he motioned to his friend. "Come with me."

He led Alex into Ethan's office. Josh handed one cell phone to Alex. "Ethan thinks the marshals will take Del and Ivy into custody as soon as the interrogation is finished. Installed a tracker. Get it to Ivy."

"We going to spring them?"

Josh leaned against Ethan's desk, frowning. "Got a bad feeling. I want to know where they are in case things go south. Not sure about Ivy, but Del couldn't find her way out of a paper bag. She got lost going to Knoxville a few weeks ago and that was with directions she'd printed out."

Alex shook his head. "She'd never make it in the military." He slipped the phone into his hip pocket. "Why won't you give this to Ivy? She doesn't know me."

Josh chuckled. "Might look funny to the feds if I play the boyfriend card with both women."

"You owe me a Porterhouse steak if she slaps me."

"Deal."

Three hours passed before the interrogation room door opened. Vance, a look of disgust on his face, shouldered past Josh and Alex who stood on both sides of the hall. Josh hadn't wanted to give the marshals a chance to leave with Del and her cousin without giving him an opportunity to hand over the phones. He wouldn't put it past them to try that to spite Ethan. Power plays were the norm for all federal law enforcement, no matter how much they spouted words of cooperation with the locals. Burns nodded at them as he followed his partner into the bullpen, phone pressed to his ear. "Atkins, we leave with the wits in ten minutes."

Josh's stomach knotted. He hated this. No idea if these marshals were any good, knew for sure they weren't as good as his team.

Ethan's voice carried into the hall. "You've got your witnesses, Jordan. You will give Ms. Peterson and Ms. Monroe time to say goodbye to Josh and his friend."

"We have jurisdiction."

"Your memory's going? My town, my people, my rules. Del, Ivy, take a break."

Ethan spotted Josh, motioned for him to escort Del and Ivy out of the room. Knowing his brother-in-law, he'd keep Jordan occupied in an argument as long as he could to give them time.

Josh clasped Del's hand and led her and Ivy down the hall to the restrooms. "We don't have long. Make it fast," he said. Two minutes later, he sent Alex and Ivy into an empty office and escorted Del into Ethan's office under the watchful eyes of the marshals. He closed and locked the door, noting the blinds were still closed.

"How are you, baby?" Josh wrapped his arms around Del. Her body trembled against his. He pulled her tighter against his chest, letting her lean against him. The questioning process, though necessary, was tedious and draining. Combined with lack of sleep, stress, and skipping meals the last few days, he was surprised Del was still on her feet.

"I can't say I want to do that again. Special Agent Jordan said the FBI knew everything that had been going on since Reece was killed."

"Feds always say that. They don't know everything."

"Figured he was blowing smoke. We told him what happened with Reece." She pressed her ear over his heart. "Are they really going to take us into custody?"

"It's to protect you." Knowing it was true didn't make the necessity of handing her and Ivy over to someone else's care any easier.

"What about my store?"

"We'll make sure it's covered." He pulled back a little, cupped her cheek. "Try not to worry."

"They took our phones." Tears pooled in her eyes. "What if something happens to Mom or my brothers?"

Josh smiled. "Got that covered, beautiful." He reached into his pocket and pulled out the small black cell phone. "This is pre-paid. No way to trace it to you. The phone's on mute. The first programmed number is mine. The second belongs to Alex. Keep this on you at all times. If you leave it lying around, the marshals will take the phone. You'll be tempted to check on the store or your mother. Don't. Only use this if something goes wrong and you need help." He bent down until he was eye level with her. "Do you understand, sweetheart?"

"Emergency only." She smiled. "Thank you." She shoved the phone deep in her pocket.

Josh watched, satisfied when he couldn't spot the phone in her pocket. "Next thing. I have another name guess."

"Let's hear it. I have another question ready."

"Delilah."

"Much better than mine."

"Huh. This might be more complicated than I thought." He grimaced. "Can't say I want to spill all my secrets this fast."

"Should have thought of that before you made the deal."

He narrowed his eyes. "You would have made a great lawyer. Okay, Ms. Peterson, hit me with your next question."

"What was the name of the girl you took on your first date?"

Some of the knots in his gut unraveled. He grinned. "That's an easy one. Rosalie Williams. She had the most beautiful red hair I'd ever seen. I almost asked her to marry me, but Mom convinced me that Rosalie wouldn't be interested in marriage even though I had a ring for her. We were both seven at the time. I found the ring in a box of Cracker Jacks and decided on the spot that it belonged to Rosalie."

Del's laughter rang out in the office. "Whatever happened to the beautiful red head?"

"She broke my heart and threw me over to marry a linebacker for the Titans. They've got three rambunctious boys at last count." Conscious of their time together growing short, Josh tugged her back into his arms. "They'll come for you soon and I promised you something." His gaze dropped to her mouth. "We might be separated for a while and I don't want you to forget me."

"Fat chance," she whispered.

He bent his head and brushed her lips with a series of butterfly kisses. When he finally settled his mouth on hers and deepened the kiss, Del sighed and tightened her arms around his neck. For a few long minutes, Josh indulged in her tastes and textures, one hand caressing her back, the other cupping the nape of her neck.

A short knock brought him back to their surroundings. Another series of soft kisses and he forced himself to lift his head. "Time to go, baby."

#

Dazed by the series of kisses she'd shared with Josh, Del walked from the office with Josh at her back. That man could kiss. How long would it be before she saw him or her mother again? Not too long, she hoped. All they had to do was wait for the police to capture the killer. How long could that take? She sighed, a ball of ice forming in her stomach. A long time. She'd read too many books about tracking killers to lie to herself.

The marshals waited in the hallway leading to the back parking lot, Alex and Ivy beside them, hands clasped.

Ethan waited at the door, expression grim. Del slowed enough that Josh bumped against her back.

"Del?"

"I don't want to do this." She swiveled to face him. "This isn't going to be for just a day or two, is it? I don't want to leave my store or...." She left unsaid that she didn't want to leave him.

"Can we get on with this?" Vance said. "You've already delayed us by several hours, Cahill."

"Can it, Vance," Ethan said.

Josh raised his hand and brushed back a few strands of hair that had worked loose from her ponytail. "You don't have a choice." He closed his arms around her, his mouth at her ear. "Trust me, baby," he whispered. "We will find out who killed Reece. You'll be back in my arms soon."

She nodded and stepped out of his embrace. Back straight, chin raised, she faced the marshals. "Ready."

CHAPTER THIRTEEN

In the backseat of a black SUV with dark tinted windows, Del pressed her arms against her stomach and glanced at her cousin's pale face. "You okay?" she whispered.

"Scared." Ivy twisted toward her. "Mad. Our life is on hold while the cops track this guy. He's running around free while we're in custody. Who knows if we saw the shooter? Truck man might have been a citizen we don't know."

Del gripped her cousin's hand. "Josh and Ethan will find him."

From the front passenger seat, Vance snorted. "Wouldn't bet on small-town cops. You'll lose."

"Enough," Burn said. "Give them a chance. It's their backyard. Maybe they'll surprise us."

The SUV accelerated onto Highway 18. An identical black SUV joined them minutes later. They left the highway and began following a dizzying number of back roads. After a while, the roads and trees appeared the same.

She prayed she never needed to make that emergency call to Josh. Del couldn't tell him where to come get her.

Finally, the pair of SUVs parked behind a white two-story farm house. The darkness prevented seeing the surroundings except for an impression of woods at the back and open space at the sides and front. She didn't think neighbors were near. Made sense. The marshals didn't want attention. Black SUVs driving in and out was sure to attract interest.

"Wait for the all-clear," Burns said.

"We know the drill." Ivy unbuckled her seatbelt and turned to watch the marshals check the area.

The back door of the house swung open. Though Del couldn't see who stood in the doorway, she knew it was someone on the small side.

Burns swung open the driver's side door. The interior light didn't come on. Another protection measure she wouldn't have thought to implement. "Welcome to your temporary home."

Vance opened the SUV door. Del and her cousin slid to the gravel drive. He hustled them indoors. As soon as Burns cleared the threshold, the woman holding the door closed and locked it. A light clicked on over the stove. Del's eyebrows lifted. Nice kitchen, about four times larger than hers. Beautiful wood cabinets, ceramic tile, stainless steel appliances.

Ivy whistled. "Makes me want to cook."

The red-haired woman's head jerked up. "You cook?"

"Not me. Del. I'm the gopher."

"Who cooks?" A tall, athletic male propped himself against the door jamb, hair the color of a raven's wing. His gray eyes gleamed in the dim light.

Ivy sidled closer to Del before she caught herself and straightened. Lee strikes again, Del thought. At least Ivy noticed the move and countered it. Too much testosterone in the room for her comfort. She stepped forward to shake hands with the new guy.

"I do. I'm Del. This is Ivy."

"Thank goodness somebody in the house can cook." He grinned. "Thought we were doomed to starve again on this detail. Deacon Creed. Deke to my friends. The short dynamo over there is Stella Grayson. We're your daytime protection."

"Nice to meet you both." Del glanced at her watch. "When do you go on duty? It's a little after one o'clock."

"In six hours," Stella said. "We made sure you didn't have any nasty surprises waiting when you arrived." She nodded toward Deke. "He'll get your gear while I show you to your room. We hoped you wouldn't mind sharing a room since you live together."

"We didn't pack anything," Ivy said.

"Your friends packed your bags," Burns said. "If you need anything else, let one of us know. We'll take care of it if we can."

"Does that include an e-reader with an unlimited expense account?" Del asked, a smile curving her mouth.

"We don't have those, but if you want books, tell us the titles. We'll do our best to find them." Stella motioned for Del and Ivy to follow her.

Deke moved aside as they crossed the kitchen. Del placed herself between Ivy and the new male marshal. Stella led them to the hallway and up the stairs. At the last room on the right, she turned on the light. A king-sized bed with a white lace bedspread dominated the room. Decorative pillows dotted the surface, the headboard and four posters a beautiful oak. Heavy white curtains covered both windows, walls painted a cool mint.

"Gorgeous," Ivy murmured. "I didn't think we'd be in a nice place."

"Most safe houses are boring. A former SEAL donated this one. It's totally off the grid. Only marshals know about this place."

"Why would he give up a home this beautiful?" Del asked.

Stella laughed. "He married into big money. He and his wife now own several houses nicer than this. She was in witness protection for a while and the SEAL wanted to give back to the people who saved his wife's life while he was deployed. Deke acted like a kid in a candy store when he learned you cook. You don't have to. We'll survive. Might be a bunch of frozen food or takeout, but you won't starve."

"I enjoy cooking, but I'm no gourmet chef. I like real food with real portions."

"Perfect. The kitchen is stocked with basics plus some canned food. Deke stopped by the grocery store before we came on duty. No telling what he bought. If you need something to fix a meal, let me know. I'll make sure you get it." She motioned for Del and Ivy to sit on the bed. "House rules. No contact with the outside world. That means no phone calls, no Internet, not even smoke signals or Morse code. The windows are covered with blackout curtains. Don't open them. Stay inside unless we tell you otherwise. If we give an order, do it without question. We have reasons for everything we ask, even if it doesn't make sense to you. Questions?"

"No questions, but I can already tell you if there aren't any books worth reading in this place, your first stop tomorrow is someplace that sells books."

"You like to read?"

Ivy grinned. "Del owns a bookstore and loves to read mysteries. I prefer romance and romantic suspense."

"My kind of women. I don't have much time to read these days. If you want specific titles, I'll try to find them. The best way to stay sane is to keep busy doing things you enjoy, even if you must do them inside. There's also a full gym in the basement if you want to work out."

Should have expected that. A Navy SEAL would need to stay in top shape for his job.

"Oh, one more thing. There's an escape tunnel from this bedroom." Stella demonstrated how to open the hidden door. "Don't use this for any reason unless it's a dire emergency."

A knock and Deke entered carrying a black backpack in each hand. He placed both on the bed. "No names on the bags. Meet you downstairs, Stel." He left the room with a nod at Del and Ivy.

"If you don't need anything, I'll see you in a few hours."

"You're leaving?" Ivy's eyes widened.

"We're on duty in pairs. Since it's so late, Deke and I will bunk down for the rest of the night downstairs. We'll leave tomorrow night when Burns and Vance come on duty."

"Good night." Del waited until the marshal left the room before facing Ivy. "You okay?"

"Yeah." She wrapped her arms around herself. "Too many big men."

Ivy didn't have a problem with Alex Morgan. He wasn't a lightweight. Maybe it was the number of men in close proximity. Del grabbed the nearest bag and pulled it toward her. "Let's see if our clothes match. No telling who packed the bags. I don't think Josh or Alex would have left the police station."

"Maybe Madison or one of her sisters. I'd feel better about one of them packing my underwear." Ivy paled. "I hope we have underwear. I don't want to send a marshal to buy them."

"Let's find out." Del unzipped the duffel and pulled open the sides. "Westie pajamas and black slippers. This one's yours."

Ivy dragged out jeans, socks, casual shirts, underwear, toiletries, another pair of shoes and two books from her nightstand. "Whoever packed this earned major points because they packed a favorite book and the current one I've been reading." She studied the pile on the bed. "Should I repack this stuff?"

Del thought about the topics she and Josh discussed in the last three days, about the phone deep in her pocket. "Yes, in case we have to run." She checked that the door was closed and moved to Ivy's side. "Did Alex give you anything?" she whispered.

Ivy nodded, face tinged with pink.

Interesting reaction. So not all men gave Ivy the creeps. She grinned. "Alex seems nice."

"He is," she whispered. "I wish...."

Del's smile faded. "Proves there are good ones, Ivy. Now, time for bed. Kitchen duty starts in about four hours."

Ivy groaned.

Josh settled his utility belt at his waist and left his bedroom. Alex, cell phone pressed to his ear, motioned toward the kitchen counter. A pile of sandwiches wrapped in plastic sat on a plate. Nice. All he needed was a couple gallons of coffee and he'd be set for the night's patrol. Unless something interesting popped up, he'd need a steady infusion of caffeine to remain alert tonight.

He glanced at his watch, wondered about Del and Ivy. His gut tightened at the thought of their safety depending on some other team than his own. Few men were as deadly and focused as his former Delta unit. Burns and Vance hadn't inspired his confidence. Unfair assessment on the basis of a short meeting? Maybe. Trusting his gut had saved his life and the lives of his men more than once. His instincts urged him to retrieve Del and Ivy and hide them with his team. His respect for the law restrained him along with an unwillingness to place a target on Ethan's back. A time might come when Ethan needed fed connections to do his job.

"How fast?" Alex asked, paused to listen, then, "Perfect. Thanks, man. Charge my card. Later." He shoved the phone in his pocket, swiveled to face Josh. "Take as many sandwiches as you want." A slow perusal with growing amusement. "Never thought I'd see you wearing a cop uniform, Major."

"Not in my career plan, either."

His friend folded his arms and leaned against the counter. "All of us planned to go the full twenty."

"Spec ops is a young man's dream."

"Thought ourselves invincible." A wry smile crossed his lips. "Shock to learn we weren't bulletproof."

"And not immune to aging." His hand dropped to his thigh. He half expected to feel bandages wrapped around his leg. "Any word on your windshield?"

"Bear put a rush on it. Should be here by noon tomorrow. Hope the feds keep a lid on Ivy and Del's location that long. Otherwise, we'll have to retrieve them with compromised glass."

"Dealt with worse." No windshield while racing across the Sand Box half a click in front of a sandstorm came to mind. Didn't miss that aspect of military service although he missed his teammates and the adrenaline rush from a mission gone south. They'd all gone south. That's why he always made multiple backup plans.

Alex chuckled. "When are you off shift?"

"Nine. Ethan covered part of my shift so I could sleep a couple hours. I'm returning the favor by working a couple hours over." He grinned. "Can't have folks around town think I'm taking advantage of family connections."

His friend snorted. "Every shift has at least one of your family on duty."

"That's the way it worked out." He reached for the sandwiches, brows furrowed. "What did you make? I haven't been home to look in the refrigerator." Usually Serena kept him well stocked. With her stomach so upset, he wasn't sure she'd been by.

Alex stared. "Your memory going?"

"Serena takes care of the grocery shopping. Wasn't sure if she'd been to the store before she passed out on my floor."

"Ah. Your sister left enough sandwich fixings to feed our unit. Not sure what you wanted, so there are three kinds. Turkey, ham and cheese, and roast beef."

"Sounds great." He chose one of each, left the rest for his friend. Knowing Alex's metabolism, there wouldn't be any by breakfast time. "Get some rest. I'll let you know if I hear anything from the women."

Josh climbed into his SUV, and radioed dispatch to log him on duty.

At fifteen minutes before four, dispatch signaled. "Unit 6."

He grabbed his handset. "Unit 6."

"10-27 at 3365 Morningstar Lane."

A break-in at Reece's place? Josh frowned. Kids or a run-of-the-mill burglar taking advantage of an empty house? Might be their shooter returning, but why? If Reece was the target, why return to the house?

"10-4. Responding Code 2. Notify Detective Kelter."

"Copy."

Josh completed a U-turn in the middle of Cotton Road, headed in the opposite direction toward Morningstar Lane, lights flashing without sirens. He hoped they'd catch the perp in the act. Even better would be to nab the shooter and spring Del and Ivy from marshal custody. Annie Jenkins was a sweetheart, but Del's customers missed her personal touch and extensive book knowledge. That beautiful lady had made a place for herself in Otter Creek.

"Unit 6."

He slid around a tight curve and swerved to miss the camel walking along the side of the road. "Are you kidding me? That camel is out again? Whoever answers that call should cite old man Lawrence." Safely around the four-legged road hazard lumbering down the asphalt, he snatched his radio from the holder. "Unit 6."

"Meet Unit 2 on tac 2."

"Copy." Josh switched his radio to tactical channel 2. "Unit 6."

Rod's voice came over the air wave. "Josh, meet me on Sunset, behind the Reece place."

"Copy that." He paused, clicked his radio back on. "Rod, call the dispatcher and have somebody roust old man Lawrence. I almost sideswiped Bonnie on Delacroix."

"Oh, man. Glad I don't have to chase that girl around town for once. Copy that."

Good thing people didn't realize Josh had captured that camel several times over the last eighteen months or he'd have Mr. Lawrence calling him personally to retrieve Bonnie any time she pulled a dromedary Houdini from the pasture. Wonder if someone left the gate open this time or if she'd learned to open the latest gate latch? Josh hoped the officer who answered that call had potato chips in his cruiser. That was the only thing the camel loved enough to follow a trail anywhere.

Two blocks from Sunset, Josh turned off his lights. He cruised to a stop behind Rod's SUV. His brother-in-law met Josh on the street. Not much of a moon at this time of morning. Good for their purposes. The air felt heavy already. He sighed. Signs of another scorcher when the sun rose. Made him glad he was on night duty for a while. Working in the heat and humidity in a black uniform left him drenched hours before the end of shift.

"Let's go around back. The Kings are out of town, so they won't cause a ruckus. No other neighbors are close enough to be a problem."

Weapon in hand, he said, "Aye, aye, Captain."

"That's General to you." Rod flashed a grin.

"Meg might call you that, but I'd probably choke on it."

"Yeah, yeah." The detective moved toward the Reece place, almost melting into the shadows. At the property line separating the King place from the Reece grounds, Rod stopped.

Josh studied the darkened windows of the mansion. "No movement."

"Nope." Rod sounded frustrated. "I hoped for some indication of where the perp is. This place is as large as a hotel. No telling where our break-in artist is located."

"Plan?"

"Back door. Room by room search."

"Cover territory faster if we split up."

"If this is our shooter and he's what you suspect, we'll have a better chance together. Agree?"

"Up to you, boss."

"I asked for your opinion, Officer Cahill. Or should I call you Major Cahill?" Rod's tone bordered on snippy.

Josh's gaze made another sweep of the darkened home and yard. Poor lighting and too many places to hide. He didn't like the set up. "A little better than even odds with the two of us together."

"That's it? Why not better odds?"

"You're a good cop, Rod. Great instincts. I respect your skills, but you aren't military trained. If that's our shooter and he served in special forces, he's several cuts above just military trained. He'll be smart, more than fast, and deadly accurate. One mistake on either of our parts and we're both dead. He won't hesitate to take us out. We're the enemy and he'll make split second decisions. If we corner the shooter, whatever happens will be over in seconds."

Rod blew out a breath. "Noted. Let's go." He took off in a crouching run.

Josh followed, alert, scanning.

They skirted the in-ground pool and traversed the patio. At the French doors, Rod crouched in front of the doorknob. "Take a look," he whispered.

He leaned in, squinted. Fine scratches around the lock. Jimmied. Not kids, then. They wouldn't have been sophisticated enough to pick a lock. A baseball bat or simple rock would have sufficed. That left a burglar or their shooter. He eyed his brother-in-law's back and scowled. Couldn't see much in the dim lighting, but he saw enough outline through Rod's jacket to know he wasn't wearing a bulletproof vest. "Let me go in first," Josh whispered.

"What? Why?"

"Because I'm wearing a vest."

Rod waved that comment aside. "No time. Let's move."

Stubborn man. If he was injured, Josh would leave him to Meg's tender mercies. His sister had almost driven Rod crazy while he'd recovered from a couple gunshot wounds before they married. Megan Cahill Kelter was as diplomatic as a hedgehog.

Rod eased open the door. They cleared the doorway, the detective going right, Josh left. Empty kitchen. He closed the door behind himself. If anyone slipped past them, the closed door would slow him down a couple seconds. Might make the difference in catching him or not.

They stood in the kitchen, listened. Nothing. If the perp remained, he could be anywhere. This house was over 10,000 square feet. A crowd could be in this house and, if they were quiet, he and Rod wouldn't know it.

A minute later, Rod signaled he was moving into the interior of the house. Room by room, they cleared the first floor. All empty. No signs of an intruder. One last room on this floor. The library. They moved down the hall in silence. The door was closed. Rod grasped the knob. He stood to one side of the door while Josh positioned himself on the other. He nodded at the detective.

His brother-in-law held up three fingers, counted down and threw open the door. Crouched, he went to the right, Josh to the left. He caught a whisper of movement. A shaft of light shining through a gap in the curtains glinted on the barrel of a gun pointed at Rod. Almost before the thought processed, he was on the move, diving in front of his brother-in-law. A cough splintered the silence and a bullet slammed into Josh's vest, mid-chest, the impact knocking him into Rod. The shooter raced for the door.

"Police! Freeze!" He got off four shots before their perp cleared the threshold, at least one a hit from the amount of swearing. Frustration twisted through Josh. Winged him or hit a shoulder. Otherwise he'd be down. Unless he was wearing body armor. In that case, he'd irritated the perp, maybe cracked a rib if he was lucky.

He scrambled to his feet and raced after the shooter. Had to be the same guy. Same movements and speed. Josh hit the edge of the patio at a dead run and, when the shooter ripped off a volley of shots in his direction, had to take a rolling dive onto the lawn and shift into a crouch behind a concrete planter. One shot decimated the planter inches to his right.

Sirens sounded in the distance. Within seconds, the shooter dashed across the expanse of lawn and disappeared into the darkened neighborhood.

Footsteps behind him. Josh swung around, one knee on the ground, weapon up and aimed.

"Whoa. It's me." Rod moved into view, gun at his side. "Dude's fast."

"Told you." He stood, holstered his weapon.

"You okay?"

"Bruised. Nothing serious."

"Good." Rod got in his face, scowled. "What were you thinking?"

"That you were about to get shot."

"So you had to play hero? Why didn't you tell me to duck?"

"Would have been too late to react. He would have gotten off the shot anyway. Next time, wear a vest."

"Thanks," he muttered.

Two prowl cars swung into the driveway followed by another department SUV. Ethan climbed out. Seeing Josh and Rod, he jogged to their location.

"Perp?"

"In the wind," Rod said.

A growl, then. "Run it down."

The detective recounted the events of the previous few minutes, outlined the steps they'd taken, and their confrontation with the intruder. "Shot at me. Josh dived in front of me and took a hit to the vest." A grin in his direction. "Ought to be checked. Might have cracked ribs."

Josh's eyes narrowed. "Cheap shot, Kelter. Won't forget it, either."

"Why the swan dive, Cahill?" Ethan asked. "Voice broken?"

He straightened, recognizing the Chief's voice rather than a friend. "Detective Kelter wasn't wearing a vest. I didn't want Meg on my case for letting her husband get hurt, sir."

Ethan's attention shifted to his detective. "Hope you like midnights, Rod, because your time on them just got extended for two months."

"Two months? Aw, come on, Ethan."

"Got a problem with that, Detective?"

A huff of air, then, "No, sir, Chief."

"Stupid move, Kelter. This guy is one of the most dangerous men you'll ever encounter. I want you around to tell the tale to your grandchildren. You hear me?"

"Yeah, I get it. Josh reminded me about the vest. I thought this was a burglar."

"That kind of mistake could put you six feet under. Don't make it again."

"No, sir."

Ethan turned his gaze on Josh. "Walk me through the scene in the library. Hospital report on my desk before the start of your next shift, Cahill. We need you mobile. More important, Del and Ivy need you mobile."

He led the way inside the house. Together, he and Rod described their steps, turning on lights as they made their way through the house. Drops of blood created a trail to the library. A zing of satisfaction curled through Josh. He'd hit the shooter.

Ethan crouched, examined the blood. "Rod, get your crime scene kit. I want to run this through our own sources. As soon as we're finished here, I'll call Jordan. Let's get this done."

While Rod retrieved the kit, Josh talked his brother-in-law through the events in the library.

"How many shots at Rod?"

"One."

"Bullet?"

"Don't know. I got off four shots at him as he ran out the door. At least one hit."

Ethan shined Josh's flashlight around the floor, highlighting five spent shells. "One of these belongs to the shooter. All of them are jackets for forty calibers." A glance over his shoulder at Josh. "I'll need your sidearm. Feds will want it for comparison. You have a backup?"

Rod returned with his kit and the three snapped pictures and gathered a blood sample. They found one bullet lodged in the wall across from the library, another in the door frame. That left two unaccounted for. "Pity we can't take the spent shells to test."

"Start a war with the feds." Ethan eyed Josh's shirt. "Unbutton your shirt. I didn't find the bullet that hit you. Maybe it's still lodged in the vest."

He tugged his uniform shirt out of his pants, unbuttoned, shrugged it off. Sure enough, the bullet was lodged in his vest. A grim expression settled on Ethan's face. The bullet was lodged directly over Josh's heart.

CHAPTER FOURTEEN

Josh slid off the emergency room bed and tugged on his black t-shirt. "What's the word, Doc?"

Otter Creek's favorite doctor, John Anderson, glanced up from making notes. "You're cleared for duty, Officer Cahill." He nodded at the chest he'd just examined. "Bruised ribs. Might need some over-the-counter pain reliever, but back to normal in a few days."

He grinned. "Good to know. I need a copy of the report so my brother-in-law will let me work tonight."

"I'll leave a copy with your discharge papers." Anderson paused, his hand on the door. "How's your family reacting to Serena's news?"

"The women are planning the nursery." And because Anderson was Madison's doctor as well, added, "Nick took Maddie out of town for some intense TLC."

The doctor nodded, his expression softening. "He's a good man. More important, he's good for your sister."

"Santana believes he's the luckiest man on the planet to be married to her. He already had plans ready for when

Megan or Serena became pregnant. Less than an hour after hearing Serena's news, he had Maddie in his Jeep."

He laughed. "She deserves every bit of pampering from her husband." Anderson opened the door. "I don't want to see you in here again anytime soon, Josh." And he was gone.

Doc Anderson was right. Madison deserved the pampering. She deserved a happy life, one Nick was determined to give her. Josh grabbed his utility belt and what was left of his uniform shirt and exited the room. He stopped by the nurses' desk, waited for his discharge papers to process.

"Cahill."

Josh turned, stared at Jordan. "Following me, Special Agent Jordan?"

"Forget your basic crime scene rules? You should have waited for me at the scene."

"Ethan's orders." Yeah, he felt a little bad for throwing his brother-in-law to the federal wolf. Very little. "He was concerned about possible cracked ribs."

"Are they?"

"Nope." He grabbed the clipboard the desk nurse pushed his direction and signed his name. "What do you want, Jordan?"

"An interview would be nice," came the sarcastic response. "Can you squeeze me into your busy social calendar today?"

"You already have my statement." Rod had taken his statement before he left for the hospital. "Nothing else to add. If I thought of anything, you'd be the first one I'd call."

"Somehow, I doubt that."

The corners of his lips curled upward. Smart man. "I'm working third shift. If we absolutely have to do an interview, we do it at the station. I'll give you one hour, not one minute beyond. I'm not getting shot on duty because of fatigue."

"Can't handle a couple sleepless days? Thought you were a big, bad Army Ranger. Lots of redacted stuff in your files."

His lips twitched at the frustration coming through in Jordan's voice. So the special agent in charge had tried to run him in the system. Almost everything in his military files was classified thanks to Delta. And, no, he wasn't concerned about fatigue on duty. Josh didn't want to be tied down with Jordan if Del needed him. He'd go through whoever stood in his way to get to her. If he went through Jordan, he'd spend some time behind bars unless he pulled a few strings. Preferred to save those strings until it really mattered. "What's it going to be, Jordan? Station for one hour or do I go home to sleep?"

A scowl, then, "Station."

That's what he figured. Josh left the hospital without a backward glance and drove to the Otter Creek police station. He nodded at the desk sergeant and walked down the hall to the bullpen. In Ethan's office, he dropped the discharge papers and his clearance to return to work on the desk.

His brother-in-law's forehead furrowed. "Why aren't you sleeping?"

"Jordan tracked me down at the emergency room, insisted on an interview."

Ethan got to his feet, frowning. "I'll take care of it. Go sleep."

"We're doing the interview in Interrogation. He has one hour."

At exactly noon, a hard knock sounded on the door. Ethan. Right on time. Josh pushed back from the wooden table and stood. "Time's up, Jordan. I'm going to bed."

"We're not finished."

The door swung open. Ethan stepped in the room. "Go," he said, spearing Jordan with a pointed glare.

With Jordan ripping into Ethan for interfering in a federal investigation, Josh walked into the sun-drenched afternoon. After parking in his assigned slot at the apartment, he glanced at Alex's SUV. A new windshield glittered in the sunlight. Bear delivered again. The former Marine rocked.

He climbed the stairs to his apartment and slid his key in the lock. Hard rock music boomed through the apartment. Josh rolled his eyes. Alex's taste in music hadn't improved since separating from the Army. The clang of weights told him his friend's location. He leaned his shoulder against the door jamb as his friend toweled sweat off his face. "Saw the new glass."

Alex grunted. "Cost me a bundle."

"I'm sure Bear smiled all the way to the bank."

"Back late, Major."

"Ran into our shooter again."

Alex's head snapped up. He draped the towel around his neck. "Get him?"

"A piece of him." He explained the events of the morning.

"The detective's lucky to be alive."

"Ethan made that point loud and clear. Rod's on midnights for the next two months." Josh straightened. "If you need to shower, I'll take one after you're finished."

His friend grabbed his water bottle and his shower gear. A minute later, water ran in the bathroom. In his own room, Josh hung up his utility belt, secured his weapon and unloaded his pockets. He glanced at his cell phone. Still nothing from Del. Good, he supposed. Meant she and Ivy were safe. He missed her.

Josh placed his phone on the nightstand and dropped on the bed on his back, eyes closing. The joke was on him. After telling Del not to forget him, she'd occupied his thoughts since she left with the marshals. No telling how long the feds would keep her and Ivy under wraps. Del thought capturing or taking out the shooter solved her problem. He wished the solution was that easy. Someone hired the killer. Until he was behind bars, Del and Ivy weren't safe. Smoking him out might take a long time.

His eyes flew open. Had Ethan talked with Milo Tyler? Someone should keep eyes on Del's family in case the shooter tried using them as leverage.

On the nightstand, his cell phone chirped. He grabbed it and checked the screen. A smile bloomed. Phone pressed to his ear, he said, "Quinn Gallagher. Long time, bro. Doing okay?"

"Better than you, Major."

At the sober rumble in his ear, Josh's smile disappeared. He sat up and swung his legs to the side of the bed. "What's up?"

"Put feelers out about the incidents in your neck of the woods. An operator's in the area. Only HVTs."

Judge John Reece was definitely a high value target. So why come after Del and Ivy? Even if they identified him, he'd reinvent himself. Good papers weren't cheap, but a skilled merc charged premium prices. He could afford the papers plus plastic surgery to fool facial recognition software.

Del and Ivy being forced into Witness Security made Josh's stomach twist into a knot. He refused to let that happen. "Anything else?"

"Guy is a ghost. Slides in, takes out his target, and is gone before anyone identifies him. No tracks, no brass, nothing."

"Had another run in with him a few hours ago. Took a bullet to the vest, so now there's brass. Nicked him in return. He left blood at the scene."

"Can you get me a sample?"

"On the way." He'd taken his own sample, knew Quinn had connections at some swanky private lab. He'd gladly foot the bill for the testing if it safeguarded Del. "Should reach you by five."

"Perfect. I'll drop it off at the lab on the way out of town."

Josh stilled. "Going somewhere?"

"Due some vacation time. So are Nate and Rio. Thought we'd fish around Otter Creek."

He missed his team. "Bring all your gear. Not sure what we'll need. Literally might be fishing if the feds luck out."

A soft huff came over the speaker.

Josh agreed. "See if there's any scuttlebutt about this ghost being black ops."

Silence for a moment, then, "Shooter was military?"

"Delta or SEALs. Same moves. Jackrabbit fast." Del and Ivy could be in more danger than the marshals knew. An operator trained by either of those teams wouldn't back down until he completed the mission or died trying.

Del put away the last of the condiments while her cousin finished loading the dishwasher. "Did you see the food in the pantry and refrigerator? We could eat for days and not run out of anything."

"Guess that's by design. Heaven forbid we escape this prison to buy sugar or milk."

Del froze at the hard edge of anger seeping into her cousin's voice. Less than one day in this posh confinement and Ivy was chafing at the boundaries. What if Josh and Ethan took several weeks to find Judge Reece's killer? She didn't know if Ivy could tolerate being housebound without sliding into a deep depression, much as she had after Lee.

"Don't look like that, Del."

She grabbed a washrag, dampened it, and started wiping the counter top. "Like what?"

"Worried I'll lose my mind in this beautiful jail."

The back door opened to admit Deke. Ivy stiffened. She turned back to her task, tossing in a dishwasher tablet, and set it to run. "I'm going to our room."

"Want some tea?" She felt a compulsive need to do something to lighten the mood for her cousin. Ivy loved iced tea more than any other drink. She said it reminded her of sunshine-filled days and lazing under a tree in a hammock.

A shake of her head, and Ivy left the room.

A minute later, a door clicked shut.

"Do I make Ivy uncomfortable?"

"Why do you think that?"

"She leaves a room every time I enter it."

She opened the refrigerator and pulled out the fresh pitcher of iced tea. "It's not you, specifically, Deke. Men make her uneasy."

"All of us? That's hardly fair. The whole male gender isn't evil."

Del waved him to the kitchen table. He looked hot and sweaty. Not surprising given the temperature outside. Well, what she heard about the weather through the news she listened to earlier. Burns and Vance refused to let them outside even for a couple minutes of fresh air. Del hadn't cared so much for herself. She loved sitting inside with a book anytime. Ivy, however, felt as though the walls were closing in. Her cousin had claustrophobia, courtesy of Lee and a weekend spent locked in an unfinished storm cellar with no light, food, or water. "Only took one."

The marshal dropped into a chair.

She poured Deke a glass of tea and set it in front of him. "She knows most men aren't evil. Takes a while to trust your assessment of someone's character when you guessed wrong and paid a heavy price for misjudgment."

"Is he dead?" Deke's voice was flat.

"Jail."

A nod. He downed half the glass before taking a breath. "Thanks for this."

"Once she gets to know you a little, learns she can trust you, Ivy will be fine."

"Needs to happen fast," he said. "She must trust me enough to do what I tell her if we have a security breach. If I have to touch her and she has a panic attack at the wrong time, it could cost all of us. If she can't do that, I'll ask for reassignment. Though I think I'm a nice guy and so does my wife, your safety and hers is more important than my dented ego."

She poured tea for herself and settled across from him. "Give her a chance. It will be that much harder on her to bring in someone new."

The marshal studied her a moment. "Does Ivy trust any man?"

Alex's face popped up in her mind, followed by Josh. "One for sure, maybe a second." Odd that a virtual stranger had wiggled past some of Ivy's defense mechanisms.

"Must be a saint," he muttered.

Del grinned. Though she didn't know Alex Morgan well, she knew enough to realize that moniker didn't fit. Alex gave the impression of walking trouble. She finished her drink and excused herself. She glanced into the security room, noted Stella watching the monitors. Nothing moved except leaves on the trees. Pretty view, but boring since the video feed was black and white.

She climbed the stairs and walked to the bedroom. Ivy, sprawled on her back with a book propped against her stomach, glanced up and smiled. "What's for dinner?"

"You ate a fully dressed hamburger along with a pile of potato chips."

She laughed. "Just wanted to get a rise out of you."

"Worked. Which book did you settle on?"

Ivy held up her favorite romantic suspense.

Couldn't beat Elizabeth Lowell, though Jayne Ann Krentz was right up there with her. So many books, so little time to read. If only she didn't have to work. "Deke's worried about you." She sat on the end of the bed and faced her cousin. "He's afraid you won't trust him to protect you."

"If that time comes."

Ivy Monroe was stubborn when she wanted to be. Well, so was the Peterson side of the family. "Make an effort to know him. You can't do that if you run when he shows his handsome face in the same room."

Her cousin's head whipped around to face her. "You think he's good-looking?"

"If you don't, you need your eyes checked."

"I thought you were nuts about Josh."

Del's face heated. "I am. Doesn't mean I can't appreciate a handsome face. Deke seems really nice."

"Unlike Vance."

"If you can't trust Deke, he'll have to be reassigned. Your safety might depend on it. Ivy, he didn't say this, but I think he and Stella are partners. If he leaves, she might be reassigned as well."

"I like her."

"Me, too. Deke's married. That should make him safer. Make an effort, okay?"

"I'll try." She moved the book back into position. "So, really, what's for dinner? It's what I'm living for right now." A wry smile lit her face.

"Something easy. Chicken Alfredo."

Ivy sat up. "Easy? Mom tried that several times, each one a total failure. She scorched it every time. The last time she tried, the kitchen caught on fire. Dad made her swear never to attempt it again."

"Must have tried making the sauce from scratch. I'm opening jars and heating the sauce to pour over hot pasta."

"And the chicken?"

"Slow cooker. Ready in a few hours."

"If I'd known cooking was so easy, I might have tried it myself."

"This isn't haute cuisine, but it'll do." Del grabbed her backpack and unzipped the front pocket. Curious what the packing fairy included for her to read, she reached in and pulled out five books. "Yes!"

"What do you have?"

"Books by my favorite authors. Carolyn Hart, Meg London, Joanne Fluke, Nora Roberts, and Elizabeth Lowell." She picked up the Nora Roberts book, frowned. "This isn't my copy."

"How do you know?"

"I started rereading the book for maybe the seventh time a few weeks ago, and I dropped the book. The corner folded, created a new crease. This book doesn't have the crease." Del passed the book to Ivy who examined it.

"You're right." Ivy tilted her head. "Is this Mae's copy? She owned every Nora book ever published."

Del shrugged. "I don't know how I ended up with her copy. We didn't take books from the Reece place."

"Don't you remember? I unpacked four boxes of Mae's estate sale finds. She brought them by the house a couple days before she passed away. One of those boxes had a copy of the book."

"That's right. She bragged about the bargains, said some relatives had boxed up all this woman's possessions and were selling them dirt cheap. I don't care how I inherited this book, as long as I have something to keep me busy for a while." She retrieved the book from her cousin. "Grab your book. Let's go into the living room."

"Del."

"We're not hiding in this room. The walls will close in on us if we stay in here. This is the perfect chance to test yourself with Deke. Burns and his sidekick aren't here."

A grin from Ivy. "If I can't trust Vance, you think we can have them replaced?"

"Our luck, the marshals would send someone worse."

"Don't see how that's possible." She sighed. "Okay, let's go."

Deke turned from one of the living room windows, his eyebrows rising, as they walked into the room and settled on opposite corners of the couch. "What's up, ladies?" he asked, his gaze studying Ivy's face which was already buried in her book.

"New scenery," Del said.

"Thought we'd keep you out of trouble," Ivy chimed in. Her voice trembled a bit, but she wiggled deeper into the couch cushions, making a statement. Had to give her points for refusing to run. The sweat beading on her forehead gave witness to the battle raging inside her cousin.

Deke's lips twitched. "Marcie, my wife, gave up on that a month after we married."

"Do you have kids?" Ivy's gaze flickered up at him for a moment, then dropped to her book.

"Two." Deke grinned. "Twin girls. My princesses are five."

The knot which formed in Del's stomach as they left the bedroom untangled. Her cousin loved kids. One day, Ivy would find the right man for her, one who wanted a house full of children. Her cousin dreamed of a home filled with laughter and love, a contrast to the home in which she grew up. "Got pictures, Dad?"

He reached into his back pocket, pulled out his wallet and withdrew several snapshots. Ivy dropped her book on the couch and reached for the pictures. While she looked at the series of shots, Deke faced Del. "What happened?" he mouthed.

Del inclined her head toward the photographs. "What are their names, Deke?"

"Isabella and Isadora. Bella and Dora unless they're in trouble."

"So beautiful," Ivy murmured. "And happy, full of life."

"Livewires, that's for sure."

"Is your wife okay with your long-term assignments? What about your girls?"

"It's no different than being in the military except the marshal service tries not to keep me on the road all the time. We're based out of certain areas. I've been lucky. Most of the time, I'm close enough to go home with regularity." He put the photos back in his wallet. "I need to make another circuit outside."

The rest of the afternoon passed without incident. Ivy engaged Deke in conversation every time he made his rounds in the house. By the time Del dragged her cousin into the kitchen for a quick lesson in easy cooking, Ivy's conversations weren't forced. "If I didn't know better, I'd say Ivy Monroe is several steps closer to trusting the married marshal."

"I feel like I ran a marathon. I haven't asked a man that many questions since Lee and we both know what a disaster that was."

"Deke would never treat you like that jerk did."

At dinner, Deke took over security camera duty, said it was time to give Stella a break. Del suspected he was giving Ivy a break from his company. Though he didn't say, he seemed pleased with Ivy's interaction and some of the tension he'd shown at lunch had dissipated.

Over dinner, Stella told several of the funnier stories about her time with the marshals.

"The man actually ran out of the bedroom in his birthday suit?" Ivy asked, her eyes wide.

"We told him not to sleep unclothed. We always anticipate the worst. What if security was breached or ʳbe a fire? He believed the car backfire was a gunshot and he leaped out of bed and ran into the security room." Stella shook her head. "Wasn't a pretty sight."

"That's an understatement," Deke called from the security room. "Dude weighed at least three hundred pounds."

"Enough," Del said, holding her sides which hurt from laughing so much in the past few minutes. "I thought you'd be wracked with tension while you're on the job."

"It can be like that." Stella drained her tea glass. "Like the military, we have long stretches of boredom interspersed with intense pressure. Nobody can handle adrenaline rushes all the time. Before I joined the marshals, I had this glamorized version of what we do in my mind. You know, protecting witnesses from the bad guys, riding in like the cowboys in white hats to save the day. Most of the time, though, we protect lesser bad guys from bigger bad guys. Sometimes, we protect the innocent, like you and Ivy."

"I'll take the bookstore pace," Ivy said. "Lots of slow periods with a lunchtime rush."

Not working with her books and customers left Del with an ache that physically hurt. She missed Josh. That special Otter Creek officer was worming his way into her heart.

"What's wrong, Del?" Stella's gaze studied her.

"Any word about the hunt for the killer?"

"Not yet."

"I have good workers, but I'm a small business owner. My profit margin is so thin you can see through it. If it takes too long to track this guy down, I may not have a business left to go back to."

"At least you'll be alive to start again," the marshal countered. "We're doing our best to track him down."

"I know. I'm sorry. I just want to go home."

"Heads up," Deke said as he strolled into the kitchen. "The night team is coming up the drive."

"Can we let them clean up?" Ivy stood, grabbed her plate and glass.

"You can leave it," he said. "It will be right here when you wake in the morning. Those two are not domestic."

"Burns is old school." Stella started collecting empty plates and glasses. "His wife takes care of everything at the house so he's come to expect other women to do the same."

"And Vance?"

"Let's just say he's not one of my favorite people to work with." She carried the dishes to the sink and scraped scraps into the garbage disposal. "Ivy, if you want to skip Vance's company, I'll help Del clean the kitchen before I leave."

Her cousin looked tempted. A grim look of determination grew on Ivy's face. "I'll be fine. If I'm not, I'll take it out on Marshal Vance."

Del bumped Ivy's shoulder with her own. At her cousin's questioning look, she winked. Yep, Ivy would be fine.

Sometime after midnight, Del woke to muffled shouting. What were Burns and Vance doing? Were they arguing? She sat up, listened. Somewhere on the first floor, glass broke. One of the marshals groaned.

She looked at her cousin, still sleeping beside her. Del reached to shake her, drew back. She didn't want to wake Ivy if this was a difference of opinion. Open the door and check? Unprofessional though it might be, if they were settling a difference of opinion she'd leave them to it.

Still dressed in jeans and a long-sleeved t-shirt, Del eased her legs over the side of the bed and slipped her feet into her tennis shoes. She and Ivy had paid attention to the story Stella told about the three-hundred-pound guy running around in the buff. They concluded being a little uncomfortable while they slept was better than being embarrassed or dead.

She grasped the knob, twisted, pulled the door open a couple inches. Soft rustling drifted up the stairs. Thankful the door didn't creak, Del eased to the landing. She moved forward enough to see down the stairs. At the foot of the staircase, Vance lay on his back, arms and legs spread eagle. Had Burns knocked him out and left him?

Red liquid spread from underneath the young marshal's fallen body. Cold chills raced down her spine. Vance was lying in a growing pool of blood.

Her first instinct was to help him. Del didn't know exactly what happened, but there were only two choices, both bad. One, Burns had shot Vance. What that meant for her and Ivy was anyone's guess. Two, their security had been broken, which meant Reece's killer could be the culprit. And if Burns wasn't already dead, he would be fighting for his life. If the killer slipped past the remaining marshal, she and Ivy were dead.

Not if she could help it. They needed help, fast. Del wanted to pull out her cell phone, but waited. If her assessment was wrong, Burns would take the phone and she wasn't relinquishing her lifeline to Josh without a fight.

Reaching the bedroom, she closed the door, locked it behind her. Stared, picked up a nearby chair, lodged the back under the doorknob. Not much of a deterrent. A few more seconds might mean the difference between life and death. Del rushed to Ivy's side, shook her cousin's shoulder. "Ivy," she whispered. "Wake up."

"Huh? What is it? What's wrong?"

"Shh! Vance has been shot. We need to get out of here."

Ivy sat bolt upright. "I didn't hear gunfire."

"Me either, but he's lying in a pool of blood at the foot of the stairs."

Her cousin threw off the covers and shoved her feet into her tennis shoes. She reached down beside the nightstand and picked up her backpack. "Reece's killer?"

"If it is him, I don't want us to be his next victims."
She grabbed her own backpack and threaded her arms
through the straps.

"What are we going to do?"

"Run."

Ivy moaned, a bare whisper of sound. "The escape
tunnel?"

"We don't know where the gunman is or if there's
more than one. You can do this, Ivy." She reached into the
side pocket of the pack and pulled out a small penlight the
packing fairy had included. Lots of free books were in the
fairy's future for this foresight. She wouldn't be surprised if
Josh had been involved.

Del opened the walk-in closet's door and tugged her
cousin inside before flipping on her light. Ivy gave a soft
sigh of relief. The wooden shoe rack moved aside as Stella
had shown them. When they'd crawled into the darkened
interior, Del pulled the rack back into position and closed
the access panel, a kind of half door. Shining the light
around the door area, she spotted a solid piece of wood,
fitted it into the slots that extended beyond the door frame.
No matter who was in the house, they weren't going to get
through this barred door without a battering ram.

Standing up to full height, she turned toward her
cousin. "Let's go." According to marshal, the escape tunnel
was really a hidden stairway to a tunnel that ran
underground about a half mile. The tunnel's end emerged
in the depths of the forest.

She didn't want to think about the woods. She and Ivy
weren't outdoors people. Del prayed the cell phones had
reception out there. No reception meant tromping around in
the forest at night with only moonlight to show where to
put their feet until they found high ground to call. Poor
lighting and unfamiliar territory at night? A sure recipe for
sprains or broken bones.

Del led the way, hand clasped tight around Ivy's wrist. Two flights of stairs later, the steps ended on a dirt floor. The tunnel curved to their left and went on as far as they could see.

"Del." Ivy drew in a stuttered breath.

"No panic attack. You can panic after we're safe." She tugged her cousin onto the sloped, packed dirt. "Maybe Alex can help you through it."

She sped down the passage at a merciless pace, ignoring Ivy's strained breathing. What if this was the only tunnel from the house? Stella said every room in the house had escape hatches built in, but not if this was the only tunnel. If the shooter knew about the escape hatches, he might not be far behind them. If the shooter caught them in this tunnel, she and Ivy were dead.

CHAPTER FIFTEEN

Josh turned right off Scenic Overlook Drive, a scowl on his face. Didn't people have anything better to do than steam up the windows in their cars? Since it was past curfew, the teens went home with minimal snarling. The adults, however, gave him the most grief. They argued their legal adult status without a curfew.

A shudder wracked his frame. Being a legal adult meant they should have better sense than to make out in a car in a deserted place. He'd embarrassed an assistant district attorney and his administrative assistant, both married to other people, not to mention the picture in his head of too much skin showing on both. He'd been kind enough not to write a ticket for these first-time offenders, but the unwanted sight seared into his brain might scar him for life.

Another two hours passed running routine patrols. A few minutes after two in the morning, Josh's cell phone rang. He unclipped it from the holder and glanced at the display. His heart rate accelerated. Del.

"What's happening?"

Gasping breaths sounded in his ear. "One marshal is down. Shot. Don't know about the other. Ivy and I ran. We're in a forest. I don't know where we are." The last was said with a hitch in her voice.

"I put a tracker on your phone, baby. I'll know exactly where you are. Are you hidden?"

"Running."

Josh flipped on his blue-and-white lights and sent the SUV racing toward town. "I need to call the station. Hold on a second."

"Okay." More ragged breathing.

He placed the phone, still connected to Del's, in the cup holder and snatched up his radio. "Dispatch, this is Unit 6. Patch me through to Blackhawk."

"Copy."

Less than a minute later, Ethan's gruff voice sounded over his radio. "Talk to me."

"Safe house was breached. I'm calling in my team."

"Del and Ivy?"

"On the run."

"You're on leave of absence as of right now. Keep me in the loop."

"Roger that."

"I'll cover the rest of your shift. Josh, you have to bring them in. The feds need to question them."

"The marshals will take them again. Not happening, Ethan."

His brother-in-law was silent a moment. "What if Del and Ivy have a better team in place, one that was former military? Can you make that happen?"

Despite the driving pressure in his gut to get to Del, a smile grew across Josh's face. He knew exactly who to contact. "Oh, yeah."

"Good. Contact me before you come in. Blackhawk out."

Negotiating a curve with one hand, he pulled the phone up to his ear. "I'm back. You and Ivy okay?"

Del was gasping in his ear. "Exhausted." A soft cry and thump sounded. "Ivy!"

Josh's hand tightened around the steering wheel. "Del?"

"She tripped over a root. Ivy, are you hurt?"

A soft murmur, then Del said, "She's sprained her ankle, Josh."

"Look around you. Tell me what's nearby." In the town proper, he slowed to a safer speed and headed to his apartment. The truck or Alex's SUV blended into the surroundings better. A police cruiser attracted attention and he wanted Del and Ivy safe without a major confrontation. He didn't have vests for them, something he couldn't take care of unless he broke in somewhere. Josh considered that, discarded the idea. No time.

"Trees, brush, rocks, a stream nearby."

Ivy couldn't run through the woods anymore. They had no chance to outrun a former spec ops soldier. He'd be stronger, faster, experienced in tracking. Probably had NVGs. They needed to hide, fast. No question, he was tracking them. Nighttime with minimal light worked in their favor as did an unfamiliar terrain. Del was resourceful and smart. So was Ivy. It had to be enough.

"Sweetheart, find a hiding place. An outcropping of rocks or a cave. Last resort would be a big, hollow tree trunk."

"She's really hurting. Can't we stay here and wait for you?"

"You're not safe in the open." Josh swerved into his apartment parking lot, shut off his engine, and ran up the stairs. He shoved his key in the lock and threw open the door. Four weapons were aimed at his chest. "Alex," he said. His partner knew what brought him home early.

"Ivy?"

"Hurt. We need to move."

Almost as one, all four heavily muscled men from his old Delta unit rose and started to gear up. He jogged to his bedroom, shifted his phone to speaker and stripped off his uniform. "Talk to me, babe."

"We're moving at turtle speed. I'm her walking stick."

"Be as quiet as you can. Sound carries. Don't use your penlight. That will pinpoint your location for anyone who's following. Stay off soft dirt. The longer it takes this guy to track you, the better." He yanked on a pair of black camouflage pants and black t-shirt which he pulled on to cover his vest. It would be a race to see who reached Del and Ivy first. If the shooter arrived before Josh did, the women wouldn't survive. "I've got you on speaker while I gear up."

Alex poked his head around the door frame. "Ready to roll, Major."

"Alex?" Del's voice sounded from the phone.

"Heard you ran into trouble."

A breathless laugh. "Understatement. Ivy's hurt."

Josh shoved his feet into black combat boots and retrieved his Go bag. Inside his head, the mission clock ticked.

"How bad?"

"Sprained ankle at least."

"She mobile?"

"With help. We won't win any races. Josh?"

"Right here."

"Why a cave or rock outcropping?"

"If Reece's killer is chasing you, he might have night vision capabilities."

"What does that mean?"

"He'll follow you because he sees heat signatures," Alex said.

"But we haven't heard anyone behind us."

"You wouldn't," he said, voice grim.

Spec ops soldiers were trained by the military to be ghosts. Wouldn't know you'd been compromised until after they were gone. Guess that's why this guy's nickname was Ghost. Untrained civilians against one of the best trained soldiers in the military. His throat tightened. He and his unit were the only chance they had to survive the night.

"Oh, dear." Del's voice sounded shaky. "That's why you wanted us in a cave. Only one problem."

He stilled, exchanging a glance with Alex. "What?"

"Ivy's claustrophobic thanks to an ugly episode with her former boyfriend. Dark, earthy places send her into panic attacks."

His friend's eyes narrowed. "Find safe shelter, Del. I'll help her. What is she passionate about?"

"Kids. Art. History."

"Good. I can work with that."

"We're leaving, Del," Josh said. He grabbed his Go bag with one hand, cell phone with the other. "Do you want to stay connected to me?"

"Will I distract you?"

"I'll tell you when I need to hang up. Fair enough?"

"Thank you. Knowing you're listening makes me feel safer somehow."

"Move out," he said to Alex. In his living room, he greeted his old unit with fist bumps. "Great to see all of you."

"Hear your lady's got a target on her back." This from Rio.

"She and her cousin, Ivy. Wrong place, wrong time." He rattled off the GPS coordinates from the current reading and gave them the tracker's signal number. With Ivy hurt, they wouldn't be far from that location when his team reached them. Turning to Alex, he said, "Okay if we take your SUV?"

"Figured you'd want to coordinate and check the topographical map. I prefer my hands on the wheel anyway."

Quinn picked up his Go bag. "I'll follow you. Nate, Rio, with me."

Two minutes later, the former Delta unit was on the move. Josh buckled up, placed the cell phone in the cup holder. "Still with me, sweetheart?"

"We heard something in the woods," she whispered.

Alex floored the gas pedal.

Frustration gnawed at Josh's gut. He needed to be with her, now. "Look for shelter. Pick up the pace."

"How's Ivy?" Alex asked as he swerved around a slow-moving truck. Josh refrained from looking at the speedometer. If they were pulled over, he'd flash his badge. His brother-in-law would cover a ticket under these circumstances.

"No worse."

Josh powered up his laptop. He signaled Alex to keep Del talking. Her voice steadied when she felt connected to them. Keeping fear at bay helped her think faster. Panic had killed more than one green solider on the battlefield.

One part of his brain kept track of the conversation. The rest focused on the map covering his screen, a map he shouldn't have access to anymore. A buddy still in spec ops had arranged a back door for Josh. Once in spec ops, always in. The units became small families. Those firefights created tight groups.

He rechecked Del's coordinates. Consulted the map. "Sweetheart, do you still hear water?"

"Yes."

"Go to the water. Should be to your right."

Silence while she and Ivy picked their way to the stream. "Okay," Del murmured. "At the stream. Now what?"

"Head east."

"Translation?"

He blinked. Directionally challenged. "Head upstream to the left. When you see a bend in the stream, look to your left again for a series of caves in the hillside."

Josh's cell signaled a text. Ethan. Vance was dead, one shot to the chest. Burns was critical, two gunshots, one in the shoulder, the other a chest shot. Marshals and FBI were crawling all over the scene, wanted to mount a search for Del and Ivy. "Alex, I need your cell." Since both marshals were down, Reece's shooter must be tracking the women. Josh texted Ethan to do anything necessary to keep the feds on the scene. His team was close. They didn't need the Ghost and the feds shooting at them in the dark.

"Sweetheart?"

"Yes?"

"The feds are at the safe house. Vance is dead. Burns is critical."

A sharp breath. "I didn't like Vance, but he didn't deserve to die for doing his job. Reece's killer is after us?"

"Looks like it. I know Ivy's hurt, baby, but you have to find shelter."

\#

"What is it?" Ivy whispered.

Del closed her eyes for a second. "Let's go."

"Del?"

"Vance is dead, his partner critical. Reece's killer is tracking us."

Ivy hobbled faster. "How far away are Alex and Josh?"

"Thirty minutes to the forest," Josh replied. "At least that much more to reach your location. We'll be playing cat-and-mouse with the shooter and the feds."

"At least an hour," Del said to her cousin.

"The marshals dumped us in the middle of nowhere, didn't they?" Ivy stumbled, righted herself. "Tell the guys to hurry. I'm cold, hungry, and grumpy."

Male laughter reached Del's ear. "They're laughing."

"Glad I amuse them." A strained smile curved Ivy's lips.

No words for a while on either side. Del concentrated on balancing herself and Ivy on the rough terrain. She tightened her grip around Ivy's waist and nudged her to limp faster. She knew it was her imagination, but she could almost feel the shooter breathing down their necks. "Josh?"

"Here, baby."

"Feels like spiders are crawling on my back."

Silence, then, "Do you see the bend in the stream?"

Del swallowed hard. He hadn't reassured her about the spider comment. That couldn't be good. Focus, she reminded herself. She scanned the surroundings. Trees, more trees, stream. Another few feet and she saw the bend. "There it is."

"There should be rocks about 500 yards past the bend. Put the rocks between you and the shooter."

His words cooled her blood. "The shooter's behind us?"

"Always pay attention to the spiders. Don't run yet."

Despite the warm night air, goosebumps surged across Del's body. They skirted a fallen tree, angled themselves away from the stream and toward the outcropping. Fifty feet. Forty. Thirty. One step at a time, she reminded herself. Don't run. Didn't want the creepy guy to know they were aware of him. Finally, the rocks loomed on their left, a few more steps, and they were in position. "We're behind the rocks."

"Run! You must reach a cave before the shooter makes it to your location. Don't choose the most obvious one unless there's no other choice."

She shoved the phone in her jeans pocket. "Run, Ivy."

She pushed her cousin at a merciless pace. A quick glance at Ivy showed tears leaving silver trails down her cheeks. She had to keep running or they were both dead because Del refused to leave Ivy. Del returned her attention to the hillside and the obsidian openings. She spotted another rock outcropping on the hillside, saw a black hole on the other side. That one. The others were closer. The shooter couldn't miss Ivy's injury. Anger burned through her. The killer was playing with them. He could have shot them by now.

Ivy stumbled again, fell. "Go. Leave me."

"Suck it up, Ivy." She reached down and helped Ivy to her feet. "I'm not leaving you." Fear clawed at Del, but refused to let it paralyze her. She dug deep and used it to fuel their flight over the rocky terrain. Her cousin pointed at the closest cave.

"No. Around those rocks. Harder for him to reach."

A shot sounded. Dirt sprayed to their left.

"Why shoot now?" Ivy's voice rose.

"Harder to reach us in one of those caves."

"Good. If he kills us, I want him to work for it."

Another shot. Pain speared through Del's arm. She hissed, gritted her teeth. If Ivy knew she was hurt, she'd want to check it. Not happening unless they wanted to bleed out on the ground.

"What is it? What's wrong?"

"Nothing. Keep moving."

"You're lying."

"No time, Ivy." Her arm throbbed. Didn't know if the idiot had actually shot her or if the bullet hit something and a shard had clipped her arm. Either way, she wouldn't make much of a soldier. All she wanted to do was sit and cry. To think Josh had been injured multiple times in the line of duty and kept going. Madison told her about the last injury that helped him decide to leave military life. Getting shot hurt. If she'd gotten shot. Couldn't think about that now. Wouldn't look at it either. Something told her if she saw the damage, the injury would hurt a lot worse. She respected the people in uniform who carried on defending others despite injuries to themselves.

"Which cave?"

"I saw a cave on the other side of those rocks."

"What if it has another occupant?"

That almost stopped Del in her tracks. Oh, boy. Wildlife. One more thing to worry over. Another shot. They ducked and scrambled faster. Dirt sprayed farther to their left. Maybe the shooter had a bad line of sight or he was playing with them. She used every bit of cover she found between them and the shooter.

Finally, they ducked behind the rocks and hustled to the cave entrance. Del stopped Ivy at the cave's mouth, urged her to lay in deep shadow, hoping to make her cousin a smaller target. What she wouldn't give to have Josh or Alex here. She was winging this based on reading and movies. Everybody knew how accurate those were. "Wait here."

"What are you doing?"

"Didn't you say something about wildlife?"

"You're going to chase the critter out? Are you crazy?"

"Not today. Just angry. I'm doing the sniff test." She figured if the cave didn't smell like a wild animal or it's last meal, the cave would serve as temporary shelter.

She approached the cave entrance, listened, didn't hear anything. Ventured further into the darkness, breathed deep. Nothing but dirt and damp. She wanted to turn on the penlight, but couldn't chance giving away their location.

"I think it's okay. No bad smells or sounds."

Her cousin climbed to her feet, hobbled toward the entrance, stopped.

She dragged her cousin into the darkened cave, parked her against the wall, and sat down beside her. Del dug the cell phone from her pocket. "Josh, we're in a cave."

"You okay?" His normally cool voice sounded odd.

"I'm fine."

Ivy felt along her arm, snatched the phone. "She's hurt, but won't tell me what happened." Her cousin slapped the phone back in Del's hand. "Maybe you'll be honest with him since you won't be straight with me."

"Del? How bad, sweetheart?"

"I'm afraid to look. Something hit my arm." As she thought about it, the pain increased by leaps. "Hope you have some aspirin."

"We each have a full medical kit. Are you safe?"

"I did a sniff test."

"A sniff test?"

"Deep breaths to see if another occupant had first claim. I didn't want to fight a bear or something." She gave a watery laugh.

"How's Ivy?"

"Her ankle's no worse." Del listened to her cousin's growing erratic breathing. "The darkness is getting to her."

"I'll pass the cell to Alex in a minute. Let Ivy talk to him. He can help. We're at the edge of the forest. We'll have to work our way around to you. It might take a while, baby. Stay away from the cave entrance. The shooter can't see your heat signature through the cave walls. Might take a few potshots to scare you into revealing your location. You can't make noise, no matter what you hear. I will get to you, no matter who I have to go through or what obstacles I have to overcome. You do whatever it takes to keep yourself and Ivy safe until I reach you."

She blinked back the tears forming in her eyes. "Can I fall apart when you get here?"

"Absolutely, beautiful. We know where you are. We're not far, baby. Hold on to that. Now, hand the phone to Ivy."

She reached over the in pitch black, found Ivy's hand, shoved the phone into it. "Alex."

Del tuned out Ivy's murmured conversation with Josh's friend. Concentrated on feeling the area around her. Dirt, something dry, hoped like crazy it was grass or moss, not something nasty like bat or rodent droppings. Moved her fingers again. A pebble. Not big enough. She reached out a little farther, bumped her fingers against a decent sized rock. She picked it up with one hand. Shaped like a baseball. Perfect. Now to find more that size. The shooter believed them too scared to defend themselves. They might not be as lethal as Josh and Alex, but he would regret trying to hurt them. Every minute they held him off brought Josh that much closer to the cave.

She prayed they didn't take too long. Del wanted to learn how this romance with Josh turned out. With Ivy's whispered conversation as background noise, she searched for more ammunition.

CHAPTER SIXTEEN

Josh positioned the webbing for his comm headset. The team switched to a preferred channel and grabbed their gear. Weapon in hand, he signaled the others to move ahead. The Delta unit spread out and slipped through the darkened forest in silence. No leaves or bushes rustled, no footfalls sounded as they passed through the terrain.

His NVGs picked up various heat signatures in the distance. Weapon aimed and ready, he eased toward the larger heat signatures. Closer in, the blobs turned into animals slinking through the underbrush. A raccoon wandered across his path, skittered away.

He checked Del's location. She hadn't moved since the last time he'd pinged her phone signal in the cave. He prayed that meant she was still safe. The shooter had taken potshots earlier, but nothing for a while. Probably searching for them. Several caves dotted the area. Locating the right one would take time. Then he'd flush them out or kill them.

Josh thought about that for a beat, suspected the killer wanted the women alive. He had NVGs. No way a spec ops soldier would miss his target that many times. Too well trained.

If he didn't want them dead, what did he want? Information or his client wanted them. Why? Word should have leaked they couldn't identify the shooter. What did they know that made them worth the trouble?

A light breeze stirred the leaves, cooled sweat beading on his forehead. He longed to race to Del and Ivy. The thought of Del bleeding in a cave drove him nuts, especially since he didn't know the extent of her injury. But impatience would lead to more injuries or death. Del and Ivy stood zero chance against Reece's shooter without at least one of his team at their side.

Checking his position, he stopped at the edge of a clearing. The hillside where Del and Ivy took shelter rose in the distance, the stream on his right. Josh crouched, keyed his microphone. "Report," he said in a nearly toneless whisper.

Each of his team responded.

"Alex, Quinn, go. Nate, Rio, into position and hold."

Alex, their team sniper, with his spotter, Quinn, circled around to take the high ground over the place where Del and Ivy hid. They would supply cover fire so Rio, the team medic, could aid Del and Ivy while Josh and Nate protected them from inside the cave. Between the four of them, they'd kill, capture or scare off the shooter. Josh knew, though, unless the client recalled him, Reece's shooter would return until he accomplished his objective.

So far, only the shooter roamed the woods hunting for the women. His team had debated various options on the drive, created a plan despite their limited intel. The plan should work unless the feds messed things up.

Josh, Nate, and Rio spread out near the rocks Del had used as a shield from the shooter, waited for Alex and Quinn's signal. He scanned the area. No sign of the shooter. Must be in one of the caves. Keying his mic, Josh asked Alex, "Del and Ivy okay?"

"Affirmative," came the response. "Almost in position."

He studied the hillside, spotted his teammates creeping from the hilltop to flank both sides of their target cave. His mic signaled and Alex whispered through the headset, "Go."

Josh motioned Nate and Rio to move forward. "Tell Ivy we're moving in."

"Copy."

A shot rang out. The rock to his right revealed a new gash in the side. Josh and his team dove for cover. "Where is he?" Josh demanded.

"Ten o'clock, behind some boulders." This from Quinn.

"We're sitting ducks out here. Lay down cover fire."

As soon as Alex and Quinn started firing, Josh and his team ran in a zigzag pattern for the cave. They slipped inside. By prearrangement, Rio took position by the entrance with Nate until the women knew of their presence. Josh scanned the interior and found the two women huddled together. Both had something in their hands from the position of their arms. Rocks? Del had taken his warning to heart. They were prepared to defend themselves with a small arsenal of rocks.

"Del, it's Josh. Three of us are inside the cave."

"Alex?" Ivy whispered.

"On the hillside, making all the racket. He's keeping the shooter busy. How are you?"

"Ankle hurts a lot."

"Can you walk?"

"The pain's much worse since we've been here." Her voice sounded tight, strained.

He walked closer and knelt by Del's side. "Hey," he whispered and cupped her face with his hand. Something wet dripped over his fingers. Tears. Del was crying. When she hiccuped, Josh's heart squeezed. "Shh, baby. Hold on. We'll get you out of here soon."

Josh cupped the nape of her neck and tugged her gently into his arms. Her body trembled. Such sheer guts and courage. He pressed a kiss to the top of her head. The last few hours had been terrifying, yet she fought panic, found shelter, and gathered rocks to use against a murderer, all while protecting her injured cousin.

"Ivy," he said, holding Del close, rubbing her back. Couldn't chance injuring her arm further. "One of my team members in the cave is a medic. His name is Rio. Will you let him check your ankle? We can't risk causing more damage."

"I wouldn't have been able to walk if I'd broken it," she protested. "I must have a sprain."

"You'd be surprised what you can do with adrenaline blocking pain. Will you let him check you?"

"Can Alex do it or you?"

He stilled his motion on Del's back. Something in Ivy's voice tightened his gut. An abusive relationship would make her skittish around an unknown male. Should have realized that sooner. Del had mentioned her cousin's ex-boyfriend. How bad was the abuse? "I have rudimentary field medic knowledge, enough to patch someone together if we're under fire and don't have another option. I want you to have the best, Ivy, and that's not me."

"I'll stay beside you," Del murmured. "Rio's part of Josh's team, Ivy. He wouldn't trust Rio with your safety unless he was honorable."

"He's the best," Josh said. "I trust him at my back on the battlefield and off. If it will make you feel better, I'll keep an eye on what he's doing. If he makes you uncomfortable, tell him. He'll stop immediately."

She tilted her head a bit, her soft laughter echoing in the stone chamber. "Alex says I should let the expert take care of me. If you do it, I might limp for life."

Josh keyed his mic. "Get back to work and stop turning the beautiful lady against me."

A snort and another round of shots fractured the silence. "Tell Ivy to save the phone battery in case we need it." More shots.

"Okay to end the call, Ivy?"

"I think so."

"What about Rio checking your ankle?"

Ivy reached over, gripped Del's hand. "Yes."

"Excellent. Rio's a good guy." To an innocent, he was a good guy. He'd seen his friend in many combat situations. Though a great medic, Rio was also a fierce fighter, not information Ivy needed to learn if his friend hoped to treat her injury.

He eased Del away from him. "Don't move. I need to cover the entrance with Nate while Rio checks both of you." He wanted to see Del's injury himself, but their safety took priority. Rio could care for their medical needs until his unit transported Del and Ivy to the nearest hospital. His jaw flexed. And they were going to the hospital, no matter how many feds littered these woods.

"Rio." Josh made himself release Del and stood. The medic picked his way over scattered rocks and branches.

His friend squatted in front of Ivy's feet. "Ivy, I'm Rio. Which foot did you hurt?"

"Left."

"I need to roll up your jeans, remove your shoe and sock, okay? I'll try to be gentle, but it will hurt." He turned his head in Josh's direction. "Major, Nate, NVGs."

Josh and Nate removed their night vision goggles and faced outside the cave. Rio would need light to check Ivy's foot and the light would temporarily blind them if they used NVGs. A moment later, a small light flashed on. Josh and his teammate readied themselves. The light, though necessary, would show the shooter exactly where they were.

Sure enough, more shots from outside the cave followed, several coming from the man who'd pursued Del and Ivy through the dark night. Ricochets from the bullets kicked up dirt and shards of rock. Josh keyed his mic. "Have a bead on him?"

"Negative. Still in cover."

Josh frowned. Why hadn't the guy moved? He had to know at least one sniper was on the hillside and knew his position. He should have moved by now. Didn't make sense. "Quinn, can you see anyone else moving?"

"Negative."

"Major," Rio said. "Looks like Ivy has a sprain, but I'd rather splint it until we're sure."

"Do it. Quinn, get behind the shooter. Flush him out or take him down. Watch yourself. He's playing with us, but that might change at any time. I didn't bring body bags on this op and I'm not carting your remains out of this forest."

"Got it. No body bags. On the move."

"Keep our guy busy, Alex."

"Copy." A series of shots rang out from the hillside.

"Major," Rio said, "I need another pair of hands for this splint."

"I can help with that," Del said.

Josh glanced at her, saw determination on her face. He nodded at the medic.

"Good enough." Rio took hold of Del's hand and said, "Hold this right here for me." Within a couple minutes, Ivy's foot was stabilized in a temporary splint, her face dotted with perspiration.

"Your turn, Del." The medic turned his light on Del. "Which arm?"

"Right."

"Don't look if you're squeamish."

Josh grinned. "Don't look, baby."

"Shut up. So I got a little woozy before. I'm allowed."

Laughing, Rio eased the sleeve higher on her arm and examined the wound. His smile faded. "Congratulations, Del. You can brag to your friends about earning a bullet wound on this adventure."

"Oh, man." Her voice wobbled.

"How bad?" Josh asked, glanced in her direction. If the bullet was still lodged in her arm, Del might need surgery to repair the damage and clean out the wound. He never should have allowed the marshals to take her and Ivy. The injury might not have happened if he'd been with her.

"Just kissed her." Rio reached into his medical kit for swabs to clean the blood off Del's arm. When the astringent-laced gauze brushed against the crease in her muscle, she hissed. "Sorry, sugar. I can kiss your arm, see if that helps the pain."

Josh sent a pointed glance at his medic. "Kissing Del is my job. I'm not sharing."

"No designs on your lady, Major." A wicked smile crossed Rio's face. "Fair warning, though. If you let her slip through your fingers, I'll spend some quality time with her."

"You never had trouble finding a date, Cahill," Nate said, gaze locked in the distance. "The rest of the unit weren't so blessed."

"Company," Alex murmured.

Josh stiffened, searched the darkened forest in vain. Couldn't see squat without the night vision gear. "How many and where?"

"Incoming from the forest, eastern flank. Ten or twelve. Hard to pinpoint. They're bunched up." Disgust rang in Alex's tone.

Had to be feds. Military men never infiltrated an area like that. The shots must have drawn them from the house. If Jordan and his cronies were like the other feds he'd worked with in his military career, they made enough noise to spook the hardiest wildlife. Sneak up on their quarry? Only in a thunderstorm or firefight. Where was the shooter? "Quinn, target."

"Crap. He's on the move."

"Alex?"

"No shot. Blended into the approaching horde."

"Quinn, back in position. Alex, hold."

"What now, Major?" Nate asked.

"Rio, is Ivy ready to move?"

"Affirmative. One minute and Del will be ready to take on the next assassin."

"You aren't funny, either, Rio," she said.

"Just honest, ma'am. Wouldn't want you after me with those rocks. Major, Ivy should be carried out. You want that duty?"

Alex chimed in over the comm gear. "Feds are almost here. Bring me down, Josh. Ivy will freak with that much testosterone in one place. I'll carry her. I doubt she'll allow you or the others to transport her to the vehicles."

"You have the right touch, huh?" Josh heard the tension in his friend's voice. Recognized Alex's driving need to be with Ivy now that his particular skills were no longer necessary. Whether his friend realized it or not, he was softening toward the munchkin.

Much as he might like to send the feds on the run with a few well-placed shots, their shooter was in the wind. It was time to pull Alex and Quinn from the hillside. Besides, if Jordan was in a foul mood, Josh might need a couple more friendlies at his side. "You and Quinn come in. I want you inside before the feds join the party. Don't want itchy trigger fingers when they realize a couple rifles with scopes are tracking their movements."

"Copy that."

"Hurry, Rio." Josh watched the flashlights moving closer. He shook his head. Nothing like pinpointing their location for anyone interested. Jordan was lucky he and his people didn't have bullets raining on their position. Child's play for a trained soldier even without the lights shining like flares at an accident scene.

"Done." The medic cleaned up the debris, stuffed the whole lot into a bag, sealed it, and shoved that into his pack. Standing, he grabbed his pack and moved it to the cave wall.

"Leave the flashlight on, directed at Ivy's foot. Everybody but Alex stay in the shadows. No need for the feds get a good look at your ugly mugs."

Alex and Quinn walked into the darkened interior. "Maybe two minutes, Major," Quinn said as he took position near the back wall of the shelter. Nate, with a signal from Josh, shifted to the opposite side. Alex moved to Ivy's side and sat beside her. "How you doing, Ivy?"

"I'd give just about anything for a painkiller."

"Rio?"

"Over-the-counter only. I'm afraid to give her anything stronger until they x-ray her foot." He dug into the medical kit and shook out a couple pain tablets, passed Ivy a bottle of water. "Sip, okay?" Rio smiled. "No indoor plumbing."

"Drink what you need," Alex said. "We'll work something out for you and Del."

After taking a few sips to wash down the medicine, Ivy passed the small bottle to Del. By the time she finished, the hillside crawled with feds, Jordan in the lead.

"Federal agents," he shouted. "Throw down your weapons and come out with your hands behind your head."

Right. "Come on up, Jordan." Josh holstered his weapon. Wouldn't give the fed an excuse to shoot him. "Stand down," he said to his unit. The badges clambered up the slope. The Washington law enforcement people weren't dressed for the terrain. Their slick dress shoes didn't have traction. One of the feds hit the dirt, face first. Josh grinned.

That dude wasn't destined for a dancing career. Graceful, he was not.

More slips, cursing. Jordan and a couple of his team crowded into the entrance, weapons drawn. "What are you doing here, Cahill?" Jordan scowled his direction before squinting around the small area. "Who are the rest of these clowns?"

"Safe house was compromised. Del and Ivy had to run."

"And you played the white knight. Isn't that cozy?" The special agent holstered his weapon, a sneer on his face. "Too bad for you this reunion is short lived. After interrogation where these so-called innocents explain how one of their protectors ended up dead, they go back into a safe house."

"No."

"Don't need your permission, Cahill." A grin. "My federal badge trumps your local one. This time we'll keep them locked down so tight, you won't remember what they looked like."

Ivy started gasping for air.

Del grabbed her cousin's hand. "Ivy?"

Alex slung his rifle strap over his head, draped it across his chest. He slid one arm under her knees, the other across her back. With one motion, he lifted Ivy into his arms and stood. "Move." The sniper hurried across the dirt and rock floor toward the entrance.

Jordan, arms crossed, shifted into the sniper's path.

Del's stomach knotted. Stupid move.

One quick movement from Josh and the FBI agent's back was to the wall, arms spread to his sides, leaving the path clear.

In seconds, Alex was outside, Ivy wrapped securely in his arms, her head buried against his neck. Thankful her cousin was out of range of Jordan's ire, Del eased back against the wall to watch the showdown between Josh and the FBI agent.

"I'll have your badge for this, Cahill. Even Blackhawk won't be able to salvage your job by the time I'm finished with you. She's faking. Ms. Monroe was fine when we arrived and two minutes later she's not? If you believe her act, I'm amazed you lasted as long as you did in your off-the-books missions."

In the shadows, his unit, almost as one, straightened away from the cave walls. Waving them off with a hand signal, Josh shifted away from the agent, seeming alert to the possibility of a physical reaction from Jordan or his teammates. She hoped the agents were smart enough not to engage him or his men. The feds would lose.

"Ivy has claustrophobia," she said.

A sneer crossed his face. "You expect me to believe that, Ms. Peterson? How could she enter this cave at all?"

Del's cheeks burned. Idiot. "Desperation makes you do anything necessary to survive. Whoever shot the marshal was shooting at us. This was the only shelter available."

Jordan's jaw hardened. "Doesn't explain why the wheezes started when we showed up."

"Maybe that says something about you, doesn't it? Can't say I blame Ivy. You don't inspire confidence in me, either. The last time we entrusted our lives to you, a killer showed up."

"Alex has been helping Ivy," Josh said, voice soft. "That's the only reason she made it this long in the cave. Look, you can argue about this with your men as long as you want. I'm taking Del and Ivy to the hospital. They're both injured."

"Wait a minute. You aren't in charge of this operation. That's not your call, Cahill." His voice rose, echoed in the stone cavern.

"Take it up with Ethan. See you in Otter Creek, Jordan." Josh signaled his men to vacate the cave and held out a hand to Del.

Her muscles loosened for the first time since their ordeal began two hours before. Fingers threaded through Josh's, Del passed the three agents and stepped outside. She drew in a deep breath. Amazing. Nothing much had changed since she and Ivy took shelter in the cave, except the hill was alive with people carrying flashlights, searching the area. Seemed like the whole world should have shifted on its axis as a result of their ordeal. How could things appear so normal when minutes earlier, a killer shot her in the arm?

"Where's Ivy?" She glanced around, didn't see her or Alex.

He pointed down the hill to the rocks that had first sheltered them. Ivy sat on a rock with Alex standing to her side, arms wrapped around her. The position still allowed Ivy the security of his presence while ensuring she didn't feel closed in. Though he hadn't known her long, Alex understood Ivy's psyche enough to provide security and freedom in one hug. Smart man.

"How's your arm?"

"Bullets hurt."

"Understatement of the year."

"Is Jordan really going to put us back in a safe house?"

"He'll try." Josh stopped their forward progress, tugged her into his arms. "I'm not letting the marshals have you again, Del. I don't know why the security was compromised, but I will find out. Until we know everything, we can't trust the feds to protect you."

"Why not?"

"Leak. That's the only explanation that makes sense." He brushed her lips with his, turned her and started them toward her cousin again.

"Don't let them take us again," she whispered. "The marshals wouldn't let us out of the house. Ivy was miserable."

"They were trying to keep you safe."

"Didn't keep the walls from closing in."

They reached the other couple, who were in a loose circle made of Josh's men. "Ivy."

Her cousin flinched. "I can't go back there. Please don't ask me to do that. The cave's too small. I can't."

"We won't let the feds do that to you," Alex said. "Right, Major?"

"Next stop is the hospital. Can you hang on to Alex for a three-mile hike?"

Del's mouth dropped open. "Three miles?"

"Amazing how far you can run when you're motivated."

"I'll be too heavy," Ivy protested. "If we go slow, I can make it."

"Ivy, you don't weigh much more than a hundred pounds." Alex swept her off the rock and settled her in his arms. "Compared to the rucksack and equipment I carried in various sand pits and cesspools around the world, you're a lightweight. You can't walk on that temporary splint. If you injure your foot further, you'll be on crutches or in a cast for a long time."

"Don't argue with the man holding you. Ask him about the time he didn't take the advice he's dishing out. Paid for it. Let's move," Josh said, squeezing Del's hand. "Quinn, take point. Nate, watch our six." When Rio, gun in his hand, shifted to Alex's left side, Josh nudged Del into the center of the loose circle.

She did her best to keep up with Josh's unit. The men had long strides and were in excellent physical shape. Not too many minutes into their trek, she was gasping for air and stumbling over exposed tree roots. She would have hit the ground if not for Josh's quick reflexes. "Sorry," she murmured.

"Do you need to stop?"

She shook her head.

"See that rise?"

Del strained to see the dark mass rising in front of her. "Did we climb that?" She frowned. "I don't remember running uphill except to reach the cave."

"We came into the forest from a different direction," Rio said. "Didn't want to run into the feds."

Josh squeezed her hand. "Get over that rise, and it's downhill from there. Thirty minutes to the SUVs."

She could last that long. Maybe. "I've had enough of the wilderness. I want our next date to be in town."

"A date that doesn't include trees. Got it."

"If you can't figure out what to do for that date, Major, I'd be happy to stand in for you," Rio said.

"Get your own woman."

"Seems all the good ones are taken."

Del grinned though she remained silent. She had a few single friends in town who would enjoy meeting the medic. He had a great smile and a snarky sense of humor.

A glance at her cousin and she caught the smile Alex shared with Ivy. If a relationship developed between Ivy and Alex, she hoped Lee had the pleasure of meeting Josh's friend. Alex had more honor in one finger than Lee did in his whole gym-buff body. Arrogant and a braggart, Ivy's ex-boyfriend acted like he was a real man. Alex simply was one. Quiet, confident, capable. Del suspected Alex wouldn't treat a woman's career as a threat to his manhood.

Quinn held up a fist and the men stopped. Alex crouched, his upper body curving over Ivy's as if to cover as much of her as possible. Josh tugged Del down into a squat, finger pressed to his lips. Her heart rate zoomed. What now? Did Quinn see or hear something? Not far away, something cracked. A person stepping on a branch or a wild animal? Neither possibility dropped her heart rate.

Quinn gave another hand signal and shifted away from them, toward where Del had heard the noise. No one moved or spoke. Minutes passed. Just when Del knew she'd shake apart from the tension wracking her body, Quinn returned. "Clear. Animal tracks."

Josh helped Del stand while Rio gave Alex a boost up. "Move out," Josh said.

"Need me to carry Ivy a while?" Rio murmured.

Her cousin darted a glance at the medic before looking at Alex. "It's okay if I'm too heavy."

Alex shook his head, settled her higher in his arms, and followed Quinn. The rest fell into the same positions as before.

Their journey passed in a blur, darkness so deep in places it seemed they were walking through a tunnel. Some sections of this part of the forest were so dense it appeared to absorb light. More than once, Josh righted her when she stepped wrong or tripped over obstacles she couldn't see. Just when she thought she couldn't go on without the rest break she'd been offered earlier, the group walked through a line of trees. Two black SUVs waited a few yards away. She staggered the last steps.

Josh caught the keys Alex tossed his direction. He unlocked the vehicle and opened the back door. Alex climbed into the back with Ivy and shut the door. "You're riding shotgun."

"Why isn't Alex driving?"

"Someone needs to help Ivy keep pressure off her ankle. She'll be more comfortable with Alex holding her leg than me."

"I could do it."

"It will make your arm hurt worse."

She wrinkled her nose. "Pass."

Josh opened the passenger door, placed his hands on her waist and lifted her into the seat. "Let's get out of here."

CHAPTER SEVENTEEN

"How much longer?"

Alex's voice had Josh checking on the couple in the backseat. Ivy's stark white face told the level of pain she was in. "Twenty."

"Make it sooner," he snapped.

As soon as they hit a straight stretch, he pressed the accelerator close to the floor. The SUV shot ahead. The miles passed in silence except for road noise and an occasional whimper from Ivy. His stomach knotted. He wanted two minutes alone with Reece's killer. No woman deserved to be a victim. Ivy was fighting her way free from the cycle of abuse. No one had the right to put Ivy back in that victim's role. Someone like Alex would help her fight back. He'd love to see that for sweet Ivy.

He grabbed his phone from the holder, punched in Ethan's number, and hit the speaker button.

"What do you need?" was his brother-in-law's greeting.

"Safe passage into the emergency room."

"How soon?"

"Twelve minutes, max."

"We'll be ready."

Josh glanced in the rearview mirror at Ivy. "A few more minutes."

"Thank you."

"Part of the service, ma'am." He turned his head toward Del. "You hanging in there, babe?"

"I've never driven Highway 18 this fast before. Why aren't your co-workers pulling you over?"

Her words had a bite to them. He'd take her ire if it focused her attention on irritation rather than pain. "They might." He grinned "Ethan will call in a few favors if that happens."

"Lucky you."

"Don't tell Meg. She'll be ticked off at the favoritism."

"What names have you guessed for Del?" Ivy asked.

Josh played along though he preferred to keep the game to themselves. "Delaney and Delilah. I don't suppose you'd have pity and throw me a few hints?"

"Oh, no." Ivy squeezed her eyes shut for a few seconds. "Wouldn't dream of short circuiting the entertainment. She'll learn everything about you before you figure out her name."

"What's this about?" Alex asked.

"Figuring out Del's first name. She challenged me to discover it on my own."

"Look it up."

"Cheating," Del said, glaring over her shoulder. "He must figure it out the old-fashioned way."

"What's the penalty for wrong guesses?"

"He answers a question." A glance at him. "Within reason. I know there are things he can't tell me."

A whistle. "Can't believe you agreed to that, Major. Softening up in your old age."

"Can't be that hard. How many names begin with Del?"

Alex shook his head. "There's a catch which means her name isn't something usual."

Josh narrowed his eyes. His partner was correct. Otherwise, Del wouldn't have agreed so easily. Hmm. Maybe this wouldn't be as simple as he thought. Still, each question Del asked helped her learn who he was, not who people perceived him to be. Allowed him to spend more time with her, too. "Love a good challenge."

He hoped she wasn't disappointed by what she learned about him. Wouldn't be the first time a woman couldn't live with his career. Would Del be the exception?

His friend snorted. "I foresee you divulging all your secrets before you guess the right name."

"No faith in my deductive powers? That hurts." Josh flipped on his right turn signal and zoomed down the deceleration ramp into Otter Creek. He weaved in and out of traffic on Main Street and hung a left on Hospital Road. His brother-in-law waited at the emergency room entrance with several other Otter Creek officers. The tension wracking his frame on the trip out of the forest and the race into town dissipated. With Del and Ivy injured, his and Alex's attention would be split, leaving Nate, Rio, and Quinn to fill in the gaps. Right now, he'd bet on sheer numbers making the difference if the shooter followed them here.

Josh rolled to a stop, the second SUV close behind. They spilled from the vehicle and surrounded Alex's SUV, baseball caps on, pulled low. He threw open the door. "Stay inside until I come around," he told Del, and climbed out.

Ethan met Josh as he rounded the vehicle, flak vest covering his chest. "Doc Anderson's ready in Room One. How bad are their injuries?"

"Gunshot to Del's arm, possible ankle fracture for Ivy. They're fed up with the Washington guests."

"They aren't the only ones. Inside. I have officers stationed outside the room." A grim expression settled on his face. "No one will reach Del and Ivy."

Josh moved to Del's door. "Heavy police presence for a ten-minute warning."

"Burns is in ICU. Marshals are at both crime scenes. Otter Creek's providing protection."

"And you're waiting to interview Burns. Very nice." He rapped once on Alex's window to signal his friend it was safe to bring Ivy inside, and opened Del's door. "Time to go, sweetheart." Josh helped her to the pavement as Alex exited the SUV, reached over and lifted Ivy into his arms. He and his partner hustled the women away from the SUV. Ethan, two Otter Creek officers along with Josh's team covered their passage into the hospital.

Rod met them inside the lobby. "Welcome back, Cahill. Stirred up a hornet's nest on your little adventure." He grinned. "Good job aggravating our least favorite fed."

"Don't thank me yet. Jordan won't be far behind. He will be your problem and he's threatening to take my badge."

Rod exchanged a glance with Ethan. "You going to let him get by with that?"

"What do you think?"

"Hey," Ivy said. "Can we go, please? I'm just about out of niceness for the day."

"Yes, ma'am." Ethan motioned them to follow him. A minute later, he pushed open the door to the room.

Doc Anderson's eyebrows rose as Josh and Alex walked in with full gear. Josh signaled the rest of his unit to take position in the hall alongside the officers Ethan had posted to stand watch.

"Ivy's first," Del insisted.

"At least you're the walking wounded." Anderson's eyes twinkled as he looked at Ivy. "Now, young lady, have this strapping lad place you on the bed and I'll examine you." He waited until Alex backed away before approaching Ivy. "A vacuum splint. Interesting equipment to have on hand. Not standard police issue, is it, Josh?"

"No, sir. My friend is a medic. He's prepared for anything."

A slight smile curved the doctor's lips. "Of course." He reached over, fiddled with the splint, and removed it, handed the contraption to Josh. His eyebrows rose at the sight of Ivy's swollen ankle. He probed her foot with gentle motions, accompanied by her hisses of pain. By the time he finished, Alex's hands were fisted.

"We need x-rays. Any other injuries before I call for an orderly?"

Ivy darted a quick glance at Alex. "No, sir."

"Excellent." He grabbed the phone handset on the wall and punched in a series of numbers, shared a murmured conversation before turning. "Orderly will be here soon, my dear. He'll take good care of you."

"Some of my men will have to go along, Doc," Ethan said from his position by the door. "Del and Ivy are protected witnesses."

"That's fine." He motioned Del to a chair at the side of the room. "Your turn. Read any good books lately?"

She grinned. "A new Clive Cussler that you'll like."

"Dirk Pitt has a way with the ladies."

"He doesn't hold a candle to you, Dr. Anderson. I know quite a few ladies who notice every time you walk down the street or into a room. Say the word and I'll start setting you up with each woman on the list of contenders as the future Mrs. Anderson."

He laughed. "I probably know every one. They turn up each week with a different casserole in their hands." He paused. "Can you keep a secret?"

"Sure."

"I started passing the casseroles along to the rescue mission. My freezer is filled with more casseroles than I'll eat in a lifetime. Now, my dear, flattering my old bones will not make your arm hurt less. Let's look at the damage." Anderson unwrapped the bandage Rio had placed around her arm and whistled. "Grazed by a bullet. Your arm looks good, though. Josh's medic did a fine job."

A sharp rap sounded on the door.

Alex moved in front of Ivy, fingers curled around his weapon's hand grip while Josh shifted position to better cover Del. Ethan opened the door, his body blocking entrance into the room.

"I'm here to take a patient to x-ray."

"It's all right, Chief Blackhawk," Dr. Anderson said. "This is the orderly I'm expecting."

Ethan moved aside to admit the linebacker-sized orderly pushing a wheelchair. The auburn-haired man pulled up short at seeing Josh and Alex and their weapons. He glanced at Ethan. "Everything okay, Chief?"

"A couple men will go with you to x-ray."

"Why?"

"To keep me from snarling at orderlies who ask stupid questions," Ivy said, a scowl on her face. "I'm not having a very good day. A wise man wouldn't test my patience."

"Be nice, Ivy," Josh said, gaze still on the orderly, assessing. Dude could flatten them. He should avoid the refrigerator and take up swimming.

"A pint-sized Bridezilla," the man muttered.

Ivy narrowed her eyes. "What did you say?"

"Don't mind Harry," Dr. Anderson said, waving aside Harry's comment. "His social skills are stunted."

"Try nonexistent."

Harry the orderly scowled at Ivy.

Alex took a step toward the orderly before Josh signaled him to stand down.

"Let's get Ms. Monroe in the wheelchair." Anderson motioned Harry forward.

Ivy shrank back from the approaching man.

"I'll get her." Alex cut the orderly off, scooped Ivy into his arms, crossed the room with a steady stride. Harry's eyes widened when he spotted the black Ka-Bar strapped on Alex's thigh and backed off, swallowing hard.

"Once you have Ms. Monroe settled, Harry has to push her. Hospital rules."

"That's fine." He eased Ivy into the chair, brushed bangs away from her sweaty forehead. "Gives me a chance to hold her hand. Another step in my plan to win her heart."

Ivy's cheeks blazed a hot pink. Josh smiled. Del's cousin appeared smitten with his sniper. And his partner was laying the boyfriend act on thick. His brow furrowed. At least he thought Alex was keeping his cover. His friend hadn't dated anyone seriously in years. To focus on Ivy meant Alex would have to fight through the protection layers she'd erected. Alex was tough. If any man could break through her defenses, it would be him. A gift for both of them. Also entertaining to watch the deadly sniper fall to the temptation of a tiny woman.

"Sure. Whatever, man." Harry moved to the back of the wheelchair. "If you'll get the door, Chief, we'll go." His tone said he couldn't get to x-ray and back fast enough.

Door open, Josh signaled Rio to accompany Alex and Ivy. He suspected Ivy would be more comfortable with Rio than Quinn or Nate. Rod trailed along behind the entourage in the hall, cell phone to his ear.

"Let's bandage your arm and I'll write a prescription for antibiotics. Make sure you take it all. Chief Blackhawk can fill your prescription at the hospital pharmacy while we wait for the x-ray results."

Ethan turned his head, listened to commotion in the hall. A pointed glance at Josh. "Your reprieve is gone."

Josh smiled. Hand pressed to Del's back, he felt her muscles tighten. Jordan would flex his muscles again, might try taking his badge. But Josh had an ace, one Jordan knew nothing about. Wasn't in his official records. Most of his missions weren't. Special Agent Jordan was in for a surprise if he pushed too hard.

An officer opened the door. "Chief, the FBI and marshals are here. They insist on seeing you and the ladies."

Ethan sighed. "Send them in."

Josh expected Jordan to barrel through the door first, but two strangers pushed across the threshold, a woman and man. They assessed the room at a glance. About the size of Ethan, the male scanned the emergency room, frowned. "Thank God you're alive, Del. Where's Ivy?"

"X-ray," Ethan replied. "And you are?"

"Sorry. Deke Creed, U.S. Marshals." He shook Ethan's hand and inclined his head to the woman by his side. "This is my partner, Stella Grayson. We were part of the protection detail for Del and Ivy."

Josh stiffened. Were they part of the leak?

"He's a good man," Del whispered. "We like him and Stella."

She didn't know if they were good officers. Del hadn't mentioned these two marshals in her recitation of the night's events. Deke and Stella hadn't been on duty. So did they call in the hit or leak information that helped the shooter find Del and Ivy? Working blind made his muscles knot. Reminded him of many Delta missions. Hard to decide who was worthy of trust. Misplaced trust meant his people died.

"Police Chief Ethan Blackhawk." Ethan shook Deke's hand, motioned to Josh. "Officer Josh Cahill."

"Who's with Ivy?" Stella asked. "Wouldn't take a rocket scientist to guess the women were brought here for medical treatment. She can't be without protection."

"Ivy's with one of my officers and two bodyguards, both former military."

"Are they good?" Deke asked.

"More than good," Josh said.

Jordan pushed by the marshals. "We'll take it from here, Blackhawk. Go back to writing tickets and helping old ladies cross the street."

"You already had your chance, Jordan. You screwed up. My people deserve the best and that's not you."

"Ms. Peterson and Ms. Monroe are under our protection."

"Didn't do such a great job of that, did you? You need local help." His soft voice belied the steel in his tone.

"From you and your merry band of hick cops? I don't think so."

"If you want your witnesses to stay alive, reconsider."

"Or we'll make you," Josh said. The body language and cockiness told him the fed's response before he opened his mouth.

Another sneer from the FBI agent. "Talk to me when you have twenty more years under your belt as a law enforcement officer, Cahill. In the meantime, leave this to the real professionals."

Josh snorted. "Don't say I didn't warn you, Jordan." At the nod from Ethan, he pulled out his cell phone and punched in a number he'd not needed to use before now, hoped never to use, then pushed the speaker button. The sound of a ringing phone filled the room.

A click, then, "Josh Cahill. How are you?" a female voice said.

He grinned. She sounded terrific. Upbeat, happy, unlike the last time he'd seen her. "I'm great, Charlotte. Heads up, sugar. You're on speaker phone. How's the baby?"

"Sam's amazing, growing like a weed, thanks to you."

"You did the hard part."

"Sure, after you rescued me from the kidnappers."

"You followed orders like a champ, showed great courage under fire. Saved yourself and Sam. Did Sam receive his birthday gift from the team?"

"Haven't you seen the stuffed elephant in the press photos? He won't go anywhere without it. How's your team?"

"Ornery as ever."

A laugh. "Although I'd love a chance to talk to you at length, you didn't call to shoot the breeze. What can I do for you? Name it and it'll be done."

"I want to speak to your father. I need a favor."

"Is that all?" Charlotte sounded disappointed. "This doesn't make us even. Griff and I owe you for our son's life."

Josh knew from the shock on Del's face and the surge of red flooding Jordan's that they knew the identity of the woman. "A phone call, Charlotte. And there's no debt owed, okay? Sam's safe birth was a gift for a bunch of grizzled soldiers."

"No way, Josh. We will always owe you and your team. Anytime, anywhere. Can Dad reach you at this number?"

Knowing he wouldn't win any argument with Charlotte Martin Abrams, he said, "Yes. Thanks, sugar." Josh ended the call.

Ethan burst into laughter. "Well played, Josh. Well played."

Del stared at Josh. "You're friends with Griff and Charlotte Abrams, President Martin's daughter and son-in-law?" How could she not know that about him?

Parts of Josh's past were shrouded in secrecy. What kind of military work had Josh been involved in? She remembered something about a special operations force being responsible for Charlotte's rescue from kidnappers. A band of terrorists had taken her hostage on one of her overseas trips representing her father at the funeral of a foreign dignitary. While escaping from the terrorists in a desert country, Charlotte gave birth to her son, Sam, a bundle of energy who ran around the White House, charming everyone. Rumors abounded that the Secret Service adored that black-haired toddler.

Josh shrugged.

"Alex and the rest of your team were involved?"

He smiled.

"Is this something I can ask about later?"

"Depends on what you ask."

She grinned. Oh, this was going to be fun. Josh Cahill, man of secrets, many he couldn't share because of national security. "I want to meet Sam. I know a series of books he'd love. The main character is a blue elephant like his toy."

Josh's cheeks flamed. Embarrassed over the toy? Blackmail fodder.

"I'll see what I can do," he murmured.

His cell phone signaled an incoming call. She glanced at the screen. Blocked number. Her heart leaped up into her throat. President Martin? She glanced at the livid federal agent staring daggers at Josh. Amusement lit Deke and Stella's eyes. Guess they weren't Jordan fans, either.

"Josh Cahill, sir. You're on speaker."

"What can I do for you, son?" President William Martin's distinctive bass voice rolled from the phone to fill the silence in the emergency room.

"My team and I want to provide protection for two witnesses in Judge Reece's murder. The feds had a breach in security that almost got these women killed. Sir, they're friends of mine. Good friends. One marshal was killed, another critically injured."

"Who's the agent in charge, Josh?"

"Craig Jordan, sir. He's listening in as well as a couple marshals."

"Special Agent Jordan?"

Jordan cleared his throat. "Yes, Mr. President?"

"Use Josh and his team for security. Their security clearance is higher than yours. You can trust them. I'll clear the arrangements with the FBI director."

"But, sir...."

"Not open for discussion, Special Agent. Josh?"

"Yes, sir?"

"Need anything else? I have a meeting on hold."

"Not right now, Mr. President."

"Whatever you need, let me know. We'll get it done. I'll never be able to repay you for the lives of my daughter and grandson. I don't know how you and your team pulled off that mission, but I'm grateful you did."

"Thank you, sir."

Josh ended the call, glanced at Jordan. "Satisfied?"

He scowled. "Keep in touch through Blackhawk. Check in every six hours or I'll consider you on the run with my witnesses." Jordan turned and stormed from the room.

"There you are, my dear. All set."

Dr. Anderson's voice dragged Del's gaze from Josh. She glanced down at her newly bandaged arm. He'd continued working during the past few minutes. Nothing seemed to rattle the town's favorite doctor.

"Stella and I want to help protect Del and Ivy," Deke said. "We also want a chance at this guy. He murdered a fellow marshal."

"Why should we trust you with their safety after the colossal failure of your last op?" Josh said.

"Check us out," Stella said. "You won't find anything suspicious because there's nothing to find."

"I intend to." Josh's eyes glittered as he stared at the pair of marshals. "Until you're cleared by my team, you won't ever be alone with Del or Ivy."

"Fair enough," Deke said. "Just remember it's a two-way street, Cahill. How do we know we can trust you? You and your team are unknowns for us. Who's to say you won't turn on us?"

"President Martin vouching for me isn't enough?"

"What mission was Martin talking about?"

"The classified kind."

Del rose and slid her hand into Josh's, laced their fingers together. "What about your family, Deke? If you stay on this protection detail, you may not be able to go home for a while." She glanced at Josh. "I don't know much about security matters, but I'd guess you'll take us somewhere unknown to the marshals for our protection. Right?"

He winked at her. And her heart rate sped up. She was pathetic. Who knew one wink from Josh Cahill would set her heart racing?

"My wife knows what happened," Deke said. "She expects me to be out of touch for a while."

Ethan's phone chirped. He stepped into the hall. A minute later, he returned and shut the door, expression grim. "Burns is out of surgery. Doesn't look good. I'm going up to ICU."

"Ken's a friend. Okay if I come along?" Deke asked, sorrow shadowing his gaze.

Del closed her eyes. So much death and suffering. And for what? No one knew why Judge Reece was killed, his death following so quickly on the heels of his mother's passing. She squeezed Josh's hand. "Is my mother okay? What if the killer tries to get to me through her?" She'd already lost her father. It would kill her to lose Mom.

"I have a friend watching her. She's safe, baby."

A breath shuddered out of her. "Thank you."

The door burst open, Alex holding it for Harry to push through the wheelchair carrying a scowling Ivy. She lifted a large white envelope the size of a regular mailer. "X-rays, Dr. Anderson." Her eyes widened. "Stella! What are you doing here?"

"Checking on you." The marshal gave Ivy a hug. "Glad you're safe. Have to admit, I expected the worst when I heard you and Del were missing."

"If Josh and his men hadn't showed up when they did," Del said, "we wouldn't be here now."

"Let's have a look at these x-rays." Anderson took the package, withdrew the film and clipped them to the lighted board mounted on the wall. After a moment, he smiled. "No fractures. We'll wrap it. Stay off it for a few days." He turned to Alex. "You make sure she cooperates."

"Yes, sir."

"Don't sound so happy about your new job," Ivy groused.

"Tough job, but somebody's got to do it." Alex grinned and ruffled Ivy's hair.

Ethan and Deke returned with Rod. None of them looked happy. Did Marshal Burns pass away? "What's wrong?" she asked.

"Problem." Ethan stared at Harry. "Wait in the hall."

Harry startled. "I'm finished."

"I'll follow you out," Dr. Anderson said. "I'll arrange crutches and have the prescriptions filled." He smiled at Ethan. "Looks like you're busy right now."

"Thanks, Doc." He waited until the door closed behind the doctor and orderly.

"What's going on?" Josh asked.

"Spoke to Burns for a minute. He recognized the shooter."

Ivy's hand clamped over her mouth. Alex moved close enough to lay his hand on her shoulder. Despite Del's dread, some of the worry she carried about her cousin lightened. Ivy needed a friend like him at her back.

"That's good, right?" Del said. "You guys can arrest him."

"It's not that easy." Ethan massaged the back of his neck. "The safe house was compromised because this guy used to be a marshal."

"He used to be one of us?" Stella's mouth dropped. "Do you know him, Deke?"

"Unfortunately. He won't stop until we take him down, Stel."

Del shivered. What kind of man betrayed his fellow marshals, killed one, critically injured another? Would she and Ivy ever be safe in the custody of the marshals? He knew tactics and places they hid witnesses.

"That's not all." Josh said. "Tell the rest."

"You sure?" Ethan's gaze shifted to Del. "Does she know about your unit?"

He shrugged. "A matter of time."

A grin. "Like that, huh?"

He smiled at Del. "She'll break my heart if she dumps me."

"Fat chance of that happening," Ivy said.

Del shifted her attention from Josh to the police chief. "Tell us everything, Ethan. The time for secrets is over."

"This guy hasn't always been a marshal. He used to be special operations." Ethan's gaze zeroed in on Josh. "He's former Delta."

CHAPTER EIGHTEEN

"Wait, Ethan." Josh motioned the rest of his team inside the room. As soon as the door closed behind Quinn, Josh returned to Del's side and said to his men, "Shooter used to be Delta."

Nate whistled softly, the rest scowled.

"What's his name, Ethan?" The sooner his unit learned the traitor's identity, the faster they could dig up information on him. Intel was key in winning this battle, and it was a battle. This former Delta operator had declared war on his brothers-in-arms.

"Curt Granger."

Josh froze, as did the rest of his team. Crazy Curt. His gaze shifted to his partner. Alex's grim expression probably matched his. The odds of solving this problem without more bloodshed just dropped into the negative range. No matter the cost, he'd make sure Granger didn't hurt Del or Ivy.

"Do you know him?" Del asked.

"By reputation only."

"Good? Bad?"

"Ugly."

"What's that mean?" Ivy asked.

Josh weighed what he could divulge without divulging too much. Most of what he knew of Crazy Curt's missions weren't public knowledge. "He was released from Delta for going beyond his orders on missions."

Alex snorted.

"Tell them, Major," Rio said. "They can handle it."

"If they want to live, they'll have to," Alex added. "We need their cooperation."

He sifted through what he knew of Granger's exploits and settled for the last mission. "Curt's unit was assigned a retrieval mission. Should have been a simple grab and go. He and his team completed the mission, were heading to the extraction point. The target's wife ran after them, pleading for her scumbag husband's release. Curt volunteered to take care of her." Josh scowled. "He murdered the wife and the village. His team thought he'd calm her down, maybe knock her unconscious. They learned different when he arrived at the extraction point covered in blood. Curt claimed the villagers were planning to give terrorists the unit's location."

"But it wasn't true?" Stella asked.

"This village was in the middle of the jungle. No way to communicate with the outside world unless one of them had a satellite phone. No one did. The villagers couldn't have gotten word to the terrorists until long after the Delta team was gone."

"How did that butcher get hired on with the marshals?" Del asked.

"He was Delta, baby, the blackest of black ops. Crazy Curt also knew a lot of secrets. Most of them were national security issues, but others were more personal, the kind his superiors didn't want leaked. He received an honorable discharge from the military. With his missions redacted, how could the marshal service know he was a loose cannon? The special forces community is tight-lipped about personnel and missions. On paper, he looks good and he was more than well trained for government service in protection."

"He's a nightmare," Alex said. "We're the cowboys of the spec ops community, but carrying the name of Delta is an honor. Curt Granger smeared us with the mud he's wallowed in. We don't sell out to the enemy."

"We don't betray our country or our morals to make a buck. Highest bidder earns Granger's services. You can't appeal to his moral compass. He never had one." Josh hated the pallor of Del's face. Was her fear strictly about Crazy Curt or was she now afraid of him? He swallowed hard, prayed she didn't paint him with the same brush as Granger. He and his unit were nothing like the other Delta operator.

"How long was he with the marshals?" Ethan asked.

"Three years," Deke said. "Granger was fired after several incidents where his itchy trigger finger injured or killed protected witnesses or their cronies. A couple times he injured his own partner or an innocent bystander. The man was poison to the marshals. We were glad to see the last of him."

"Did you work with him?" Stella asked.

"Guy has an ego the size of Texas."

That might come in handy. He'd never believe he could be taken down. That arrogance could be used against him.

"What now?" Del asked.

"Set a trap," Ethan said. "Use what he knows against him. Draw him in when we're ready. He's coming anyway. We'll make the confrontation happen on our turf, our terms."

"Won't he know the tricks from both Delta and the marshals?"

"He never worked with my unit." Josh cupped her beautiful face between his palms. "We worked a lot of ops with Navy SEALs and Marine Recon. Plus, we have Ethan, Rod, Deke, and Stella to contribute their knowledge."

"Will you have to kill him?" she whispered.

"Not if we can avoid it. We need to know who's pointing him at you and Ivy. That's where the next threat lies."

"But if he's dead, wouldn't this stop? Granger's after us because we saw him, right?" Ivy asked.

"That's why we need to bag Crazy Curt," Alex said. "We might be able to squeeze information out of him."

"Might?"

He shrugged. "The military spent a fortune training us to resist interrogation, even under extreme conditions."

Josh's lips curled. A gentle euphemism for torture. Not wanting to explain that to Del, he slid one hand to cradle the back of Del's head, eased her against his chest. Her trembling renewed his fury at Crazy Curt. Women like Del and Ivy shouldn't be afraid of someone who had once sworn to protect American lives. "If we can't uncover the person who hired Curt, that person will keep hiring others. Now that we know the shooter's identity, we'll make some discreet inquiries. Curt's client had to talk to someone to come up with his name."

"How do you know?"

"He can't put up a killer-for-hire website." Nate shrugged. "His name circulates by word-of-mouth. Some are desperate enough to contact him and pay his fee."

A light tap on the door had Quinn shifting to the side. At a nod from Josh, he opened the door, peered down at Dr. Anderson. The doctor smiled, held up a white bag, a bandage to wrap around Ivy's ankle and a pair of crutches. Quinn motioned the doctor into the room, took up position against the door.

Alex took the crutches. When Rio held out a hand for the bandage, Anderson's eyebrows raised. "The medic, I presume?"

"Yes, sir. Name's Rio."

"Very good work with Del's arm, young man." The doctor turned to Del. "Here are your antibiotics, my dear. I also included pain pills should you need them. If not, any kind of anti-inflammatory tablet will suffice."

"Yes, sir."

"Anything else I can do for you, Chief Blackhawk?"

"Not unless you have a cure for morning sickness that lasts all day. Right now, the scent of any cooking food sets off Serena's nausea." A smile. "Makes it tough to keep her cooking schedule. So far, her customers have been very understanding. A couple left caffeine-free soft drinks to help."

"Hmm. If Serena isn't better by next week, call my office. I'll call in a prescription that should help. I'd like to see if the problem resolves itself first."

"Appreciate it, Doc."

"A nurse will be in soon with discharge papers." With a wave, Dr. Anderson left.

"So what now, Ethan?" Rod folded his arms across his chest.

"Need a place for Del and Ivy, one we control access to. The marshal safe houses are out since Granger knows them. That also means places connected to Deke and Stella's personal holdings as well as those of other marshals. Any suggestions?"

The detective's brows furrowed. "How about a cabin that belonged to my first wife's grandfather? Is that a distant enough holding to be safe?"

"Where is it?"

"Middle Tennessee, just outside of Murfreesboro."

Alex's head jerked up. "Isn't that near Nashville?"

"Less than an hour. Why?"

"Fortress Security is based in Nashville," Josh said. "They've been recruiting us, hard."

Ethan scowled at that. "They'll be available for backup?"

"If we need it."

"They better be more than good."

"They recruit former special ops," Alex said. "Lot of SEALs, Recon, Rangers, a couple PJs. Their CEO, Brent Maddox, brought on a former Secret Service agent a few months back. We worked with a couple SEALs that are now employed by Fortress."

"Eli Wolfe and Jon Smith," Rio added. He tossed the bandage up in the air, caught it, and moved toward Ivy. The medic motioned for Ivy to extend her leg so he could wrap the ankle. Alex supported her leg for Rio.

Ethan's eyebrows shot up. "You serious?"

"You know them?"

"Not personally. I still have connections in the spec ops community. Wolfe and Smith made an impression on many people."

"They're good?" Del asked, her gaze shifting between Josh and Ethan.

"They make Curt Granger look like an amateur," Nate said, a grin spreading across his face. "Those frogmen have honor in spades."

"They'd like nothing better than to bag a dirty special forces operative working in their backyard," Quinn put in from his spot against the door. "They'd fit in seamlessly since we already worked with them in the field."

"We trust them," Josh said. "Wolfe and Smith would give us an edge. An added benefit is Granger doesn't know about them."

"But there are five of you, plus two marshals, and Ethan and Rod, all against one man."

"One very dangerous man." Ethan leaned back against the wall, watching Rio work with the bandage. "All special forces soldiers can do a lot of damage. They might go down, but they'll make you wish you hadn't crossed them before they do."

"But you're special forces, too," Ivy said. "Aren't you as dangerous as he is?"

"Maybe. But I can't go with you."

"Why not?"

"Serena needs him," Rod said. "Second, somebody has to ride herd on Jordan. And though I'm more than happy to antagonize the fed, our police force isn't large enough to cover Ethan and Josh being gone."

"We also don't want to alert Granger that we're on to him." Alex patted Ivy's knee. "Shouldn't raise suspicion for Josh to ask for personal leave to protect his girlfriend. I've already flashed the new boyfriend card with you. Granger won't question me signing up for protection detail."

"What about the rest of your team?" Del asked. "Won't it be strange if they just disappear?"

"No one knows Nate, Rio, and Quinn are in town except the doctor and the orderly." Josh turned to Ethan. "I assume you'll take care of them?"

"Let me tackle Harry." Rod grinned. "Made his acquaintance the last time I was in the hospital. He's a good guy. Kept an eye on Meg for me while I was knocked out."

"I'll touch base with Doc before I head out. Have a cabin key, Rod?"

The detective dug in his pants pocket, dragged out a key ring. He flipped through and pulled off a couple keys, handed them to Josh. After rattling off the address which Josh plugged into his phone, Rod excused himself to track down the orderly.

Rio stood, surveyed his handiwork. "You're good to go, Ivy. Stay off your foot the next few days. We'll ice it frequently, see if we can bring down the swelling faster."

"We should split up," Deke said. "Let me take Ivy with Stella. I swear I'll protect her with my life."

Ivy blanched and shrank against the back of the wheelchair.

"Over your dead body." Alex's expression darkened. "Got a short memory, Marshal?"

"Ivy's hurt. What if Granger comes after her? The best defense for her is to run and she can't."

"No." Josh watched the male marshal carefully for any sign of deception. His instincts told him the marshal was honest in his expressed concern. But what if he was wrong? "I already laid out the ground rules, Deke. You and your partner will not be alone with Del or Ivy until you're cleared by my team." Even then, he doubted his partner would leave Ivy in Deke and Stella's care. "We can't afford to split our resources. Egos aside, as good as you might be, you aren't one of us."

"Wait a minute."

"No." Stella placed a restraining hand on her partner's arm. "He's right. Burns and Stone didn't stand a chance against Granger, and Burns had years more experience than we have. I want this guy as much as you do, but I don't care who captures him. All I care about is keeping Del and Ivy safe."

"Burns is my friend, Stella. I want a piece of this guy."

"Not at the expense of an innocent life," his partner insisted. "Besides, you heard President Martin. It's Josh's op. We're backup."

Deke held his hands up in front of him. "Okay. When do we leave?"

Another knock on the door.

"Let me take care of this," Ethan said. "The fewer people who see your team's ugly mugs the better. It's probably the discharge papers." He slipped into the hall.

Josh turned to the marshals. "I hope you have bags with you because we're leaving as soon as Del and Ivy are released. I assume you have wheels?"

Deke snorted. "Fed issue."

"Good. Should make a splash when you leave town. You're going to do some acting to help with our cover story. Spread the story around town that you've been relieved of duty because of the screwup at the safe house. Make a production of being ticked off about the injustice of it."

"That should work," Deke said. "I'll make a couple calls, spread the word we've been kicked to the curb. The director will go along with the charade if it nets us Granger."

"Agreed." Josh pulled out his phone and, after exchanging numbers with Deke, sent the marshal the cabin's address. "Attract attention around town. When you finally leave here, take the long way around."

"Check for tracking devices on your vehicle," Alex added. "Wouldn't put it past Granger to attach one to your fedmobile."

"Give us a four-hour head start," Josh said. "We need to make a couple stops for equipment."

Ethan eased back into the room, papers in hand. "You're free to leave."

"Great. Let's get out of here," Ivy said. "Is there a safe place to shower and change clothes?" She indicated her dirt-streaked attire. "I'm tired of wearing forest and cave dirt." She shuddered. "Who knows what kind of stuff is embedded in this dirt?"

"We'll stop by Mom and Dad's place as soon as we leave the hospital." Josh eyed the rest of his team. "Here's what I want you to do." For the next couple minutes, he gave orders in rapid-fire fashion, much as he did with them while they were in the military. "Ethan, can you bring their SUV around to the back?"

He held out his hand. "Keys." Ethan snagged the key fob in mid-air from Quinn, paused with his hand on the doorknob. "Watch your back, Josh. I don't want to make a death notification with Liz and Aaron." He glanced around at the others remaining in the room. "Same goes for the rest of you. We've already lost three people. Don't give Granger more blood to brag over."

Josh gave his brother-in-law a salute, waited until he left before addressing his team. "Nate, Rio, Quinn, I assume you're fully loaded. Need extra supplies?"

Nate grinned. "More C-4 is always better than less. Blasting caps, too."

Quinn rolled his eyes. "The two bricks you have isn't enough?"

"You never know."

Del closed Ivy's bedroom door behind her and, with backpack in hand, crossed to the stairs. On the first floor of the Cahill home, she dropped her pack on the couch and followed the soft murmur of voices into the kitchen. Alex sat on a barstool while Josh hugged his mother.

"It's safer if you don't know the details, Mom."

"This situation is that dangerous?"

"When will Dad return?"

"He's been delayed. Probably Saturday afternoon."

Josh sighed. "I'll call him." He cupped her face. "In the meantime, stay with Madison so I won't worry about your safety."

"Aren't you worried about your sisters?"

"Why should I be? Their husbands eat nails for breakfast."

Liz Cahill finally nodded. She turned, saw Del. "Looks like I'm going on vacation." She squeezed Del's hand on her way upstairs.

Josh held out his hand to Del, drew her into his embrace. "Feel better?"

"Clean clothes, clean hair. What's not to like?" A chuckle rumbled under her ear. "Your mother's traveling?"

"Dad will take her away for a few days."

"What if Granger remains loose?"

"Liz will be away from Otter Creek long enough to bait Granger's trap," Alex said.

"Bait?" Del scowled.

"Beautiful bait." He raised an eyebrow. "You signed on for that."

"I feel like a Happy Meal at a kid's party. On display and on the verge of being devoured by the biggest kid in the room."

"Who doesn't love Happy Meals?" Alex tilted his head toward the stairs. "Ivy ready?"

"Should be."

Alex stood, strode from the room.

"Sure you want to do this, sweetheart?" Josh threaded his fingers through her damp hair. "Say the word and I'll hide you and Ivy while we run the Ghost to ground."

"Ghost?"

"He moves through strike zones like a ghost."

Del shivered. She hated paranormal movies. Hopefully, she and Ivy wouldn't be too-stupid-to-live heroines.

He kissed her, then said, "Got a few minutes before we leave. Ready for my next name guess?"

"Go for it."

"Della."

A soft laugh. "As in Della Street? Very nice. Wrong, but classy."

He sighed though his eyes twinkled. "Be gentle with me, baby."

"Would you ever consider returning to black ops work?"

Josh seemed to turn to stone under her hands. Del tilted her head back. "Breathe," she murmured. "Sore subject?"

He released her, paced to a barstool and sat, regret and sadness in his eyes. "The truth or a pretty lie?"

Cold chills rolled down her spine. Guess that answered her question. "Always honesty, Josh. You've been telling me to trust you. The combat boot's on the other foot. Time for you to trust me."

His gaze locked with hers. "Fortress Security is recruiting me and my team as a unit."

"What do you want?"

"I like my job, Del."

She heard the unspoken in his voice. "But?"

He sighed. "It's not enough though I don't want to work for Fortress full-time."

"Can you take some missions?" As soon as the words left her mouth, understanding dawned. For her to consider a relationship with a man who may be gone for weeks, her feelings ran deeper than she'd acknowledged on a conscious level. Was she in love with this wounded warrior?

Josh's gaze grew more intent. "Brent's teams are contract workers. I spent years apart from my family. I don't want to be gone for months. I refuse to be an absentee uncle." He paused. "Or an absentee husband and father."

"Will you keep your job here?"

"Hope to."

"What about your team?"

"A question I can't answer yet. We'll need to train together. Quinn and Alex live in the same town, but Rio and Nate live a few hours apart from each other and the rest of us."

Del's stomach knotted. "Who's moving?"

Footsteps sounded on the stairs. Ivy's complaints about crutches drifted into the kitchen. Del gripped Josh's hand. Not much time, but she could ease his mind. "Do what you're called to do, Josh, whether it's work for Ethan or Fortress. Details surrounding your decision will work themselves out."

He lifted her hand, pressed a kiss to her knuckles. "If I take contract work, will you still be part of my life when I return?"

Ivy hopped into the kitchen, stopped when she noticed the silence between Del and Josh. "Bad timing? I can go in the living room." She stumbled in turning.

"No need, kitten." Josh stood. "Where's Alex?"

"Grabbing his bag and your mother's suitcase."

"I'll give him a hand. Mom never travels light." A lingering glance at Del and he left the room.

She dropped onto the nearest barstool.

"What was that?" Ivy whispered. "Spill."

How did she explain? The words were simple enough. The undercurrent? Not so much. "Josh guessed another wrong name."

"What question did you ask?"

"If he'd return to black ops work."

Ivy maneuvered to sit at the counter as well. "What was his answer?"

"Maybe part-time." She tried to swallow, discovered her throat resembled a desert. Deciding Josh wouldn't mind if she stole a sip of his Coke, Del uncapped his bottle and downed a couple swallows.

Her cousin's hand fisted. "Alex will do the same. The team won't let Josh go without them. What about his job here?"

Del shook her head. Something Josh and Ethan would work out. She didn't mention he might move to train with his team. Long distance relationship? Not her first choice. If she didn't take a chance, she'd lose him. How many frequent flyer miles did she have? She might be cashing them in soon.

Alex strode into the room, carrying two suitcases. A wry grin curved his mouth. "Can't believe Liz packed so much in a short time."

"Told you Mom never packs light," Josh called from the stairwell.

"Hush, Josh," Liz said. "If I had more time, I could combine everything in one case."

A snort. "Right." He walked behind his mother, carrying a garment bag and a make-up case. "Don't lie when I'm standing this close. I'd prefer not getting caught in the lightning backwash."

Liz rolled her eyes and, with dignity befitting a queen, strolled out the back door, Josh close behind.

"All right, ladies," Alex said. "Time to roll. Need a piggyback ride, Ivy?"

She scowled. "I'll get the hang of these crutches if it kills me." She hopped and stumbled across the kitchen and out the door.

Del grinned. "Fierce little thing, isn't she?"

"Tiger in training. Grab Ivy's pack. It's beside yours." He pivoted toward the door.

She stood. This was the only way to end Granger's reign of terror in Otter Creek. If they didn't draw him away from town, how many other people would he hurt or kill before he got who or what he wanted?

CHAPTER NINETEEN

Josh backed out of Madison's driveway, guided Alex's SUV toward Highway 18 and the 350-mile journey to Murfreesboro. Like the rest of his team and the marshals, he planned a wandering route to Rod's cabin. They needed time to plan a welcome party for Granger.

Once he reached cruising speed on the highway, Josh grabbed his cell phone and punched in his father's number. One ring, two, three, then his father's voice greeted him. "What's going on, son?"

"Can you talk?"

"Wait." His father whispered to someone nearby. A pause. "I slipped out of the meeting into the hall. Good enough?"

"Be careful what you say, Dad."

"I'll find a place more private." Another pause, footsteps, a door closing. "I'm in an empty room. Door's locked. What's happening?"

"Take Mom on a short vacation."

Seconds of silence greeted his blunt statement. "I'll have someone cover for me."

He'd expected grilling from his father. His throat tightened. Dad trusted his assessment of the situation that much? "That's it? No questions?"

"Can you tell me more?"

Josh weighed the advisability of sharing info with his father, knew he didn't have a choice. His parents' safety depended on his father. In as few words as possible, Josh shared the shooter's identity and his military reputation without divulging too many details. "This man doesn't have a conscience, Dad. Won't take him long to realize Alex and I are with the women. He'll use any means necessary to learn our location, including hurting Mom. I need you both out of his reach."

"Are you safe, son?"

"For now. Granger doesn't fail in his missions. He won't back up or quit." The idea this man might lay one finger on Josh's mother made him want to hurl. Liz Cahill was no match for Curt Granger. The man would hurt, perhaps kill his mother without regret to achieve his objective. His lips curled. The Army did a great job training him. Too bad they couldn't program a conscience into him.

"Where's your mother now?"

"With Nick and Maddie. Nick promised to stay with her until you returned."

"I'll touch base with him. Anything else I can do?"

Josh glanced at Del, whose nose was buried in a book. Her posture brought a smile to his lips. What would she think about his next request? "Got a pen and paper?"

"Sure. Shoot."

He rattled off Dee Peterson's name and phone number. Del closed her book with a slap, head whipping his direction. "Wait an hour, then call Mrs. Peterson. She's as much a target as you and Mom. Take her with you."

He glanced at Del. Her gaze was glued to his face. At least his parents knew what was happening with Del and Ivy. Mrs. Peterson didn't have a clue. What she was told would have to be limited because she didn't have much discretion. His team needed every minute available before Granger tracked them down. He also wanted to protect the woman who gave birth to Del. He didn't want to be responsible for her losing another parent because of his negligence.

"We'll take care of her, Josh. What about Ivy's family?"

"They should be safe. Ivy hasn't contacted her folks for a while." He'd contact Brent Maddox, Fortress Security's CEO, and have one of their operatives watch Ivy's parents.

"Be careful, Josh."

"Always. Love you, Dad."

He handed his phone to Del. "Call your mother. We have an hour to convince her to leave town."

She clutched his phone in both hands. "You're kidding, right? I'm supposed to tell her the man who killed Lily is after me and Ivy? She's convinced Charles killed Lily. She'll panic."

"You're not giving her enough credit," Ivy said. "She's tougher than she lets on."

"This is the same woman who calls me when a light bulb needs changing at the house, even though I'm an hour away and my brothers are across town and capable of changing light bulbs."

"She just wants to be part of your life. You don't need her for anything, but she desperately wants you to. Your father's gone. Your brothers have their own lives. You moved." Ivy sighed. "She loves you to the extreme, yes, but I'd give anything for my parents to love me that much. I wish mine loved me enough to ask favors instead of silence or emails and phone calls blasting me for being an ungrateful daughter and a disappointment to the family name."

Josh caught Alex's scowl in the rearview mirror. He was grateful his parents loved him and his sisters enough to get in their business and their faces when it was deserved. Growing up, he never doubted he and his siblings were the center of Liz and Aaron Cahill's world. As the Cahill children grew older, his parents began letting go, allowing them to make decisions and reap the benefits or suffer the consequences of those decisions. No matter what, he never doubted Liz and Aaron Cahill loved him, even if he made stupid choices. "Call your mother, baby. Put the phone on speaker. I'll help if you have problems."

Del dialed, pressed speaker. The SUV filled with the sound of a phone ringing and Mrs. Peterson's greeting. "Hi, Mom."

"I'm glad to hear from you, Del. Are you coming to home soon?"

"I'm not sure. Why?"

"I met the most wonderful man this morning. Quite charming."

She darted a glance at Josh.

"He's new in town."

"Where did you meet him?"

"At the coffee shop. You know how I love my lattes."

Del smiled. "You and Dad had a standing coffee date every Saturday morning while we watched cartoons and threw pieces of cereal at each other."

"I miss your father so much." She sighed. "Anyway, Curt stopped by my table and asked if he could join me. The other tables were empty, but he said he hated to drink coffee alone." She laughed. "Can't imagine a man several years my junior actually making time for a grandmother."

Josh's stomach knotted. Curt? What was the chance of two men named Curt showing up in the same case? Slim, edging toward zero. A glance in the mirror showed Alex's grim expression matched his own.

"Curt?" Del's voice wavered. She drew in a deep breath. "Did he tell you his last name, Mom?"

"Gardner, Grace." Dee paused. "No, Granger. That's it. His name is Curt Granger."

His hands tightened around the steering wheel. "Mrs. Peterson, it's Josh. Del has you on speaker. What did Curt say to you?"

"He asked about me, my life, my family. Curt was so interested in everything I had to say." She sniffed. "I've missed having someone listen to me. Why? Do you know him?"

"Only by reputation." And what he knew would cause Dee Peterson many sleepless nights. He'd never tell her everything, just as he wouldn't Del. "Did he ask questions about Del?"

Her soft gasp sounded in the vehicle's interior. "How did you know? Curt was so sweet, anxious to hear everything about my wonderful girl. You'll have to be careful, Josh Cahill. Curt may fight you over my girl's heart."

He didn't have to wonder whether Granger knew his name. Another glance at Alex who was shaking his head. Yeah, his partner caught that, too. Before long, Granger would know about Alex. The only thing Granger couldn't confirm was whether the rest of Josh's unit was involved in protecting Del and Ivy. So much for the element of surprise.

"Mom, I need you to pack a bag or a suitcase."

"What? Why?"

"Curt Granger is a very dangerous man."

"He was a perfect gentleman. That's a terrible thing to say."

Del bit down on her bottom lip, sent Josh a helpless look.

"Mrs. Peterson, I'm helping investigate a crime in Otter Creek, a crime in which Curt Granger is a key suspect. Del was a witness and Granger wants to find her and prevent her from testifying against him."

"Del?" Her mother's voice rose, shock reverberating in her tone. "Is that true?"

"Please, Mom, go pack. Josh's parents will came get you soon. Nothing is more important to me than making sure you're safe."

"Oh, but that's not necessary. I can stay with one of your brothers."

"Mrs. Peterson," Josh said. "You don't want to bring danger to your sons and their families. It's best for everyone if you leave town. Mom and Dad are looking forward to spending time with you." Tension rolled through his body. Convincing her of the seriousness of their request was critical to Mrs. Peterson's cooperation.

Ethan needed to contact Milo Tyler. Josh blew out a breath. Oakwood PD should know what was going on, critical to their safety if they came into contact with Granger. He didn't want to be responsible for another officer's injury or death because he walked into a situation with Granger without knowledge of the former Delta operator.

"This is really necessary?"

"I wouldn't ask if I didn't believe that."

Silence, then, "Did you come with Del as a police escort?"

His eyebrows rose. Sharp lady. Ivy was right; Dee Peterson wasn't what she projected. "I came with Del as a cop protecting a citizen and a man who's crazy about your daughter. She caught my attention when she moved to Otter Creek."

A soft laugh. "You redeemed yourself with that answer. How long before your parents arrive?"

He calculated, allowing a few minutes for checking out. Knowing Aaron Cahill, he'd already filled the gas tank and was ready to roll, especially since he knew it was possible he'd leave before the banker's meeting concluded. "Two to three hours, max."

"You'll keep my daughter safe?"

"I'll protect her with my life, Mrs. Peterson."

"Let's hope that's not necessary. I expect the whole story once this man is behind bars."

"I'll tell you what I can."

"I expect you to stay for dinner the next time you come home with my girl. Del, be careful. I'm pretty sure I don't want to know exactly what you're involved in, but it must be dangerous."

"It is dangerous, but Josh is the best. Thanks for doing this, Mom. I couldn't bear it if I lost you." Her voice broke.

"I'll be fine. Is Ivy all right? Is she with you?"

"I'm here, Aunt Dee." Ivy leaned forward. "You'll love Josh's parents."

"Hope Josh doesn't have skeletons in his closet. I plan on asking a lot of questions. You and Del were together when she witnessed this crime?"

"Yes, ma'am."

A sigh came over the phone. "Then you are in danger, too. Who's watching out for you, Ivy?"

"Alex. Don't worry, Aunt Dee. He's as well-trained as Josh."

"Good. Let me know what's happening when you can." And she was gone.

Del returned his phone. "That wasn't as bad as I thought."

"Nice job," Alex said.

Josh patted Del's hand. He checked the side mirror and took an exit off Highway 18. Stopping at the back of the building he'd visited days earlier, Josh sent a text and waited. Two minutes later, the back door opened and Harry Willis trotted outside, large bag in hand.

Alex climbed out and took the bag which he placed in the cargo area.

"Got everything you asked for plus a few other surprises," Harry said. "Let me know if you need anything else." With a wave, Harry retraced his steps into the building.

"What surprises is he talking about?" Ivy asked.

Alex settled into the backseat beside her and shut the door. "Stuff to help us greet Granger in style."

"Things I don't want to know about?"

"Smart lady."

Josh pulled away from the building. After a few minutes of turning squares to lose potential tails, he returned to Highway 18, headed for Interstate 40 and Nashville. While driving, Josh recounted for Del and Ivy the events of the days after the marshals took them into custody.

Del gasped when Josh admitted to being shot. "Granger tried to kill you?"

"He tried to kill Rod. I happened to step in the way."

A snort from Alex. Josh glared in the mirror. So it was a deliberate step. Meg still had a husband because Josh chose to step in the line of fire. Good thing Granger hadn't used armor-piercing bullets or a head shot.

"You're okay?" Ivy asked.

"Ribs are sore, but I've had much worse."

"If he'd been hurt," Alex said, "you'd know about it. He's downright mean when injured."

Del shifted in her seat, hissed.

"What's wrong, baby?"

"Arm."

He glanced her direction, noted Del's pallor. Pain must be bad, considering the way she was holding her arm. "Take a pain pill."

"What if we run into Granger?"

Josh smiled. "How? He doesn't know where we're going. I used evasive maneuvers in case a fed was on our tail. If he did find us, Alex and I can handle him. We have plenty of fire power. Take the meds, Del. You didn't sleep last night. I need you alert when Granger does make an appearance."

She dug the pain med out of her bag.

"Same for you, kitten." He glanced in the mirror in time to catch Ivy wrinkling her nose. "You're short on sleep, too."

"Yes, Dad." She rolled her eyes, but scrunched down in her seat, let Alex drape her jean-clad legs over his thighs, and closed her eyes.

Josh drove the next twenty miles in silence before murmuring to Alex, "They asleep?"

Alex grinned at the quiet sigh from Ivy. "Yep."

With another glance Del's direction, Josh dialed the number for Fortress Security.

"Wake up, sweetheart."

Del's eyelids flew up. She straightened in a hurry, moaned at the sharp pain in her arm. Bullet. Right. Don't lean on that arm. "What's wrong? Is it Granger? Did he find us?"

A soft chuckle. Josh leaned over and kissed her, a kiss soft as a butterfly's wing. Warmth spiraled out from her heart through the rest of her body. "We're at the cabin."

Her mouth gaped. She glanced out the windshield. They were parked behind the other SUV used by Nate, Rio, and Quinn on a cement driveway. To the right, Rod's cabin rose two stories. The wraparound porch drew her attention. Four rocking chairs sat along the log wall, two on either side of the front door. It looked so inviting. The only thing lacking was a porch swing. In normal circumstances, she could imagine passing a peaceful hour or two, rocking in the evening breeze. Trees ringed the property, so dense in places she couldn't see the surrounding countryside. Wide open spaces encompassed the cabin.

She eyed the forest again. The shooter could still take potshots at them from the trees, like he had the night before. Unlike her and Ivy, Josh and his team had guns and could shoot back. Best not to put a weapon in her hands unless it was a book. A spark of humor lifted her spirits. A heavy hardback dictionary ought to do the trick. Webster's unabridged dictionary could stop even a tough guy like Granger in his tracks. "Ivy's inside already?"

"Alex carried her in a minute ago. Feel better, babe?"

She took stock of her aches and pains. "Minus the arm pain, I'm a little stiff." She smiled. "I'm excellent considering where I was last night."

"You mean you didn't like the accommodations in the cave?" His eyes twinkled.

"My idea of roughing it is the Holiday Inn."

"Guess I'll have to think of something other than camping for a date."

Her eyes narrowed to slits. "I've had all I want of communing with nature for a while."

Josh grinned. "Why don't you go inside and check out the place? I'll bring in the backpacks along with the rest of our gear."

"Need help?" She eyed the bags in the cargo area, skeptical of her ability to lift anything Josh and Alex had brought.

"I've got help." He inclined his head toward the porch where, one by one, his team members came through the door. All but Quinn swarmed the back of the SUV and hauled in bags of equipment. Quinn remained on the porch, rifle in hand, eyes scanning the area.

Despite the humidity and heat, Del shivered. Though Josh didn't believe Granger could have located them this quickly, she couldn't help but feel as if he were hidden in the trees, watching every move, waiting to kill her and Ivy.

She drew in a deep breath, opened the passenger door, slid to the ground and made for the porch. She wanted to run. A lot. Because of that, with her jaw clenched, she forced herself to walk as if nothing were amiss, as if she didn't feel a killer zeroing in on her back, bringing his target into focus, caressing the trigger. Del didn't want to tangle with another bullet.

Quinn stopped scanning long enough to grin at her and wink.

Dismay wound through her. So much for acting like a courageous woman. Hey, she was only a bookseller, after all. Her greatest adventures came inside the covers of a book. Inside the front door, she stopped. Wow. The living room was spacious with an open floor plan, tall ceiling, and a large staircase leading to the second floor. The sun-drenched interior looked warm and inviting.

Ivy sat in the recliner, footrest propped up, an icepack on her ankle. "Beautiful, isn't it?"

"Amazing." Her visual sweep came to a halt at the river stone fireplace. "Wish I had one of those."

"As small as your place is, a fireplace that size would take up most of one wall and heat your house inside of ten minutes."

She grinned. "Think what a small heating bill I'd have each winter. More money to buy bookshelves."

"And put them where? You don't have any walls available."

The men muscled through the doorway, each bearing at least one bag. Josh brought up the rear, backpacks clenched in one hand, cell phone pressed to his ear with the other. He didn't look happy.

"Appreciate the info, Jon. Email me whatever you learn. See you at 7:00."

Alex strode into the room, a bottle of Coke in each hand. He handed one to Ivy, the other to Del. "Jon already doing his thing?"

Josh nodded and positioned the backpacks against the wall, out of the path of foot traffic. "Granger's already burning up the phone wires and Internet. He's searching for our Delta unit."

Rio grimaced as he stowed one of the equipment bags near the stairwell. "Knew he would, Major."

"I hoped he'd look for me and Alex, not all of us. He won't miss the significance of you, Nate, and Quinn being out of circulation."

"No spec ops soldier would go into battle for him," Nate said, "but Durango's known for having each other's backs, anytime, anywhere. Might be more suspicious if we weren't with you."

"Our real advantage isn't hiding our presence," Quinn added. "It's the fact we worked as a team for years. We'll take him down, Major. He'll have to go through us to get to Del and Ivy." His lips curved upward. "We'll make it hurt when he tries."

"Jon and Eli are stopping by tonight." Josh rubbed the back of his neck. "Is there food in the kitchen?"

"Already made a grocery run, Major," Nate said. "We're stocked for a few days. If this op runs longer, I'll buy more supplies."

Del exchanged glances with Ivy. Wonder what quiet, intense Nate had put in his grocery cart? Frozen food? Canned stuff? "Do you cook, Nate?" Were they expecting her to cook for this crowd? Josh's unit were all big guys in fabulous shape. They probably ate like a bunch of linebackers for the Cowboys.

"Nate's parents own a restaurant," Rio said. "He's been cooking since he was a kid. Makes the best beef stew I've ever eaten."

"He's no slouch at anything to do with food," Quinn said.

"I don't bake." Nate's mouth moved into a crooked smile. "Never could get the hang of delicate stuff like cakes or pies. I've a fair hand with cookies, though."

"He's neck-in-neck with Serena," Josh said. "We never worried if our rations ran out while in the field. Nate made almost anything taste good. Did amazing things with whatever wildlife was at hand."

Del grinned at Nate. "I hope you didn't buy anything too exotic at the grocery store. My food tastes are pretty tame."

"Well, I did catch a deal on rattlesnake."

When the rest of the team laughed, she figured he was teasing. Two could play at that game. "I have the perfect recipe for rattlesnake. I do some mean stuff with curry powder."

He wagged his finger at her. "Not nice, Del. Just for that, I might send Alex hunting in the woods."

She waved her hands in front of her. "Sorry. Don't make me eat Bambi or his friends."

Nate chuckled. "She's a keeper, Major."

"You'll get no argument from me." He winked at her and turned his attention back to his team. "Anything from the marshals?"

"An hour out," Quinn said. "Deke drove for an hour like they were headed back to D.C. Had a tail he ditched. Drove in circles for a while to make sure they were clear."

A nod from Josh. "How many bedrooms do we have?"

"Four," Rio said. "We'll put the women in one room. Figured Stella would prefer that. The rest of us will split up in the other rooms."

Alex and Quinn almost bristled with tension. What was up with that?

"You okay staying with Deke, Rio?" Josh asked.

"As long as he doesn't snore the roof down on me."

Del blinked at the exchange, the room awash with subtle undercurrents. Something she couldn't put her finger on. Did Alex and Quinn not trust the marshal? Her stomach churned at that thought. She liked Deke and Stella. Had the men picked up an attitude or behavior that raised a red flag in their minds?

"Move the equipment upstairs. Harry packed surprises for us."

"Yes!" Quinn pumped his fist, grabbed a couple bags, trotted toward the staircase. Nate and Rio grabbed the rest of the bags and followed their teammate. Alex picked up the backpacks and left the room.

"You know how to clear a room," Ivy said, a smile curving her mouth.

"What wasn't being said about Deke?" Del asked. "Is there a problem with him?"

"Why?"

"Alex and Quinn don't want to stay in the same room with him," Ivy said.

"Alex and Quinn have had each other's backs in some tight places and don't trust others easily. Neither would sleep well with a stranger in close quarters."

"Would you have a problem with him?" Del's eyebrows rose.

A slight smile. "He's not in my room, either, is he? Rio's more easy going than the rest of us. He's as tough as they come, but not as alpha as the rest of us."

"And if you do learn there's a problem with the marshal?"

"You'll be among the first to know. No secrets, baby. I promise." His gaze shifted to Ivy. "How you doing, kitten?"

Her cousin bared her teeth. "Grumpy. What's that tell you?"

"That I should stay out of your way, let you sharpen your claws on Alex."

"I heard that," Alex said. "Mean, Major."

"To survive, I'd happily throw you under the bus."

Nate and Rio returned, smirks on their faces. Must have heard the volley between Josh and Alex. If these guys were anything like her brothers, it wouldn't be long before mudslinging devolved into wrestling on the floor to determine superiority. "Nate, should we start on dinner?"

His eyes lit. "You cook?"

"I'm not a chef, but I know my way around a kitchen."

"Great. The rest of these slobs don't know a spatula from a strainer." Amid a chorus of protests and Ivy's laughter, he waved his hand for Del to follow him.

Ninety minutes later, while spaghetti sauce simmered in a large pot on the stove, the marshals arrived. Stella breathed deep, moaned. "That smells amazing. You cooking again, Del?"

"Nope. This is Nate's work. I was the gopher this time."

Stella smiled. "Hi, Nate. I'm Stella." She shook his hand. "I'm glad to know someone else in this group can cook besides Del. Got a feeling you guys can put away the food."

"That's why the pantry and refrigerator are stuffed." He tilted his head. "We're growing boys."

Del burst into laughter.

"When will dinner be ready? Deke hasn't fed me for hours."

"As soon as our guests arrive."

Her eyebrows rose. "Guests?"

"Big, bad Navy SEALs."

CHAPTER TWENTY

Josh greeted Jon Smith and Eli Wolfe on the driveway. Like every other time he'd been in their company, Eli was the more outgoing. Jon Smith was one intense, scary man, a lot like Alex. Come to think of it, every sniper of his acquaintance shared the same qualities. Chaos might break out around them and, instead of panicking, they grew calmer. None of them broke a sweat on missions. If he didn't know better, he'd swear ice water ran through their veins.

"Looking good, Cahill." Eli clapped him on the shoulder, a grin on his face. "It's great to see your homely face. How's the family?"

"Doubled in size. My sisters are married and Serena's going to make me an uncle."

"Congratulations, man. And your folks?"

"About like you'd expect with a loon like Granger prowling around."

"Worried about their boy, huh?" The smile slid off Eli's mouth. "Good reason for concern."

Josh held out his hand to the other man. "Jon."

The Navy SEAL's eyes changed from ice cold to moderate warmth. Amused, Josh grinned. Guess that was the best he would get from the sniper.

"He wasn't that funny, Jon. Show a little restraint, why don't ya?"

The response was a snort and lip curl. Yep, same old Jon. "Dinner's ready. Come eat."

"Real food?" Eli's gaze brightened. "Not the frozen kind? Or the kind covered in paper and delivered in a bag by a perky teenager?"

"Smelled real to me. Del mentioned spaghetti and salad, maybe dessert."

"Who's Del?" Jon asked.

"She's amazing." He paused, shrugged. "Mine," Josh finished.

"Yeah?" Eli's eyebrows rose. "Now my curiosity's buzzing. Let's meet the lady who captured our boy's heart, Jon."

Josh led them through the door. His team stood as Jon and Eli walked into the room, all except Quinn who patrolled the perimeter. After dinner, Rio would take his place while the rest of the team plus the SEALs talked strategy.

One glance at Jon and Eli had Ivy's eyes widening. She cast an uneasy glance toward Alex. His partner, though he claimed to have no sensitivity where women were concerned, winked at her, then stepped forward to greet his fellow sniper with a grin and handshake.

Durango didn't trust easily. When they did, it was a long-term deal. His team greeted Jon and Eli like they were long-lost friends back for a visit.

"Where's Rio?" Eli glanced around. "My second favorite medic's here, right? And what about Quinn?"

"Rio's stirring the sauce," Nate said, "and trying to make time with our pretty U.S. marshal. Quinn's on the perimeter."

Eli laughed. "Ah. The medic must be doing a good job because the food smells great. I assume the meal is your handiwork, Chef Nate?"

"Had help. Josh's lady is handy in the kitchen." He frowned. "Gave her sissy work this time, though."

Josh straightened. "Why?"

"Arm."

"Pain bad?"

"Enough. She hasn't complained. One tough lady."

"And that's why Rio stayed in the kitchen. I'll talk to her."

A smirk from Nate. "Yeah, good luck with that, Major. Your woman has a stubborn streak like the Cahill women."

Josh flinched. Not what he wanted to hear. If Del was anything like his sisters, he might have to get creative.

"And who is this beautiful lady?" Eli asked, his gaze on Ivy.

Alex laid a hand on Ivy's shoulder. "Ivy Monroe, meet Eli Wolfe and Jon Smith. Eli's the mouthy one. You almost can't get anything out of Jon."

A smile from Ivy even as she settled deeper into the couch cushions. Her grip on the empty Coke bottle whitened her knuckles. Jon zeroed in on her hands. A raised eyebrow was the only response.

"Looks like you're the walking wounded, sugar." Eli tilted his head to get a closer look at her ankle without moving nearer. "What happened?"

"I fell running from Granger," she whispered. "Twisted my ankle."

"How did you escape?" Jon asked.

His voice was so gentle Josh did a double take. He'd never heard that tone from the cold, focused sniper. Of course, the few times he'd been around Jon when he was interrogating terrorists, the man never raised his voice. He didn't have to. Never failed to get information, either. Had to admit, he wouldn't want Jon Smith questioning him about anything.

"Del harassed me into running anyway. I tried to get her to leave me behind, save herself, but she wouldn't." She grinned. "Told me to shut up and get moving."

A nod from Jon. "Soldiers do the same for each other, Ivy. We never leave a man behind."

Josh swallowed hard. Ivy had no clue she'd connected with one of the most dangerous men on the planet. She also had no way of knowing what Jon had gone through in recent months. Captivity at the hands of human traffickers had left indelible marks on his soul and body. Word was Jon's team had been sold out to traffickers. Eli had sustained injuries himself rescuing his partner.

Rio walked in, wiping his hands on a towel. He brightened at the sight of the two newcomers. "Jon, Eli." Another handshake with Eli, a nod at Jon. Very few people risked touching the SEAL sniper.

"Table's set," Rio said. "Don't let the food grow cold. Hate to disrespect Nate's work."

Eli stopped by the couch. "Need help to the table, sugar?" he asked, southern drawl pronounced.

Alex waved him off. "I'll carry her."

Eli trailed his partner. Alex lifted Ivy, her arms locked around his neck.

Josh's lips curved. Guess Ivy trusted a few men. He heard the introductions for Del, Deke and Stella. Someone found four extra chairs for the table. Tight quarters. Instead of waiting on the others to decide the seating arrangement, he signaled Jon to take the end seat so his back was to the wall. Eli dropped into the chair on his left. When the subtle tension in Jon's body disappeared, he caught a slight nod from Eli. If Josh didn't trust these men to watch his back, he would have the same fake spiders crawling over him, too. His gaze stopped on Deke and Stella, not sure about them. He'd wait until the reports came back before relaxing his guard.

He slid an arm around Del's shoulders. "Sit down, beautiful," he murmured. He guided her to a seat across from Rio and seated himself next to her. The medic watched her, eyes narrowing.

"How long ago did you take pain meds, Del?"

She remained mute.

"Too long," Josh said.

"Don't wait. If you let the pain get ahead of you, it's harder to kill. Eat something so the meds won't upset your stomach."

"What's up with your arm, sugar?" Eli asked.

"Ran too close to Granger's bullet."

That's what he wanted to hear. Smart-mouthed attitude. Mindful of the women's recent trauma and need to rest without more nightmares, he said, "Shop talk after dinner."

From that point on, every topic introduced fell on the light side. Unfortunately for him, several discussions centered on some of his less-than-notable escapades in the military. Alex shared about the time Josh had been treed by a wild boar the size of an SUV. Rio contributed the story of his ignominious fall into a briar patch. The rest of his unit tattled about his encounters with snakes, scorpions, and aggressive children looking for American money. "Thanks a lot, guys. Way to impress Del with my abilities."

"Sorry, Major." Nate grinned. "You should have told us to stretch the truth."

Del and Ivy sported broad grins on their faces. He hated being the center of conversation, but if airing his more ridiculous exploits gave them respite from the tension and fear, Josh would take the abuse.

After finishing his meal, Rio stood and gathered his plate and utensils. "I'll send in Quinn. Del, take your meds."

She saluted. "Yes, Doctor."

He laughed and strolled out of the dining area. Josh and the rest of his team rose and gathered dishes and plates. When Del started to rise, he placed a hand on her shoulder. "We'll clean." He turned his head to eye Eli. "Ask Eli about the time one of the village elders decided he was the perfect husband for his granddaughter."

The SEAL scowled. "Dirty pool, Cahill."

"Someone else should be on the hot seat for a while."

"Sounds like a great story," Stella said, her eyes sparkling. "Talk, Eli."

He sighed. "Our team was on a mission in an unnamed hot zone."

Josh carried his dishes into the kitchen. The men scraped plates and dumped dishes in the dishwasher. Josh shook his head. "I'd rather not buy my brother-in-law a new set of plates because you clowns hate kitchen duty."

That started a whole new round of good natured ragging on him and his domestic diva tendencies. Right. He relegated that duty to Serena. Madison and Megan burned water, though they could both clean. Mom had made sure of that.

As he shut the dishwasher, Quinn's voice sounded in the dining room, followed by laughter. Josh trailed his men into the other room, held out his hand to Del. Surprise registered on her face. "Let me walk you to your room. Take pain meds so Rio doesn't come after me with a stick."

She gave him a slight smile. "Can't have that. I like your face."

"Oh, sugar, you shouldn't tell him tales. His head will grow so big he won't fit through the doorway." Eli grinned at her.

Del turned back to Josh. "Some friend." She gripped his hand and rose.

He scowled at Eli. "I'm rethinking his status on my friend list."

"Won't help." Jon's lip curled. "He's like an overgrown puppy. Thinks everybody loves him."

"Well, he is cute," Del said.

Stella laughed and Ivy shook her head. The guys threw out catcalls. Eli waited until the furor settled down before sighing. "You wound me."

"You'll survive."

Still chuckling, Josh laced his fingers through hers and escorted her to the second floor. Behind him, he heard Alex climbing the stairs with Ivy in his arms. He got the impression Alex liked carrying Ivy.

He opened the last door on the right and ushered her inside. On the king-size bed sat her backpack and Ivy's. A large dresser was against the wall by the door, an armchair in each corner, and a door leading to a bathroom. Crutches were propped against one of the chairs. "We gave you the master suite. Alex and I are across the hall. We don't want to be more than a few feet from you during the night."

Alex angled Ivy through the doorway, trailed by Stella. He placed her on the bed. "Same instructions, Ivy. Take your meds. Get some sleep."

"What if Granger finds us?"

"If he shows, we'll handle him."

"Okay if I stay with Del and Ivy?" Stella asked.

Josh's text tone chimed. "Excuse me," he murmured, grabbing his phone. He scanned the coded message from a former teammate working in intelligence. He raised his gaze, zeroed in on the marshal. "Keep your weapon close. Anything feels weird, yell. We'll update you on the plan as soon as we hash it out." He dropped a quick kiss on Del's mouth, tapped her nose, and signaled Alex to follow him.

In the hall, Alex grabbed his arm, pulled him to a stop. "We're leaving Stella alone with them?"

"Zane cleared both marshals. Let's set a trap."

"We got sent to our room while the big, bad military men plot to save our skins."

Del grinned at Ivy's outrage. "Did you really want to sit in on that discussion?" She couldn't imagine her cousin wanting to hear the war plans being discussed in the dining room. She hoped the plans were overkill, but knew better.

The men standing between them and Granger were the best. If they weren't, Ethan wouldn't trust their safety to Josh and his team. Made her wonder what the man who'd won her heart was capable of.

Her arm ached something fierce. Hated to admit Josh and Rio were right. She needed pain pills. The throb was becoming unwieldy.

Ivy wrinkled her nose. "Probably not. I would like to sleep sometime this century." She shuddered. "When I close my eyes, I see a shadowy figure stalking us with a gun."

Stella grabbed the crutches. "Why don't you get ready for bed? Even if you can't sleep, at least you'll be comfortable."

Del and Stella helped her stand. Once her cousin was balanced, she hopped toward the bathroom. When the door closed, Del turned to Stella. "We slept in clothes at the safe house."

"You were ready to run." She studied Del. "How did you get help from Josh and his friends?"

She raised her chin. "Cell phone."

A wry smile from the marshal. "I won't scold since it saved your life."

"The phone was a safety net. We weren't to use it except in an emergency. When I saw Vance on the floor, bleeding, I wasn't sure who shot him."

"You must have wondered if Burns turned on his partner." She nodded. "I'm glad you had the phone, Del." Stella sat on the side of the bed. "Why is Granger after you? I thought you didn't see him."

Del dropped beside the marshal. "He had on a baseball cap, pulled low. We saw the side of his face. We wouldn't recognize him if we ran into him on the sidewalk."

Stella frowned. "Doesn't make sense he's so determined to kill you."

"If this guy is a former soldier, how could he miss us? Our progress didn't break speed records."

"I thought about that, too," Ivy said from the bathroom doorway. She hopped back into the room, collapsed on the bed in a huff, and laid the crutches on the floor. "I know we were wobbling all over the place, but he should have nailed us."

Stella furrowed her brow. "Maybe he wanted to scare you."

"For what reason?" Del moved toward the bathroom to start her bedtime routine. "We can't identify him. Scaring us seems pointless. If he doesn't want us dead, then what does he want? That's what we should figure out."

Minutes later, she returned to the room to find Ivy asleep on top of the quilt. Del's heart clenched. Her cousin looked exhausted. Hopefully, Granger's information network wasn't good enough to find them for a few days. The longer Ivy had to recuperate, the better chance she had to escape if he located them and blew past Josh and Alex.

"Try to sleep," Stella whispered.

"What about you?"

"Night watch. I'll sleep tomorrow after you're awake."

Del crawled beneath the covers, still clad in jeans and long-sleeved t-shirt. She lay still for a few minutes, couldn't still her mind. She rolled to her back. Waited. No dice.

She sat up, shoved her hair away from her face. Cross, Del swung her legs from under the covers and stood.

"What's wrong?" Stella whispered.

"Can't sleep. Arm hurts and my mind won't shut down." She sighed, grabbed her book from the backpack.

"I'll read a while." She tiptoed across the room and eased the door open. The murmur of male voices drifted up the stairs. She considered joining them in the dining room, shelved the idea. Ivy was right. Too many details about Granger and what the Durango team might have to do to stop him. Not the best idea to join the war party.

Del eyed the open doorway across from their suite. Would Alex and Josh mind if she sat in their room to read? Probably not. She stepped into their room, closed the door to a crack and turned on the light. Twin beds with pine headboards and matching log cabin quilts occupied either side of a nightstand made from the same material. A small glass lamp sat on the table.

Perfect. Using the hall light to illuminate her steps, she turned off the overhead and substituted the soft lamp light. She studied the open bags at the foot of each bed. Two Robert B. Parker books lay on top of clothes in one of the bags. Must belong to Josh.

She propped the pillow against the headboard. After settling on top of the quilt, she relaxed, book on her stomach. Before long, she was lost in the story. She finished one chapter, began the next. Halfway down the following page, she noticed different letters on the page were underlined. Same on the facing page. Her eyebrow shot up. She'd seen sentences underlined in used books, but never individual letters. With a shrug, she continued reading.

A couple chapters later, the same pattern of underlining popped up again. What did it mean? Yawning, she closed the book, laid it on her stomach. She'd rest a minute before returning to her room.

Josh scowled at the two SEALs sitting across from him. His expression matched those on his team's faces. None of them liked the news the computer guru was giving them.

"You won't convince him to talk," Jon said. "Not only does he have training to resist interrogation, pain isn't a motivator. He has no feelings about pain. Considers it one more thing to conquer because that's what a super soldier does."

"Super soldier?" Nate shook his head.

"That's how he thinks of himself. More machine than man. He truly has no conscience."

"Why don't we just take him out?" Alex asked.

"Because I'm a cop," Josh said. "I can't sanction a kill. This isn't the Sand Box with everybody out to murder us." A noise upstairs made him pause. He held up his hand, listened a minute. Voice lower, he continued. "Granger had more than one chance to kill Del and Ivy." A world without Del didn't bear thinking about.

"Why didn't he?" Quinn asked. "If the point of this cat-and-mouse game is to take them out, what held him back?"

"Maybe he wants to know who they told," Nate said.

"For what purpose?" Alex shook his head. "Even Crazy Curt can't kill all the cops who know he's connected to Reece's murder."

"So what does he want?" Deke asked. His voice echoed the frustration boiling in all of them.

Eli downed part of the Coke in his bottle. "They know information or have something Granger's client wants."

"And if he gets what he wants?" Alex asked.

"They're dead." Jon folded his arms. "Granger doesn't care if they recognize him. He's nicknamed the Ghost for a reason."

"His client." Josh rose, paced the length of the dining room and back. "He's afraid Del or Ivy will connect Granger to him. Look, when Rod and I ran into Granger, he was tearing apart the library."

"Maybe the client wanted something hidden in there."

"Must not have found it," Eli said. "He still wants them."

"Is it possible Del or Ivy have what Granger's after?"

Josh frowned. "They didn't take anything from the crime scene except Del's computer."

"What about before that day?" Jon asked. "Were they in the house before Reece's death?"

"Probably. Mae Reece was one of Del's best customers. She collected books like some people collect fine art."

"Hardbacks?"

"She had several hardbacks. Her passion, though, was mass market paperbacks. She had thousands in the library." He paused. "What if Judge Reece was killed for something involving his mother instead of a political vendetta?"

"Should we return to Otter Creek?" Alex's hands clenched.

"No." Josh dropped into his seat again. "I'm not taking them home until Granger's under wraps. He'll use my family as leverage. Though Mom, Dad and Del's mother are out of town, my sisters are vulnerable when their husbands are on duty."

"Then we need to draw Crazy Curt down here. Should we take out an ad in the classifieds?"

"We leak our location after we're ready."

"I'll take care of that," Jon said. "Still have contacts in the right places. I'll drop crumbs." A baring of his teeth. "Make him work for the information. Too easy and he'll suspect a trap."

"And once he's here?" Quinn asked. "If we play it straight, what do we do with him?"

"Tranq him," Eli said. "We know he won't talk because we wouldn't, and we have more at stake than he does. We can make sure he doesn't talk to anybody."

Jon glanced at him, nodded. "Black site. Fortress can put him on ice."

"We'll spread the word he's dead, killed in a firefight," Eli continued. "His client needs a replacement since he still doesn't have what he's after."

"You want the job?" Jon asked, his gaze locked on Josh's.

"Oh, yeah. I'd love to meet Curt's client. Have to bring in Jordan, though." His mouth curved. "I'm out of jurisdiction. We need the feds to make this work in court."

A general round of complaints filled the room. Josh held up his hand like a traffic cop. "I hate it, too. I'd hate even worse for this dirt bag to keep hiring guns to come after Del and Ivy. If it means playing nice with Jordan, so be it."

After finalizing their plans, the men dispersed to their rooms; Jon and Eli left, promising to remain available and to scour the Internet for more information. Outside his room, Josh noticed a light shining from inside. He eased open the door. Del was asleep on his bed, a book on her stomach. He held up his hand, signaled Alex to wait. He approached the bed with silent steps.

Josh sat on the edge, heart turning over in his chest. So beautiful and so vulnerable. He cupped her cheek.

Del nuzzled into his palm. "If you're not Officer Cahill, go away. I was just getting to a really good part of my dream."

"Hope you're dreaming about me."

"Not telling unless I'm offered an outstanding bribe."

He smiled into her green eyes. "What's your price?"

"A goodnight kiss after you walk me to my door."

"I think I can accommodate you, love."

The sleepy haze cleared from her eyes. "You have a great bedside manner, Mr. Cahill."

He chuckled. "It's late. Let me walk you home, Ms. Peterson. Can't be too careful this late at night." Holding out his hand, he helped Del to her feet, kept her hand in his.

As soon as they cleared the doorway, Alex slipped into the room and closed the door.

"Is Alex okay? He didn't say anything."

"It's part of the best friend code not to interfere with the after-date kiss."

"Some date," she whispered. "Lasted all of two minutes."

He turned her so her back was to the wall beside her door. Josh tugged her into his arms. "Rain check for a longer date after Granger's behind bars?"

"Deal. Did you finish laying out the war plans?"

"Yes. It's late. You're tired. I'll tell you tomorrow." He leaned down, took his time kissing the woman in his arms. When he lifted his head, Josh nudged her toward the bedroom door. "Better go on to bed." While he still had some self-control left. Del Peterson went to his head, fast.

Hand on the doorknob, she glanced over her shoulder. "You're going to bed, too?"

He shook his head. "I'm on watch in fifteen minutes. I'll be back in a few hours. Alex is across the hall if you need him." If she felt the need to rouse Alex, it meant he'd miscalculated Granger's resourcefulness and they were all in deep trouble.

CHAPTER TWENTY-ONE

Del woke to Ivy's grousing as she hopped to the bathroom. She glanced around the room. No Stella. She rolled over, grabbed her watch. A little after six. Time to either start breakfast or help Nate feed this crowd of big eaters.

She changed clothes and dragged a brush through her hair. Down the stairs and into the kitchen, she slid to a stop. Josh was leaning against the sink, steaming mug of coffee in one hand, cell phone pressed to his ear with the other, hair wet from a recent shower. A smile lit his face when he noticed her. He put down the mug, held out his arm in invitation, a request she was happy to fulfill.

A sigh escaped as his arm snugged her against his side. He pressed a kiss to the top of her head. She angled her head up to smile at him, took a minute to revel in his presence, then eased away from his hold.

"Hold off for forty-eight hours, Jon. After that, we should have Granger on ice and we'll leak the info to his employer."

Sounded like the guys made many plans last night. Should be an interesting discussion with him. She opened the refrigerator, scanned the contents. Scrambled eggs, bacon, and biscuits sounded good. Del loaded her arms with the necessary ingredients.

As soon as the bacon started sizzling, sending an enticing aroma upstairs, Del heard footsteps overhead. She grinned. Worked every time with her brothers, too. Biscuits in the oven, she broke two dozen eggs into a bowl, mixed them with milk, salt, and pepper. She poured the concoction into a large skillet.

By the time the eggs and biscuits were ready, the kitchen overflowed with hungry men and a grumpy Ivy. She grabbed a mug, poured her cousin coffee. Ivy's first sip elicited a moan of appreciation.

Stella didn't show. She set aside a plate of food for their nighttime bodyguard. Once she'd wrapped it in plastic and placed it in the refrigerator, Del set up the plates, silverware, butter, and jam on the counter and started another pot of coffee. "Food's ready."

"Smells great." Deke smiled. "Much better than anything I put together. My wife's the chef in our house. I just man the grill."

"Yeah?" Quinn turned to stare at the marshal. "What kind of grill?"

That started a conversation on the pros and cons of gas versus charcoal grilling. Del shared a look with her cousin. Ivy rolled her eyes, sipped more coffee.

Alex grabbed a plate and piled on food. "Does Ivy like all this?" he murmured, indicating the plate in his hand.

"Yes, but not as much. She eats that amount spread over the day."

He scowled. "She's not eating enough."

Delight raced through Del. Alex Morgan was a keeper, like Josh. "You should tell her that sometime. She'd appreciate your comment."

Speculation lit his gaze. "Maybe I will." Alex set the plate down on the counter, grabbed a clean one and filled it with smaller portions for Ivy. He placed the food in front of her cousin. Ivy's face turned pink, but she smiled as though he'd given her a priceless gift. Her former boyfriend, Lee, had told her repeatedly that she needed to lose weight. Del thought her cousin was perfect. Alex agreed with her. Now to convince Ivy she didn't need to change her appearance. Maybe that job belonged to the Delta soldier.

She glanced at the guys congregated at the table. Nate wasn't there. Durango always had someone watching the area. Looked like the chef had drawn guard duty this time. She filled and covered another plate, made a return trip to the refrigerator before returning to the counter.

Josh refreshed his mug with freshly brewed coffee. He leaned over, kissed her. "Thanks for cooking for this rowdy bunch, sweetheart."

"When will you tell me the plan?"

He grinned. "Patience, love. Eat first." Josh snatched a plate from the dwindling stack, placed it in her hand. "The cook needs to eat as well. I'll tell you what I can while we clean up."

"Will you go on patrol?"

"Not until later this evening. We're on four-hour shifts. Keeps us fresh. One slip could be our last."

Not something she wanted to hear from his lips. Her appetite vanished. Del swallowed hard, tried to return the plate to the stack.

Josh gave her a pointed look. "You have to eat. Your body needs fuel. I need you in top form."

"Why?" Her gaze dropped to her feet. "You and your team are doing all the work. Ivy and I are window dressing."

"Hey." He tilted her head up so he could see her face. "What's this?" he whispered, concern growing in his eyes.

"I feel useless. You're doing everything; I'm doing nothing to help."

"You're doing exactly what I need you to do. You're keeping Ivy's spirits up, helping her maintain equilibrium in a bad situation for her."

She shook her head. "Alex's work."

"Don't fool yourself, babe. He helped Ivy in the cave, but she wouldn't have made it to shelter if you hadn't used your sharp mind. Now, come sit with me and save me from my team's clutches. I'm still bruised from the abuse I took last night at dinner."

Though skeptical, she complied. The men turned on him as soon as he sat and tucked into his meal. The quips came at Josh, hot and fast, keeping Ivy laughing. Del did her best to deflect their attention to other topics. She started conversations about fishing, baseball, and the upcoming football season, none of which she knew anything about. Her brothers loved to discuss those topics, sometimes almost coming to blows. She figured Durango could be diverted by them as well.

Josh winked at her when the men chased the topics she introduced like a pack of dogs chasing a rabbit. Within minutes, every bite of food was gone. One by one, they rose from the table and left to carry out the tasks Josh assigned. Only Deke and Alex remained.

"What do you want me to do?" Deke asked Josh. "I don't have the expertise to set traps."

"Your partner's asleep. Watch over Del and Ivy. Alex and I will be in and out, helping set traps for Granger. One of us will always be close if you and Stella need backup."

"You think Granger might show?"

"I don't put anything past Curt. However, I think it's a little soon." He shrugged. "I won't chance Del and Ivy's safety if I guessed wrong."

Deke narrowed his eyes. "I thought you wouldn't let me watch them without one of your team present."

"You were cleared last night. And, no, I'm not apologizing for digging into your background. Did the same with Stella."

A faint smile curved his lips. "Can't say I blame you. I wouldn't trust anyone I hadn't personally checked out to protect the woman I love, either."

Del blinked, expecting Josh to deny the statement. He didn't. Her heart thudded against her chest wall. Maybe he felt something more than friendship for her. She drew in a deep breath. She hoped so because she definitely felt something a good deal more than friendship for the Otter Creek police officer.

"If the intel was wrong about you and Stella, and you're in cahoots with Granger or his employer, Del and Ivy are smart. They outwitted Granger; you and Stella don't stand a chance." His eyes twinkled.

"Nice to know you think so highly of my intelligence."

"Not a matter of intelligence. It's a matter of motivation. They have it in spades."

"Fair enough." He rose. "I'll get familiar with the layout and the views from different windows. Any place off limits?"

"Don't mess with our equipment. Other than that, the place is open."

A nod and Deke left.

"What now?" Ivy asked.

"We clean and talk." Del waved at the table and the spread of dishes across the surface. She laughed at Alex's wince. "Don't like kitchen duty, Alex?"

"Not if I can avoid it."

"Well, you're helping today. I'm not the maid." She stacked plates and utensils and began loading the dishwasher. Footsteps sounded behind Del. She pivoted to see Alex set Ivy onto a barstool so she could participate in the discussion. With a scowl he trudged into the dining room and aided Josh in clearing the table. A sigh of relief from Alex as he loaded the last of the dishes in the dishwasher.

Del dropped onto a stool beside Ivy. "Enough stalling. Talk."

Josh and Alex sat across from Del and Ivy. Josh folded his arms on the counter and leaned toward Del. "We're setting multiple traps for Curt. First line of defense is motion sensors and cameras, some Granger will see, some he won't."

"How?" Ivy asked. "If he's as sharp as you say, won't he see them all?"

"Some perfect hides, a few not," Alex said. "Granger's too well trained for us to make everything obvious. Trick is to make him think he's clever enough to find them all."

"Smart." Del said. "What else?"

"Flashbangs. Hides for my team. Holes for him to step in. Clear out some brush."

"What's a flashbang?"

"Stun grenade. Brilliant flash of light and a loud noise. Disorients the enemy for a short period of time."

"Why not clear all the brush?"

"We don't want to make it impossible for Granger to approach." Josh grinned. "We're leaving the brush with long thorns. If he wants cover, and he does, Granger has to crawl through."

Ivy clamped a hand over her mouth, but not before he caught a glimpse of the grin curving her mouth.

"Why won't he go around?" Del asked.

"He'll be too exposed," Alex said. "If he gets tired of thorns and takes a chance, any decent shooter will pick him off. Granger will research before he attempts to grab you and Ivy. Won't take him long to realize Durango's here, including the team's spotter and sniper."

Ivy's eyes widened. "Who's the sniper?"

He hesitated a moment, glanced at Josh. Dread glittered in the depths of his partner's eyes. Josh sighed. Ivy seemed so fragile. What would she think of the man who toted her around the forest, the hospital and the cabin when she discovered he'd been trained to kill people? He was a world-class sniper, a fact Josh and his team would always be grateful for. Without his skills, most of them wouldn't have made it home in one piece. His friend had been rejected by his own family and survived. As tough as Alex seemed, however, Ivy's rejection was sure to hurt worse than that of his family. Still early days, but Ivy's opinion mattered to his friend.

"I am." Alex said, his voice soft.

Josh waited for Ivy's reaction. He glanced at Del. Her gaze rested on her cousin.

"And the spotter?" Ivy asked.

"Quinn." The sniper leaned forward, gaze intent. "You're okay?"

She blinked. "Why wouldn't I be?"

Alex appeared stunned. "It doesn't bother you I'm a trained killer, Ivy?"

Del's cousin frowned. "You take out the world's garbage and keep the rest of us safe. Why should it bother me?"

The sniper burst into laughter. "Why, indeed. You, Ivy Monroe, are an angel with a spine of steel."

She beamed. "I like that description. Thank you."

"It's well deserved," Josh said. "The point is we have many surprises for Granger. Hopefully, he won't evade them all. The goal is to capture him."

"And get answers from him?"

He glanced at Del, caught the uneasiness growing in her eyes. "We'll try. Chances are almost nil we'll be successful. Our plan is to bag Curt and put him on ice."

Her brow furrowed. "What good will that do?"

"Jon has connections in the intelligence community. He'll leak Curt's untimely demise and spread the name of another assassin, one who is more skilled."

Alex snorted. Yeah, Josh thought it was funny, too. The SEAL insisted the description was necessary.

"Who?" Del asked.

"Me."

Color drained from Del's face. "It's too dangerous. Granger's employer will kill you if he realizes you're undercover."

"This shadow employer will send more people until one captures you."

"Capture?" Ivy sat up straighter. "Not kill?"

"Granger had multiple chances to shoot you," Alex said. "He didn't take any of them."

"Tell my arm that," Del said, a scowl on her face.

"Your back's a bigger target. The arm injury was probably from a ricochet off the rocks. I found a gouge in the rock near the place where your blood dripped on the ground while I was outside with Ivy. Granger's a good shot, Del. He hits what he aims for. Trust me, he wasn't trying to shoot you."

"But what does his employer want?" Del asked. "The only crime we've been around is Reece's murder and the break-in."

"A good question," Josh said. "Did you take anything from the Reece place besides your laptop?"

"We were packing books, many I would have sold in the store because Mae left me her paperbacks in her will. My job was to catalog and box the hardbacks for Judge Reece to ship to his home in Washington, D.C."

"Did you take books from the library to your home?" he pressed. Granger had to be after something in that room.

"Nothing."

"What about earlier? Had you been in the house before the day the judge was killed?"

"Several times. Mae invited me over to help her reorganize the bookshelves. She didn't want to climb the ladder to move the hardbacks to the top shelves." A shadow crossed her face. "She worried about falling."

His blood cooled as suspicion surfaced. Mae Reece had fallen to her death three weeks ago. Made him wonder if Mae's death was an accident. When he had a chance, he'd ask Ethan to check into Mae's death a little deeper. "Did Mae give you anything to take home or to the store?"

"Every time I visited. Mae loved yard sales and picked up books by the bags or boxes, many times without checking the contents. Mae said she found bargains and the best surprises using that technique. She loved estate sales. She found rare first editions in one sale not long ago and added those to her library. In that same sale, she bought three boxes of paperbacks she already owned. Those she gave to me."

"When did she give you the books?"

"A few days before she died. Why?"

"Where are they?" Was it possible Granger was after those books? But why? The paperbacks weren't valuable. Something in the books maybe? A piece of paper someone might kill to retrieve? If the books had been transported to the store and sold, he might never find what Granger's boss wanted. Del's employees and his sister, Madison, were also at risk.

"At my house. Josh, you can't seriously think someone would kidnap me and Ivy over a bunch of paperbacks. They aren't worth the risk."

"Might not be the books, baby. It might be what's in the books. Have you been through any of them, noticed a piece of paper sticking out, or something odd?"

"No paper." She stopped, a thoughtful look settling on her face. "I don't know who packed our backpacks, but whoever did slipped some of Mae's estate sale books in my bag. I noticed strange underlining in the book I read last night before I fell asleep. It didn't make any sense."

"Strange?" Alex frowned. "Explain."

"People underline sentences, even whole paragraphs in their books. I do it, too. The previous owner of this book underlined specific letters."

"Did it spell names or words?" Ivy asked, her eyes sparkling.

"Not that I could tell, but I was exhausted when I came across the passages. I planned to show it to you today." She turned to Josh. "If anybody can figure out a puzzle, it's Ivy."

"My art history degree's got to be good for something," her cousin said, a wry smile on her lips.

"You said passages. You saw the underlining in more than one place?" Josh asked. Was it possible Del had the key to Granger's pursuit? A stroke of luck if that were true. The odds of her having the one book with those markings in her possession were astronomical.

"Two that I found so far."

"The pattern was the same?" Alex asked.

Del shrugged.

"Get the book," Ivy urged.

Maybe they would catch a break. As far as he was concerned, they were due one. He needed to nab Granger and his employer soon. Del couldn't be away from the store indefinitely and the longer this cat-and-mouse game dragged on, the greater the risk to his family and Del's.

She hurried out of the kitchen and upstairs.

"What are you thinking, Major?" Alex asked.

"Might be a fluke or some kid underlining for kicks."

"But?"

Josh's gaze locked on his friend. "This might be the key to taking down Granger and his boss."

CHAPTER TWENTY-TWO

Del opened the bedroom door, scanned the room for the book she'd read the night before. It wasn't on the nightstand or the floor. Where, then? The last time she had the book in her hands was in Josh's room. Maybe it fell off her stomach when she fell asleep.

She replayed the short conversation with Josh, the blistering kiss. The book had been in her hand.

On a hunch, Del turned back to the bed and knelt. Quilt flipped up, she peered underneath. Aha! She reached under the bed and snatched the Nora Roberts book. She carried it to the kitchen and dropped the paperback on the counter in front of Ivy. "Chapter 8 and Chapter 10."

"You remember the chapter numbers?" Josh asked, eyes filled with mirth.

"You know guns. I know books."

"I need paper and a pen." Ivy's gaze was glued to the page where the strange markings occurred.

"I'll get it." Alex left the room. Less than a minute later, he returned with the requested items in hand.

Her cousin copied the underlined letters on the paper, spun it around so Josh and Alex could see what she'd written. From their puzzled expressions, they didn't know what to make of the markings.

"The pattern's the same in both chapters?" Alex asked.

Ivy nodded. "I'll check the rest of the book, see if the pattern shows up elsewhere and if it's different." She paused. "This might turn out to be nothing."

"Maybe," Josh said. "It's the best lead we have, thin as it is."

"What do you want me to do?" Del asked.

"Check the rest of the books in your pack. See if more have those markings."

"You can brainstorm with me," Ivy said. "Between the two of us, we should figure out if the underlining means anything."

"Good plan." Josh stood. "We'll return later. Our cell phones are on if you need us. Find Stella or Deke if anything makes you uneasy. Don't second guess yourself, sweetheart. Trust your gut." He rounded the counter, dropped a quick kiss on Del's mouth.

The sniper trailed after Josh, paused behind Ivy's stool. "You should keep your foot elevated. Want a lift to the living room?"

Ivy blinked, looked up from her work, pen motionless in her hand. "What?"

He chuckled. "Never mind, angel. Del, make her behave."

The men grabbed their duffel bags and left.

"What did Alex say?" Ivy demanded.

"Keep your foot elevated. Where are your crutches?"

"Dining room."

Del retrieved the crutches and handed them to her cousin. "Might as well be comfortable. Let's go to the living room couch. I'll bring the book, your notes and some ice."

Ivy sighed. "My ankle is hurting."

"Want pain meds?"

"Only the over-the-counter kind. The prescription stuff will have me taking a nap within fifteen minutes."

"I'll see what I can find. Take your time. The last thing you need is to lose your balance and break a bone."

"Yes, Mother."

She smiled at her cousin's grumpiness. Guess the coffee wasn't enough to sweeten her disposition. Wonder if there was any chocolate in this place? If Meg had been here after she and Rod married, there was a stash of Snickers bars somewhere.

She searched through the kitchen cabinets, drawers, and the pantry, where she struck chocolate. Oh, yeah. Meg had been here. Del picked up a candy bar, packed ice into a storage bag, grabbed a kitchen towel to wrap it in, and scooped the book, pen and paper off the counter on the way to the other room.

Ivy was sitting with her leg stretched across the length of the couch, ankle propped on a pillow. She glanced up as Del cleared the archway. Her gaze dropped to the stash in her hands. "Chocolate!"

She handed her cousin the candy bar. "Thought you might like a chocolate chaser to round out breakfast."

"Perfect." Ivy unwrapped the treat and handed half to Del. "You need this as much as I do, maybe more for putting up with me."

"You're not that bad. We're due for a small bout of self-pity. After all, how many family members discovered a dead body, survived a break-in, were placed in protective custody, then chased from that protection to find themselves hours from home, and now wait for a killer to track them down for another shot at them?"

A quick smile from her cousin. "You're right. We deserve a treat."

"Exactly. So, eat the candy bar and let's get to work." She handed over the book, paper, and pen, then positioned the ice pack on her cousin's ankle.

When Ivy was once more at work on the strange markings, Del retraced her steps to the kitchen, put some chicken breasts in the crock pot with chicken broth to use for dinner later. She climbed the stairs again, grabbed the other five books stashed in her backpack. She was almost positive two of the books were hers. The other three might be from the estate sale.

Back in the living room, she sat at the opposite end of the couch from her cousin. Their luck, the underlinings were somebody's bored doodling, though how anyone could be bored with a Nora Roberts book was beyond her understanding. Trying to make sense of the marks would occupy Ivy for a while. She hated to let go of a puzzle until she'd solved the thing. Made her a good teacher.

Del checked the two books she suspected were hers, nodded in satisfaction when she was proved correct. No odd markings. Just the well-worn creases of much loved books and a chocolate smudge on the edges when she'd pushed the books across her kitchen table without realizing she had candy on her fingertips. The summer heat had melted her chocolate bar and left a sticky residue.

She examined the other three books. No funny markings that she noticed while skimming the pages. The inside front cover of the books, however, contained a name. Catherine Wright. Del frowned. Sounded familiar. She searched her memory, came up empty. Maybe she heard the name on the news. "Ivy, look at the inside front cover of your book. Is there a name written?"

Ivy flipped open the cover. "Catherine Wright. Is her name in your books, too?"

She nodded. "The question is, did the markings mean anything to Catherine?"

"Who's Catherine?" Deke walked into the room and dropped onto the recliner. "What did I miss?"

"Catherine Wright is the person who owned most of these books," Del said. "The book we're most concerned with is the one Ivy has. It has some interesting markings in chapters 8 and 10."

His eyebrows rose. "May I see it?"

Ivy tossed the book to the marshal. He flipped to the first chapter, stared at the underlining. Turned pages. "What do you make of the markings?"

"Code, maybe." Del bit into her Snickers bar, chewed before continuing. "Got any ideas? Ivy wrote down all the letters. We were going to put our heads together, see if we might crack the code." She winced. "Now I sound like one of my favorite detective novels."

Deke grinned. "I've heard worse. Do the letters spell anything?"

"No." Ivy held out the piece of paper. "I'm not good at word search or crossword puzzles, but the letters don't seem to mean anything."

The marshal took the paper, studied it a few moments. "What about numbers? Hand me the pen." He spent a few minutes writing on the sheet, then handed it to Ivy. "What do you think?"

Del lifted Ivy's foot from the pillow, slid closer to her cousin so they could study the paper together. Numbers ranged across the top of the letters. "The numbers represent each letter's position in the alphabet?"

"What do the numbers mean?" Ivy asked.

"That I don't know. Could be anything." He stood. "Time for another security sweep around the cabin." Deke eyed Ivy. "Stay inside, okay? Rouse Stella if something spooks you, but I won't be far. I'll be outside, searching the grounds."

"You won't go far?" Ivy's voice wavered a little.

That made Del smile. Her cousin was adding one more man to the list of trusted ones.

Deke snorted. "Not if I want to stay healthy. There's no telling what these crazy yahoos are setting up for Granger. Since they didn't tell me where their traps were located, I'd be risking life and limb traipsing in the surrounding countryside. Yell out the door or window. I'll hear you."

A nod from Ivy and she settled against the couch arm again.

"Do your rounds." Del smiled. "Ivy and I will work on the numbers."

With a nod, the marshal left.

Del slid out from under Ivy's foot. She lifted the bag of melted ice and towel and stood. "I'll bring your pain meds. Want a Coke?"

"Thanks."

She detoured to check on Stella. The marshal still slept on the library couch, pillow stuffed under her head, blanket pulled to her chin. After a stop in the kitchen, with two Cokes and pain meds in her hands, she returned to the living room. Ivy was curled on her side, sound asleep.

She tiptoed into the room to leave the Coke and medicine on the coffee table, then retrieved her books. She settled on a barstool. Del's Coke was the perfect chaser to the chocolate. She opened the Nora Roberts book and slipped back into the story.

Josh shoved the collapsible shovel into his Go bag and stood. "That's the last hole. You set?" He examined the area where they dug. They had cleared the area of their presence, so no one would know they disturbed the earth. The more information he received from Jon, the more concerned he grew. Curt didn't have anything to lose. He didn't care if he lived or died while Josh had many reasons to keep breathing, starting with the beautiful bookseller who'd stolen his heart.

"Done. What's next?"

Josh consulted his to-do list from Nate. "Tripwires and motion sensors in the fourth quadrant."

His partner stilled. "That's too far from the cabin."

"Quinn checked in. He's working one hundred feet from the cabin."

Alex grabbed his Go bag and trotted toward their last assigned area. Josh followed on his partner's heels, erasing their trail as they went. One misstep on his part and he could trip one of the surprises they'd left for their adversary.

Halfway to their destination, Josh's cell phone vibrated. He pulled it out, glanced at the screen. His stomach knotted. "Hey, sunshine. Everything okay?"

A few feet ahead, Alex skidded to a halt and turned.

"We had some excitement in the store."

Josh's free hand fisted. "What happened? Anybody hurt?"

"Granger showed up. We were pretty scared. He didn't like the answers we gave to his questions."

"What did he ask?" Though he suspected, he needed it confirmed.

"If we knew where Del and Ivy were." She drew in a deep breath, one that sounded shaky to him. "He cornered me in the office, grilled me about you and Alex."

Josh's face burned. "Did he hurt you, Maddie?" When she paused, he knew the truth. "What did he do to you?"

Alex stepped closer, a scowl growing on his face.

She gave a shaky laugh. "Nick says I'll have a shiner by day's end."

Granger would be lucky if Josh stuck to the plan and simply bagged him and put him on ice. "I'm sorry, sunshine." If Curt had gone after Megan, she would have fought dirty enough to get in some good licks. Rod had been sparring with her at the gym since they married last winter. Of the triplet sisters, Madison was the most fragile. He'd never admit he worried about her more than the others. Since Serena was pregnant, though, that might change. "What about Serena and Meg? Did Granger try for them?"

"Guess I drew the lucky straw." She sniffed. "Sorry. I'm glad he didn't try to hurt the others, especially Serena. It makes me sick to think of what he might have done if Serena had been here or if he caught her by herself."

If anything happened to his niece or nephew because of Granger, the former Delta operator wouldn't be able to run far enough or fast enough to get away from him or any of his brothers-in-law. Ethan wouldn't rest until he'd tracked the man down. Personally, Josh would rather have any man but Ethan on his trail. The former Ranger was smart and ruthless when he needed to be. "I'm glad you're okay. How's Nick holding up?"

"I've never seen him so angry. Nick wanted to kill him for hurting me. Do something about that maniac, Josh. I don't want to visit my husband in the state penitentiary."

"You have my word on that, sunshine. Are Del's employees all right?" Josh knew that would be one of her first questions when she heard the news. He motioned for Alex to move ahead and fell into step beside him.

"He didn't touch them."

"Did Granger do anything besides interrogation?"

"That's the funny thing. He made one of Del's people round up the Nora Roberts books in the used book section."

He grinned. This was good. A break they desperately needed to end this nightmare. "All of them?"

"Every one. The feds don't know what to make of that. Can't imagine he has a sensitive side and plans to read them."

Josh knew what to make of the information. Del had the key, a used book. Had to be the book with the underlining. If they could figure out what it meant, Del and Ivy would reclaim their lives and he could romance a certain lady. "Is Ethan handy?"

"He's here. Ethan declared both stores a crime scene and sent the workers home. He's lifting fingerprints and fending off Jordan's attempts to take over. I'll get him."

"Madison?"

"Yes?"

"I love you."

Another sniff. "I love you, too. Stay safe. It would break my heart to lose you."

"I hear you, sunshine. Hand the phone to Ethan."

Some fumbling, a few muffled words, then his brother-in-law's deep voice came over the speaker. "How much longer do you need?"

"Twenty-four hours. We're setting traps now."

"Run it down."

Josh told Ethan the details of their plan. When he mentioned bagging Granger and sending him to a black site, his brother-in-law grunted. "And the point for that?" More explanation followed.

"Dangerous," Ethan said. "Is it necessary?"

"To stop the boss from sending more and more men after Del and Ivy, yes."

"Bring in the feds during the second phase of this op."

"Yes, sir."

"Keep me informed. Watch your back. And Josh?"

"Yes, sir?"

"You get one shot at this. If he slips through, he's mine. Granger's not coming after my wife and child. You hear me?"

"Roger that." Josh blew out a breath. Granger didn't stand a chance against Ethan Blackhawk. No one was as good a tracker as that Ranger. His brother-in-law had been a legend in the Rangers and still received calls from law enforcement agencies to track dangerous fugitives. He didn't take as many out-of-state cases since he married Serena. The only cases he never turned down involved abducted children. The last time Josh checked, Ethan's success rate hovered near ninety percent.

"What happened to Madison?" Alex asked.

"Granger clocked her."

"She okay?"

"Black eye. Curt wasn't happy when she couldn't answer his questions." He grinned at his partner. "Guess what else he was looking for? Used Nora Roberts books."

Soft laughter from his partner. "Beautiful. So we do have what he's after. What are the odds of that happening?"

"Almost nil. About time the tide turned in our favor." He signaled Alex to step up the pace. They needed to finish their work and return to the cabin. He had a puzzle to solve and another guess at Del's first name.

Ten sensors, several hundred yards of tripwire and a fifteen-minute jog later, Josh and Alex opened the door into the kitchen. Del turned on the stool, finger to her lips. "Ivy's sleeping in the living room," she murmured.

Alex headed toward the stairs. "I'll put up my bag and check on her."

Josh stashed his bag against the wall. "How are you, baby?" He gave her a quick kiss. "And what smells so good besides you?"

"You smell chicken for tonight's dinner." She studied his face. "What happened?"

His eyebrows shot up. She caught something from his expression? Interesting. Most of his teammates couldn't read him. Alex had his facial expressions down cold, but they'd been friends since basic. No use delaying the inevitable. "Granger showed up at the store."

Her hand clamped on his arm. "Did he hurt anyone?"

"Gave Madison a black eye." Fury still burned in his gut over that. "Everyone else is fine. He probably singled Maddie out because she's my sister."

"I'm sorry, Josh. Should we go back? Maybe if we're close by he'll come after us and leave your family alone."

Color drained from her face. "What if he goes after Serena? We must go home. I can't let him hurt her or the baby."

He laid his finger across her lips. "We stick with the plan and draw him here, away from my family and yours. By day's end, Jon will start connecting with his contacts. If all goes well, by tomorrow night Curt won't be a threat." He placed his hands on the counter, one on either side of her body, caging her. "Hang in there a little longer. I promise you, Ethan will double security on the triplets. Granger won't get to them again. Besides, I doubt Curt will try for the other two. He saw Madison as the weakest of the three. Since she couldn't give him information, he'll assume I didn't tell anyone where I went."

"Would he go after Ethan, Rod, or Nick for information?"

He grinned. "That would be the biggest mistake of his life. He wouldn't get squat from them, but they would take great pleasure in making Granger regret taking them on. All three are out for blood because of Madison."

She swallowed hard and buried her face against his neck. Josh's arms closed around her. He needed a distraction or the distraught woman in his arms might dissolve in tears. He could handle a lot of things, but her crying wasn't one of them. "Hey, I thought of another name." Actually, he'd surfed the web on his encrypted phone and noticed a name that was sure to make her smile. He doubted the name was correct. The timing wasn't right for her mother to choose that name even if she did read the book series.

Her laugh was muffled against his neck. "Let's hear it."

"Delia."

She lifted her head, a smile blossoming on her face. "As in Delia Peabody, Eve Dallas' partner? Nice, but no. That's not right, either."

He let out a dramatic sigh. "Fine. Ask your question."

Her smile faded. "Is what we're feeling for each other real?"

Josh lifted a hand, cupped her cheek. "It's as real as it gets, baby. This situation with Curt and Reece's murder brought it on faster, but the interest has been growing for months." He paused, struck with a serious case of uneasiness. Maybe the feelings were on one side. Was he so out of touch with the dating scene he'd misread the signals from her? "At least on my part."

"I felt the same. However, I convinced myself you weren't interested since you never asked me on a date."

He chuckled. "I was trying to figure out a way to ask without getting shot down or causing awkwardness between us if you weren't interested." Josh sobered. "I didn't want to cause problems between you and Madison."

"I love your family. I'd never allow anything to interfere in our friendship."

"Good to know. Anything happen while Alex and I were gone?"

Del handed him the paper Ivy had been working on when they left. Over the letters were a series of numbers. "What's this?"

"Deke wrote the numbers. He wondered if the letters represented numbers based on their position in the alphabet. It made sense to us, but we couldn't figure out what the numbers meant."

Josh studied the numbers, searched for a pen. He took the numbers and moved them to the bottom of the page in the order they were listed, frowned. There was something about those numbers. Couldn't pin it down, though. "I'll run these by Jon. If it's possible to figure this out, he will. Did you and Ivy come up with anything else?"

"A name. Catherine Wright. The books belonged to her."

He stilled. Dread built until it felt like a giant ball of ice in his stomach. That is not what he wanted to hear.

"You knew her?"

"Recognize the name. She died about six weeks ago."

She dropped her hands to his and laced their fingers together. "Go on."

"She was murdered. The police don't have any idea who killed her." Man, he didn't want to tell her more even though she needed to understand the danger in pursuing his plan. The stakes were higher than he realized. Now that he knew Catherine's name, he also knew who was after Del and Ivy. Never in his worst nightmares would he have connected the name with Del. Perhaps the best course of action was to get her and Ivy out of the country. He could call in a favor with Fortress or one of his former Delta teammates. "Catherine Wright was tortured."

CHAPTER TWENTY-THREE

"Tortured?" Del swallowed hard, hoping her stomach stayed in place. "Did Granger kill her?"

"Maybe. Now that we have a connection, law enforcement might be able to place Granger in the area." He sounded doubtful.

"But it's not likely?"

"He's called Ghost for a reason."

"What did he do to her?"

"You don't need to know anything except the M.E. had to use DNA to identify her."

Del slipped out of his arms. She needed a Coke. Now. In the refrigerator, she slipped two bottles of the soda from the plastic rings, handed one to Josh before opening hers and drinking a third of the liquid.

He gulped most of his, watching her as she settled on the stool again. "I'm sorry. I should have found a better way to tell you."

"I hate that Catherine suffered. Why was she tortured?"

"Don't know for sure, but I suspect it has something to do with her gun dealer brother."

"Gun dealer? Are you talking about Xavier Wright?" A shiver raced over Del's body. She was familiar with his reputation from his frequent mentions in the press. The government was always bringing charges against him for dealing guns to terrorists. He beat every rap because the evidence was either misplaced or contaminated and useless against him.

"Unfortunately. There have been rumors the last couple months about problems in his organization. Law enforcement hasn't been able to get anyone inside to find out what's happening."

She frowned, glancing down at the paper with numbers and letters scribbled all over it. "What does the book with underlining have to do with Wright?"

"Not sure yet. I have some calls to make. Maybe we have enough pieces to start making sense of this." He cupped her face between his palms and kissed her. "Good work, sweetheart." Between one heartbeat and the next, Josh was outside.

"Where's Josh?" Alex cleared the doorway with Ivy in his arms. He set her on the stool next to Del and crossed the kitchen to the refrigerator. A minute later, he returned with two Cokes, one for Ivy, the other for himself.

"He's outside making phone calls. Ivy, Josh recognized Catherine Wright's name."

"No kidding?" She broke the seal on the cap and took a few swallows of the sweet drink. "So who is she?"

"Was." Nausea swelled in her stomach. Oh, boy. Del took a few more swallows herself before continuing. "Catherine Wright was the sister of Xavier Wright."

Clutching the bottle, Alex's hand stopped halfway to his mouth. He muttered something under his breath, pivoted on his heel and followed Josh outside.

"What's going on? Who's Xavier Wright and what happened to Catherine?"

"He's a gun dealer. The government's been trying to put him in prison for years. According to Josh, Catherine was murdered about a month ago."

Ivy's eyes narrowed. "And Mae went to her estate sale and bought her books. Do we know if the underlinings mean anything?"

"Not sure. Did Alex tell you what happened at the store?"

"Yes." She frowned. "Granger's a menace. Is Madison okay?"

"Black eye."

"Guess now we know why Granger's so desperate to catch us." She shivered, her hands wrapped around the drink. "What will he do if he slips by Alex and the rest of the guys?"

"He won't. Durango's been coming through here in waves for water and food while you slept. The traps are almost complete. One more day, Ivy, and they'll have Granger."

The sound of footsteps grew louder as somebody approached the kitchen. Del knew the marshals were close. Didn't stop her from grabbing a skillet. No point in getting a knife. If Granger had slipped by everyone and gotten into the cabin, she would have to get too close to use the knife.

Stella traipsed into the room, covering a wide yawn with her hand. "Morning," she murmured. "Or rather, afternoon. Didn't think I would sleep that long. Where's Deke?"

"Patrolling. He rolls through here every fifteen minutes." Del set the skillet on the stove top. "Hungry?"

"Starving."

"I saved breakfast for you. Would you like me to warm that or cook something else?"

"Anything, as long as coffee comes with it." She sat beside Ivy. "How are you?"

"Not bad. Rio's dogging me to keep my foot elevated with ice on it."

"Do what he says, kiddo. We need you mobile as soon as possible. What did I miss?"

Del retrieved Stella's plate from the refrigerator and removed the plastic wrap. While the food was heating, she summarized the events of the past few hours.

Stella whistled when Del mentioned the connection to Xavier Wright. "No wonder Granger is persistent. May I see the paper you worked on?"

Ivy slid the paper to Stella. The marshal studied it a moment, frowned. "The two strings of numbers are too long to be GPS coordinates. Bank account numbers?"

Del stared at the paper. "Is there any way to check?"

"We need a computer geek."

"According to Josh, Jon is a computer geek." The microwave beeped, signaling the end of the reheating cycle. Del retrieved the plate and handed it to Stella along with utensils and a steaming mug of coffee.

Stella's first bite elicited a sigh. "This is fabulous. Your handiwork, Del?"

"Nate was on patrol this morning."

"This might be the cushiest protection detail Deke and I have ever had. Maybe we should find an excuse to keep you and Ivy sequestered for a while."

"No, thanks." Del smiled. "I miss my books." She also missed her customers and the Christie Club with their busybody ways and noses for mysteries. Though she didn't think she would, Del missed her mother. She knew the Cahills would take good care of her, but she couldn't help the concern for her mother's safety. What if Granger tracked them down?

The door opened to admit Josh and Alex. "Stella." Josh smiled. "About time you woke up."

"Heard about all the excitement in Otter Creek. How's your sister?"

"She'll have a black eye to brag about, but she's fine." He waggled his cell phone. "I just talked to her husband. He made her go to the emergency room. Doc Anderson says she has a slight concussion and needs rest for a few days."

"Good thing Ethan closed the stores," Ivy said. "Now Madison won't fight Nick to return to work."

Josh snorted. "It's a crime scene. She'd lose the argument."

"We might have something else for Jon to look into," Del said. She handed the paper to Josh. "What are the chances these are bank account numbers? Or maybe one account number with a password?"

Speculation lit his gaze. "Decent. If Wright is after the numbers, it would explain Granger's determination. If Jon figures out what bank this account is in, might be interesting to know when the account was opened."

"About the time Wright's problems began?" Alex settled on the stool beside Ivy. "Maybe his sister created the issues he's been experiencing."

"Interesting supposition." Josh positioned his phone and took a picture of the paper. He typed in a quick message and hit send. "Jon will get back to us as soon as he hits on something. Excellent work, ladies." He leaned over and brushed a light kiss on Del's lips. "We know where the real brains are in this unit." He ruffled Stella's hair and tapped Ivy's nose with his finger. "Guess Alex and I should shower before we get too close." He gave a wry smile. "Hot and dirty work don't make us very pleasant to be around right now."

"Are you hungry?" Del asked.

"Do you have to ask?" Alex scanned the kitchen. "What do we have?"

"I'll make sandwiches while you shower. Roast beef sound good?"

"We'll hurry." And they were gone.

"Guess that was a yes." Stella hopped down from the stool and gathered her empty plate and utensils. "I'll help you."

By the time Josh and Alex returned, Nate, Rio, and Deke were seated around the dining room table, having washed up in the other bathroom. Del handed each a plate filled with two sandwiches, piled high with meat, cheese, lettuce, and tomato, and a side helping of chips. She figured they had lost a lot of salt sweating in the heat.

"Thanks, sweetheart." Josh dropped into a chair beside the medic and started eating. He motioned for Del to sit on his other side. While he and his unit ate their meal, Josh told them the latest news and speculation.

Nate pushed his plate aside and sat back. "Wright will be hard to pin down, Major. He lives in a fortress. Security is tight. They have double guards patrolling the grounds with trained dogs. He never goes anywhere without at least two bodyguards."

Del's body jerked. Armed guards? Trained dogs? She twisted in his direction. If Wright found out Josh was a cop, he would kill him. His team wouldn't be able to reach him in time.

Under cover of the table, Josh reached over and clasped her hand in his. "I'm not going unprotected, Nate," he said, his tone mild. "Get the estate plans and map out multiple escape routes. I need contingency plans."

"You need a miracle."

Josh's head swiveled in her direction. "You don't believe I can do this?" Disappointment gleamed in his gaze.

"I know you can. I don't want you to."

"Even though it will free you and Ivy from constant fear?"

"I'd rather be afraid and have you alive and unharmed."

"I'm not going alone." He lifted his free hand and trailed the backs of his fingers over her cheek. "I have no intention of dying on this op. I have a strong incentive to live."

"What's that?" she whispered.

"You."

"You said you're not going alone." Ivy's stare grew intense. "Who's going with you?"

"I am," Alex murmured.

Her face drained of all color. "Why?"

"Someone has to watch his back, angel. He stands a better chance coming out in one piece with a partner and we've been through similar ops together."

"And it has to be you?"

"We're partners, best friends. It was always going to be me."

"There's no other way?" Del asked.

"Sure." Deke set his glass on the table with a thud. "You can go back into protective custody. Stella and I will relocate you to a different part of the country and hope Granger doesn't break our security a second time. Of course, you wouldn't have Josh and his friends to keep you safe and there's no telling when law enforcement will catch Granger and lock him away. Could be years. That means a new identity for each of you and no contact with family or friends for the duration. In the meantime, Granger keeps hunting you. Eventually, he'll get to your family and friends to smoke you out. The real problem isn't the shooter. The problem is Wright. He's desperate enough to hire more than one hunter. As long as Granger makes progress or is close, Wright won't hire someone else. While he searches for you, your life is on hold." He paused, letting his gaze touch Alex and Josh for a few seconds. "All parts of your life are frozen. Your family and friends, though, go on without you. If you're gone from Josh's life indefinitely, Del, he might meet someone else. Do you want to take that chance?"

"Low blow, Marshal." Del sighed. Even if she might be willing to chance protective custody again, she knew her cousin couldn't live in terror for possibly years into the future. Ivy had done that for months and was just starting to rediscover herself. She couldn't do that to her cousin. Ivy might not survive a second round of virtual imprisonment with her sanity intact.

Besides, she wanted to see where this relationship with Josh headed. Del believed Josh Cahill was a very special man, one she would be honored to walk beside the rest of her life. That wasn't going to happen if she disappeared from his life for a few years. What if the marshals never found Granger? Her gaze locked on Josh's hazel eyes. She might never see him again. That thought sent a spear of pain so deep into her body, she almost couldn't breathe. No. A thousand times, no.

Del's grip on Josh's hand tightened. "Promise to be careful." She couldn't make him promise to be safe. She had to trust his partner. He and Alex had survived their dangerous missions in the military to arrive at this point in their lives. Could this be any more dangerous?

"Always," Josh said.

She gave a short nod. "What's the plan?"

After an amazing dinner of chicken and dumplings along with some kind of green bean casserole and a fruit salad, Josh held out his hand to Del. "Walk with me?"

"I should help clean."

Josh glanced around. Everyone was pitching in to clean except Ivy, who sat on a stool again, and Rio, who was on patrol. "I think they can handle it."

Del glanced at the back door, fear in her eyes. "What about Granger?"

He cupped her face and gently turned her toward him. "I'll know if he shows. We're not going far, baby. I have something I want you to see."

A quick glance at Ivy. "She needs to get out, too."

Josh bent down so his mouth pressed against Del's ear. "Alex is planning to take her to the porch swing in a few minutes. He'll take care of her. Let me take care of you."

He slid his arm around her waist and guided her to the door. A glance at Alex followed by a hand motion garnered a nod of agreement. Once outside the cabin, Josh took Del's hand and lead her to the back of the detached two-car garage. Behind the building, a faint footpath led into the forest. He followed the trail in silence. Though he didn't expect Granger yet, Josh remained vigilant as he moved deeper into the woods. Birds chirped, squirrels chattered in the distance, all giving him confidence in his assessment of their safety.

Josh led Del to a fallen log beside a burbling creek. Though only about one thousand yards from the cabin, the path they'd taken wound through the forest, around rock outcroppings and bushes, making it seem the place they sat was miles from civilization, an oasis of peace in the midst of chaos and danger.

He sat beside her, watching the water flow by at a decent pace. Must be fed by an underground spring. The drought should have dried the creek to a trickle. For the past two months, Murfreesboro's rainfall total was about the same as Otter Creek's. Though the humidity in this part of Tennessee was worse than at home, sitting in the shade beside moving water made the air temperature feel several degrees cooler.

After about fifteen minutes of sitting in silence, Del leaned her head against his shoulder. "Thank you."

"For what?"

"Letting me brood."

He pressed a kiss to the top of her head. "I did my own share of brooding when you were in protective custody. Figured you could stand a few minutes of normal."

"I'm scared, Josh."

"You have reason to be."

Soft laughter from the woman next to him. "You don't pull punches."

"Fear will keep you alert." He turned her toward him. "I want you safe, baby. I'll do anything necessary to make that happen."

Heat simmered in her gaze. "Even compromise your own safety."

"You know the answer to that." He'd already put his life on the line more than once and would again within hours. "A few more days. We will end this so you can get on with your life."

She watched him. "What role will you play in my life?"

Josh stilled. He longed to tell her how he felt, but the timing couldn't be worse. He wanted the kind of marriage with her that his parents had, the forever kind. "Any role you'll allow me. What would you like me to be?"

She started to turn away. He caught her, gently turned her back. "Tell me what you want, sweetheart." He prayed she wanted the same things he did.

"You," she whispered.

"As?"

"Mine."

A grin grew on his face. Thank God she felt the same way or was at least starting that direction. "As long as I can claim you as mine, too." Josh cupped her face between his palms and kissed her. Minutes later, he eased back. "Enough. You're a serious distraction and we should go back. The sun's going down."

Cheeks flushed, she stood. "I don't relish another nighttime jaunt through the woods. I've had my fill of running scared in the dark, waiting for a bullet to smash into my back."

In the cabin, Josh noted Ivy's pink cheeks as she sat beside his partner on the couch. His eyebrows shot up as he caught Alex's gaze. A wink was his response. Interesting. "How's the foot, kitten?" He nudged Del to sit in the recliner near her cousin and dropped to the floor at her feet.

"Rio says the swelling is down." She scowled at her foot. "I'm tired of ice packs. And I hate crutches. They make my arms hurt."

"Rio said another few days and she should be able to walk," Alex said. "He suggested a brace. Says it'll be weak for a while."

"Do what he says, Ivy. Your ankle will heal faster if you follow his advice."

"Where is everybody?" Del asked.

"Nate and Quinn are keeping watch. Rio and Deke are asleep," Alex said.

"Stella?"

"Monitors," Ivy said.

Josh glanced at his watch. Not late enough to suggest Del and Ivy get some sleep. He suspected they wouldn't have a full night's rest. None of his team planned to sleep tonight. If Granger didn't show overnight, Fortress would keep watch during the day tomorrow. "We have a few minutes before you should rest. Tell me about your family."

Pressed against his back, Josh felt Del stiffen at his question to Ivy. He reached back and patted her foot. Yeah, he knew the subject was touchy for her cousin. Still, she needed to get her mind off the circumstances and it would give Alex a chance to learn her family background. Couldn't be any worse than his partner's family. They were something. He'd told Del a slice of Alex's background. The rest would be up to his partner to share.

Ivy's eyes darkened. She glanced at Alex, bit her lip.

"General stuff, Ivy," Josh encouraged. "I want to know you better." At those words, Del's muscles relaxed. That pleased him. She never had to worry he'd embarrass Ivy. He liked her cousin. She had backbone hidden beneath fear. With enough time, the fear would ease and the real Ivy would shine through, the one he'd caught glimpses of in the last few days.

"My parents live in Belle Meade. It's the part of Nashville where people with old money live."

He thought about her word choice. "Did you grow up there?"

She nodded.

A telling statement. Ivy was from old money, just like Alex. Both rejected by their families. "Any siblings?"

"Only child." A sad smile. "Sometimes I think my mother became pregnant by accident. She and my father are very polite to each other. Their marriage was a society match."

"How are you and Del related?"

"Mothers are sisters," Del said. "Marigold and Dahlia Whitmore."

"They go by Mari and Dee," Ivy added.

"What about your side of the family, Del?" Alex asked. "Brothers or sisters?"

"Brothers. The rest of our families had a mixture of boys and girls."

"Were there any siblings besides Mari and Dee?"

"Two more sisters, Rose and Peri."

Alex blinked. "Perry? As in Perry Mason?"

Del laughed. "Short for Periwinkle."

"What about your brothers?" Josh asked. "What are their names and what do they do?"

"Evan is a lawyer, Grant a contractor. Malcolm owns a gym. What about your family, Alex? Do you have brothers or sisters?"

"One brother. Porter. Dad's a huge country music fan."

"What do your parents do?" Ivy asked.

Behind Josh, Del drew in a quick breath. Again, he patted her foot. She must not have told Ivy about Alex's family. Alex could handle it. He'd been fending off questions for fifteen years.

"My father is Senator James Morgan. Mom's name is Cynthia. She's heavy into Washington, D.C. society."

Surprise registered on Ivy's face. "I've heard stories about your parents and brother in the news. Why haven't they said anything about you?"

"They disowned me fifteen years ago, Ivy. I haven't spoken to them since I enlisted in the Army."

She laid her hand over his arm. "I'm sorry, Alex. I didn't mean to hurt you."

He leaned over and kissed her forehead. "Don't let it bother you, angel. I don't."

Over the next hours, they covered everything from fishing to books to movies. Nice to know Del and Ivy shared many of the same interests with the exception of outdoor activities. Reminded him of his mother and sisters.

When the grandfather clock struck eleven, Josh stood and pulled Del to her feet. "You and Ivy need rest."

"What about you?"

He smiled. "Not for a while."

Alex rose, plucked Ivy from the couch. "Need a drink before I take you upstairs, angel?"

"Water."

"Kitchen, then second floor." He glanced over his shoulder at Josh. "Meet you here after I wake Rio and Deke."

"He's really good with her," Del murmured after Alex had left the room. "I wish Ivy had met him sooner."

"She's healing." He squeezed her hand. "Come on." He walked her to her room. Conscious of Alex's imminent appearance, he kissed Del and nudged her inside the doorway.

"What if Granger comes?"

"I'll let you know if the perimeter security is breached. Rest, beautiful." Hearing footsteps behind him, something he knew was deliberate as his friend normally moved in absolute silence, Josh turned and strode down the hall. He met Alex and Ivy at the top of the stairs. "Night, kitten." He tweaked her nose as he passed.

At the bottom, he turned right and headed for the security room. Stella sipped on a Coke as she scanned the monitors. "All quiet?" he asked.

"A couple deer, a wolf. Nothing on two legs."

"Won't last."

"You're that positive he'll show?"

"I would."

She shot him a glance, returned her attention to the screens. "How long?"

"Three, four hours. Heaviest part of the sleep cycle."

A shower kicked on upstairs as Alex stepped through the doorway. "Any word from Jon or Eli?" he asked.

"Should be here any time." At that moment, Josh's text signal dinged. He glanced at the message. "Jon's at the back door. Says he has something for us."

The Navy SEALs were clad in black. Just as in Delta, nothing on Jon Smith and Eli Wolfe reflected light as they stepped inside. Jon carried a small duffel bag in one hand. "Communication gear from Fortress," Jon said. "Brent has a full team on standby. They'll cover the roads if Granger gets past us."

"Thanks." If they needed Fortress to shut down the roads, it meant his team was down and Granger had captured Del and Ivy. He couldn't let that happen. Josh knew if Granger took Del and Ivy to Wright, they would be killed as soon as the arms dealer got what he wanted. "As soon as Granger breaches the perimeter, signal Fortress to get in position. Under no circumstances is he to escape with the women."

"Roger that," Eli said. He took the bag from Jon and unzipped it. "The gear is similar to what we used in the Teams, but better." After demonstrating and testing the equipment, he and Jon slipped into the night, their own headgear in place, promising to signal when they were in position.

Josh doused the lights on the first floor and turned to his partner. "Now we wait."

At 2:30 a.m., the motion sensor on the first perimeter was triggered.

CHAPTER TWENTY-FOUR

Josh cleared the security room door seconds after the alert signaled on his wrist monitor. "Where?" he asked Stella. Staring over the marshal's shoulder, he studied the screens. One showed a figure moving through the forest, picking his way with care. Satisfaction bloomed in his gut. Nice to know his instincts were still good two years after leaving the military.

"Quadrant 4." She glanced over her shoulder. "This guy is good, Josh. He hasn't tripped any of the traps yet. How can he see? It's pitch black out there. I stepped outside a few minutes ago while Alex spelled me. I couldn't see anything."

He watched the figure a moment. Definitely a man. "NVGs." He sensed movement behind him and turned.

"Not for long," Alex murmured. "Thunderstorm rolling in fast." His words were punctuated by a crack of thunder and lightning flash.

Josh blew out a breath. Great. Not only could they not use NVGs with the lightning, footing would become tricky as the rain fell, turning the ground into a slippery mud bath.

Granger would be just as blind in the night as Durango and Fortress.

He keyed the mic on his headset. "Breach in quadrant 4. Execute phase 1."

Whispered responses acknowledged his orders. He squeezed Stella's shoulder. "Keep track of him. Update his position in five-minute intervals unless something changes." Maybe they'd get lucky and Granger would be caught in one of their traps. Unlikely, but possible given the weather conditions.

Deke entered the security room and leaned down to observe the monitors. "That him?" He turned back to Josh.

"Let's catch him and find out." He inclined his head toward the shoulder holster and weapon the marshal wore. "How many magazines do you have?"

"Two."

"Got a third one?" Alex asked, his voice soft.

Deke looked startled. "Will I need it?"

"Get it." The sniper turned his attention to Stella. "Same for you, Stella. If Granger gets past all of us, you'll need every bit of fire power you have to stop him. You can't let him take Ivy and Del. He'll kill them as soon as Wright gives the word."

The female marshal swallowed hard, glanced at her partner. "Watch the screens, Deke." She hurried from the room.

Deke eyed Josh and Alex in turn. "Level with me. Is this guy as bad as you're making him out to be?"

"Worse." Josh signaled Alex to grab his gear. He had one more thing to do before he joined his partner. "We're depending on you, Deke."

"We won't let you down. You have my word."

"I'll hold you to it." Josh hated to leave Del and Ivy in the protection of the marshals, even knowing they were professionals. Still, they were no match for Granger. At least if Durango went down along with Eli and Jon,

Granger would be injured. No way all those trained operatives wouldn't do damage to the Ghost. Might be the only edge Deke and Stella would have. "You'll only get one chance, Deke. Don't miss."

A solemn nod from the marshal before he turned back to the computer screens to track their quarry.

Josh took the stairs two at a time. At Del's door, he knocked and pushed the door open. Two figures sat up.

"What's wrong?" Del asked.

"Perimeter breach. You and Ivy need to dress, fast."

"Already ahead of you. We slept in our clothes. We just need to put on shoes."

A soft chuckle escaped. Beautiful and brainy. Couldn't ask for more than that. "Good job, both of you."

"Josh?"

"What is it, kitten?"

"I still can't run and I'm not very fast with those crutches."

"If Granger slips past us, Deke and Stella will get you out. We need Alex in the field. You okay with Deke carrying you if it's necessary?"

"I'll be fine. I promise. Make sure Alex doesn't worry, okay? I don't want him distracted." Her voice quavered a little at the last.

"He'll know, Ivy. Do everything the marshals tell you." A brush of fabric told him Del slid from the bed. Her feet pattered across the floor in his direction. He opened his arms and she slipped her arms around his waist, head nestled over his heart. Probably not comfortable for her since he had on a bullet-proof vest. Josh dropped a quick kiss on her lips. "I need to go. Alex is waiting. No lights. It will shine like a beacon and draw Granger right to this room."

"No lights. Be careful, Josh."

"Always." A last squeeze, then he forced himself to let go and slipped from the room.

Del turned away from the empty doorway. "Where are your tennis shoes, Ivy?"

"Here by the bedside. Del, what are we going to do?"

"Everything Deke and Stella tell us to." She bent over and grabbed her cousin's shoes. "Do you need help with these?"

"No. Aren't you scared?"

"Terrified. We got away from him before. We'll do it again."

"Are you kidding? He was playing with us. You heard Alex. The guy shouldn't have missed us in the forest. Maybe he's come back to finish the job."

"You're not helping. I'm ready to barf as it is."

"I wish Alex were here."

"They need him. Based on what I heard from the rest of the guys, Alex is the best at what he does. With him watching their backs, the team has a better chance to come through this in one piece." Though that was important, to Del the most pressing reason for Alex to man his post was his ability to protect Josh. An invisible band squeezed her chest. Now that she'd gotten to know Josh, losing him would break her heart. He might not realize it, but there was no one else for her. She was depending on Alex and the rest of Durango to bring Josh Cahill back to her.

Ivy grabbed her tennis shoes and started tugging them on and tying her laces. "I know. Did Josh say anything else before he left?"

"No lights and to do what Deke and Stella tell us to."

"If we balked, they would bully us for our own protection." Finished tying her laces, she sat up and grabbed her crutches. "Let's go."

"Where are you going?"

"Down to the first-floor security room. At least we'll see what's happening." Ivy hopped toward the door. "There's the additional benefit of being on the first floor if

Granger does get past the guys." Her breath hitched. "Makes it easier for Deke to haul me out the nearest door or window."

Del laughed softly as she grabbed their backpacks in case they had to make a run for it. Wouldn't do to let Granger have the book. Something told her that might be a huge mistake. "Lead the way. Take your time. If you fall, you might break a leg this time."

Ivy stumbled, did a hop and skip combination. She glared at Del. "Shut up. Now you're the one who's not helping."

They managed to navigate the stairs without more than a couple minor scares. They both blew out a breath when they stepped onto the first floor. Ivy turned toward the security room. "I'll follow you in a minute."

Ivy skidded to a stop. "Where are you going?"

"To get the paper and the book. I left them in the kitchen."

"Hurry."

She felt her way to the kitchen. Deep shadows messed with her depth perception and generally gave her the creeps. Finally, she reached the entrance to the kitchen. A flash of lightning lit the room like the noon sun for a few seconds. Her gaze zeroed in on the white paper and Nora Roberts book on the counter. Del swept both into her backpack. If she and Ivy were taken, she'd use everything at her disposal to safeguard her cousin. All she had to do was convince Granger she would give him what he wanted if he left Ivy behind. Her cousin was vulnerable. No matter what, Del couldn't let him take Ivy.

A loud rumble of thunder made her jump. Time to get into the security room. She was spooked. Another flash of lightning sent her scurrying from the kitchen and racing down the hall, backpacks in hand. She slid around the corner. Both marshals turned to glance at her. "What's happening?"

"Granger's here," Deke said, pointing at a motionless green blob on one screen. "The others are ours."

"How far is he?" Ivy asked.

"Half mile. Closing fast." Stella touched her mic, gave another position update.

Del leaned the packs against the wall near the door. "And our guys?" Fear for Josh beat like a living thing under her skin. She knew he would confront Granger.

"Closer to Granger than to us." Deke shifted the camera view, tracking Granger or whoever that was. "That was the point of their plan. Confront Granger before he got into the cabin. Don't want him that close to you."

Del dropped into the nearest chair, gaze glued to the screens. One of the men on the screen gave a series of hand signals. She leaned as close as she could without obstructing the Stella's view. That had to be Josh. Tension ratcheted up several degrees. From the way the men fanned out, they were closing in on the intruder.

CHAPTER TWENTY-FIVE

Rain poured down in a blinding waterfall. Good thing the Fortress comm system was waterproof. Josh signaled Alex to find high ground. Quinn followed, close on his heels. Nate and Rio swept in from either side, flanked his position. They moved in tandem toward Granger.

In his ear, Stella relayed the Ghost's position at one-minute intervals. At the coordinates he and Alex had agreed would be ideal positioning for the sniper to be the most effective, Josh stopped, keyed his mic. "In position."

"Roger that," came Alex's response.

"Still on the move," Jon whispered. He rattled off the coordinates.

Josh estimated the distance to his present position. Granger was slowing. His lips curled. Granger knew he was out here. The rain hampered his senses. All the better to catch Granger off guard. No way Granger caught all the cameras, not in this deluge. Right now they had the upper hand. His unit knew where Granger was while the Ghost suspected Durango was in the wet darkness.

He snorted. Granger wouldn't know their location until his men revealed themselves. Josh trusted his men, knew from long months in the field how good they were.

"In position," Alex murmured.

"In position," Quinn added.

"Copy." Josh signaled Rio and Nate to take cover. He moved behind a stand of trees and waited. Five minutes passed. Ten. At the thirteen-minute mark, Jon signaled he and Eli were in position. Anticipation zinged through his veins as a shadowy figure moved from one source of cover to another. Yeah, good luck with that. Durango thinned the coverage about 15 feet ahead. Granger would hate being in the open. No choice if he wanted Del and Ivy. He wasn't getting near them. Even if Josh went down, his team and the SEALs knew the stakes.

At the edge of the clearing, the black-clad figure stopped. Soft swearing reached Josh's ears. He mentally urged Granger to take a chance. The figure hesitated, eased two steps closer. Good enough. Josh moved in silence, not that it mattered at that moment. A rumble of thunder covered any noise he might have made. "That's far enough."

The figure froze. "I just want to talk, Cahill."

Right. Fury rose in Josh's gut. Was this the man who had terrorized Del and Ivy for days, killed Judge Reece and maybe Mae? "So talk."

The intruder took a step forward. "Your woman has something that belongs to my employer. He wants it back. I get that, I'm gone. You won't hear from me again."

"The man pulling your strings will simply let the women walk?" Fat chance. Granger must think he was an idiot. Xavier Wright couldn't afford to let Del and Ivy live. Law enforcement would love any excuse to take down the gun runner.

"I'll tell him I killed them."

Josh stared at him. Granger had researched him, knew he was a cop. Did he think the promise of safety for his girlfriend would blind him to the law? Josh couldn't let the Ghost slide back into the mist and disappear again. No telling how many more people would die if he did. "He'll want proof."

Lightning flashed at that moment and lit the area enough for Josh to ID the man feet from him. Curt Granger. Disgrace to the Delta name. Seeing Granger behind bars would bring great satisfaction.

Granger shrugged.

Ice water surged through his veins. Curt would provide two bodies for his employer. A casual shrug as he planned to murder two other women and claim they were Del and Ivy. "I'm a cop. I can't turn my back while you murder two innocent women."

"You're a bleeding heart, Cahill. Too soft. No matter. You should take my offer."

"Threatening me?"

"A fact. Give me what I want and I'll disappear."

"And if I don't?"

In his ear, Alex murmured, "Don't react. He's trying to make you lose control. If you do, you're dead."

Josh mentally took a step back and shoved his emotions behind wall of ice. He knew the game Granger played. Josh had too much at stake to lose at mental chicken.

"I'll kill you and your men, then take your woman and, after I have the information I need, gut her like a fish." The sound of the last word hadn't died in the night when Granger moved.

Though Josh realized Curt was planning to attack, he was unprepared for the burst of speed. For such a beefy man, Granger was on Josh before he could draw in a breath. One second he was standing, the next he was on his back fighting for control of the knife in Curt's hand. He hadn't seen him pull the weapon. He shot his left arm between Granger's knife arm and his head. Josh wrapped his arm around Granger's, his hand grabbing the shirt at the back of the guy's neck to hold him in place. He bucked his hips up, knocking him off balance. Again he bucked, using his right leg, and flipped Granger onto his back, knife arm still pinned. Josh shoved his right forearm into Granger's neck and leaned with all his weight. Curt punched Josh in the ribs, but the punches were ineffective because of the bullet-proof vest. More resistance from the assassin, but the struggles were becoming weaker. Twenty seconds after Josh had trapped Granger's knife arm, the man slid into unconsciousness.

Breathing hard, he sat back, wiped mud from his face. The rain finished what he missed. Nate and Rio moved in from the trees, weapons in hand. In Josh's ear, Alex said, "Good job, Major."

"Hold position. Make sure he didn't bring friends."

"Copy."

"Copy," Quinn added.

Nate aimed his weapon at the downed former Delta operative. "Covered, Major."

Josh stood.

"Injuries?" Rio asked.

"Left arm."

The medic shifted position. He whistled. "Need a new shirt and some stitches."

"I can live with that."

"Your lady won't be happy."

Josh grunted. Since Granger's plan to slice his throat failed, he counted a cut on his arm a victory. He keyed his mic. "Jon, move in."

"Roger that. One minute."

Rio dropped his bag on a rock, keeping it out of the mud pit that used to be a clearing. "I'll wrap this for now.

When we reach the cabin, I'll give you a local and stitch you up." He ripped Josh's shirt sleeve.

Jon and Eli trotted into the clearing, saw an unconscious Granger on the ground.

"Very nice," Eli said. "And here I was hoping the SEALs could ride to Delta's rescue." He grinned. "Just like old times."

"Their sniper has you in his sight. Don't make him angry." Jon eased his pack to the ground, unzipped the inner pouch. He pulled out a hypodermic needle. "Let's make sure this clown stays out." He inserted the hypodermic into Granger's vein and depressed the plunger. "This stuff is guaranteed to keep Granger unconscious for about 12 hours. More than long enough to transport him to Fortress's black site."

"Hate to think I was injured in the line of duty only for Fortress to lose him. He won't be happy when he wakes."

"Don't worry." Eli knelt beside Granger and methodically searched him for weapons. "Brent is heading the team escorting Curt to his temporary home." By the time he finished searching, a pile of knives, guns, grenades and a little C-4 along with detonators lay at Eli's feet. "When will you call in the feds?"

"As soon as Fortress is out of here. He's a hard case about mercenary groups."

"Incoming," Alex murmured in Josh's ear.

"This is Maddox," a deep voice rumbled over the comm set. "Coming in soft."

"Copy," Josh replied.

"Hold still." Rio tugged him around by his vest. "If I don't cover this, your lady will freak."

"You think she won't insist on seeing the injury?"

"Probably. At least we can prepare her. I'd rather she not faint. She and her cousin have been through enough."

He and Alex weren't the only ones feeling protective of Del and Ivy. Durango acted as though they'd adopted the two women. Suited him fine. The more eyes on the cousins the better, at least until Xavier Wright was behind bars.

Five men, all clad in black, strode into the muddy clearing. A buzz-cut blond separated himself from the others. He stared down at Granger, a sneer on his face. "Curt Granger. Look forward to a long talk with him."

"Why?"

"We've crossed paths several times over the years. He's been a pain in my backside since I started Fortress." He turned, held out his hand to Josh. "Brent Maddox. Nice job on this op."

"Thank you, sir. I appreciate you letting us borrow the comm system."

"Sweet, isn't it? Paid too much money for it." Maddox motioned two of his men to haul Granger up. One of them slung the unconscious man over his shoulder like a sack of grain and started back the way he'd come. Two of his teammates flanked him, weapons in hand. One remained behind, waiting for Maddox.

"Worth every penny."

"Think so, huh? You'll get to play with that and other very cool toys if you work for us."

Josh grinned. "Bribery, sir?"

"If it gets me what I need. Fortress needs you and your team, Josh. Your unit operates like a well-oiled machine. You would be a huge difference maker. Save a lot of lives."

"After Del and Ivy are safe, we'll talk."

"I'll hold you to that." Maddox turned on his heel, eyed Eli and Jon. "Keep me posted. I'll have men ready to assist in the next phase."

Eli saluted his boss.

With a wave, Maddox joined his remaining man and followed his team into the rainy night.

Josh keyed his mic. "Alex, Quinn, we clear?"

"Affirmative," his partner said.

"Head to the cabin."

"Copy."

He signaled Nate, Rio, Eli and Jon to follow as he headed back to Del.

On the computer screens, two men left the clearing. "What's happening?" Del demanded. She wished for a communication headset herself. She hated being left in the dark. Why couldn't the cameras come equipped with sound capability? That would have brought her blood pressure down at least a dozen points.

"Our guys are coming back to the cabin," Stella said.

"Everybody okay?" Ivy asked.

Stella exchanged glances with Deke.

"What is it?"

"One injury." Deke's gaze shifted to Del.

Her heart sank. Josh was injured? "How bad?"

"Cut. Needs stitches." He shrugged. "He's walking so it's not too bad."

"How was he injured?"

"Granger had a knife. He went after Josh. Took your boyfriend about a minute to take him down."

Ivy frowned. "I thought Granger was scary good at this soldier stuff."

"Josh is better," Stella said.

"How long before they're here?" Del asked.

"Maybe ten minutes," Deke answered.

"Should I brew coffee? They've been in the rain a while."

"Sandwiches, too. They burned a lot of energy. They'll be starving."

Seems like all she'd done was cook since this nightmare began. Maybe when Wright and Granger were behind bars, Josh would take her out to eat. She hurried to the kitchen. The end was in sight. Before long, she would be in her store, ordering and sorting books. She missed the smell of Madison's coffee and the scent of books, craved the thrill of opening boxes of new books and shelving them for others to browse and buy.

Del made several trips to the refrigerator to retrieve bread, condiments, several types of lunchmeat, cheese, lettuce and tomato. She arranged things so it was easy for the men to grab and make their own. She started the coffee pot and brought out Cokes for those who preferred a cold drink.

As she set the last Coke on the countertop, the back door opened and the men streamed into the kitchen, Josh the last one through the door. Water dripped on the floor as they unloaded packs and rifles.

Deke walked in, towels in hand. "Here, dry off with these." He tossed one to each man.

Del stepped forward, stopped, gaze fixed on Josh. With him at the back of the pack, she couldn't reach him without making a spectacle of herself. The rest of his team must have noticed her hesitation because they shifted position, leaving an aisle for her.

A slight smile curved Josh's lips. He dropped the towel and spread his arms.

That was all the encouragement she needed. Del raced into Josh's arms. In a distant part of her mind, she registered her clothes absorbing water, but she didn't care. She buried her face against his neck. "I was so afraid for you," she whispered.

"I'm okay, sweetheart."

"Granger?"

"Out cold and out of our hair. Fortress will keep him under wrap until this op is finished."

"Hope they lock him up and lose the key."

He tightened his grip around her. "Got a mean streak, do you?"

Alex dropped his towel. "Where's Ivy?"

A thump sounded in the hall. The woman in question hobbled through the doorway. "Here. You okay?"

He grinned. "Wet and hungry."

"I can't help the wet part," Del said, still holding Josh. "The coffee is hot and food's ready."

"Perfect, sugar," Eli said. He reached over and ruffled her hair. "Josh, can one of you drive us to our SUV after we eat? I don't want another drenching."

"I'll take them, Major." Nate toweled his short hair. "Rio needs to work on your arm."

At that, Del tried to pull away from Josh, but he refused to let go. "I want to see."

"In a minute."

"How bad is it?"

"Needs stitches." He tipped her face to his. "It's not your fault. The first rule in a knife fight is you will get cut. The key is to keep the injury from a vital organ or a major artery. No matter how bad it is, the injury could have been worse."

Granger could have stabbed him, perhaps killed him. She reminded herself again that this is what Josh had been trained for. Either she trusted him or she walked away. Walking away was not an option. "Do you want to eat first or have Rio work on your arm?"

"Arm." Rio grabbed his bag from the floor. "Main bathroom. Light's better in there."

"Come with me." Josh left his right arm around her waist. "You can hold my hand. I'm afraid of needles."

More than one bark of laughter broke out in the kitchen. Yeah, she didn't believe that one either.

Rio pointed at Ivy. "Park yourself somewhere, missy. I don't need another patient."

"Hey, I'm not a toddler. I can take care of myself." Her cousin's voice bridled with outrage at the command from the medic.

Alex picked her up and set her on the nearest barstool. "Make two sandwiches for me while I grab some coffee. And make yourself one while you're at it. You can't weigh more than one hundred pounds soaking wet. You're gorgeous, angel, but you need to gain some weight."

Del saw the blinding smile on Ivy's face as she and Josh turned into the hallway and headed upstairs. "Alex is good," she murmured. "He's letting Ivy take care of him while he takes care of her."

"Yeah? I taught him all he knows about sweet talking women."

This time it was her turn to laugh.

In the main bathroom, Rio placed his bag on the closed the toilet lid. The medic washed his hands, then pulled out a pair of latex gloves. Josh tugged Del back into his arms.

She frowned. "Won't I get in Rio's way?"

"Nope." Rio unwrapped the arm and gently eased bloody gauze from the cut. "Keep your gorgeous eyes on his face. Don't want you passing out and hitting your head."

"Quit flirting with my girl."

"Just laying the groundwork for when she tires of you and wants someone better."

"Not going to happen. I'm making it my mission in life to keep her guessing."

Del tried to lean around Josh to see the extent of the damage. "Is it bad?"

Josh nudged her back into place. "You heard him, sweetheart. Look at me."

Rio wiped Josh's arm with an alcohol pad and picked up the hypodermic needle he'd prepared. "Little stick," he said.

She kept her gaze glued to his. This close, she would have seen any telltale flinch at the prick of the needle. There wasn't one. So much for him being afraid of needles. Rio produced more alcohol swabs and created a growing pile of soiled wipes.

"Tell me if you feel this." Rio reached around the back of Josh's arm and did something Del couldn't see.

"Just pressure."

"Perfect." He stripped off the gloves and grabbed a new pair. "A couple stitches might sting, Josh. Cut's deeper on one end."

"Go ahead." Josh's gaze dropped to Del's lips. "Where would you like to go on our first official date?"

"Picnic by the lake."

"And if it rains?"

"Movie."

Josh moved closer until his lips brushed against hers. "What kind of film? Please tell me you don't want a sob story romance."

"Action or adventure with a romantic subplot are perfect."

"If we can't find a movie in the theaters we agree on?"

"I have several in my DVD collection that work." She shared a series of light kisses. "I want dinner out first."

His eyes twinkled. "Tired of cooking for me already?"

"I've been cooking for a regiment for over a week. There's also the added benefit of warning off the other women in town. I've overheard more than one plotting your downfall. There's a line forming to entice you into marriage."

Rio leaned closer to his work. "I need more light for these last two. Hug your girl close and shift toward the sink."

With his free arm, Josh hugged her tight to his chest as he moved. He dropped a kiss on her neck which caused a shiver to wrack her body.

A minute later, Rio straightened. "I put on a water-resistant bandage. Try to keep that arm dry, though. I'll check it tonight for signs of infection. Let me know if you need pain meds when the local wears off." He gathered the trash he'd created, picked up his bag and left the room without a backward glance.

Del wrapped her arms around Josh's neck and leaned in for a long kiss. When she came up for air, she whispered, "I'm glad you're okay."

His gaze was solemn. "This won't be the last time I'm injured on an op. Hazards of the job."

"I'll handle it."

He studied her face a moment, appeared satisfied with what he saw. "Yeah, I believe you will. Come on. Let's join the others. I'm starved."

Her hand wrapped in his, Del trailed him down the stairs. Her gaze dropped to the bandage, a stark white against his tanned skin. From the shape, the cut was a long one. Almost over, she reminded herself. Then they could heal and move forward.

In the kitchen, Durango and the SEALs wolfed sandwiches and chips. The coffee pot was empty and only two Cokes remained on the counter.

"Sit beside me, sugar." Eli patted the chair to his right. "You're a far sight prettier than all these rowdy guys. You and Ivy brighten up the place."

Ivy rolled her eyes, reached for the last bite of sandwich on her plate.

Del grinned. Eli Wolfe was a charmer.

"Are you hungry?" Josh asked. He grabbed a plate and assembled sandwiches for himself.

"No, thanks. I'll brew a cup of tea."

His gaze darted to her face. "I'll take care of it. Go sit with Eli."

"You're the one injured. I should take care of you."

"Come sit with me. I'm lonely," Eli complained.

Josh scowled over his shoulder. "Watch it, frog boy."

A chuckle was his only answer.

"What kind of tea, babe?"

She sighed. Alex wasn't the only man in this room great at taking care of those who mattered to him.

"Chamomile mint." The sooner she gave in, the sooner Josh would sit and fuel his body.

She dropped into the seat beside Eli. One by one, Durango finished their meals, bussed their own plates and cups or bottles, and filed out to change clothes and rest.

Josh slid a steaming cup of tea in front of Del and sat beside her. He downed one sandwich before he asked Eli, "You guys staying here?"

"No." Jon exchanged a glance with his partner. "We'll return before 10:00."

"Wright will expect a report from Granger within the next 24 hours."

"One phone call to leak information."

"Do it."

A nod. "Be ready, Josh. We'll have to move fast when Wright contacts."

"Sure this is how you want to play it?" Deke asked, his expression somber.

"Only way. I'm finishing this. My family and Del's are at risk. That's bad enough, but I refuse to live looking over my shoulder, wondering if another one of Wright's goons has us in his crosshairs."

"Cut off the snake's head, the body dies?" Eli asked.

"That's the plan."

"Let's hope you haven't miscalculated," Jon said softly.

CHAPTER TWENTY-SIX

Josh lifted the cell to his ear, listened to the phone ring on the other end. He leaned against the outside cabin wall, watching the sun peek over the horizon, shooting strands of golden light over the terrain and bathing the landscape in peace after the chaotic night.

"Blackhawk."

"How's Serena?"

A retching noise came through the phone's speaker. Josh flinched. Oh, man. "Guess that answer's my question."

"I don't know what to do for her," Ethan said, frustration evident in his voice. "The only thing I've been able to do is keep her from collapsing on the bathroom floor. The nausea is wiping her out. This baby might be an only child. I'm not sure I can watch her go through this again."

Frowning, he thought about all those times the triplets had shared stomach bugs. "Have you tried Saltine crackers and Coke? Mom used to give her that when she was sick as a kid. Seemed to be the perfect combination to settle her stomach."

"She can't have caffeine," Ethan snapped.

Josh blinked, pulled the phone away from his ear to stare at it. Who was on this phone? Couldn't be his extremely intelligent boss. Maybe Serena's morning sickness had rattled Ethan's brains. "So get her the kind without caffeine. Just make sure it's not a diet drink. Mom found out the hard way diet drinks made Serena's nausea worse."

His brother-in-law blew out a breath. "Hold on."

A few muffled words later, Josh heard a door slam.

"Don't say it." Ethan's SUV motor cranked.

Josh grinned. "Wouldn't think of it."

"Give me some good news while I race to the store."

"Hey, if I raced anywhere, I'd get a ticket which you would happily require me to pay."

"Shut up. Sit rep."

Yeah, Ethan Blackhawk was a complete wuss when it came to his petite wife. Josh hoped Serena had a girl because he couldn't wait to see his tough brother-in-law melt in the face of his daughter's tears. Figuring he'd better get on with his situation report before Ethan tore a verbal strip off his hide, Josh summarized the night's events, ending with, "Fortress is providing backup."

"You're going to work for them, aren't you?"

Josh froze. "I don't know."

"Don't lie to me, Cahill."

"I haven't decided for sure." He sighed, admitting the truth to Ethan as well as himself. "Whether or not I accept the offer depends on Del. Look, the truth is I'm restless."

"Saw that a year ago. You're late to the party, bro."

"You could have clued me in. I didn't recognize the restlessness until recently."

"Small-town policing isn't the adrenaline rush we get on the battlefield." He stopped, chuckled. "At least not most of the time. I chose to walk away from the battlefield because of Aunt Ruth. I stay away from it because of Serena. Don't tell my wife, but I'm also not capable of that kind of duty anymore, no matter how much faith she has in me and my abilities. It's a young man's game, Josh. You and I both took some heavy injuries defending our country. My priorities changed. I decided I had given enough. Only you can decide when you've given enough. Just don't wait too late to get out of the game alive."

"I know I can't handle private contractor work full-time." He wasn't the only one facing the decision. Either all his team signed on with Fortress or none of them would. War had impacted them all, some more than others. Durango wanted to keep their skills sharp without committing to full-time mercenary work. If Ethan wouldn't go for a compromise, Josh might have to turn Maddox down. He found satisfaction in rescuing people and pets and didn't want to give that up. Walking away from his law enforcement job was not an option. "Would you be willing to work with me if my team decides to go in with Fortress part-time?"

"How part-time?"

"Case by case. Maybe once a month."

"I get first rights to your time."

"Agreed. All this is tentative, Ethan. Del says she's okay with it, but we haven't had much time to talk."

"She might change her mind, Josh. After what she's experienced and your recent injuries, a wise woman would reconsider. Can you live with that?"

He dragged a hand down his face. "I can't live without her."

"Like that, is it?"

"She's everything."

A soft laugh drifted through the speaker. "I know exactly how you feel. Your parents know?"

"When would I have had time to tell them? Mom probably suspects. She's sharp. Besides, she's the one who put the idea in my head when Madison first opened the store with Del. Do you know how embarrassing it is to admit she's right?"

"It's time to call in the feds."

"In addition to checking on Serena, that's why I called. Text me Jordan's number."

"As soon as I return to the house. Sorry, buddy, but Serena comes first."

"Tell her I love her."

"Will do. And Josh?"

He straightened, recognizing the switch in tone from brother-in-law to boss. "Yes, sir?"

"Do not let down your guard. You can't truly trust anyone except your own team. Keep your operations base in Murfreesboro. It's better to keep a degree of separation between you and the town until you bag the target. Great job on this op so far. Don't screw it up now by moving too fast. I know you want this over with. So do I. We need you coming out of this without any new holes."

"Yes, sir."

"I want updates every two hours."

Josh walked to the porch steps and sat. Based on the sounds coming through Ethan's phone before the call ended, he had a few minutes before the text came through. Might as well enjoy the peace of the morning. He had a feeling moments like these would be rare in the coming days.

Behind him, the door opened. A moment later, Del settled on the stair beside him and handed over a mug of coffee. She looked incredible for such a short night of sleep. "Morning, baby."

She smiled, leaned her head against his shoulder. "Morning. Any news from home?"

Josh kissed the top of her head before replying. "Serena's still battling nausea. Nothing from your mother or my parents."

"No news is good. Ethan would have heard by now if there was a problem."

"Sleep well?"

"No nightmares for the first time since Judge Reece's death."

He gave her a one-armed hug, touched she remembered which arm had the stitches and had seated herself on the opposite side. "Thanks for the coffee."

"Have you eaten yet?"

"Nate had breakfast ready when I came downstairs." He leaned in, kissed her. "What about you?"

Del wrinkled her nose. "Too early to think about food."

Josh's text tone dinged. He set aside his mug and retrieved his phone. Ethan. He sighed. Hated to make this call. Jordan would not be happy when he discovered he couldn't have Granger yet. The feds, however, couldn't keep him locked down. The man knew more ways to escape than a criminal with a ten-page rap sheet. The Army had done a great job training all of Delta to escape captivity.

"What's wrong?"

"It's time to call in Jordan."

"Great."

Her lack of enthusiasm made him smile. "I'm not happy about it, either. Jordan has jurisdiction because Granger killed people all over the country. I'll let the feds fight over who prosecutes him for the overseas assassinations."

"I should go inside while you talk to Agent Jordan."

"Stay." He punched in the number Ethan had sent.

The snarly fed answered with a grumpy, "Jordan."

"Agent Jordan, this is Josh Cahill."

"Cahill, where are my witnesses?"

"With me." A string of blistering profanity spewed through the phone in response to his words and fired Josh's temper. "Watch your mouth, Jordan. My girlfriend can hear everything you say."

"What do you want, Cahill?"

"You have the jurisdiction I need."

"Talk."

For the several minutes, Josh outlined the overnight events and suppositions as to Granger's employer and his agenda.

"Explains the turmoil we've noticed in his organization. What's your plan?"

He explained replacing Granger as a killer for hire. "A friend's going to drop my name as a better hired gun than Granger."

"Got an ego problem, Cahill?"

"Not in real life, but Wright doesn't know that."

"You won't give that bozo your real name, will you?"

"Nope. He'll want to make sure I'm not a cop."

"Have enough expertise to lay a false trail?"

"I don't. A friend does. Wright will see only what I want him to see."

"Your friend is that good?"

Josh considered what he knew of Jon Smith. Not a lot. Smith didn't share with people. What Josh had learned about him was learned under fire and holed up in caves in the Sand Box. "He's magic with computers."

"Maybe he'd like to work for the FBI."

"Not in a million years."

"Whatever. I want Granger."

Yeah, he knew that was coming. "You'll get him after this op is finished. The federal cop shop leaks like a sieve, Jordan. I'm not getting shot because Wright has a bunch of your buddies in his hip pocket."

"Where is he?"

"Locked down so he won't blow my cover. By the way, you can stop stalling now. My cell is untraceable."

More muttered swearing from Jordan.

Since he doubted Del had heard him, Josh let it slide. "So, you in?"

"When?"

"Within the next 48 to 72 hours."

"We'll be on the road within two hours of you telling me your location."

The corners of his mouth twitched. Jordan might want in, but he wasn't happy about handing over leadership to someone else. He'd get over it. Josh wasn't putting his life on the line in a mission he hadn't planned.

He gave the cabin's address. "A few warnings, Jordan."

"What?"

"First, you and your team aren't staying with us. Get rooms nearby. Second, Del and Ivy are under my protection. Interfere with that, they'll disappear again, and this time you won't have access to them. Third, you will not antagonize or harass them in any way. If you break that rule, Alex and I will set you down, hard. They mean everything to us. You don't. Fourth, you will not take over this op. My team follows only my directions. Alex is second in command. Any attempt to wrest control from either of us will be ignored by my team and could end up costing lives. Am I clear?"

"Like playing hardball, Cahill?"

"When my life and the lives of my team are on the line, you better believe it. Now, you in or not?"

"I'll see you in a few hours."

Josh shoved the cell into his carrier.

"Agent Jordan didn't sound happy," Del said.

"He will be when I let him take credit for capturing a killer law enforcement's been trying to nail for years."

"You should receive credit. You're the one taking the risks."

"The people who matter will know who's responsible. The only thing I care about is keeping you and Ivy safe."

"He better not try to intimidate Ivy or I will make him sorry."

"You'll have to wait your turn, honey. Got a feeling Alex will be the first to plant his fist in Jordan's face. The rest of Durango will be lined up behind him." He smiled down at her anger-flushed face. "You can have what's left after we're finished."

Del stood at the counter shredding cooked chicken as the back door opened and the two SEALs strolled into the kitchen. She glanced at her watch. Ten o'clock. They looked well rested, too. She scowled. The men had to have slept fewer hours than she had, but didn't show the late night. Not fair.

Eli drew in a deep breath. "Sugar, what smells so good?"

"The makings of chicken salad. If you wait a couple hours, I'll feed you lunch."

"Deal. Where is everybody?"

"Alex and Ivy are in the living room. She's sleeping. He's pretending to read a book while watching her sleep." Gave her a warm, fuzzy feeling. Alex was a good guy. "Stella's asleep, too. Deke's gone to the grocery store since an apparent locust plague swept through here and ate everything in sight. Nate, Rio, and Quinn are patrolling and checking that Granger didn't leave any nasty surprises behind. Josh is in the security room, watching the monitors."

"Ah." He glanced at his friend. "Go report. I'll stay with this beautiful lady."

Eli Wolfe was quite a southern charmer and she might fall for it if she hadn't seen him eat the last two days. The man was an eating machine. And, of course, not an ounce of extra weight sat on his frame. Double unfair. "You just want first dibs on lunch."

"Busted." Jon smirked. He left the room with a soft chuckle.

"Oh, now, that hurts." Eli's hand covered his heart. "You wound me with your skepticism, Del."

"Hush." She grabbed a second cutting board and knife and slid them in Eli's direction. "Make yourself useful. I suspect SEALs are handy with knives." With that, she handed him three stalks of washed celery. "Chop these."

"SEALs rock at knife work, sugar. You would do well to find yourself one of us elite warriors as opposed to a run-of-the-mill Army grunt."

"I heard that," Josh said. He opened the refrigerator door, grabbed a bottle of water. "Making a pass at my girlfriend is dangerous to your continued good health, frog boy."

"Misunderstood on every side." Eli sighed in mock heartbreak.

Josh came up behind Del, leaned over her shoulder and planted a hard kiss on her lips. One more glare at the unrepentant SEAL before he left the room.

"You're baiting him. Not smart, Eli."

"Good for him. Makes him appreciate the treasure he has."

Del's eyes misted. Oh, man, whoever won his heart would have a keeper. "Stop it, Eli. You'll make me cry."

Horror flashed over his face. "Oh, no. Not that. Can't handle a woman's tears. So, what drew you to owning a bookstore?"

She grinned at the quick subject change. It was a good one, though. Nothing she liked better than talking about her business. "What better job for a woman who reads obsessively?"

"Yeah? What do you read?"

"Almost everything. Can't take horror or speculative fiction, but other than those genres, I've probably read a bit of everything."

"Broad reading taste. If you were to go into your own bookstore as a customer, where would you head first?"

"Mysteries and romantic suspense." She paused, put down her knife, swallowed hard against the knot in her throat. "Well, they used to be my favorites. Not sure I'll read one of those books the same way now."

Eli finished chopping the last bit of celery. He reached over and clasped her hand. "Give it time. You'll find joy in those books again. In the meantime, try reading those cozy mystery things. You know, the ones with the old ladies who knit and solve murders from their armchair. And if that doesn't work, try a few sappy romances." He grimaced. "Maybe you can find a few that aren't too lame. Anyway, the point is the aversion you feel is normal and will dissipate in time."

"How do you know?"

"Experience. Instead of reading, though, I watch cowboy movies when memories from various ops crowd in."

Del made another trip to the refrigerator for mayonnaise and sour cream. She detoured to the pantry for a box of golden raisins and laid everything on the counter. "PTSD?"

Eli stiffened. "Some," he said, voice rife with caution.

"I think Josh deals with that as well. He stocks up on books. Sometimes he'll go through two or three a week. I've noticed he reads more when he's had a tough week on the job."

"Most of us have coping mechanisms." He tilted his head. "Does it bother you?"

"Why should it? People who've never been to war can have PTSD because of trauma."

The SEAL sat in silence a moment, gaze fixed on her. "You are smart and beautiful. Cahill's a lucky man. Enough sap for now. What do we do with this other stuff?" He waved a hand at the condiments on the counter.

She handed him two spoons, a measuring cup and a mixing bowl. "I need three cups of mayonnaise and two cups of sour cream mixed in this small bowl." While he measured and stirred, Del added onion powder, salt, pepper, and raisins to the larger bowl of chopped chicken.

She combined the ingredients from the two bowls and, after covering it, placed it in the refrigerator.

"Hey, where's my sample?"

"There's food?" This from Quinn who walked in from the living room, looking hopeful. "Something smells great."

"Lunch," Del said. "You'll have to wait until Deke returns with bread and pita pockets. Before you say it, no, you can't sample now."

Josh came into the kitchen, spotted Quinn. "Where are Rio and Nate?"

"Living room."

"I'll meet you there in a minute."

With a smart salute, the spotter spun on his heels and retraced his steps.

"Something wrong?" Del asked.

"Come sit with me while Quinn and company report. You've been on your feet for hours."

She glanced at the clock. No wonder her feet hurt. "Ivy awake? Maybe we should meet in the kitchen."

"I'm awake," Ivy called from the other room.

Josh held out his hand and led her to the couch. Ivy curled up on one end, leaving room for her and Josh. Alex was seated on the floor in front of Ivy, her hand draped over his shoulder. Del winked at her cousin and Ivy's cheeks flamed. She hoped Alex stayed around a while. It would be a lot of fun to watch this friendship develop into something more.

The rest of Durango sprawled around the room. Eli brought in a barstool for himself. When Nate snorted, smirking because of the stool, Eli just shrugged.

"Wuss," Nate muttered.

"Smart, if you ask me." Eli grinned.

"Didn't."

"What did you find?" Josh asked.

"A few rigged concussion grenades, a stash of weapons, bunch of flashbangs."

"What's a concussion grenade?" Ivy asked.

"A grenade meant to stun rather than kill," Alex said. "Makes you go deaf temporarily, causes a bad headache. Disorients the enemy."

"You have experience with those things?"

"Courtesy of the Army."

"Why leave his stuff?" Del asked. That didn't make sense to her. Granger had to know Durango was here and well armed.

"A few options," Josh said. "One, he thought he could slip in undetected, snatch you and Ivy, get out fast. Two, he planned to sneak in, steal the book, and leave without us knowing he'd been here. Three, he wanted to talk and didn't want to show up heavily armed."

"Four," Alex added, "he wanted to prove he was better than Durango."

"Failed," Quinn said.

"Granger lost the hardware because he wanted to move fast," Nate said, voice quiet. "Most likely scenario is he planned to take you to Wright. Couldn't afford to take Ivy because her injury would slow him down. He knew we'd be after him like a hunting dog on a rabbit."

"Thank God he planned to leave Ivy alone," Del said. She clasped her cousin's hand for a few seconds. "At least I could have run if I got the chance." She pretended not to notice the grim looks exchanged by Josh's team. Guess it was a high probability she wouldn't have had the opportunity.

"What about your planted story, Major?" Nate asked. "Any nibbles?"

"Jon says he's floated the story in the right places and set up a throwaway email account. Still waiting for Wright to take the bait."

CHAPTER TWENTY-SEVEN

A light tap on the door of Josh's darkened bedroom woke him. He glanced at the time. Three o'clock. Sighed. Who needed a full night's sleep or as close as he ever came to it?

He slid out of bed, weapon in hand. Didn't suppose one of Granger's buddies would be tapping on the door, but it never paid to trust blindly. Back pressed against the wall in case shots were fired through the door, he murmured, "Yeah?"

"Contact," Eli said. He and Jon were taking turns keeping watch on the monitors and the throwaway email account.

Looked like they might be on the move soon. "Five minutes." Wouldn't be wise to jump on the email too fast. Might look desperate. Plus, after two weeks of little sleep, Josh wanted time to fully wake up before taking on Xavier Wright.

The SEAL said nothing more, but Josh heard him moving down the hall. Deliberate on his part like it had been with Alex. Eli and Jon moved in silence unless they wanted to be heard.

"What is it?" Alex murmured. He sat up and swung his legs over the side of the twin bed he occupied.

"Wright."

His partner pulled on his jeans, yanked a t-shirt over his head. "I'll make coffee." He shoved his feet into running shoes and fist bumped Josh on the way out the door.

Josh laid his weapon on the nightstand. Pit stop to splash his face with cold water and a couple gallons of coffee and he'd be awake. Maybe. He was feeling every one of his 35 years. Maybe he should rethink the plan to work with Fortress. He shook his head, laughing at himself. Not wise to make decisions this important before the sun came up.

After drying his face, he headed for the kitchen and the promised coffee. True to his word, Alex had a fresh pot ready, a large steaming mug in his hand which he held out as Josh neared. "Thanks. Anything from Del or Ivy?"

"Not so far."

Good. Both women were exhausted, like the rest of his team. Difference was, his guys were trained to handle it and still function. "Stella still with them?"

"Yep."

Josh finished half the mug before his brain cells fired at almost full speed. He refilled the mug, motioned for his friend to follow him to the security room.

Jon sat in front of the bank of screens, typing at supersonic speed on a laptop. Good grief. The screens flew by at an incredible rate. How could Jon even know what was on those screens? "Sit rep."

The SEAL held up one hand, kept typing with the other. A minute later, he slowed and an email popped up. "Take a look." Jon slid the computer over the desk to make it easier for Josh to read.

He snorted. Not much to go on. Just a request for Chase McKenzie to contact Black Knight, that he had a job for him. Black Knight was the moniker Wright used when online. He offered premium pay. Yeah, this job was going to cost Wright a great deal more than he wanted to pay. Heat burned him from the inside out. This was the man who wanted his hands on Josh's girlfriend. If he had anything to do with it, Xavier Wright wouldn't get within one hundred miles of Del.

"Dude's careful." Jon sent him a pointed look. "He may not give us what we need without the women."

"I know."

"No," Alex said, his body stiff. "The two of us can't protect both Del and Ivy. My focus would be split between you and Ivy. Don't ask me to do that."

"Ivy's a liability," Eli said softly. "You can't let her go on this op."

A ball of ice formed in Josh's stomach. He didn't want either of them in danger. "Don't you think I know that? I never planned to take her into Wright's estate. I want to hurl at the idea of taking Del in there. To bag Wright, I may have no choice." He'd promised to protect her, but in order to do that he might be forced to drag her into the heart of danger. If anything happened to her, it would finish what the war on terror had started.

"We'll protect her," Alex said. "Without Ivy, there will be two of us in there to cover her."

"Might not be enough." Josh's hands fisted. "One second of inattention, one ricochet from the enemy's gun, and Del's life ends in a river of blood." And his own life would be over because if Wright or one of his men killed her, he would take out as many of them as possible before they killed him. If he was lucky, he'd be able to cover Alex's retreat. Except the stubborn sniper would rather die beside him than leave him behind.

"One of our teammates has a bullet-proof vest we can borrow for Del," Eli said. "We'll do what's possible to swing the odds in our favor, but there's always a risk. If the time comes, give her a crash course in survival." He grinned. "Number one rule? Do exactly as we tell her. Fortress has ear pieces for you. Wright's people won't see them and the gear will allow us to keep in contact. We'll know if things are too hot. The SEALs will ride to the rescue."

Alex glared. Eli laughed, voice soft in deference to the early hour.

"What should I tell Wright?" Jon asked.

"I want details, face-to-face. Send it in a few hours. Let him stew for a while, long enough to realize he doesn't have complete control of the situation." For a man used to ruling his world, Josh's power play was sure to leave Wright unsettled. He needed every advantage he could get.

Jon nodded, swung around to the keyboard, started typing.

Didn't take him long, only a few keystrokes. Josh eased closer to the screen. He chuckled. "Nice." The SEAL had typed four words. *Details. Face-to-face.*

"He's used to people kowtowing to his every wish. He expects respect." Jon inclined his head toward the screen. "This will irritate him. Might make him careless. The message will be sent at 6:00."

"Perfect. I assume you created an extensive cover story for Chase McKenzie."

A grin. "Eli helped with that. By all accounts, you're a very dangerous man to cross, McKenzie."

"Let's hear the details."

Del woke to the scent of bacon and something baked. Muffins? Hmm. No, not sweet. Maybe rolls or biscuits? She glanced over to the other side of the king-sized bed. Ivy was still sound asleep.

She eased from under the covers, grabbed clean clothes, and locked herself in the bathroom. Twenty minutes later, she emerged, refreshed and ready for the day's challenges.

Expecting to find Nate whipping up those amazing scents, she pulled up short when she saw Josh manning the stove and Alex using a spatula to transfer biscuits from a hot pan to a waiting platter. Also on the counter were butter, grape jam, strawberry preserves, apple butter, another platter heaped with scrambled eggs, a container of white gravy, and gallon jugs of apple juice and orange juice. Good grief. This was a feast.

She ventured closer to the counter. "How long have you been awake?" Hours by the looks of their growing mound of food and the alertness she saw in their eyes.

Josh glanced over his shoulder, smiled. "How are you, baby?"

The guys must have been awake a good while and Josh was hoping she wouldn't worry if she didn't have facts. Ha. He ought to know better. The man grew up in a house full of women. "Better. What's happened?" If her handsome boyfriend knew what was good for him, he wouldn't brush her off or deny anything had changed. Then again, she'd never known Josh Cahill to lie to anyone, except maybe in the course of his job when unavoidable. She could tell by the way he looked and his avoidance of her question that something had occurred while she was sleeping. At least this time, she and Ivy hadn't been awakened and forced to race through the woods overnight.

Alex placed the pan in the sink. "I've got this. Why don't you talk before everyone stirs?"

Josh blew out a breath. "Yeah, okay." He handed Alex the tongs he'd been using to turn the bacon and grabbed the travel mug Del hadn't noticed near his hand. He passed Del the mug.

"What's this?"

"Hot tea. Figured it was about time for you to come down. Walk with me?"

"Sure." She took his outstretched hand and followed him out the door. She sipped the hot liquid and moaned. "This is fabulous. What is it?"

"Green tea with ginseng and honey. Thought you could use some natural caffeine."

Another sip or four later, she squeezed his hand. "Bad night?" How did you ask a man you were crazy about if he was having PTSD issues because of the situation they were trapped in?

"Short one."

They walked around the back of the cabin, headed for that same trail Josh has chosen before. Del didn't push him to spill the news though curiosity was a wild lioness inside her, demanding answers yesterday.

Josh sat beside her on the same fallen log, still silent. Del watched the water flow by, the stream higher because of the rain, and sipped more tea. His tangible gesture of caring touched her heart. The only way she could thank him without breaking the peaceful atmosphere was to remain quiet and wait for Josh to fight with himself. She knew a battle was raging inside him, a battle between what he knew to be right and what would keep her safe. No other dilemma would cause such turmoil that he was reluctant to share details with her.

Minutes passed, the solitude broken by birds calling to each other, the whoosh of water washing over rocks and tree roots. A bee meandered by on his hunt for nectar. When she'd enjoyed her last sip of tea, Del closed the lid and set it by her feet. She twisted on the log, faced him. His grim, fixed expression sent her heart into a rapid rhythm. She laid her hand on his arm and said, "Tell me."

"Wright contacted me. Alex and I will meet him this afternoon."

She leaned her head against his shoulder. In a few short hours, Josh and Alex would stride into the center of a target. She hadn't forgotten the discussion of Wright's defenses. "You'll be armed?" Of course he would. She hoped her question got the response she wanted.

He grinned. "Can't be a world-class assassin without weapons, love."

"This is what you wanted."

"Yeah, I did. However, Wright was very careful with his wording. If I printed that email and took the paper to court, the words would tell the judge nothing." Josh sighed. "This sting might take a couple meetings with Wright. I'm afraid the second one will require you to be with me."

A shudder wracked her frame. After all the warnings about how ruthless and evil Xavier Wright was, Del had no desire to meet him in person. Worse, things were bound to turn ugly. When they did, Josh would disregard danger to himself to protect her. Breath strangled in her lungs. She might be the death of him. And that would kill her just as surely as any bullet Wright or his cronies might fire at her.

He kissed her, then pressed his forehead against hers. "I'm supposed to protect you from him and if things go like I think they will, I'll be dragging you into the presence of a killer."

CHAPTER TWENTY-EIGHT

Josh strapped on the bullet-proof vest, his actions as natural as breathing from years of repetition. He glanced at his partner who was slipping a black t-shirt on top of his own vest. "What's your gut say?"

"He'll be cagey. He'll say just enough to convince us the job will be a piece of cake. Snatch the women, grab the book, bring them back to him. Easy money."

Josh paused in the act of tying his combat boots. "Does he know about Durango?"

"Doubt it. Bet Granger kept details to himself until he defeated us so he could brag to his boss. Quite the prize to bag a whole Delta unit by yourself."

"And since Curt's supposed to be dead?"

Alex shrugged. "Wright will hope we're a great deal better than Granger."

He snagged his own black t-shirt from his bed and tugged it on. He hoped the sniper was correct. If Wright knew Josh's real name, he might unearth a photo to ID him. Jon's last scan revealed no searches on the name Josh Cahill. The Army had made sure no images of him were posted online while he was on active duty. He'd made an effort to stay out of the limelight or at least out of camera range since he'd transitioned to civilian life, but there was a chance snapshots had been posted without his knowledge. For that reason, he remained wary. From all accounts, the man was arrogant enough to believe he'd best an undercover cop and get what he needed. He was wrong. Josh had the best motivation in the world to keep Del safe. He loved her.

He grabbed his Go bag at the foot of the bed. "Ready?"

"Oh, yeah. Let's bag a gunrunner." Alex slung his bag over one shoulder.

At the bottom of the stairs, Del and Ivy waited. Alex motioned for Ivy to come with him. The two of them made their way to the living room. Josh set his bag on the floor and hugged Del. Her contented sigh made him smile. "One step closer to ending this nightmare, beautiful."

"I wish you didn't have to do this."

"It's necessary. Trust me to do my job, baby."

In answer, she hugged him tighter.

She was breaking his heart. He foresaw a fast trip to a jewelry store as soon as this was over. "Rio is staying with Deke and Stella. They'll watch over you."

"What if you get hurt? You might need him."

He cradled her face between his palms. "One of Fortress's medics will be on hand if Alex or I need treatment. I want Rio with you and Ivy. My medic is fierce in a firefight. He'll offer another layer of protection and, if something happens here, medical help. Ivy trusts him. He may be able to do more with her than Deke."

A sigh. "As long as you have medical help if you need it."

"Jake Davenport is as good as Rio. I've seen him in action on the battlefield. He's saved countless lives. Ivy okay?"

"Worried."

He grinned. "About Alex."

"I'm sure you're on the list as well."

"Right. Near the bottom, I'd guess." He leaned down, kissed her, a long expression of how he felt about her. No words necessary, he hoped. Later, when he wasn't watching over his shoulder, waiting for one of Wright's goons to take another shot at him, he'd give her the words he prayed she wanted. Josh lifted his head, eased her back a step. "We need to go. Listen to your bodyguards. Stay inside. Ivy will probably feel the walls closing in more with Alex gone. Distract her."

"If she has problems, we'll work on the string of numbers. Maybe we can figure out if those are Swiss bank account numbers."

"Excellent idea. Jon said that's probable, but he hasn't had time to locate the bank."

"I can't wait to see how much is in the account. Must be a substantial amount if Wright's that determined to recover the information."

Another kiss and he picked up his Go bag and strode to the living room. Alex sat on the couch beside Ivy, arm around her shoulders, her face pressed against his neck.

Josh raised an eyebrow in query.

Alex nodded. He cupped the back of Ivy's head. "I have to go, angel. Stay out of trouble."

She smacked his shoulder. "I'm not the one meeting a criminal. You stay out of trouble."

"I will if you will."

"Just remember, the sight of blood makes me woozy. You get injured, I might throw up on you, but I'll bandage your injuries." She grinned. "I'll use the pretty pink bandages I found in our bathroom to patch you up. Should stand out nicely with your tan."

He chuckled as he stood. "Deal." Alex grabbed his Go bag.

Eli and Jon waited in the backseat of their SUV. Alex dropped both their Go bags in the back of the vehicle, then climbed behind the steering wheel. "We've got some justice to shell out."

An hour later, the second SUV with Quinn and Nate parked behind a stand of trees. Alex slowed to a stop and let Jon and Eli bail from their SUV with their equipment. The rest of the Fortress Security team would rendezvous with them. They'd been delayed by a traffic accident. "Slow down a little. Let's give Fortress time to get in position."

"Roger that."

Josh took the opportunity to scope out the landscape surrounding Wright's estate. Dense trees and bushes hid the estate well from the road. His lip curled. Plenty of places to hide. Through the ear piece, Jon murmured, "Fortress is in position. Two minutes to go time."

"Copy."

"Cameras, Josh."

Only half a mile from the entrance of his estate. Wright's security wasn't as good as it was touted to be. A true assault team could be at the gates in under a minute from this position. With no near neighbors to complain, camera coverage should have started much farther out. Sloppy.

"Camera coverage half a mile out," he reported to Jon and the rest of the team. "Anything from our fed friends?"

"Oh, yeah." Eli chuckled. "They weren't happy about taking a backseat on this one. They're a mile from our position."

"Have one of your men watch for them. There's a good chance Jordan will horn in."

"Copy."

Alex guided the SUV around a corner and black wrought-iron gates loomed 500 feet ahead. A high stone wall rose on either side of the gates and appeared to surround the estate. As their SUV approached, a pair of armed guards stepped from the guard house inside the fence perimeter, a dog at the side of one man.

"Roof," his partner murmured.

Josh's gaze zeroed in on the weapons battery and men on the roof. He whistled softly. "RPG," he reported to Fortress. "Weapons battery. Men on each corner. Two armed guards at the wrought-iron gate. Guard dog."

"Copy."

The SUV slowed to a stop, grill inches from the gate. "Camera's looking us over."

Alex grunted. "Won't do much good."

Not with that special coating on all the windows which distorted the camera's view of the SUV interior and its occupants. That was sure to frustrate whoever was manning the security feeds. He and Alex weren't exiting the vehicle. Too many weapons pointed their direction. The guards at the gate weren't authorized to do more than ask for ID without directions from inside the estate. "Two minutes and they'll ask us to get out."

"Not happening."

The guard without the dog leashed to him walked to the gate, hand on his sidearm. Stupid move. Weapon should have been in hand and ready. Josh's estimation of the security dropped another notch.

Alex lowered the driver's window enough to hear the guard without compromising safety.

"Get out of the vehicle. Bring your IDs."

"McKenzie and Malloy," Alex said. "Tell Wright he has 30 seconds to open the gate or he hires new troubleshooters."

The guard turned away, cell phone pressed to his ear. The other guard watched them, dog standing at his side and focused. "Dog's better trained than the guards."

"These bozos are disposable. The real talent's inside, closer to Wright."

"Time?"

"Fifteen seconds."

The mission clock in Josh's head ticked off the seconds. At the 30 second mark, Alex shifted into reverse and backed up. When they rounded the curve and were out of sight of the guards, his partner would swing the SUV around and get them out of there. Before they drove more than 10 feet, the gates slid into the stone walls.

"Alex."

The sniper stopped the SUV. "Orders?"

"Go. Jon, we're going in."

"Copy. Watch your six."

"Roger that." As soon as the SUV's bumper cleared the wall, the gates closed, locking them inside Wright's estate.

Del watched Ivy make another circuit of the living room. Well, this wasn't good. Her cousin had lasted 30 minutes before fidgeting. At the 45-minute mark, she'd trekked to the kitchen for water. Again for a Coke. Last time she returned with a cookie. Now she would wear the shine off the wood floor if she didn't distract her.

"I have to go outside."

"Can't. We have a job, though."

She hopped around to face Del. "What? Anything."

Del grinned. "Be careful making that promise. I might con you into doing my spring cleaning at the store."

"I'm not stupid. Notice that I didn't make that statement while in your store. What's the job?"

"Jon didn't have time to trace those numbers, but he does think they're connected to a Swiss bank account. We need to find the bank, plug in the numbers and see what Wright wants so badly."

"Is that all?" Ivy's voice sounded faint.

"There's a laptop we can use in the security room."

"What's in the security room?" Stella stopped in the doorway, a couple bottles of water in her hands.

"A laptop."

"Why do you need one?"

"For the Swiss bank that matches those numbers."

"Tall order."

"Is there another computer?" Del asked. "I want to research Catherine Wright. Not sure it will help, but knowing her might give us something we can use."

"Agreed. I brought a laptop. You can use mine."

"Thanks." Kept her mind occupied. Knowing Josh was on a dangerous mission made her skin crawl with anxiety. Future missions probably meant overtime at the store. In fact, she might save the store's spring cleaning for the next time he planned an operation with his team. She smiled. Perfect game plan to survive his absence and the lack of communication. Whatever it took to give him his dream. She loved Josh Cahill enough to let him do what he was trained to do. She prayed, though, the missions would be spread out. Too many close together might give her an ulcer.

"I'll meet you in the security room." Stella climbed to the second floor.

"What are you hoping to find out about Catherine?" Ivy asked.

"I don't know. Since Catherine was murdered, there should be a bunch of information out there. Reporters love to dig up dirt on people." Including the things Josh didn't want her to know. She hadn't forgotten the pointed looks he and his team shared when she asked what happened to Catherine. Del hoped the reporters weren't too descriptive because if she found out exactly what Xavier Wright was capable of, she might not be much help to Josh.

Ivy grinned. "I'm telling Meg Kelter you said that."

"Nobody heard me but you, Ivy. Who will corroborate your story?"

"I will," Deke called out from the security room. "I heard every word you said." Amusement rang in his voice.

"Remember who has power over your meals," Del warned.

"Ouch. Good grief, lady, I thought you liked me."

"I do, but I'm not above blackmail. Meg has a mean streak and I don't want it turned on me. You can leave Otter Creek. I live there."

"Is she really that bad?" He glanced over his shoulder as they trooped into the room, skepticism evident in his expression.

"Worse. Once she bites down on something, she doesn't let go. That includes a good grudge."

The marshal made a face. "Can't say the press are among my favorite people."

"She's one of mine," Del said, pulling out a chair near the laptop for Ivy, then laid the paper with the numbers beside the computer. "Meg is one of my best customers."

"She's also Josh's sister," Ivy added. She stowed the crutches under the table.

"Here's my laptop." Stella placed the computer on the desk next to Ivy. She rattled off the password and seated herself in front of the bank of monitors. "Take a break, Deke. I'll keep the ladies out of trouble."

"Good luck with that," he muttered and made good his escape before Del and Ivy had finished protesting their innocence.

"He's been awake more than 24 hours," Stella said. "The jerk let me sleep instead of waking me to take my normal shift."

Ivy glanced at the doorway. "What if someone tries to take us while he's sleeping? Will he wake fast enough?"

"Oh, yeah. Deke completed a four-year stint in the military. He'll be alert as soon as I say his name."

"Must be nice," Ivy said as she began searching Swiss banks. "Takes me at least two cups of coffee to be coherent in the mornings."

"Same here." Stella adjusted one of the monitors. "What about you, Del?"

"It's green tea or a Coke for me. Never did learn to like coffee."

"Good thing you like the scent of it," Ivy said. "Madison keeps the coffee pot filled at The Bare Ewe."

"Who's Madison?" Stella asked.

"Another of Josh's three sisters." Del booted up Stella's laptop and keyed in the password. "We share retail space and we're business partners."

"Books and knitting go together?"

"Absolutely. There are a lot of good books that mention knitting, not the least of which is Agatha Christie's Jane Marple."

"She was some old lady who solved mysteries, right?"

Oh, boy. Del hoped the Christie Club members never heard Stella talk about Miss Marple that way. "If you stop by my store, I'll give you one of her books to try."

"I read biographies, not fiction." She sounded skeptical.

"I have biographies about Ms. Christie. I'll include one of those as well. What do you have to lose?"

"True. All right, I'll take you up on the offer."

Del used her favorite search engine to call up information on Catherine Wright. More than a million hits. She clicked on the first link and started reading. The more articles she scanned, the sicker she felt. No wonder Josh hadn't wanted her to know what Catherine suffered. His determination to keep her a long way from Wright and his utter frustration that he might be forced to change his plan was understandable. However, if that was the only way to capture this monster and dismantle his organization, Del would find the courage. With Durango and the SEALs, how could she lose? A sigh escaped. Right. Didn't matter who was with her, fear would play a big role in that meeting. Her fear. She figured Wright for the kind of man to gloat over his victory in capturing his elusive prey.

One report mentioned Catherine's two sons, ages 8 and 10. "Huh." That would explain the strange markings in chapters 8 and 10.

"What is it?" Ivy's hands hovered over the keyboard.

"Catherine's two sons are 8 and 10."

"Nice. Anything else in the news reports?"

"Nothing good. Xavier Wright is ruthless. If he was behind his sister's death, he is cruel and evil."

"You can bank on it," Stella said.

"Yes!" Ivy pumped her fist into the air. Her eyes sparkled, a big grin on her face.

"You found the bank?"

"Oh, yeah, baby, I found the bank."

"What's all the ruckus?" Rio leaned against the door jamb, a light sheen of sweat on his brow, a bottle of water in one hand.

Del's eyes narrowed. He looked more heavily armed than the last time she'd seen him in uniform. If she had to hazard a guess, she'd say his medic kit was close by as well.

"I found the bank with Catherine Wright's money."

"What's the balance in account?"

"A lot of reasons for Wright's desperation. Thirty billion of them."

CHAPTER TWENTY-NINE

As soon as Josh stepped from the SUV, he took on the persona of Chase Mckenzie just as he knew Alex became Dean Malloy. The bronze double-doors were opened by a genuine butler. Josh walked through the doorway, followed by Alex. Gaze sweeping the interior of the palatial home, he decided he much preferred Del's cozy house or his apartment to this museum. A showplace, to be sure, but no heart. Home should be a place to relax, a refuge from the world. Wright's house was not a home.

Two big bruisers appeared. One stepped forward. "No one sees Mr. Wright with weapons on them. You'll hand over all of them before you see him."

Josh's lip curled. "No."

Thug One scowled. "Wasn't a suggestion."

"Tell Wright to find someone else." Though it went against every instinct he had, Josh turned his back on Thugs One and Two and started for the door. He knew Alex would watch the two men as he headed outside, his back to Josh's. He'd taken five steps when a voice stopped him.

"Mr. McKenzie, Mr. Malloy. Forgive the overzealousness of my employees. They are protective and loyal."

He turned, stepped to the left side of Alex. A man about six inches shorter than Josh stood on the other side of the foyer, black eyes cold, hard. So this was the infamous Xavier Wright, the man responsible for Catherine's death whether or not he actually took part in it. He took his time committing every detail to memory. "You pay them to be loyal."

Color suffused Wright's face at Josh's reminder that the gunrunner was not in control of this transaction.

"Come with me." Wright eyed both men. "A word of warning. If you harm me in any way, you won't leave this house alive."

Neither Josh nor Alex responded. Wright either took them into his confidence or he didn't. If he didn't, they'd fight their way out of the estate.

After another few seconds of the standoff, Wright caved and led them to an opulent office. A large Persian rug covered the hardwood floor. Josh took in the L-shaped Teak desk, paintings by Monet on the walls, and two doors. One led outside. He bet the other opened into a panic room or another avenue of escape.

The gunrunner waved at two delicate chairs in front of his desk. Neither accepted the invitation. Harder to maneuver if they were caught in a chair. The move also served to irritate Wright since his short stature already put him at a disadvantage. Because they remained standing, he also had to stand to avoid giving them the upper hand.

"Details of the job." Josh folded his arms across his chest.

"Find two women. They have a book which belonged to my sister. I want it back."

"A book. Why don't you buy another copy?" He smiled. "Be a whole lot cheaper."

"My sister is dead. She meant the world to me. I want her book."

The fake heartbreak over Catherine's death made Josh want to plow a fist in his face as did the fact this man threatened his girlfriend and her cousin. "Not buying it. Lie to me again and our negotiations are finished."

Wright frowned. "I'm the one paying for your services. My motivation doesn't matter."

"You aren't paying us yet. What's so important about this book? Is it a rare book or a first edition?"

A snort in response to Josh's suggestions. "It's a recent paperback by Nora Roberts."

Josh cocked his head. "Something in it, perhaps?"

He stiffened. "What do you know about it?"

"What you just told me. The name of the book?"

"How should I know? I don't read that stuff."

Yeah, he suspected the gunrunner didn't read anything. His glance around the room had revealed no books. Of course, the man could have been an ebook fanatic, but Josh didn't think so. Being around Meg and Del had educated him on the book habits of serious readers. "You want us to find two women and bring every Nora Roberts book in their possession to you?"

"Exactly."

"And the women?"

"Bring them to me. I'll extend my own special brand of hospitality to them."

In his ear, Jon whispered. "Feds on the move. Headed your direction."

Josh clamped down on his temper, forced his hands to remain relaxed. Knew Jordan would screw this up. Question was could the fed carry off whatever power play he'd concocted without giving Josh and Alex away.

He stared at the human snake standing a few feet from him. Josh had seen the M.E.'s report about Wright's hospitality. The only way this man would touch Del and

Ivy was if he managed to kill Josh, Alex, the rest of Durango, the marshals, and the Fortress operatives. In other words, not happening in this lifetime.

And just as Josh had feared, he needed Del to bring down Xavier Wright. "Transportation of the women is extra. They won't come willingly."

"Just get them here. Money is no object."

"Good. One million for each woman and an extra million for carting books."

"That's outrageous!"

"You asked for the best," Alex said. "The best doesn't come cheap. We always achieve our objective."

"For that price, you better." Wright's cold eyes glittered. "Failure comes with a steep penalty."

A knock on the door. Thug One stepped in. "We have a problem, sir. The FBI is at the gate, demanding entrance."

"Let them in." He returned his gaze to Josh, then Alex. "We should introduce them to our new friends."

Ah. Had to give the man points for double-checking that they weren't a plant. Unfortunately for Wright, Josh and Alex were working for more than one cop shop. Now if the feds didn't give away the game, they might have a chance to pull this off and get out in one piece or at least with no extra holes in their bodies.

"I need names, Wright. Can't track down your books without the names of the women."

"Del Peterson and Ivy Monroe. They live in some podunk town in east Tennessee. The man tracking them didn't say which town."

"We'll find them," Josh said as feet tromped down the hall. He steeled himself and turned to the door.

Jordan was through the door first, followed by another flunky Josh recognized. To his credit, Craig Jordan showed absolutely no recognition of Josh and Alex as his gaze slid over them. He flipped his cred wallet open for Wright to examine. "Special Agent Craig Jordan. My associate, Gil

Townsend. We have questions regarding the death of your sister, Catherine."

"Again? I answered questions for hours several times. The cops came up with nothing."

"Yeah? Those weren't my questions, Wright. You don't have to answer them. However, I'll take that as a sign you have something to hide and you'll move up on my list of suspects for her murder."

Josh shifted, eyed Wright. "We'll be in touch." He moved toward the door only to have his progress impeded by the junior agent in his path. He waited while the younger agent sized him up.

"ID," Townsend said. His eyes glinted with a serious case of dislike.

Slow and easy, he reached into his back pocket for his wallet with the fake identity inside. Wouldn't give Junior a reason to haul him out in handcuffs. Townsend examined the driver's license. A measure of respect showed in his eyes as he returned it. He gave Alex's fake ID a mere glance.

A nod at Wright, and he and his partner left the house, climbed back into their SUV and drove out the gates.

After sending Ivy, romance book in hand, to the couch to elevate her foot, Del trekked to the kitchen. She needed to do something with her hands, something which required concentration to distract her from what she'd learned about Catherine's death. She swallowed hard. How that poor woman had suffered.

A hunt around the kitchen turned up a Betty Crocker Cookbook. She knew just which recipe to use if the ingredients were available. Del checked the pantry and found chocolate chips, vanilla extract, sugar, and flour. Now if the guys hadn't run through every egg in the refrigerator, she was in business. Finding eggs and butter, she collected the ingredients she needed for chocolate chip cookies. Nothing beat the scent of fresh-baked cookies.

She measured and mixed ingredients, dug out baking sheets, and dropped spoonfuls of the gooey goodness on the pans. A quick wipe of her hands and she popped the first batch in the oven.

By the time she finished cleaning the pan from her final batch of baked cookies, Del had eaten more than one. Okay, no use kidding herself. She'd downed four of the cookies while they were piping hot. Best way to eat them.

"Hey, you sharing or what?" Ivy hopped into the kitchen, dragging her crutches in one hand.

"Crutches work better under your arms."

"My arms are sore." She climbed on the barstool, held out a hand. "Hand them over."

With a laugh, Del placed four cookies on a small plate for her cousin. "Drink?"

"Iced tea if the herd of men in this house didn't drink it all."

"Do you think Stella might like a few?"

"Who wouldn't? These are amazing."

She grinned and pulled out two more plates, suspecting Rio would like some as well. Maybe a carbonated drink for each. Del carried the cookies and drinks into the security room on a tray she'd found in a cupboard.

Stella and Rio turned at her entrance. Rio's eyes lit up. "Cookies. That's what smells so mouthwatering."

"I brought enough for you both."

Stella's eyes widened at the pile of cookies on the plates. "We can't possibly eat that many cookies."

"Speak for yourself, lady," the medic said, grabbing his first treat from the tray. "I'll eat what you don't." He paused, cookie halfway to his mouth. "Do we need to save some for the rest of the team?"

"I doubled the recipe. There's plenty."

Satisfied his teammates would share in the bounty, Rio devoured the cookie in his hand and reached for another when a chime sounded in the room. He swung around, scanned the screens, rose. "Durango's back. Stay on the screens, Stella. And don't eat all the cookies." He strode from the room, Del close on his heels.

"Ivy, the guys are back."

A thump greeted her call, along with muttered words, followed by the sound of crutches. By the time she heard gravel crunching beneath SUV tires, Ivy had joined her in the living room. Within a minute, Josh and Alex entered the doorway, followed by the rest of their team. None of them looked happy.

"What happened?"

"Let's sit down," Josh said, then stopped, breathing deep. "Wait. What smells so good?"

"Chocolate chip cookies. Have a seat. I'll bring some for all of you."

One by one, Durango and the SEALs stowed their bags out of the way. "I'll help," Josh said. "We need drinks as well." He scowled. "Couldn't afford to stop anywhere along the way."

Hmm. Wonder what that was about? In the kitchen, she found a large platter and loaded it with cookies while Josh grabbed bottles of water for his teammates.

Josh leaned over and kissed her. "Missed you, baby," he murmured.

"Same here. You okay?"

"I will be as soon as Wright is behind bars and you're safe."

With a nod, Del lifted the tray, carried it to the coffee table in the living room. Men from every part of the room surged toward the treats, grabbed handfuls of cookies and the water Josh handed out.

Silence reigned in the room for a number of minutes while the men wolfed cookies and guzzled water. She and

Ivy exchanged glances. Del suspected the worried expression on her cousin's face matched one on her own. She sat next to Josh, waited for him to break the silence. The rest of his teammates settled against the walls or dragged in barstools from the kitchen.

"We would have been here an hour sooner except Wright had us followed." Josh scowled. "We ditched the tail and rode all over the countryside to make sure we didn't lead anyone to you."

"Tell us what happened," Ivy demanded.

Del glanced at her cousin, a grin on her face. The real Ivy Monroe was making an appearance. About time. She'd hidden from life for months.

Josh filled them in on the events at Wright's estate. "Went just like I feared it would." He rubbed his face with his hands, expression showing fatigue.

Del's heart clenched at the sight. "He didn't give you enough to arrest him."

"I'm sorry, sweetheart."

"When do we leave?"

"What do you mean by that?" Ivy twisted on the couch to stare at Del. "We can't go anywhere near that man."

"Not you, Ivy. Just me."

"What? No!"

"We don't have a choice, kitten," Josh said. "We have to take Wright down before he hires someone else. Right now, Alex and I know there's no one else hunting for you." He grinned. "The price we're charging is too high for him to hire anyone else."

"How high is too high?" Del asked.

"Since you two aren't going to be cooperative, one million each plus another million for carting books to the estate."

"Three million dollars?" Ivy's voice resembled a croak.

"We're expensive because we're the best, and you two ladies are a lot of trouble for us bad boys to handle," Alex said.

Ivy smacked his shoulder. He laughed at her mock outrage.

"How long before we leave?" Del asked again.

"Can't be too soon or we'll tip our hand." Josh wrapped his arm around her shoulders and hugged her. "Maybe tomorrow night. If something goes wrong, I want as much advantage as we can get. Working in darkness is second nature to spec ops soldiers. That's when we do most of our work."

"Won't you have to take me, too?" Ivy asked.

"No." Alex said. "You can't maneuver with those crutches. We'll either tell him we killed you or you were out of town when we went after you two."

"I'd rather be out of town if it's all the same." Her voice came out a notch above a whisper.

He shrugged. "Doesn't matter. One way or the other, after tomorrow night, Wright won't be a danger to you or Del."

Del thought about the way he'd phrased that, the grim determination on his face. A glance at Josh revealed the same from him and the rest of his team. She couldn't help but be thankful these men were using their skills to help her and Ivy. "Thank you," she said, catching the gaze of each team member. Most looked uncomfortable at her words. Eli winked at her. When Josh drew her closer to his side, a scowl on his face, she figured he'd seen it. She patted the hand clasping her shoulder.

"How soon will we have the bullet-proof vest you mentioned for Del, Jon?" he asked.

"Two hours, tops."

"I'll take care of it," Eli said. He rose, strode from the room, cell phone in hand. Seconds later, his soft murmur could be heard from the hallway.

When the SEAL returned, Josh nodded his thanks.

"Is this a good time to tell you we found the Swiss bank and Catherine's account?" Ivy asked.

Alex jerked around to stare at her. "You serious?"

"You bet your boots, buddy." She grinned.

"Excellent. So how much is old Xavier desperate to retrieve?"

"In round figures, just over thirty billion dollars."

Stunned silence filled the room. Del and Ivy grinned at each other. Yep, that was the same reaction in the security room earlier.

"Perfect blackmail material," Jon said. "Tell me the bank name. I'll access the account and transfer the money into untraceable accounts around the globe. He doesn't get his money unless Josh, Alex, and Del walk out of that estate in one piece."

"You're not going to give him that money, are you?" Del stiffened as she stared at the SEAL. "The money was a gift from her grandfather, a legacy she died protecting for her sons. Don't let her suffering be in vain."

"Never," Jon replied, voice soft. "But Wright doesn't know that. Josh needs leverage to get you out of the estate. Dangling this money will do it."

"The only people with account numbers and passwords will be law enforcement," Josh said and pressed a kiss to her forehead before turning to the others. "Time to plan this op."

The next hours passed in a flurry of ideas, some retained, others discarded. All dangerous in Del's estimation. How could they talk about these options without tossing up the cookies she'd fed them? Each man, however, treated this as normal and that amazed her. They had the skills to do what was necessary and the heart to carry the mission out to its final conclusion. She just prayed they all returned from this one unharmed.

CHAPTER THIRTY

They slowed to a stop in front of Wright's estate. Josh's stomach knotted. Man, he hated this. Del being in the same room as Xavier Wright made Josh want to puke. But he wouldn't let her see his fear for her. She needed him to be confident in his and his team's ability to pull this off. He knew, however, one stray bullet and her life would be over. So would his.

He glanced at her, seated beside him in the backseat of Alex's SUV. "You ready, baby?"

"Let's get this over with before I lose my nerve." Her voice shook.

Josh leaned over and kissed her, hard and deep. He drew back, cradled her face between his palms. "Remember what I told you?"

"Follow your orders without question or hesitation. It's okay to be scared and to show it, but freezing will be fatal."

"Can you do it?"

She pressed a quick kiss to his mouth. "I will. I trust you to take care of me. You make sure you protect yourself as well, you hear me?"

"I hear you, love." He drew in a deep breath. "I'm going to open the door and drag you out. I need you to fight me and make it look real, like you're scared to death and desperate to escape."

"Easy enough since it's true." She paused, a worried look on her face. "What if I hurt you?"

He grinned. "You won't. Ready?"

She nodded.

"Go, Alex."

After a last glance around the immediate vicinity, his partner threw open the driver's door, grabbed the cloth bag of books, and slid to the ground. He rounded the back of the SUV and approached the back door.

"Remember you're onstage every minute until you're back in this vehicle," Josh murmured with a last caress of her cheek. As soon as Alex opened the door, his expression changed to one worn by Chase McKenzie. He'd warned Del how it would be, prayed she understood his actions weren't his, but those of Chase.

He grabbed her wrist in a firm grip, one he made sure didn't hurt. Josh dragged her out of the SUV. "Fight me, baby," he whispered. Immediately Del tried to break away from his firm grip and, when she couldn't, tried to punch him in the face. He jerked his head back just in time to avoid a bloody nose, yanked her into his arms, clamping her arms by her side.

She screamed, still trying to break away. A small foot stomped down on his boot. Didn't really hurt, but he had to squelch a grin. She was quite the wildcat. No wonder he loved her so much. "More," he murmured.

Del redoubled her efforts to get away from his grasp. He scowled over at Alex and said in a raised voice, "Get over here and help me with her before she gouges my eyes out."

Alex laughed. "Can't handle one little woman?"

"Wildcat, you mean." His wildcat. "Just shut up and get over here."

Another laugh and his partner gripped Del's arm in an unbreakable hold no matter how much she struggled. Together, they dragged a still fighting Del into the mansion.

"Please, don't do this. Let me go," Del begged. "I won't tell anyone, I promise."

If he didn't know she was acting as he'd instructed, his heart would break at her impassioned, fear-filled pleas. "Shut up," he snapped, jerking her around to face him. "Close your mouth or I'll do it for you. I'm sick of your whining and crying."

She gasped at his words.

Josh kept his expression as hateful as he could manage staring into the face of the woman he loved, but his thumb brushed over her wrist in silent apology. He didn't dare do more than that because the ruckus Del raised had drawn an audience.

"Mr. McKenzie, I see you were at least partially successful." Wright's pleased voice drifted across the room.

His hand tightened on Del's wrist. "She's been a boatload of trouble. Might charge extra for this one."

Fury spread across Xavier Wright's face. "You'll get what I agreed to pay and not a penny more. Bring her to my office." He turned and strode down the hall.

Shudders wracked Del's body, so much so that he and Alex were practically carrying her to Wright. Josh yanked her into his side as if she'd tried again to escape. The action brought her close enough to whisper in her ear, "Okay?"

A slight nod, then a furious, "I hate you."

"Ask me if I care, Ms. Peterson. You're nothing but a pain in my backside I'll be happy to leave behind."

He and Alex dragged a fighting Del through the doorway into Wright's office. Alex closed the door behind him. Better for Del's safety if the gunrunner's flunkies weren't witnesses to their meeting.

Wright's eyes glittered as his gaze swept over Del, imprisoned between him and Alex. Made Josh want to punch the man for looking at his girl that way.

"Is that all of them?" Wright demanded, gaze on the bag in Alex's hand.

"All they had in the house." He dropped the bag on the desk and resumed his position at Del's side.

"And the other woman?"

"Out of town," Alex replied. "We'll track her down, bring her here."

"No." Del went after Alex with a vengeance. "Leave her alone. She doesn't know anything."

Josh lifted her away from his partner, spun her around to face him, his back to Wright. "Enough," he yelled. Josh raised his hand as if he meant to slap her. She cringed away from him, an action which lanced his heart, but was the perfect reaction for Wright.

"Spirited. Good. I like them that way."

Josh's jaw flexed. With her body hidden from the sleaze bag's gaze, he took a second to squeeze her hand, willed her to realize he'd never hurt her. In response, she stroked his hand. The band around his heart eased. He pivoted to face the snake across the desk, Del at his side.

Wright snatched the bag and dumped books on his desktop. One by one, he thumbed through the books until he reached the one with the underlining. Triumph flooded his expression. "Excellent work, gentlemen. I'm so pleased you just might receive that extra payment for the trouble this one's caused you."

"What do you want us to do with her?" Alex said, inclining his head toward Del.

"Leave her. Go after the other one."

Josh scowled. Yeah, that wasn't happening. "What will you do with her?"

"Does it matter? Your duties with this one are finished."

"Talk or we take our sweet time retrieving the other one. Every day we search, we'll charge an extra $100,000. And she'll have that much more time to tell the world who wants her and why."

Josh saw the exact moment Wright made up his mind to answer. "She'll be my guest for a while, but eventually, when I tire of her, she'll die."

Del shuddered, a small moan escaping her throat.

Fury boiled in his gut while his face remained impassive. He owed Xavier Wright for scaring her and more than intended to pay up. "You're going to kill her?"

"Was there any doubt as to the outcome of this transaction? Why do you care? The Peterson woman's nothing to you. I won't have loose ends to strangle me or my operation."

"Got him," Jon murmured in his ear. "Get out of Dodge. Let the feds collect the garbage."

"That's where you're wrong," Josh said, his voice hard. "You got what you paid us for. The book, the woman in your office." He bared his teeth. "I changed my mind. I'm taking her with me."

"Are you insane? That is not an option."

"What do you care? You want her dead. We'll take care of it. Eventually."

"You, Mr. McKenzie, will do exactly as I tell you to do."

"I don't think so." With the end of those words, he and Alex had their weapons out and aimed at the gunrunner. "Not if you want the money."

"Money? What money?"

"Oh, in round figures, $30 billion. You won't see a penny unless we walk out of here in one piece with the woman."

"Blackmail is pointless." He held up the book with the markings. "I have the information I need."

"Not all of it," Josh said, voice soft. "The money is no longer in Catherine's account. You can have the money. For a price."

"And that price is the woman?" Hatred burned in the gunrunner's eyes.

"Both of them." Alex moved a step closer to Wright. "I like the looks of the other one." He nodded at the book. "You still get what you want. Money. Once we have the women secure, neither will see the light of day again. As soon as we clear the gates, we'll send you the information."

"You expect me to believe you'll walk away from that much money? Why should I trust you? You've already deviated from my instructions." Wright slowly shifted his right hand along the desk.

"Uh uh, Xavier." Alex shifted Del to stand behind Josh without taking his gaze or aim from the man. "A smart man would take his hand away from that panic button. Unless, of course, you don't mind leaving this room with a few extra holes. What's it going to be? Rich and intelligent or dead? Just so you know, I would prefer the latter option."

"Who are you?"

"Forgotten our names already?" Josh shook his head. "I'm hurt, Xavier. Get on your knees."

"I will kill you for this." The man sank to his knees, his venomous gaze fixed on Josh.

"A lot better men than you have tried and failed." His weapon remained steady while Alex yanked the gunrunner's hands behind his back and cinched them with zip ties. After tying on a gag, his partner darted Wright. Within seconds, he was on the ground with a moan. Josh waited for Alex to confirm the man was out before he lowered his weapon.

"Package is wrapped," he murmured to Jon as he helped roll the man into a large duffel bag that had been folded and stashed under his partner's vest. Alex hefted the gunrunner over his shoulder.

"Roger that. Feds are at the gate."

"Copy."

He swung around, grabbed Del's arm. "Let's get out of here, sweetheart. Look defeated. Drag your feet a little, but not enough to slow us down." Josh pressed his back to the wall as he opened the door, checked for foot traffic. Nothing. He pulled Del toward the front door.

Shouts from the yard had him tightening his grip on Del. "Do exactly what I tell you."

The front door opened. Two of Wright's foot soldiers pulled up short at the sight of them in the hall, weapons drawn but not aimed. Yet. "Thought Mr. Wright planned to keep her around a while," one demanded.

"Decided she was more trouble than she was worth." Josh scowled down at Del. "Told me to dispose of her."

To her credit, his girl played her part to perfection. She kept her gaze downcast, her slender shoulders slumped in defeat.

"Take the back way. Cops are at the front gate." Thug Two aimed his chin at the duffel over Alex's shoulder. "What's he got?"

"Trash," Alex said, his expression blank.

"Go," Thug One ordered. "The feds can't see her. Might lead to questions Mr. Wright won't want to answer."

Josh motioned his partner out the door first as he was the most vulnerable with Wright's added weight. With a nod at the thugs, he followed Alex to the SUV with Del at his side. He yanked open the back door, picked Del up and tossed her onto the seat, followed her inside just as Alex slammed the hatchback where he'd heaved his burden into the luggage compartment. A quick jog to the driver's seat and he cranked the engine.

Shouts as Thugs One and Two raced toward their SUV.

"Back way. Go!" With the feds blocking the front gate, he didn't want to be caught between the good guys and the bad guys.

Alex took off, thugs running after them, firing at the vehicle.

"Down." Josh pushed Del flat on the seat. "Don't sit up unless I tell you it's safe." He glanced at the luggage area. "How much of the drug did you give Wright?"

"Enough to take down an elephant. He won't wake up until tomorrow."

One less thing to worry about. Ahead, another gate loomed. Didn't look as solid as the front. "Ram it."

Alex grunted and floored the pedal. Five men raced toward their vehicle, guns drawn, firing. A spiderweb of cracks spread on the right side of the windshield. "Just had that thing replaced," he groused.

"This one's on me." As they sped toward the opening in the wall, concrete posts began rising from the ground in front of the gate.

The sniper growled. "I'm tired of these bozos."

"Jon, the back gate has concrete posts locked in place. The feds are at the front. We're sitting ducks out here."

Alex swung the SUV around and steered the vehicle straight for three more guards racing their direction.

"Copy. Fortress is moving in. Two minutes."

"Machine gun," Alex barked, swerving away from the weapon.

"I thought those were illegal," Del said.

"Tell them that," he snapped. Another evasive maneuver. A burst of machine gun fire. The SUV's engine locked up.

CHAPTER THIRTY-ONE

"Are you kidding me?" Josh dived into the front seat. He glanced at Del. "Drop to the floorboard and stay there. It's the most protected place in this vehicle." He reached into Alex's Go bag and yanked out the dart gun. "Loaded?" he asked his sniper.

A snort in response. Yeah, he figured as much. With Del's life on the line, though, he wasn't taking chances. He handed the gun to her. She flinched. "It's loaded with a dart. Just point and shoot."

"What are you going to do?"

He never wanted to hear absolute fear in her voice like that again. "Alex and I are on garbage detail. We'll do our own pointing and shooting. We can't let them take you or Wright. Help is one minute out." Josh didn't bother to tell her a lot of bad things could happen in one minute. From the tears streaking down her face, she suspected as much anyway.

"Forty-five seconds," Jon murmured.

"They're aiming for the windshield," Alex said, drawing his weapon.

"They know Wright is in the back and the windshield is compromised. A few more well-placed shots and the windshield will shatter." A last glance to be sure Del remained in place. "Let's do this. I'm ready for a big, juicy steak and baked potato."

"Sounds good to me. You're buying. I'll take the left. I want the gunner who killed my ride. Jon, the clowns on the roof?"

"I solved the problem. Thirty seconds," Jon said.

"Go." Josh and Alex threw open the doors and rolled to the ground, firing as they went. A hail of bullets struck the SUV. He refused to consider a hull breach by one of the small metal missiles. Focus on the mission, he reminded himself, then ride into the sunset with the girl.

The roar of the machine gun cut off abruptly. Alex Morgan strikes again.

"Fortress incoming," Jon said. "They're dressed in black. Don't mistake them for the bad guys."

Laughter burst from Josh as he took down another tango. Shots sounded behind him, shouts from the bad guys. One scream. His blood froze in his veins. Del. He needed to get to her. She'd never scream unless someone had gotten past Alex. He rose into a crouch, scanning in front of him for another tango, saw no one. Movement to the right was his only warning. The next second he was flat on his back, staring down the barrel of a Ruger aimed at his head by a grinning Thug One.

"Not so smart, are you?"

Josh saw the movement of his trigger finger and, with his booted foot, kicked Thug One's kneecap. With a scream of pain, the man collapsed to the ground, writhing in pain. Josh dived on top of him, pinned his gun hand to the ground and, after several vicious punches to Thug One's head and face, knocked him unconscious.

He leaped to his feet and yanked open the vehicle's back door, weapon up, ready. What he saw astonished him.

Somehow, Wright had freed himself, escaped the duffel bag and climbed over the seat. Del's face was bruised, which ticked him off, but she held the gun aimed at the gunrunner who was unconscious, sprawled across the seat with a dart protruding from his neck.

"Tangos down. Area secure," Jon murmured. "Tell your girl she's amazing."

He'd do that as soon as he stopped shaking. "You okay, baby?"

"Is he down?" she asked, gaze still focused on Wright.

"He is. Besides, the gun's empty."

"You said he was down before. He got up."

He grinned. Had to love a woman with such spirit. "Blame Alex for that."

"Hey! Don't send her after me," Alex protested. "She's dangerous with a gun."

Not yet, but soon. "You're lucky there isn't more ammunition." He planned to turn his sweet girl into a marksman. Never did he want to feel the kind of fear he had today, knowing she couldn't defend herself. Never again. "Let's get out of here, love. The feds can take care of the rest."

"We did it?" Del crawled over to his side of the vehicle, grasped his outstretched hand.

He enclosed her in his arms. "He's going down hard. We have backup on the recording. No way he'll slide out of this one."

"Can we go home now?"

"Josh owes me a steak," Alex groused. "He's paying up."

"Tomorrow soon enough?" Josh asked Del.

"Tomorrow," she agreed.

He took the dart gun from her unresisting hand, grabbed his Go bag and secured the weapon inside as Alex hefted his own over his shoulder. Josh hugged Del. "We injured or killed many of Wright's men. It's better if you don't see that as we leave."

"You'd blindfold me?"

"Carry you. Wrap your arms around me and whisper sweet nothings in my ear until we're clear." He dropped a soft kiss on her lips. "Let me do this, sweetheart. You've been through enough."

She nodded.

"Where is he?" Jordan strode across the estate grounds toward the trashed SUV.

Josh motioned to the vehicle. "He's all yours, Jordan. See you at home."

"Wait a minute. You can't run off. I need statements."

"You know where to find us. This is your collar." He ignored Jordan's further protests about having his badge and swept his girl into his arms. "Let's go home, sweetheart."

The next two weeks passed in a flurry of interviews with the FBI and Ethan, dodging the press, and a couple visits to the recovering Marshal Burns. Del reveled in her store with it's perfect scent of brewing coffee and books. The Christie Club made an appearance in the store minutes after she opened the first day back and grilled her for information. Being warned not to share too much information, she gave generalities. All but Ethan's aunt were satisfied. When Ruth grew too persistent for days on end, she pointed the mystery writer to her police chief nephew.

Ivy's laugh bubbled out as the door closed behind a disgruntled Ruth. "That is one determined lady." She slid off her stool behind the counter and limped over to the coffee bar.

"How's your ankle?"

"Better. Have you seen Josh?"

She shook her head. "Durango is meeting this morning. They have something they want to talk over with him."

"It's been three hours."

"Worried?"

"Hungry. Alex promised to deliver lunch."

And maybe a little worried, though her cousin wouldn't admit it. "They should be here soon."

Lunch customers came and went in a steady stream. Still no sign of Josh or his team. At 1:15, the door opened and Durango walked in, big grins on their faces. All except Josh. He looked serious, a huge contrast to his teammates.

Del's stomach knotted. Had something gone wrong with the case against Wright? Did he escape? Would they need another sting? She frowned, not knowing if such a thing were possible. After all, Wright had seen the faces of Josh and Alex. She didn't trust anyone else with her safety or Ivy's. She came around the counter and hurried to Josh. "What's wrong?"

"Nothing if you answer his question right," Quinn said, his eyes twinkling.

Nate laughed. "Not if she's smart."

"I don't need you clowns to help." Josh scowled at his laughing friends.

Alex clapped him on the shoulder. "Face it, Major. This is a team operation now. We have a vested interest in her answer."

"Fine." Josh turned away from Durango and held out his hand to Del. "Can you take a break?"

"Go on," Ivy said. "I'll keep the monkeys busy."

"Aw, now, that wasn't nice, Ivy," Rio said.

"You're the one who said I should stay off my foot as much as possible and there's work to be done." She picked up a stack of books and handed them to the medic. "Shelves those, please. The rest of you come get your stacks."

357

Amid protests, Josh ushered Del outside and down the sidewalk. He said nothing while they walked and that made her uneasy. He only nodded at people who greeted them when normally he'd stop and talk.

"Where are we going?" Del asked.

"The park."

More silence until they reached a bench under a maple tree near the pond. Josh drew her down to sit beside him and faced her.

"How was your meeting with Durango?"

"What? Oh, fine. We're opening a bodyguard school outside town. Well, the rest of Durango is opening the school. I'll teach a class as they need it. Ethan's talking to Durango about being his volunteer SWAT team."

Del blinked. A bodyguard school? Guess such an institution had to exist. "What about working for Fortress?"

He lifted his hand, brushed the back of his fingers over her cheek, his touch gentle. "That, love, depends on you."

"I don't understand. I thought you already decided to work with them, at least part-time."

"That was before you had an up-close-and-personal view of a mission. Knowing what a mission might entail, can you still handle it if I work for Fortress?"

"And if I can't?" she asked. Del had nailed down her answer to his question at the cabin. She was curious what Josh would say, though, and promised herself not to let him suffer long.

His face lost all expression, which told Del volumes about his feelings on the matter. "I can live without Fortress. I won't live without you."

Joy exploded in her heart. "Josh."

He raised her hand, still clasped in his, and kissed the back of it. "You mean everything to me. I was partially alive until you walked into my life. I'm not willing to live in numbness anymore. If you can't handle my working with Fortress, I'll pass on that opportunity."

"Why would you give up work you love? Think of the lives you'll save."

"It means nothing if I lose you. I love you, Delphinium Peterson. I love you enough to walk away from Fortress without one second of regret if that's what you need to be happy."

"You figured out my name. Joshua Cahill, all I need to be happy is you." She leaned in and kissed him. "I love you."

"Then I have a couple questions for you."

She smiled, eased away. "Ask."

"Would you like to see your mother tonight?"

"She's back?"

"She had a blast with Mom and Dad on the cruise. Mom says they all have a tan."

"I'd love to see her. Wait, don't you have to work tonight?"

"Ethan agreed to patrol my sector for a couple hours so we can celebrate."

Del's brow furrowed. "Celebrate what?"

He withdrew a small, gray velvet-covered box from his pants pocket, and knelt in front of her. "I hope we're celebrating our engagement." He opened the box and pulled out a platinum ring.

She gasped as a diamond solitaire glittered in the sunlight. "Josh, it's beautiful."

"Will you make my life complete by marrying me?"

"Oh, yes," she whispered.

"Soon?"

She nodded, too overwhelmed to speak as he slid the ring on her finger.

"What did she say?" Quinn shouted across the park.

Josh burst into laughter and drew Del to her feet. He leaned down, kissed her before turning to his waiting team. That's when he noticed a lot of other town and family members eagerly anticipating his response. "Yes!"

Applause and cheers broke out across the park. Del grinned and leaned into Josh's side. The perfect place to be with the perfect man for her.

ABOUT THE AUTHOR

Rebecca Deel is a preacher's kid with a black belt in karate. She teaches business classes at a private four-year college near Nashville, Tennessee. She plays the piano at church, writes freelance articles, and runs interference for the family dogs. She's been married to her amazing husband for more than twenty-five years and is the proud mom of two grown sons. She delivers occasional devotions to the women's group at her church and conducts seminars in personal safety, money management, and writing. Her articles have been published in *ONE Magazine*, *Contact*, and *Co-Laborer*, and she was profiled in the June 2010 Williamson edition of *Nashville Christian Family* magazine. Rebecca completed her Doctor of Arts degree in Economics and wears her favorite Dallas Cowboys sweatshirt when life turns ugly.

For more information on Rebecca . . .
Sign up for her newsletter: http://eepurl.com/_B6w9
Visit her website: www.rebeccadeelbooks.com

Made in United States
North Haven, CT
14 October 2021

10334324R00215